MOVING TARGETS
The Sixth Cal Claxton Oregon Mystery

"With *Moving Targets*, Warren Easley delivers another humdinger of a tale featuring the City of Roses. But there's so much more to like about this story than just its evocative Portland setting. Cal Claxton is a guy worth rooting for, and the gang who aid him in solving the complex and dangerous mystery involved are a fun bunch to follow. If you're not familiar with these gems out of Oregon, now's the perfect time to give Warren Easely and Cal Claxton a try. You won't be disappointed."

—William Kent Krueger, award-winning, bestselling author of *Ordinary Grace* and the Cork O'Connor series

"Intelligent dialogue, evocative descriptions of the Oregon landscape, and sly pokes at the current cultural climate make this a winner."

—*Publishers Weekly*

"Easley continues in every installment of this series to get a better handle on his characters and the vital balance between principal and supporting plots."

—*Kirkus Reviews*

BLOOD FOR WINE
The Fifth Cal Claxton Oregon Mystery

A Nero Wolfe Award Finalist for 2018

"I've been a fan of Warren Easley's Cal Claxton series since I read his first book, and they've gotten better with age, like the fine wine at the center of this complex novel of suspense. If you enjoy wine and a really good mystery, *Blood for Wine* is a must read."

—Phillip Margolin, *New York Times* bestselling author

"Warren C. Easley blends my favorite subjects—wine, food, a really cool dog and, of course, murder—into a tasty thriller set in Oregon wine country. With more twists and turns than a rain-swept coastal road, *Blood for Wine* is the fifth in this series with a tantalizing backlist just waiting for me to get my hands on. It promises to be a mystery maven's haven."

—Roz Shea, *Bookreporter.com*

"In Easley's fine fifth mystery featuring Portland, Ore., lawyer Cal Claxton, Cal is shocked to learn that vintner Jim Kavanaugh, a friend and neighbor, is the prime (and only) suspect in the brutal murder of Jim's estranged wife, Lori.... As Cal delves into Jim and Lori's troubled marriage, he stumbles onto other community secrets—including a blackmail scheme—all tied to the area's booming wine business. Meanwhile, senseless acts of violence that hit too close to home upend Cal's personal life—but only serve to strengthen his resolve. Oenophiles and aspiring vintners will enjoy the wine lore in this well-wrought tale of love and betrayal."

—*Publishers Weekly*

NOT DEAD ENOUGH
The Fourth Cal Claxton Oregon Mystery

"Masterfully crafted, this tale of greed, deception and revenge has an added benefit—the stunningly beautiful descriptions of the lush landscapes of Oregon's Columbia River country. Easley's characters bring enough complex complications to keep you reading long after regular bedtime."

—Anne Hillerman, *New York Times* bestselling author

"The narrative spends much time absorbing sights and smells of the glorious outdoors and detailing the political fights they engender.... fans of Tony Hillerman and C. J. Box won't mind...Advise readers not to jump to that last page. Easley deserves his surprises."

—*Booklist*

"With a very likable sleuth, *Not Dead Enough* is sure to appeal not only to mystery lovers, but also to those interested in Native American history, Oregonian culture and environmental issues like salmon migration. Although *Not Dead Enough* is the fourth in the series, it can easily read as a standalone, allowing fans of Tony Hillerman or Dana Stabenow to dive right into Cal Claxton's life."

—*Shelf Awareness*

NEVER LOOK DOWN
The Third Cal Claxton Oregon Mystery

"*Never Look Down* is an impeccably crafted novel that hits every note. Memorable characters, a unique plot, and a wonderful sense of place. By all means, get this book and settle in for a great read."

—Philip Donlay

"Easley exquisitely captures Portland's flavor, and his portrayal of street life is spot-on. Readers of John Hart and Kate Wilhelm will delight in trying a new author."

—*Library Journal*

"From four stories up the side of a building, a young graffiti artist, 'a runaway teenager,' witnesses a murder, and then finds herself in the killer's sights. Oregon attorney Cal Claxton teams up with the young artist to identify the killer and uncover a smuggling racket, along the way working with Portland's homeless and helping members of the Cuban-American community whose lives were affected by the murder. The Portland cityscape is as much a character as are the colorful graffiti artist and the lawyer who walks Portland's streets with his dog, Archie."

—*Ellery Queen Mystery Magazine*

"The killer, who leaves a bloody trail in his wake, and Cal race to find her, but Kelly avoids them both, not knowing whom she can trust. When Cal and Kelly do connect, they make a formidable and unlikely team as they try to find justice for the killer's victims. Cal's name is on the title page, but plucky and resourceful Kelly steals this tense adventure."

—*Publishers Weekly*

DEAD FLOAT
The Second Cal Claxton Oregon Mystery

"A fast-paced, tightly woven who-dunnit that kept me guessing to the end. Easley's vivid landscapes and well-drawn characters evoke comparisons to James Lee Burke, and Cal Claxton is as determined and resourceful as Burke's Dave Robicheaux."

—Robert Dugoni, *New York Times* bestselling author

"*Dead Float* starts with a man's throat cut ear to ear and Claxton's fishing knife found nearby, and gathers momentum like the midnight freight trains nearby. As a Deschutes [River] aficionado myself, I'll never listen to those lonesome whistles again without thinking of this story, and thanking the stars it was only fiction."

—Keith McCafferty, bestselling author of the Sean Stranahan thrillers

"When someone tries to drown Cal, he uses his fishing skills to good advantage. What a showdown finish! Easley's folksy style belies an intense drama revolving around corporate greed and espionage. The second outing for this action-packed Oregon-based series succeeds in quickly bringing readers up to speed. Pairs nicely with other boomer thrillers such as those by H. Terrell Griffin and also with fly-fishing mysteries by Keith McCafferty and Victoria Houston."

—*Library Journal*

MATTERS OF DOUBT
The First Cal Claxton Oregon Mystery

"Warren Easley has created a character you can root for—a man who has experienced loss but still believes in a better future, a lawyer who vigorously pursues justice for the most vulnerable clients. *Matters of Doubt* proves that legal thrillers can indeed be thrilling."

—Alafair Burke, *New York Times* bestselling author

"A fast, fun read with a fascinating defendant and our hero, Cal Claxton, a small town lawyer who risks his life to solve a big time cold case."

—Philip Margolin, *New York Times* bestselling author

"Easley brings alive the world of street kids and the alternative social groups they form..."

—*Publishers Weekly*

Moving Targets

Books by Warren C. Easley

The Cal Claxton Oregon Mysteries
Matters of Doubt
Dead Float
Never Look Down
Not Dead Enough
Blood for Wine
Moving Targets

Moving Targets

A Cal Claxton Oregon Mystery

Warren C. Easley

Poisoned Pen Press

Library of Congress Control Number: 2018935812

ISBN: 9781464211300   Hardcover
ISBN: 9781464210150   Trade Paperback
ISBN: 9781464210167   Ebook

Poisoned Pen Press
4014 N. Goldwater Blvd., #201
Scottsdale, AZ 85251
www.poisonedpenpress.com
info@poisonedpenpress.com

Printed in the United States of America

For educators everywhere, especially the ones who influenced me:
Marion A. Porter
Gilbert Morales
Carroll Dirkes
Leo Eves
Bob Musick
James F. Hornig
Sunney I. Chan
Theodore Von Laue
David A. Shirley
Norman Edelstein
William Weltner, Jr.

"No, all we need to do is buy up the ground from under their feet—and evict them. We're buying up the planet, Bishop, fair and square. We're turning it into the most exclusive gated community in history..."

—David Marusek, *Mind Over Ship*

"Forces beyond your control can take away everything you possess except one thing, your freedom to choose how you will respond to the situation."

—Victor E. Frankl, *Man's Search for Meaning*

Acknowledgments

Once again, I owe much to many for all manner of assistance during this project. First and foremost, Marge Easley, my wife, my muse, my "in-house" editor, kept me on track and daughter Kate provided sage advice on a central, young adult character. Thanks always to the brilliant crew at Poisoned Pen Press, especially editors Barbara Peters and Annette Rogers, who provided invaluable suggestions and insights. A group of talented Portland writers—Lisa Alber, Debby Dodds, Alison Jakel, Janice Maxon, and LeeAnn McLennan—critiqued this manuscript and let me hang out with them, too. Thanks again, guys! I owe a debt of gratitude to Dr. Shawn Easley, who advised me on several civil aviation issues that arose in this book. If any inaccuracies crept in, it's on me not him. In a similar vein, barrister and former Navy fighter pilot John advised me on the legal scrapes Cal got himself into this time around, which were legion and gnarly. Thanks, John!

Finally, and significantly, I took inspiration for this book from courageous people everywhere who are standing up to greed, hatred, and racism.

Chapter One

I've got one rule in the morning—drink two double cappuccinos before I do anything else. I occasionally make exceptions, however, for fly fishing or a pre-breakfast run with my dog. On the morning this case began, one look out the window signaled a run was in order. I was in Portland and the early spring day broke clear and bright. As I put on my jogging shoes, Archie spun in circles and barked in high-pitched, crazed excitement. I leashed him up and we headed out, working our way over to Burnside from Couch, then down the steep steps at the bridge and across to Tom McCall Park.

Not that many spring days break clear in Portland, so half the city, it seemed, was out that morning. Walkers, runners, bikers, 'boarders, and even a couple of Segway riders vied for right-of-way on the broad promenade running along the west side of the rain-swollen Willamette River. I was hoping my favorite, the kilted, unicycling bagpiper, would be out, but I didn't see him. The cherry trees edging the walkway were in full bloom, and out on the water, slanting sunlight silhouetted the low profiles of multi-oared sculls. It was spring in Portland, there was light, and like a living organism, the city surged with newfound energy.

Archie and I wove our way north and crossed the river at the Steel Bridge, then headed south on the Eastbank Esplanade, a series of floating sections, ramps, and concrete paths that hugged the Willamette and afforded an unobstructed view of Portland's skyline across the river. That morning the U.S. Bancorp Tower—known to locals as the Big Pink—glowed rosily in the sunlight, and ten blocks south, the Art Deco KOIN Center looked like a Jules Verne rocket ship poised to blast off. Arch and I crossed back over on the Hawthorne Bridge, and by the time we got back to my Portland office I was breathing pretty hard. I stood at the front door fumbling for the keys in my sweats when I heard someone clear her throat behind me.

"Excuse me, but could you tell me where Caffeine Central is?"

I turned to face a twentysomething Hispanic woman. She was small in stature, a couple of inches more than five feet, and wore boots, scruffy jeans, and a tee-shirt that had *Hands Off My Hood* emblazoned across the front. "This is it," I said, pointing upward. "The sign's a little faded."

"Oh," she said, glancing up, "I didn't see it. Are you Cal Claxton?"

I offered my hand and smiled. "In the flesh. Uh, this is my office. The place used to be a coffee shop called Caffeine Central before a Starbucks moved in up the street and squeezed it out of business. I've been meaning to replace that sign." What I didn't say was that that had been my intention for the decade I'd been running this part-time, pro-bono law practice in Portland.

She grasped my hand with surprising firmness. "I'm Angela Wingate." She had a lovely, heart-shaped face dominated by brown eyes that mirrored the color of her short hair. "I've come to talk to you, Mr. Claxton."

I glanced at my watch. "We don't open for another thirty minutes. If you'd like to wait, I'll be back down as soon as I shower and change." Drops of sweat dripped from my eyebrows as if to emphasize the point. She nodded, and I added, "Archie, here, will keep you company. You want some coffee? I'm making some."

She declined the coffee and followed me through the small waiting room into my office. Archie sidled up next to her with his stump of a tail twitching. "An Aussie," she said. "Love his markings. He's very handsome."

"Careful," I said over my shoulder as I climbed the stairs up to my studio apartment, "it'll go straight to his head."

Twenty-five minutes later I joined Angela, carrying a steaming mug of coffee. Archie left her side, took his favorite spot in the corner, and lay with his white paws extended and his ears up, as if he, too, were curious about our first visitor of the day.

Before I could say anything, she pointed to a small sign hanging behind my desk that read:

Start where you are. Use what you have. Do what you can.
—Arthur Ashe

"I like that." She showed a wisp of a smile.

I nodded. "Me, too. So, Angela, what can I do for you?"

She shifted in her seat, squeezed one hand with the other, and teared up. "Oh, shit. I promised myself I wouldn't do this."

I got up and handed her a tissue. "Hey, crying's allowed in here. What's the problem? Take your time."

She dabbed her eyes, blew her nose, and sat up a little straighter. "It's my mom. She was killed five weeks ago. Hit-and-run. Right up in the posh-ass hills of West Portland." She shot me an angry look. "Someone's Mercedes is probably in the shop right now, having the bumper fixed and the blood cleaned off."

I winced, as much at her cynical response as at her loss. "I'm so sorry to hear that. I think I read about it. Was your mom Margaret Wingate?" The story had hit the front pages since Margaret Wingate was well-known in Portland's charity circles.

She nodded, and her eyes filled again. "She and I, we'd just made peace, you know, as mother and daughter." She managed a half-smile. "My teenage years, well, I was a selfish little bitch with a rotten attitude. Drove my parents crazy. Chuck, he was my dad, finally disowned me, but Mom always kept in touch, even when she was angry and freaked out by my behavior." Her look turned wistful. "She never gave up on me."

I knew Charles Wingate, a prominent developer, died of a stroke a year earlier. "I know about your dad's passing, too. Again, I'm sorry."

She forced a laugh, but her eyes were etched in pain. "An orphan twice over. My biological mother used to clean the Wingates' house, and when she was killed in a car wreck on I-84, the Wingates adopted me." The wisp of a smile again. "That's why I'm brown and they're white. The adoption was mainly Mom's idea. I knew from an early age that Chuck never really considered me his daughter. I was just a prop to show they were, you know, good liberal Portlanders."

"Was that why you acted out?"

She looked at me straight on. "No. No excuses. It's all on me. After I lost my biological mom, I was pretty screwed up, didn't feel like I belonged anywhere, and I made a lot of really shitty choices. You know, I had to do every reckless thing out there to prove how cool I was." She shook her head. "God knows Mom and Chuck tried to help me. I did every program there is for messed-up kids—Outward Bound, behavioral therapy, counselors, and a half-dozen shrinks with all the latest antidepressant drugs, three stints in residential rehab…You name it, I've done it."

It was an all-too-familiar story. Given the pits and snares our culture throws at kids, it was a wonder any of them made it through unscathed. I looked at her again and saw a quiet determination. It wasn't hard to spot. "Looks like you have new priorities now."

"I have. I'd like to say it was because of some miraculous event or strength in my character, but the truth is I think a couple of synapses in my brain finally connected." She laughed self-consciously. "You know, the teenage brain's not all there. And I finally quit putting shit in my body that messes with my head."

I smiled, admiring her honesty. "What brought you and your mother back together?"

Her face brightened. "I'd been working on making amends,

you know, as part of the Twelve Steps. Anyway, I wrote her a long letter of apology, she called me, and we met at a coffee shop." She laughed. "We cried right there in public. It was ridiculous. At the end of that first meeting, I happened to mention my wanting to go to the march in DC, and Mom jumped on it."

"The Women's March?"

"Yeah. That's what sealed the deal." A smile creased her lips. "It was an epiphany for her. I mean life-changing. That sea of committed women from all over the country, the funny signs, the angry signs, the speakers—my God, she was blown away. All the way home on the plane we talked about ways she could become more engaged, you know, to start to make a real difference. She was like a new woman, and after years of battling, we were finally good again, too. It was like we'd found this common purpose."

I nodded, aware of how ill-timed and wrenching her mother's death must have been. "I'm glad you had that experience with your mother, Angela. How can I help you?"

She leaned forward in her seat. Angela was small, but her dark chocolate eyes, which were almost too big for her face, had an intensity that commanded attention. "I hear you're good at solving crimes, stuff the cops might give up on. They're too busy busting the homeless or hassling street kids. Finding some rich dude up in the West Hills who killed my mom? Who knows? Might cause a scandal."

I knew where this was going. Was there a millennial in this town who trusted the cops? "The police in Portland have a tough job, Angela, and my guess is your mom's case has a high priority. What are they telling you?"

"Nothing to me directly, but Melvin, that's my mom's attorney, says they're doing everything they can. But he's full of shit most of the time."

"Do the police have any leads?"

"*Nada.* I guess nobody saw anything when it happened. Melvin said they're checking all the body shops, but nothing's turned up." She met my eyes and held them, her eyes beseeching. "Could you just take a look? It's been over a month. I know you work pro bono here, but I can pay you."

I should have said no. After all, what could I bring to a garden variety hit-and-run case? But the thought that someone was walking around free out there, someone who had taken this young woman's mother from her in such a brutal way, stuck in my craw. "Okay, I'll make some inquiries, but I can't promise a thing." I pointed in the direction of the waiting room. "It's probably filling up out there. Give me your contact information. I'll want to talk to you again in more detail, but that can wait. I'll be in touch."

She jotted down her cell phone number and e-mail address and left, but not before shaking my hand and giving Archie a hug. With the door to the waiting room closed, I leaned back in my chair with my fingers laced behind my head for a few moments. Angela's story was familiar, I realized, because a decade earlier a young man came to me with a similar request. The death of his mother was a cold case, but it heated up in a hurry. Would something similar happen here? I had no way of knowing, of course, but a feeling just short of a premonition stirred in my gut that it might.

I looked over at Archie, who stood looking at me with his head cocked. "What?" I asked him. "Things are slow right now, so no big deal." He blinked a couple of times, and shot me a look, the one that says, Yeah, heard that one before.

Chapter Two

I kept a small studio apartment above my office at Caffeine Central, but that Friday night I opted to return home—an old farmhouse up in the Red Hills above Dundee, a small burg south of Portland in the heart of Oregon's wine country. My daughter, Claire, had christened the secluded five acres "the Aerie," and it was, at least to me, a fortress on a hill, a place where I could escape and recharge after doing battle down in the world. I fed Arch, scraped together leftovers—a bowl of vegetarian chili, a couple of homemade biscuits, and the last of a bottle of pinot noir—and hit the sack early.

As soon as sunlight torched the Douglas firs out in my yard the next morning, birdsong erupted. It's great that birds happily greet the new day, but do they have to start so early? I heard Arch stir, but I rolled over and tried to squeeze in a little more sleep. It didn't work—it never does—so I got up, got dressed, and followed my dog down the back staircase to the kitchen.

I'd just finished my double cappuccino when I heard a dull thump and felt a shock wave pass under my feet that rattled the glassware on the counter. I'm from L.A., so I knew an earthquake when I felt one. I looked down at Archie, who was making little whimpering sounds. "Easy, Big Boy. Just a tremor." I glanced out the kitchen window and saw a cloud of dust rising from the abandoned gravel quarry that lay on the other side of my south fenceline. "What the hell? That was no earthquake."

I loaded Arch in the car and drove around to the entrance of McCallister Quarry, a narrow, one-hundred-and-fifty-acre swath of rocky terrain running east-west below my property line. The broad gate was wide open, the first time I'd ever seen it without a padlock. I parked next to the gate and just as we got out of the car another thump shook the ground, followed by an even larger plume of dust. Arch pushed his trembling body against my leg. I knelt down and comforted him until the trembling abated. "You stay in the car, Big Boy. I'm going to find out what's going on."

The dust came from the east end of the quarry, where the terrain sloped off sharply. I worked my way through the rusty detritus of the previous mining operation and a scattering of scrawny cedar trees until a couple of pickup trucks and a half-dozen workers in fluorescent orange vests and yellow hard hats came into view. One of the workers saw me, elbowed another, a big man wearing a full beard and an annoyed look. He put up a hand and said, "Whoa, buddy. You need to turn around and leave. We're blasting here."

I kept walking, and when I reached him said, "I'm Cal Claxton." I swung my arm around and pointed in the direction of the Aerie, which was barely visible from that low spot in the quarry. "I live right over there. What the hell's going on? I thought it was an earthquake."

Beard nodded in the direction of the rocky embankment that formed the north boundary of the quarry. Two men were picking through a pile of rocks below a crater that was still belching dust. Another worker was hoisting what looked like a hydraulic drill next to the carved-out section. "Like I said, we're blasting," Beard answered.

"I can see that," I said with anger rising. "Why?"

He nodded in the direction of the workers again. "We're trying to confirm there's a viable seam of blue basalt running through there, that's why."

Viable? A rocky escarpment surrounded by fertile soil on all sides, the quarry always seemed like a geological anomaly to me, and I'd assumed that whatever was mined there had been fully extracted long ago. "Who authorized you to blast in here?"

"My company. We own this property. Look, mister, we're getting ready to pop off another charge. You need to leave right now. You don't have a hard hat, and I can't guarantee your safety."

I fished my wallet out of my back pocket, extracted a business card, and handed it to him. "Give this to your boss. I'm a lawyer. Tell him I'll be in touch." With that, I spun around, and as I retraced my path questions swirled around in my head. Blue basalt? They weren't thinking about resuming mining here, were they? They couldn't do that, could they? When I got back to the car, I figured the next blast was imminent, so I got in the backseat and wrapped my arms around Archie. When it came, he whimpered and began shaking hard again. I did my best to calm him. My big Aussie had the heart of a lion, but he obviously couldn't cope when the earth trembled.

By the time we got back to the Aerie, Arch was still panting rapidly but had stopped shaking, and thankfully that third blast was the last of the day. I looked up the company whose name I'd seen on the door of one of the trucks—McMinnville Sand and Gravel—and called them. I got a recording and left an angry message for the president of the company.

What a way to start the day.

A bank of fast-moving clouds to the south threatened rain, so after breakfast I hurried outside to squeeze in some gardening chores I'd been putting off. I re-anchored the windblown plastic sheeting I used to control the winter weeds in my vegetable garden and had just finished fertilizing my raspberries and blueberries when the rain arrived, drumming across the quarry and then clattering in the Doug firs that began swaying in the stiffening breeze. No fan of the rain, Archie led our dash back into the house. My cell phone rang with Steve Job's digital version of the blues while I was eating lunch. It was my friend, private investigator Hernando Mendoza—Nando to almost everyone in Portland—returning my call. We spent several minutes catching each other up before he said, "What can I do for you, Calvin?"

"I'm wondering if you know how to contact Semyon Lebedev? I tried the last number I had for him, but it's no longer in service." A naturalized U.S. citizen from Russia, Semyon and I had a violent history, but he saved my life several years back in an incident that had forged an unlikely but strong friendship.

Nando chuckled. "Ah, the mad Russian. I believe he retired from the cage fighting and has become a bouncer at one of the strip clubs in town. I'm not sure which one. There are so many."

"What about the automotive business? I heard a rumor a while back he might be involved with one of the Russian theft rings."

"Yes, I have heard this, too." Nando chuckled again. "Perhaps the profession of bouncing does not pay so well. Why do you desire to speak to him?"

"I just want to pick his brain a little about a hit-and-run case I'm looking into."

"Oh. Hit-and-run cases are very difficult to solve."

"I know," I said, and as a former prosecutor I did know. "Just a preliminary look."

"Very well. I will see what I can do."

After the call, Archie followed me into the study and stood there with his head cocked, looking at me with his big coppery eyes. I snapped my fingers. "You're right, Big Boy. It's Saturday, and I owe you." I went back into the kitchen and gave him a nice bone—his once-a-week treat—that had been defrosting on the windowsill. My dog had me well trained.

Back in the study, I started some online research on Margaret Wingate to get a better sense of her and how the hit-and-run had gone down. I read her obituary first. A native of Seattle, where she graduated from the University of Washington, Wingate had moved to Portland twenty-five years earlier with husband Charles. It was a familiar upper middle class American story. While he built a successful real estate development company, Margaret dove into charity work, serving on a number of committees and boards, including the Make-A-Wish Foundation and later the Portland Cancer Society. A lifelong sports enthusiast, she also belonged to the Multnomah Athletic Club and Oregon Golf Club. She was survived by a brother in Seattle, a sister in Los Angeles, and Angela, whose full name, I noted, was Angela Morales Wingate.

An article in *The Oregonian* business section caught my eye. The headline read, "Wingate Properties Names New Head," and went on to say that the CFO of the company, a man named Brice Avery, took the reins following the death of Charles Wingate. Margaret Wingate was quoted in the article: "I'm delighted that Brice Avery has accepted my offer to become CEO of Wingate Properties. I have great confidence that Brice will pick up where Charles left off and guide our company to even greater heights."

I wondered what would become of Wingate Properties now that Margaret was gone as well.

I read through the coverage of the hit-and-run. Margaret Wingate was struck while jogging in the Kings Heights neighborhood, a prime piece of acreage with commanding views of the city from the hills that form its western boundary. She was a mile from her home, jogging east on NW Monte Vista Terrace, and had just entered the intersection with Vista Court when she was hit. The impact threw her forty feet, and she apparently died instantly. Tire marks at the scene suggested the car that struck her then proceeded eastbound on Monte Vista. According to the reports, she wasn't using earbuds that might have distracted her. The make and model of the vehicle was unknown, although I knew the investigative team might be holding back sensitive information like that. It was also reported that a canvass of the Kings Heights neighborhood turned up no one who saw anything suspicious relating to the incident. All the reports ended with a plea for anyone having information regarding the case to contact the Major Crash Team at the Portland Police Bureau.

I wasn't encouraged by what I read, but what did I expect? From my experience as a prosecutor in L.A. I knew hit-and-run cases were tough. Hell, seventy to eighty percent of them went unsolved, if memory served, and I was sure it wasn't much different in Portland. In the absence of someone coming forward because of a guilty conscience—which was unlikely in a fatality case—the only hope was to find a witness or the car. But witnesses were hard to come by, mainly because John Q. feared getting involved, and only the most naïve perpetrator would take a damaged car to a legitimate body shop.

I pushed back from my computer screen, rubbed my eyes, and slowly exhaled a breath. I knew all this going in, and attempting to enlist the help of Semyon Lebedev was a Hail Mary pass at best.

"Damn," I said out loud, "what was I thinking?

Chapter Three

Spring weather in the Northwest is always a mixed bag, as if Mother Nature can't seem to make up her mind which way to play it. But the "sunbreaks" are always welcome, and the rain... well, we Oregonians may curse it at times, but we know it's what makes the landscape so verdant. It rained most of the following Tuesday night, but Wednesday morning announced itself with spirit-lifting clarity. Archie lobbied hard for a run, but I told him we had an early appointment at my law office in Dundee. He wasn't impressed, but at least the blasting had ceased, and he was back to his old, confident demeanor. I'd called a contact at the Yamhill County Planning Commission to ask about the status at McCallister quarry. She hadn't called back yet, and neither had anyone from McMinnville Sand and Gravel.

I saw three new clients that morning—two scheduled appointments and a walk-in that showed up a half hour before noon. The latter was a young woman wearing spandex, an array of tattoos on her arms, and body language shouting her anxiety. I understood why when she explained that her ex-boyfriend was threatening to go public with a sex tape they'd made back in happier times. This wasn't my first brush with revenge porn, a sign of the times, I suppose. I took her boyfriend's contact information and told her I'd look into it.

After lunch at the little bakery across the Pacific Highway, a call came in from a number my phone didn't recognize. "Hello, Cal, this is Semyon. Nando Mendoza said you wanted to talk to me."

"Semyon," I answered. "How are you?" He said things were good, and after a bit of small talk I said, "I need some information about the car business in Portland. Thought maybe you could help me."

A pause ensued at the other end. Finally: "This is something I know nothing about, but it would be good to see you. I am working at a club on the east side, the Scarlet Hideaway. If you come after nine tonight, we can share some vodka and talk about old times."

"I'll be there," I told him.

Back in the office, I made a couple of calls to clear my afternoon calendar. I was relieved to see the next day was clear as well, so there was no need to hurry back to Dundee. I turned to Arch. "We're going to Bridgetown."

After stopping by the Aerie to throw a change of clothes in my backpack, I took the Pacific Highway north to I-5 and forty minutes later parked at the intersection of NW Monte Vista Terrace and Vista Court, the scene of the Margaret Wingate hit-and-run. I wanted to walk the scene, even if the crime was cold by better than a month.

Arch was happy to walk up the incline of Vista Court, which I knew connected back into Monte Vista Terrace a mile or so up the road. We walked a couple of hundred feet and then turned around to face in the direction the car was travelling when it struck Wingate. A car coming down Vista Court would have had a clear view—at least a block in either direction—of anyone jogging on Monte Vista Terrace. I pulled out my cell phone and asked Siri, "What was the weather like in Portland on March sixteenth?" I read the answer a moment later—light rain and no mention of fog. I looked down at Arch and shook my head. "I hope we don't have a texting teen." On top of a life taken, a young life surely damaged. A depressing thought.

Most of that first block was wooded and undeveloped. We kept walking until we came to the first two houses on the street. They sat opposite each other like two contestants in an architectural contest—stacked stone, local softwoods, and acres of plate glass. I felt no need to ring doorbells. I was certain Portland Police Bureau's Major Crash Team had put a full court press on the folks living there and on the rest of the houses further up Vista Court.

I considered that for a moment. If the team had found something, there's a good chance they would have gone public, since they would be under a ton of pressure to show progress in a high-profile case like this. But there were no additional press reports on the accident, so the investigative team had probably accounted for and cleared the cars owned by the families living on the loop, as well as those of any visitors, repairmen, and the like.

If that held, then the perpetrator had to have been someone driving through the neighborhood.

Once back in the car, I sat mulling this, oblivious to the view of Portland that spread out to the south and west. One thing was certain. If the perp wasn't associated with one of the houses on Vista Court, then this case got a lot harder. That triggered another thought—why would someone drive through if it simply brought them back onto Monte Vista Terrace a mile or so later? A shortcut? Maybe, but since the street cut a serpentine path on its way through, not much of one. A wrong turn perhaps, resulting in the driver looking at a screen map instead of the road? A possibility.

There was another possibility. I didn't give murder much credence, but it did make me want to learn a little more about Margaret Wingate's personal life.

Chapter Four

Despite a surround of threatening clouds, the sky in the city stayed defiantly clear that afternoon, so Arch and I snuck in a good run. I was low on provisions in my galley kitchen at Caffeine Central, so I texted an order into a little artisanal pizza joint off Burnside and picked it up on the way back. I did have beer, so after feeding Arch, I settled back with the pizza, a Mirror Pond pale ale, and a Jo Nesbo classic, *The Snow Man*, that I'd somehow missed reading.

A couple of murders later I took a break to look up the address of the Scarlet Hideaway. Across the river on NE Columbia Boulevard, the strip club's website promised "The finest nude dancing in the Portland area," with a bonus feature of "Private VIP sessions with an exotic dancer of your choice." I was surprised when I first learned that Portland was a veritable Garden of Eden of strip clubs, which numbered more per capita than any city in the country, including Las Vegas. Yet I now see that the fascination for strip clubs makes perfect sense for a city that celebrates its eccentricities and fiercely guards the right of free expression.

Semyon Lebedev wasn't at the door, so I paid the five-dollar cover, gave my name, and asked for him. The bouncer at the door nodded and summoned another hard-looking man who escorted me through the club. Music throbbed near the pain threshold, and the interior—a study in faux leather, chrome, and mirrors—smelled of stale beer, human sweat, and bad perfume. Hard-ass led me between two oval stages, sprouting floor to ceiling poles, both of which had young, gyrating women attached to them. I followed him through a set of swinging doors and into a poorly lit, narrow hallway. As we entered, two dancers who still had their tops on passed us hurriedly on their way to the stages.

"Third door on the left," I was told. "He's expecting you."

Semyon, a big, expressive man, hugged me like a bear, then held me at arm's length and beamed a smile that included a gold tooth. "Good to see you, Cal." He wore Doc Martens, black chinos, and a black silk shirt with the top button unfastened, owing to the wide expanse of his chest and shoulders.

"You, too." I raised my eyebrows. "Your own office. Looks like you're not just a bouncer here."

He smiled with modesty and showed me to a seat across from his desk. "You know what they say about the blind pig rooting up an acorn. I'm the head bouncer here." He laughed. "But we don't call it that. I'm the floor manager."

"Impressive. Congratulations."

Semyon produced a bottle of Stolichnaya vodka, poured us each three fingers, and after we toasted our friendship he said, "So what is on your mind, Cal?"

"On March sixteenth, a woman was killed up in the West Hills by a hit-and-run driver. She was a prominent Portlander, so I'm sure the case has a high priority, but the police are apparently not making any headway. The woman's daughter asked me to look into it, and for some reason I said yes."

Semyon laughed. "Knowing you, I am not surprised."

"Anyway, suppose someone had a damaged car but was afraid to take it to a legit body shop. What could be done?"

Semyon sipped his vodka, gazed at me, and smiled. "You are assuming I have knowledge of such things?"

"Come on, Semyon."

He shrugged and suppressed a smile. "They could sell it to a chop shop, then report it stolen."

"They would have to know about chop shops, right?"

He shrugged again. "It is not a big secret in Portland, although the police seem incapable of shutting these shops down."

"What happens to the car?"

"It is stripped of all useful parts and sent to a crusher. It would be done in one night. End of story."

I nodded. The next question was the tricky one. "Suppose I wanted to know if anyone dumped a car with a damaged front end in one of these chop shops, say, in a five-day window following the sixteenth?" I could have asked for a larger time slot, but figured that if this was the direction the guilty party chose they would act fast to dispose of the evidence.

His brow, burnished with scar tissue from his cage fighting days, lowered a bit, and his face hardened. "That's a risky question, Cal."

"I know. Look, Semyon, it's a long shot, but it's the one avenue I can check that the cops can't. The girl's mother was tossed across an intersection like a rag doll and left there to die."

He poured us more vodka, then leaned back in his chair. "When I said risky, I meant risky for me. I am not involved in the automotive busi—"

"I heard you were."

His eyes narrowed. "I was, but I am not now. This club isn't either. Here it is small-time prostitution, drugs, and, since the immigration crack down, supplying forged green cards, a very lucrative business. You're talking about the Boyarchenko operation, the Russian Mafia. They are frying the bigger fishes."

"Can you get me that kind of information?"

He downed his vodka, crossed his thick arms, and considered the surface of the desk separating us for several beats before raising his eyes. "I have a contact who owes me. I will make some inquiries. Killing a woman, someone's mother, is a shameful crime." He smiled unexpectedly. "And it would be enjoyable to cause some trouble for that bastard, Ilya Boyarchenko, even if it puts my ass at risk."

I thanked him, and we talked about old times for a while. At the door he said, "Cal, the things I mentioned going on here, I want you to know I'm not involved. I am just the floor manager."

"Good," I said, losing my hand in his massive grip. "Glad to hear it."

On Thursday morning I called Angela Wingate and left a message saying I wanted to talk to her. Meanwhile, I returned some phone calls and worked on a couple of briefs that needed filing, the kind of work that pays the bills. Caffeine Central was open for business most Fridays, but I knew from experience people would wander in, so I kept the door to the street locked out of necessity. These days a growing portion of my work consisted of defending tenants evicted by landlords with dollar signs in their eyes, Portland currently being one of the hottest real estate markets in the country. Gentrification was transforming the city I loved, and I was engaged in a rearguard action to protect a growing number of its victims.

Angela called back midmorning, and at half past one I parked across the street from the address she gave me, a two-story industrial building on North Williams in inner northeast Portland. "I'm at the Bridgetown Artists' Co-op," she'd told me. "Just ask for me in the showroom. And Cal, can you bring that handsome dog of yours? I've got a crush on him."

I'd heard of the cooperative but had never been there. I leashed up Archie and crossed to the entry, which was marked by vertical helixes of rusty iron standing about my height, one on either side of the door. The helix on my left was capped with a shiny chrome sphere; the one on my right sported an equally polished cube balanced on a corner. The showroom walls were filled with paintings, prints, ink sketches, even macramé. A jewelry counter and shelves holding pottery lined a back wall, and the sculptures on the floor caused me to zigzag my way to the counter, where a young man with a full beard and a beret awaited me.

"She's on the second floor, last studio on the left at the end of the hall," he told me. He took a ring of keys out of his pocket and opened a door behind the counter for me. "Stairs are on the left." He smiled at Archie, not the least bit concerned that a dog was in his showroom. This was Portland, after all.

The stairs and second-floor hallway were poorly lit, and I was relieved when someone emerged from a studio halfway down. I pointed to the end of the hall. "Angela's studio?" The young man stopped and held his hand out for Archie to sniff. "Last on the left," he repeated, as Arch gave him permission to adore him.

I rapped on the door twice before it opened. Angela Wingate greeted me, wearing welder's goggles on her forehead and a heavy leather apron. "Hi, Cal. I see you brought Archie." She dropped to one knee to hug him. "He reminds me of a Bernese we had when I was in middle school."

"Yeah, a lot of people say that. Same markings, and he's almost as big as a Bernese."

"Give me a sec," she continued, "while I shut down. I sculpt metal, in case you haven't guessed."

Brightly illuminated by overhanging fluorescent lights, the studio had two windows in the wall running parallel to North Williams and a workbench on an adjoining wall with a cluster of gas cylinders chained in the corner next to it. A heap of scrap metal lay against the opposite wall next to a large anvil and what looked like a gas-fired forge. An exhaust fan droned in one of the windows facing the street. In the center of the studio, a skeletal cylinder, maybe six feet tall, stood on a wooden platform. Wide in the middle and tapered at each end like a vase, it was formed by a series of gracefully curved rods welded in place to a series of horizontal rings. It looked like Angela was in the process of cutting a gaping hole on one side of the cylinder and bending the vertical bars outward.

I studied it for a moment and smiled. "Nice. I think that butterfly has flown the coop."

She laughed, and her eyes lit up. "You got it. The working title's *Chrysalis.*"

"Did you do those helices at the entry to the Co-op?"

"Yeah. Those were early pieces I used to pay a couple months' rent here." She laughed again. "But I still haven't quit my day job."

"Which is?"

"I'm a courier. I deliver for a big cannabis shop in southeast." I must have looked surprised, because she smiled and went on. "Pot delivery's a thing since the legalization last year. It's the perfect job for me. Most of the work's at night and the money's good."

After doffing her protective gear and shutting off the exhaust fan and the acetylene and oxygen tanks, she ushered me to a small table and two chairs in one corner. "I can make some herbal tea. You want some?"

I declined the tea, and when we were seated said, "As I mentioned on the phone, I'm checking some sources but don't have anything yet. The chances that I can shed any light on your mom's death are still pretty remote."

Her face grew solemn, and her eyes locked on to me. "I know that. I'm thankful you're taking the time, Cal. At least I can say I tried."

I nodded. "I looked the crime scene over. That intersection was completely open, and since it was still light when it happened, whoever hit your mom must have been totally preoccupied."

She grimaced. "Someone texting?"

"Maybe. And that person now has a damaged car to deal with." I went on to explain my approach—looking at the illegal body shops in Portland. "Of course," I warned her, "whoever did this might simply hide the car somewhere until he thinks the heat's off."

Her big eyes grew even larger, and I knew my caveat hadn't registered. "Sure, a chop shop. That would be the place to take a car like that."

"Only if you know about them," I responded. "That narrows the field down considerably."

She cocked her head and looked at me. "You know about that scene?"

"I know a guy who knows a guy."

"Cool."

"We'll see. We're talking about a long shot, Angela. Tell me about your mom. What was going on with her around the time she was killed?"

Angela sighed. "After the Women's March, she was powered up, looking around for new issues to get involved with, you know, more radical stuff. Suddenly her charity work seemed pretty tame, I think. I'd been telling her about what was happening in Portland, how all this new development was ripping up established neighborhoods and pushing out the long-time residents, the whole cluster fuck we're living right now."

"Your mom owned a big development company and didn't understand that?" I asked, a bit incredulously.

"She was kind of oblivious. She'd never taken any real interest in the business. That was always Chuck's thing. Her thing was her charities and her board work, you know, safe stuff, no controversy. She bought the bullshit, too, that Wingate's developments were all great for Portland."

"So how did she react to what you were telling her?"

"She actually started to listen, which was a shock, believe me. She began to see beyond her manicured neighborhood up in the West Hills, you know, to get what was really happening at street level. She started taking an interest in the projects Wingate had on the drawing boards and even started questioning some of them." Angela flashed a sly smile. "I was getting to her."

"What happened at the company?"

She laughed. "She told Brice Avery—he's the guy who runs it now—that she wanted to move the company toward more socially responsible projects. I know that they got into it over some humongous project on the North Waterfront. She wanted it redirected."

"Did she prevail?"

Angela shrugged. "I'm not sure how it came out. She did say that both Brice and Melvin were upset with her."

"Melvin's the family attorney?"

"Yeah, and he works for the company, too. He was tight with Chuck. They went to school together. Stanford. He's, um, not a big fan of mine."

"Did your mother leave a will?"

"Yeah. She left me the house up in the hills, and some stocks and shit. I'm going to sell the house with Melvin's help." She laughed. "He acted like he'd just given me the moon and stars, but money scares me. Rich people seem pretty fucked up. They're so attached to their money they choke on it and forget to live. I'm into my art, and social justice, I guess. Stuff like that."

"An authentic life."

She cut a look at me to insure I wasn't mocking her, then smiled. "Right, an authentic life."

"Do you have a copy of the will?"

She shrugged. "I guess I didn't ask for one at the reading."

"What about the Wingate Company? What's going to happen to it now?"

"They're going to sell it, I think."

"Does Melvin have a last name?"

"Turner, Melvin Turner."

I knew him by reputation. The firm, Turner, Ross, and Steinman, was a big player in the city and the state. "Do you mind if I talk to Turner? I'll have to tell him I'm working for you, which may put his nose out of joint. At the very least, I'll get you a copy of the will."

"Sure, go ahead. I'd love to see the look on his face when you do. Me with a lawyer. Speaking of which, when do I pay you and how much? I've got money in the bank now."

"Send me a check for three hundred dollars. If this case gets legs, we'll talk about fees, okay?"

She agreed, and the conversation wound down from there. Before leaving I nodded at the sculpture. "How did you make those graceful curves?"

She pointed to a forge. "I heated the rods in that oven over there." She pointed again, this time to a metal plate propped against the wall with the curved shape outlined on it by a double row of closely spaced pins. "When the steel was soft enough, I shaped it using that mandrel as a guide. I made the rings that hold the piece together the same way."

"Nice." Then out of curiosity I added, "I met one of your colleagues coming in. How many artists work here?"

"The dude you ran into must've been Darius. He's a photographer, just moved in. That makes ten of us, two up here and eight on the first floor. We pay a fee in exchange for a private studio and a chunk of the retail space. I tried working in the garage where I live, but some tweakers broke in and stole my tanks and torches one night. Took me six months to save up enough money to replace the equipment."

"You lease the space?"

Her face clouded over. "Yeah, but not for long. We just got a heads-up from the landlord that our lease is not going to be renewed."

"When does that happen?"

"We have three months before we get kicked out. They're going to convert the building to condos or something, double or triple the rent, probably. She looked at me, her eyes brimming with passion. "Artists, musicians, all kinds of creative people flocked to this town because of the vibe and affordability of creative space. Now we're getting pushed out. It really sucks."

We kicked the gentrification dilemma around for a while, then Arch and I watched as Angela went back to work. We left her perched on a stepladder, her torch flashing and hissing as she worked on a form that was at once graceful and imposing, and which touched on some longing in my heart I couldn't quite put my finger on.

As I drove back across the river, my mind was weighed down by thoughts of the city I loved and what was happening to it. It was almost a relief when those musings were finally pushed aside by the questions I intended to ask the Wingate family lawyer, Melvin Turner, concerning Margaret Wingate's estate. Something just didn't add up.

Chapter Five

"It's all in one piece," I said into my phone, standing in the center of Winona Cloud's apartment later that afternoon. Winona was, for lack of a better term, my girlfriend. She was away, and I'd promised to keep an eye on her place.

"No broken water pipes, huh?" She'd been gone better than three weeks and needed her plants watered and reassurance that her beloved collection of paintings—mostly Native American art—was still safe and sound on the brick walls of her loft, the second floor of a converted liquor warehouse in Portland's Pearl District.

"Not a one, and your art's as beautiful as ever. Are you okay?" It wasn't an idle question. Winona, a Wasco Indian and member of the Confederated Tribes of Warm Springs, had gone to Standing Rock, North Dakota, to stand in the fight against a crude oil pipeline project that threatened sacred and water-critical Sioux tribal land. The protest was disintegrating, but Winona chose to stay. I worried about her.

She laughed, which I read as an effort to reassure me. "I'm fine, although I can tell you that getting drenched with a fire hose when it's eighteen degrees out is no fun." I groaned and started to say something, but she cut me off. "We're trying to figure out our strategy, now that the environmental impact report has been waived by executive order, giving the bastards a green light."

She took me through some of the options they were considering, none of them reassuring at all. "Is it going to get more violent?" I asked, fearing the worst.

She laughed defiantly. "That's up to them."

The call went silent for several moments. "Be a voice for non-violence, Winona."

"I will," she promised. "What's happening at your end?" I brought her up to date, mentioning Angela's nascent case last. She said, "That cage fighter and the Russian Mafia? Sounds dicey, Cal."

I laughed at that. "Look who's talking." She didn't respond, which was a response of sorts. After we signed off I stood there thinking about this woman, who along with my daughter, Claire, occupied the piece of my heart that hadn't been shattered by my wife's death. I was lucky to have found her, and I knew it.

The pro bono work at Caffeine Central that Friday was uncharacteristically slow, so I closed up shop early and headed for Dundee to beat the traffic. Just past the curves on Wilsonville-Newberg Road a call came in. "Cal? It's Marnie. Sorry for the slow response. Took some time off this week. What can I do for you?"

Marnie Stinson was a senior staff member of the Yamhill County Planning Commission. I'd handled her divorce a few years back, which included slapping a restraining order on her abusive husband. That act and the favorable settlement earned me her undying appreciation. "Thanks for returning my call, Marnie. Hey, I'm wondering if you've heard anything about a quarry being reactivated—the one that's just below my place."

"McCallister?"

"Yeah, that's the one. A crew was in there blasting last Saturday. The foreman told me they were assessing a vein of blue basalt. Scared the crap out of my dog."

"Sorry about your dog. It's not surprising. Animals, particularly dogs, are very sensitive to blasting. Haven't heard a thing, but gravel is in high demand these days, and blue basalt's the best substrate."

"They can't just start mining again, can they?"

"Well, they'd need to apply for a permit, unless they're grandfathered in. How long has the site been inactive?"

"Ever since I've been here, so better than ten years."

"Twelve years is the cutoff. If they've idled that mine for that long, they lose their right to reopen without a permit, which they won't get in today's environment. The Red Hills area is wine country now."

I thanked her, hung up, and went out on the front porch. Sure enough, my neighbor to the north and my intrepid accountant, Gertrude Johnson, was out doing what I'd been avoiding—working on her garden. I walked up to the north fenceline and called out to her. She put her hoe down and joined me. Streaked with veins of pewter, her dark hair was pulled back and tied off, and the smile lines on her handsome face were deeply etched by the slanting afternoon light.

After some gardening and shoptalk, I said, "Did you feel the tremors the other day?"

"I did. Reminded me of when they used to blast down in the quarry."

"That's what it was." I went on to explain the situation. "Do you remember how long they've been idle down there?"

She pushed a strand of hair off her forehead and paused for a moment. "Twelve years and ten months," she answered.

"You sure?" I wanted confirmation, even though I knew she had a steel-trap mind.

"Yes. I remember because my husband died a month before they shut down. It pissed me off that he didn't get to see it. He hated that damn pit."

I explained what Marnie Stinson just told me. Gertie said, "Well, I hope you're right, Cal. The quarry starting up again would be a nightmare for all of us on the hill, but you'll get the brunt of it because you're on the lip. The mining industry in this state's powerful and well connected, so beware."

Her warning notwithstanding, I felt relieved as I walked back down to the house. I still hadn't heard back from McMinnville Sand and Gravel, but when I did, I was looking forward to breaking the sad news to them.

A big front moved in off the Pacific that weekend, which put a crimp in my plans to get the vegetable garden ready for planting. The sun made a brief but dazzling appearance on Sunday morning while I stood at the kitchen window sipping a freshly made cappuccino. As if a switch had been flipped, the valley suddenly rippled with vivid spring colors, and in the foreground the emerging buds and tendrils shrouded the distant vineyard in a green haze. Meanwhile, the neighborhood finches, nuthatches, and sparrows commenced a friendly game of musical chairs at my feeders.

I took my cappuccino into the study, and after perusing the news, did a more thorough computer search of Wingate Properties. While it hit the front pages, the death of Margaret Wingate and its impact on the company hadn't been covered in the business section of *The Oregonian*. I figured that was because the details of her will and estate were still being sorted out. There was, however, plenty of coverage of the company's activities, which ranged from buying land for speculation to spearheading developments impacting every quadrant of the city.

There were a couple of recently completed projects, including a large one on SE Division that had torn down a block of existing houses and built new, upscale condos and trendy shops in a neighborhood that was once one of Portland's blue-collar strongholds. The opening of the development, it was reported, attracted a rowdy crowd of angry Portlanders protesting yet another loss of affordable housing. It was a familiar story in Portland, where battle lines had sharpened even more dramatically since the presidential election.

An article on an upcoming project caught my eye.

Portland's Vision for the North Waterfront Takes Shape

Brice Avery, CEO of Wingate Properties, unveiled a master plan on Thursday, that if realized would put Portland's North Waterfront on the same footing as its affluent, highly successful sister on the south end of the city's west side. The ambitious plan spans 28 acres between the Steel and Fremont Bridges, which the development firm quietly purchased over the past three years. The property would be developed to accommodate 2,000 high-end residential units, 1.2 million square feet of office space, a retail anchor, a private pitch-and-putt golf course, and waterfront access to the Willamette River. According to Avery, the centerpiece would be a 200-room luxury hotel called Tower North.

In describing the project, Avery said, "This development is going to be best in class and provide Portland with a North Waterfront that we can all be proud of and will be the envy of the other West Coast cities."

The article went on to mention that the project had the support of the Portland Design Commission, whose chairman, Fredrick Poindexter, was quoted, "We're solidly behind this project. The plan is as bold and innovative as anything we've seen in Portland." A dissenting voice was noted, however. City Councilwoman Tracey Thomas said of the project, "We don't need a gilded tower in Portland for the one percent. We need affordable housing."

I pushed myself away from the computer, put my hands behind my head, and leaned back in my old roller chair. Led by Brice Avery, it looked like Wingate Properties was aggressively pursuing, if not leading, the high end of the Portland real estate market. I thought about what Angela told me—that Margaret Wingate might have been questioning that strategy. I had to laugh. The current political climate was minting new social activists at a heady clip, and I was willing to bet that socialite Margaret Wingate's *epiphany*—the term Angela used—came as quite a shock to Brice Avery. And I wondered again about Wingate's will, which bequeathed a house to Angela, her next of kin, but apparently nothing related to the multimillion-dollar Wingate Properties.

I wasn't suspicious at this juncture, but I was curious about how all these disparate parts fit together in the run-up to Margaret Wingate's death.

Chapter Six

Beep, beep, beep. The sound was distant yet incessant. Beep, beep, beep. The sound got louder. Beep, beep, beep. That did it. I was awake. I looked over at Arch, who was already standing with an annoyed look on his face. "What the hell's that noise?" I asked him. I took the backstairs, fed my dog, and made a coffee, all the while being serenaded by the beeping, which was clearly coming from the quarry.

I left Archie in the house this time and drove around to the quarry entrance. I parked outside the gate and got out just as a truck loaded up with the rusted remnants of the previous mining operation pulled out. A bright yellow front-loader was filling another truck further into the quarry. When the tractor backed up, I realized it was the source of the beeping. My friend with the beard stood off to the side with a sheaf of papers in his hand. He saw me at the same time I saw him, and when I approached, he said, "Sir, you're trespassing again, and you can't be in here without a hard hat, either."

"Good morning to you, too." I pointed at the front-loader. "I just stopped by to disconnect that goddamn backup beeper. It woke me and my dog up."

He flashed an exasperated look and glanced over at a couple of workers who had paused to listen to the exchange. "Sir, I'm asking you to leave."

"If you're just cleaning up the area, which is something you should have done years ago, fine. If you're thinking about mining again, think twice. You have no permit to do so. Tell your boss that. Tell them if they try to mine here, I'll slap them with an injunction so fast their heads will spin." I turned around and walked out, my face hot with anger.

By the time Arch and I got down to my office that morning, I'd cooled off some. I called McMinnville Sand and Gravel again and got a human this time. I asked for the president—a man named Mason Goodings, according to their website—and was put through to his voicemail. I left a measured response in which I informed him that it would be illegal to commence mining at McCallister's Quarry unless they obtained a new permit from Yamhill County. And good luck with that, I said to myself as I hung up.

That week was slow in my Dundee office. The spring pause, I'd come to call it. It was as if the arrival of the sun, or at least more frequent sunbreaks, had moderated the urge to drive drunk, assault someone, file for divorce, or commit any number of willful acts of stupidity. Whatever the cause, I used the time to beat back some paperwork, a task I put just ahead of having my fingernails extracted. Midweek I drove over to McMinnville and managed to find the young man who threatened my client with disclosure of a sex tape. He was just getting out of his fire engine red Mazda MX-5 outside his apartment. I introduced myself, told him who I represented, and handed him a copy of the Hulk Hogan judgment, which delineated the one-hundred-forty-million-dollar judgment the TV wrestler won from a media outlet after public disclosure of a sex tape similar to what this guy was threatening. "Read this carefully," I told him. "If you don't burn that tape, and it shows up *anywhere*, we'll see you in court." I started to leave, then turned back to him and pointed at his car. "After you lose in court, your Mazda will be the first thing to go, trust me."

He looked back at me like I'd just threatened his firstborn. Not going to be a problem, I told myself as I walked away.

The law offices of Turner, Ross, and Steinman were on the thirty-first floor of the Fox Tower in downtown Portland. On Thursday afternoon, I announced myself at the front desk, having set up a meeting with Melvin Turner after playing a round of phone tag. The high-rise went up in the nineties, but the office décor was old Portland with darkly stained wood paneling, brass fixtures, original art—mainly Northwest landscapes—and oriental rugs on the marble floors. A well-dressed woman ushered me to Turner's office and rapped softly before opening the door.

Melvin Turner rose to greet me but stayed behind his massive desk. He was short, on the pudgy side, with a balding pate and gold wire rims that magnified his liquid eyes. A picture of him with his family—a wife and three smiling kids—was front and center on his back bar. He motioned for me to sit but remained standing and furrowed his wide brow. "So, Mr. Claxton, what's this all about?"

"As I mentioned on the phone, Angela Wingate has retained me to look into the death of her mother. I'd just like to ask you a few questions for clarification."

He held the perplexed look. "Are you an investigator or an attorney?"

"A little of both, I suppose. I'm a one-man law firm, so I do some of my own investigating."

He took his seat, the whole time shaking his head. "I know Angela's frustrated that the police are stymied at the moment, but I can assure you they're pursuing this matter aggressively. What could you possibly add?"

"Probably nothing, but I told her I'd give it a fresh look. She understands the odds of my finding anything are low."

He laughed. "That's an understatement. Are you sure you're not taking advantage of the situation, Mr. Claxton?"

I smiled. "I can understand that you might feel that way, but that's not my motive here. And, frankly, I'm a little surprised to hear all the concern for my client. She tells me you haven't exactly been a mentor of hers."

He laughed again dismissively. "Oh, that's rubbish. It was my job to look after the Wingates. A young woman, out of control like she was, could have been a real liability. And she's not even a blood relation. But Angela seems to have put most of that rebellious behavior behind her."

"I understand she and her mother recently reconciled."

"Supposedly. I counseled Mrs. Wingate to take it slow, to make sure of Angela's sincerity."

"Did you also advise her regarding the direction of the North Waterfront Project?"

Turner looked incredulous, but an instant before that his eyes flared ever so slightly. "I don't know what you're talking about, and I suspect you don't either. Mrs. Wingate had no problems with the direction of the business."

"She wasn't concerned about the impact some of the developments would have on the character of the city?"

"*Please*. Did Angela tell you that? Like a lot of her generation, she has some rather naïve beliefs about economics and how the real world works. The Wingate developments will add jobs, tax revenues, and prosperity to a city that badly needs it. What in the world could be wrong with that?"

I shrugged. "That reminds me. Angela mentioned she didn't receive a copy of Mrs. Wingate's will."

Turner waved a placating hand. "That must have been an oversight. I'll make sure we put one in the mail for her today."

"If you give me a copy, I'll see that she gets it. It'll save you a stamp."

He stood up, his face taking on a little color. "That won't be necessary. We're finished here, Claxton. I'll show you out."

Noting that he'd dropped the Mr. in front of my name, I followed him in silence. When we got to the lobby, he turned to me, and the overhead lights reflected off the droplets of sweat that had formed on his brow. He said in a low voice, "I'd advise you to drop this fool's errand. If you don't, I'll make sure the Bar hears about this. Preying on a young girl who's grieving over the death of her mother is very unseemly."

I gave him my best smile. "Nice meeting you, too, Melvin. I'll be in touch."

At the car, I leashed up Archie and strode off for the Park Blocks, a tree-lined swath of green cutting through the center of Portland. Thoughts about what makes for a good city crowded into my head. "What in the world could be wrong with that?" Turner had asked. Hard to argue with, I supposed, but what about the creative class, the less powerful, and the most vulnerable? Could there be any balance in this city, or would it all eventually roll to the highest bidder?

I had no answers, but I was sure of one thing—Melvin Turner definitely didn't want me poking around in Margaret Wingate's death and his handling of her estate. I laughed at that. If he'd intended to discourage me, it had the opposite effect, like waving a red flag in front of a bull.

Chapter Seven

On the way back to the car from the Park Blocks, I called Angela to say that Melvin Turner might be calling to warn her about my *unseemly* behavior and try to talk her out of using me. "I'll tell him to go to hell," she shot back. "He's such a dick."

"No, don't get into it with him. Just say you're an adult with the right to choose your own lawyer. Leave it at that, okay?"

She agreed, albeit a bit reluctantly.

At the car, Semyon Lebedev called to say he had some information for me. I told him I was in town, and we agreed to meet. He pressed me for a spot, and I suggested the basement bar at Ringlers Annex, across from Powell's Books. He laughed. "This is a good spot, Cal. No Russians go to yuppie bars downtown."

I was sure Archie had had enough of the backseat, so I swung by Caffeine Central and dropped him off, offloaded my backpack, and filled his water dish. At least he could have the run of the inside of the building.

"Guard the castle, Big Boy," I said, and he gave me that look, the one that means "you always say that."

I got to the Annex before Semyon and watched as he came down the stairs to the bar. He looked fit, his hair cut high and tight, military style, and the tattoos on his muscled arms a swirl of ink in the low light. He glanced around first, nodded to me, and came back from the bar with the same thing I was drinking—a pint of the house amber. We clinked glasses and exchanged greetings. He said, "My contact in the automotive business was not anxious to talk to me." A grim smile split the dark, three-day growth on his cheeks. "I had to...ah, remind him of the favor he owed me."

"I appreciate that, Semyon."

His eyes flashed a warning. "The organization you're messing with is dangerous. Car theft is where it started, but they have diversified. The big boss is Ilya Boyarchenko, a scumbag who gives the Russians in this town a bad name. He is slippery, has good lawyers, and denies any criminal connections." He laughed derisively. "In Russian, we call him *ubiytsa*. He rules without mercy. People with loose lips are dealt with harshly."

I nodded as my gut tightened a little. "Understood."

Semyon took two long swallows of his beer. "So, my friend took a look at the shops where the car you are interested in could have been taken, shops where records of ownership are not an issue. There are several such shops in the area, but one shop received cars during the time you are interested in. This one has the highest volume." He removed a folded piece of paper from his shirt pocket, opened it, and squinted in the low light. "Four cars were brought in: a 2016 Lexus GS on March sixteenth, a 2015 Prius C on March nineteenth, and a 2017 Honda Civic and a 2016 Lincoln Navigator on the twenty-first." He waved the paper. "I'll give you these notes. They include the timing of each drop."

I nodded. "Did your friend notice the condition of the front ends of these cars?"

"*Nyet.*"

"Registration? Colors?"

Semyon shook his head. "I'm sorry, Cal. My friend swore he did not have this information."

My heart sank. "That's it, then?"

"There was one other thing. He told me the Lexus was a

stolen car driven up to Portland by a man called Lenny the Fox, a well-known car thief and friend of my friend. The reason he mentioned it, I think, was that this man, Lenny, killed himself the same night he dropped the car off. This bothers my friend. He said he thought it was strange."

"What's Lenny's full name?"

Semyon glanced down at his notes. "Bateman. Leonard Bateman."

I nodded. "So, these cars are stripped and sent to a crusher. What happens next?"

"They're stored until they're shipped off to a scrap recovery operation."

"How long does that take?"

Semyon shrugged. "Hard to say. Weeks or the next day, depending on when they have a full load to ship."

"Are the cubes stored inside or outside?"

He shot me a so-what look. "Some of both, mostly outside."

"Got it." At this point, I ran out of questions, and Semyon seemed anxious to leave. He finished his beer, handed me his notes, and sauntered out, but not before warning me again to be careful. I sat there nursing the last of my beer and turning things over. I was disappointed he didn't have more for me, but I reminded myself this had been a long shot to begin with.

If whoever killed Margaret Wingate *did* use the Boyarchenko ring to get rid of the car, my decision tree split into two branches—accident or murder. If an accident, then it could have been any one of the four cars. I knew the makes, models, and years, but nothing else. If not an accident, then at least I could eliminate the Prius and the Honda. No way a small, light car like either of those would have been selected for such a job, I figured. That left the Lexus and the Lincoln, both of which were stoutly built and could be relied upon to keep going after colliding with a human body.

Another thought occurred to me. If it was a paid hit designed to look like an accident, then using a car from out of town, like the Lexus, would make sense. A car stolen in Portland for the job would have presented a much higher risk of being noticed by the cops.

That was okay, as far as it went, but I finished my beer and left the Annex feeling deflated. Accident or murder, my Hail Mary pass felt like a dud. There was the question of the suicide. I didn't have a clue what it meant, if anything, but I did call Nando Mendoza and asked him to run Leonard—Lenny the Fox—Bateman through his databases.

After a hard run along the river with a happy dog, a whirl-wind shopping tour through Whole Foods for provisions, and a plant-watering stopover at Winona's, I was starved. I'd scored some fresh Alaskan rockfish at the market, which I sautéed in a little butter and lemon juice and topped it with toasted sliced almonds, broiled asparagus drizzled with olive oil, and a nuked sweet potato. The first glass of chilled Sancerre I had with the meal tasted so good I had a second.

I was cleaning up when Nando called back. "This Lenny the Fox…" he began as if we hadn't terminated our previous conversation, "has only the one conviction—grand theft auto when he was twenty-two. He was from L.A. and had a reputation as the Houdini of car thieves. Apparently, he learned well from his one mistake."

I chuckled. "Any family in L.A.?"

"A brother in Highland Park named Kenneth Bateman."

"What about the details of his death? Anything?"

"He was found on the morning of March seventeenth by the maid at Swanson's Motel just off Southeast Foster on 111th. She discovered him hanging from the bathroom door using a noose fashioned from bedsheet strips."

"The bathroom door? Was he a midget?"

Laughter. "No. He apparently put the noose around his neck and simply folded his legs."

"This happens?"

"If the will is there…. I investigated a case once where a man hung himself with his belt from a doorknob."

"Was Lenny's death ruled a suicide?"

"Yes. The case is closed."

"Anything else?"

"Nothing of note except many of the rooms at Swanson's Motel are rented by the hour."

I thanked Nando and told him to put the search on my tab. That alone would eat up the retainer I'd received from Angela. *You've got to be more realistic about your rates*, I told myself, echoing the recurring theme of my accountant, Gertrude Johnson.

I was curious what, if anything, Kenneth Bateman might be willing to tell me about his car-thief brother. I found a phone number for him in the White Pages and had him on the line a couple of minutes later. "I'm sorry for the loss of your brother," I said after introducing myself and emphasizing I wasn't a cop.

"What exactly do you want, Mr. Claxton?" he asked, his tone wary.

"I just have a couple of questions. I'm trying to determine if your brother's death has any bearing on a case I'm involved with."

He puffed a sarcastic breath. "I can tell you Lenny didn't kill himself. That's bullshit."

I popped to attention. "Why do you say that?"

"Lenny was no angel, and he drank a lot, but he'd never kill himself. We received his belongings when they shipped his body down. A switchblade knife was included. The Portland cops said he used it to cut the sheet strips that he tied together to make a noose. My brother was not the type to carry a switchblade, you know?" He laughed. "And Lenny wasn't handy at all. No way he makes a rope out of a bedsheet. No fucking way."

"Did you tell the police this?"

"Yeah, I did, but it was clear they had their minds made up."

When I asked about when and why Lenny went to Portland and who he might have been in contact with, Kenneth cut me off in a hurry. "Lenny never discussed his business dealings with me," his brother said. That ended the conversation.

Afterwards, I sat there in the study, a little stunned. Lenny the Fox stole a Lexus in L.A., drove it to Portland, and then, after dropping the car off at the chop shop, went to a motel and was either murdered or hung himself. That same day, Margaret Wingate was struck and killed by a hit-and-run driver. I got up and retrieved the notes Semyon had given me. I knew from the newspaper report that she was struck around five-thirty p.m. I checked the time that the Lexus was dropped off—six-forty p.m. "That could work," I said out loud, "if the Lexus was driven directly from the crime scene to the chop shop."

I turned to Arch as a small swirl of excitement stirred in my gut. "Damn, Big Boy, the timing fits."

Chapter Eight

That Friday morning I watched as a stream of viscous, aromatic coffee collected in the upper chamber of a small, steam-driven espresso maker, the one I took on fishing and backpacking trips. A little added milk heated on the stove and a sugar cube, and *voilà*—not a cup for a purist but a passable way to start the day. I'd been meaning to get a decent espresso machine for my galley kitchen at Caffeine Central, but like replacing the sign out front, I hadn't gotten around to it.

By the time Archie and I came down to open up, a sizable line had gathered out on Couch Street, promising a busy day. In addition to the usual problems of abrupt lease terminations, evictions without cause, and various complaints about landlord neglect, I was experiencing a sharp uptick in undocumented immigrants looking for advice and reassurance. I was no expert in immigration law, which is highly specialized, but I had a stack of cards on my desk of lawyers who were. If the clients were Hispanic and challenged by English, I sent them off with a reminder that Portland was *una ciudad sanctuaria*.

Around midday, Angela called to say Melvin Turner had contacted her, as I predicted. "He was pissed, Cal," she said. Then, in an exaggerated imitation of his voice, she went on, "'I don't understand why you saw the need to hire some hick lawyer from Dundee. He'll take advantage of you, Angela.'"

I chuckled. "How did you respond?"

"Just the way you told me."

"Good. Listen, I asked him to send you a copy of your mom's will. Keep an eye out for it."

"Will do. Uh, there's something else—I also got a call from a newspaper reporter today. She said she was doing a story on Portland gentrification. I don't know how she got my cell number, but it was pretty cool. She asked me some questions about Mom and the North Waterfront Project."

"What was her name?"

"Cynthia Duncan. She seemed really sharp, Cal."

Uh oh, I said to myself. I knew Cynthia well—an aggressive, thorough investigative journalist. "She *is* sharp. What did she ask you?"

"She asked about Mom, what her role in Wingate Properties was, and how she felt about North Waterfront."

"And how did you respond?"

"I told her about the will and her unexpected death, and that I'd hired an attorney—you—to represent me with all the legal stuff. I told her about Mom's epiphany after the Women's March, and how she wanted to change the direction of Wingate Properties. She started boring in on North Waterfront and Turner and Avery, and that's when I realized I was talking too much, so I shut up. God, I hope I didn't say too much."

I shrugged. "Well, what's done is done. If she calls again, tell her you don't have anything more to add. The problem with reporters is that they have their own agenda and timing, and it might not square with ours."

That's how I left it with Angela. *Great*, I said to myself. I'd worked with Cynthia on an earlier case and knew how relentless she was. I thought about calling her but decided against it. Better to keep a low profile at this point. Maybe this won't go anywhere.

The day flew by, and when I finally closed up shop, I walked with Archie over to Deschutes Brewery for a beer and sandwich and to let the afternoon traffic abate somewhat. I leashed my dog to one of several unoccupied outside tables and took a seat at the window, where we could see each other. Packing seventy muscular pounds with a broad back, a deep chest, and a one-master attitude, Arch was no mark for dog-napping, but we were both more comfortable when connected visually.

I glanced at my watch when I finished eating. I was tired and anxious to get back to the Aerie, but I had one stop to make on the way out of town—Swanson's Motel. *The timing's ideal,* I thought. *By the time I walk back to the car and fight my way over to Southeast Foster, the night shift at the motel should be on, the people who might've seen something the night Lenny the Fox died.*

The Ross Island Bridge was still snarled to a standstill, and I didn't get to the motel until half past seven. The night manager had a poker face marked by a set of vertical lines on either side of his mouth that became deep crevasses when he smiled, which was too often. "Sorry," he told me, "but I don't know spit about that suicide."

"I'm just wondering if Mr. Bateman checked in alone or had any visitors that night."

The crevasses opened up. "I got nothin' to tell you, buddy. Even if I knew something, I don't talk about our clientele. Company policy. Got our reputation to protect."

I swung my eyes around the dingy office. "Of course. If your policy changes, give me a call. I could make it worth your while." I watched his beady eyes as I said the last sentence, but he didn't react in the least.

The motel consisted of two rows of two-story units. I was parked in front, and, when I left, I drove between the two units instead of pulling out on the street. Too early for any John and hooker traffic, the back unit was quiet except for a white panel truck parked in front of a first-floor unit with its door open.

I parked next to the truck, as a small, squat man with sloped shoulders came out of the room carrying a toolbox. I got out and smiled at him. "Keeping the place running, huh?"

He smiled back and shook his head. "Plenty of work around here. You know, doesn't matter what the signs say in the bathroom, the idiots keep trying to flush rubbers down the toilet."

I barked a laugh. "Job security."

He smiled even broader. "You got that right."

I introduced myself, telling him I represented an insurance company. "I'm wondering if you remember anything about the suicide that happened last month, on the sixteenth?"

His face stiffened, and he measured me through rheumy eyes. "Hey, got strict orders not to talk about what goes on at this place. Job security."

I laughed again. "Understand. Just wondering if you were around that night. Whatever you tell me's strictly confidential. I'm not a cop."

He took a furtive look around before answering. "I was around. So what?"

"Did you see the man come in?"

He crossed his arms, and his look turned calculating. "I'm not sure if I remember that exactly."

Shit, I said to myself. *Should have brought more cash.* I took out my wallet, emptied it of two twenties, and extended them. "Would this improve your memory?"

He took the bills and tucked them in a shirt pocket without thanking me. "Had a toilet backup four doors down that night. I was in my truck, seen 'em drive by."

"*Them?* Someone was with him?"

"Yeah, another guy was drivin'."

"How do you know the victim was the passenger?"

"I seen 'im get out. Little, skinny guy. He was wobbly-legged drunk. The maid who found 'im told me what he looked like."

"What about the other man? What did he look like?"

The handyman scratched his head and wrinkled his brow. "Didn't get a good look."

"You didn't see *anything?*"

"Nope. Sorry."

"Did you see the other man leave?"

"Nope."

I knew I'd lose him on the next question, but I had to ask it. "Would you be willing to tell the police what you saw?"

His eyes grew wary. "If you send the cops to talk to me, I'll get amnesia in a hurry. Job security."

"No worries," I said. "What about other people who might've—?"

His phone buzzed, he took the call, and after listening for a moment said, "Gotta run, bub." I handed him a card and told him to call if he thought of anything else, but doubted that the request registered with him. I watched him hurry off, suspecting he might know more than he told me. But at least I saw the vague outlines of something now, and my instincts were to keep pushing.

When I got back in the car, I turned to Archie. "I know you're anxious to get home, Big Boy, but how about one more night in Portland? I'll throw in a river run tomorrow morning." He wagged his stump of a tail and whimpered a couple of times, which I took for a yes. The promised run must've clinched the deal.

I called Angela, and when she picked up asked if she'd gotten a copy of her mother's will yet. "No," she answered.

"Maybe it'll come tomorrow. If it does, call me. I'll be in town, and I want to look it over."

"Okay. Have you found something, Cal?"

"No, nothing like that," I said, not wishing to stir her hopes. "Just laying some groundwork. Call me one way or the other as soon as your mail arrives, okay?"

I called Semyon Lebedev next, got his voicemail, and left a message. He called back just as I let us into the studio apartment.

"Yes, Cal?" he said, his voice clearly surprised but barely audible over the staccato beat I now associated with pole dancing.

"Can you meet me in the parking lot of your club in twenty minutes? I have a quick follow-up question," I said a bit disingenuously. It was a quick question but loaded, too.

The phone went quiet except for the grinding beat. Finally, "Jesus, Cal."

"I know. A friend in need's a pest. Look, it won't take three minutes, I promise."

I heard him exhale over the music. "Okay. I'll be at the north end of the parking lot at eight-thirty. We're busy as hell, so this has to be fast."

Semyon was right on time, emerging out of the shadows between two cars like a big cat. I told him I was interested in the name of a man seen with Lenny the Fox at the motel the night he died. "I'm thinking this guy might have been with Lenny when the Lexus got dropped off at the chop shop."

"Names are harder to come by."

I nodded. "Yeah, I realize that."

Semyon grimaced and stroked his stubbly chin, making a scraping noise in the stillness. "You are putting us both at risk," he complained, but agreed to talk to his friend for me once more.

I thanked him, then thought of one more thing. "Any way your friend could arrange to have the Lexus cube held back, you know, stash it somewhere?"

He shot me a puzzled look. "Why?"

"It might be a murder weapon," I said. "Evidence."

"I will ask him." After a Russian eye roll he disappeared back into the shadows.

By the time I got back to Caffeine Central the second time, I was beat. I took Arch out for a quick stretch and turned in, knowing I wouldn't get many more pages of *The Snow Man* read.

My eyelids were lead-lined, but I was glad when Winona's call came in. I'd tried her earlier without success and was beginning to worry. She asked about me first, and after I brought her up to speed she said, "The thought of someone being killed that way sickens me, Cal. There's no honor among these thieves. Are you sure you can trust this Russian?"

"With my life," I answered. I swung the conversation around to her, knowing things at Standing Rock were in disarray. "What's the latest out there?"

She sighed deeply. "It sucks, majorly. We lost our bid for a temporary restraining order. The camp's been razed, and everyone's leaving the area. They won, Cal."

"What about the courts?"

"We're filing a couple of last-ditch motions. We're saying the pipeline under Lake Oahe could degrade the water, which would interfere with the Sioux Tribe's religious freedom. Their water's sacred." She sighed again. "The motions don't have much of a chance."

The phone went silent for a while, and I listened to her breathing, realizing how much I missed her. "Have you thought about coming back to Portland?"

Her voice grew thick. "How can I leave when these people are suffering so?"

"Maybe there's nothing more you can do at this time. Why don't you come home? I miss—"

Click. She hung up on me. "Damn, damn, damn," I said out loud. The decision to give up the fight was hers to make and hers alone. I knew that. And I sounded like I was putting my feelings ahead of everything else. "What an idiot!" I started to call her back but resisted. I knew her temper well. An apology might escalate the situation even further.

I sat like a lump for a while, then snapped off the light and lay back, staring up at the darkened ceiling. I thought about how to fix it with Winona, but the last thing to drift through my mind before I fell asleep was the despicable crime that had taken place at that intersection up in the West Hills. That was something else I needed to fix.

Chapter Nine

I slept restlessly and got up feeling stiff and tired. It rained most of the night, but a cool east wind had swept the clouds away by the time Arch and I hit the jogging trail. I took my phone with me, hoping Winona would call, but she didn't. She must be really pissed, I decided.

When we got back I called her and when she didn't answer, left a conciliatory message. That didn't make me feel much better, but after a shower and a three-egg omelet with spinach, bacon, and Gruyere cheese I was ready to soldier on.

I spent the morning tidying up the files in my downstairs office, which were a godawful mess. Record keeping wasn't one of my strong points, and I couldn't justify hiring a clerk. Billable hours weren't as important in my *pro bono* practice, but without clerical help I lived in fear of missing a court appointment or a filing date for one of my clients, because I was juggling such a big workload. At one point I looked over at Archie, lying in the corner, chin on paws, with a contented look on his face. "You want to trade jobs?" He raised his chin off his paws and yawned a no thanks.

At eleven ten, Angela called with the news that her mother's will had arrived in the mail from Melvin Turner. She said she was on her way to the Bridgetown Co-op, and I agreed to meet her there. Twenty minutes later Archie and I wove our way through the art gallery, buzzing with shoppers that morning, and found Angela right where we left her last time—in her studio on top of a stepladder working on her chrysalis. This time she was brandishing a wire brush instead of a torch.

"That would look great in my flower garden," I said, after knocking and letting myself in. "I'd put it right next to a couple of my butterfly bushes."

She laughed, a sound I was growing fond of. At that moment I realized why—it reminded me of my daughter Claire's laugh. Not the sound of it, particularly, but the insouciant attitude it reflected—that most things, big and small, deserved a laugh as a first response. It was an attitude Angela obviously shared. "It's spoken for," she said, "but you're right, it belongs in a flower garden. I'd be glad to make you something. I've been known to barter."

My turn to laugh. "Me, too. Maybe we can work something out."

She hung her brush on one of the curved ribs, got down from the ladder, and fetched a large envelope from her workbench. "Here's what came this morning." She extended it to me, her fingers leaving smudge marks on the envelope, then mounted the ladder again, saying over her shoulder, "I'll work while you read. This piece's scheduled for a powder coat in two days and needs a ton of finish work."

I nodded and sat down to read through the will. By the time I finished Angela had switched from using a wire brush to fine grit emery paper, which was giving the piece a burnished, polished look. "Okay," I said, "can you take a break?" She nodded, climbed down, and pulled up a chair. Wearing a black bandanna, pirate style, grime under her short nails, and bandages on a couple of fingers, she eyed me expectantly. I'd gone back and forth with myself about how much to say about the stolen Lexus, the suspicious death of Lenny the Fox, and the man seen with him the night he died. I decided against saying anything.

"Your mother's will is interesting," I began. "She did leave you the house and everything in it, furnishings, computers, flat screens, the riding mower." I smiled. "You could have a blow-out yard sale, or I suppose you can sell the house furnished. The Cadillac SUV and the his-and-hers Jaguars were purchased through Wingate Properties, so they don't belong to you. Same with the boat at the marina."

"Good. I don't want anything to do with those ridiculous cars or that speedboat."

"When you're thirty-five, you'll get the investment portfolio, too. Do you know the value?"

"Melvin told me it was worth around two hundred thousand at the moment. The broker's a guy named Chrysler."

"Huh, I would have expected a higher balance."

She shrugged. "Chuck plowed everything back into the business, so the savings weren't so hot." She laughed, although a bit nervously. "It's more money than I know what to do with."

I nodded. "The disposition of the company's very surprising. The will instructs the executor, Melvin Turner, to sell the company and split the proceeds among the charities your mom was directly involved with."

Angela shrugged. "Yeah, I know. Mom said that Melvin was bugging her about updating her will. She asked me if I had any interest in the company. After I stopped laughing I said something like, "If I owned Wingate Properties, I'd make it a nonprofit for affordable housing."

"How did she react to that?"

"She said maybe that wasn't such a bad idea."

"So are you surprised at the way the will turned out?"

Angela blinked into the middle ground between us. "Well, I know that Brice and Melvin talked to her about selling the company before the accident. She said she told them absolutely not."

"Did she say why they wanted to sell?"

"Some outfit with deep pockets was interested." She laughed. "You know, they'd have more money to rape and pillage."

"Are you surprised it's going to be sold now?"

"Not really. I figure Mom was trying to honor Chuck's feelings. You know, it was his company, and he really didn't approve of me. If I inherited Wingate Properties, he'd start spinning in his grave."

"You're the sole heir to this estate, and that provision cuts you out of the largest portion of it."

"I don't care about that. The only thing I don't like is that she's giving all the money to charities that already have tons of support. There are more deserving causes. I thought she got that."

"The will is dated March first, just fifteen days before the accident. I was surprised the date's so recent," I continued. "Does it surprise you she waited so long after your father's death to update it?"

"Not at all. Mom wasn't what you'd call the organized type. I'll bet she drove Melvin crazy, putting off that chore. I could barely get her to sign my report cards."

I paused at that point to allow myself time to think. Angela got up and made herself a cup of tea, some concoction called rooibos. "Sure you don't want some this time?" She was half teasing. "It's from South Africa. Loaded with antioxidants."

I waved her off, and when she sat back down said, "You have the right to contest this will."

She rolled her eyes. "No way I want to do that. I respect Mom's decisions."

"I know that, and I'm not suggesting you should contest it. But I'd like to give Melvin Turner the impression that after having seen the will we might be considering it."

"Why?"

"Because it'll give me better cover for nosing around."

"Nosing around for what?"

I hesitated for a moment, searching for the right words. "I think there's something odd about the will and about the circumstances of your mother's death."

Her hand rose involuntarily to her mouth, and her big eyes got bigger. "My God, you think it wasn't an accident, that Melvin's involved?"

I raised a hand in caution. "No. There's nothing to suggest anything like that. I just have more questions to ask."

She cocked her head and eyed me skeptically. "You're not telling me everything, are you?"

I smiled, impressed but not surprised by her perceptiveness. "It's better I don't at this point. Trust me."

She hesitated for a moment, then gave a knowing smile. "Okay, that's cool."

As I was leaving I asked her how she got into metal sculpting. "I love to read and draw," she said, "but school wasn't my thing. Too freaking regimented, you know? I decided I wanted to learn auto mechanics. Hands-on, that's me." She laughed. "Mom was horrified, but she was desperate to find something I could do, so she enrolled me in an auto mechanics course offered through the school system. I didn't like it, but I became intrigued with the parts. I mean, have you ever looked, *really looked*, at a piston, for example, or a crank shaft?"

"Uh, no, not really."

She laughed again. "It's form following function, but there's more—a kind of elegance in the form, at least to me. Anyway, I decided I wanted to make stuff out of metal. I talked Mom into springing for some courses at Pacific Northwest Sculptors, and after I got sober, it just took off from there." Her eyes filled with passion. "You know, we think of a material like steel as something rigid and unyielding, but that's not the case. I love bending it to my will, to some vision in my head that I hope has beauty and integrity."

I looked at the nearly finished piece in the center of the room, then back at Angela. "I'd say you've come a long way."

Driving back to Caffeine Central, I thought about the items in the will I hadn't asked Angela about, items I knew she had little interest in. First, the will stipulated that in the event of Margaret Wingate's death, the sale of Wingate Properties was contingent on maintaining the law firm of Turner, Ross, and Steinman, with Marvin Turner as the sole legal representative of the company, and second, if Brice Avery were still CEO of the company, he would remain so. Turner and Avery could only be fired for cause and would both retire at age seventy. I wasn't that familiar with these kinds of arrangements, but I assumed that clause was added to provide some protection for them, and to insure continuity of operation, at least from the point of view of Margaret Wingate. From a buyer's perspective, who would normally want to put their own people in place, this could be a serious impediment.

I was curious to see what Brice Avery and Melvin Turner would have to say about that.

I brought the will with me and told Angela I'd get the original back to her after I made a copy. I'd examined the back pages carefully, which were witnessed by two Turner, Ross, and Steinman employees and duly notarized, all attesting to the document's legitimacy. It looked in perfect order, but I wanted to talk to the two witnesses. I was sure Turner would be loath to cooperate with me. But now I had a new angle and maybe some leverage—the threat of a legal challenge to the document that significantly benefited both Turner and Avery and ran counter to my client's interests. Of course, I had no proof of fraud, and my client really wasn't upset by the will's provisions, but the prospect of depositions and the resultant publicity could hold up the sale of Wingate Properties.

I was fishing, for sure, but my gut told me it was worth exploring.

Chapter Ten

Archie and I arrived back at the Aerie that afternoon. A rain shower had just left the smell of damp earth in its wake, and the spectral trace of a rainbow lay half hidden by the towering firs bordering the east side of my property. As I swung the heavy gate open, my dog sprinted into the yard, scattering a flock of robins busy poaching earthworms from the sodden grass field above the driveway. Standing where the robins had been, Arch turned back to me and barked a joyous chorus, making it clear how glad he was to be back in his kingdom.

It was quiet over in McCallister Quarry, which was a relief, although it was a Saturday and the crew I'd seen in there earlier might've taken the weekend off. I gave Arch his weekly bone and took a sandwich and a beer out on the side porch, which afforded a restricted view into the sunken area where the blasting had taken place. I saw nothing, but after lunch I pried Arch away from his bone and walked the half mile down to the gated entrance to the not-so-abandoned quarry. A big, extended cab pickup with Patterson Engineering Consultants written on the side was parked next to the gate, which was closed but not locked. We let ourselves in and followed what was now a wide, cleared path that looked disturbingly like a road-in-the-making.

I stopped dead in my tracks. Arch sat down next to me and whimpered softly, as if he too sensed a threat. A large piece of machinery painted Caterpillar green had been moved into the quarry in my absence. Resembling the ugly offspring of a tank and a locomotive, it sported the mother of all hoppers resting on the center of an elongated body topped with conveyor belts. The body, resting on a combination of tank treads and balloon tires, was powered by a built-in engine that looked big enough to propel an aircraft carrier. Two men wearing coveralls and ear protection were hunched over the controls of the engine, and as if on cue, fired it up. The behemoth sprang to life, shaking the ground and belching black smoke, the whine of the belts rising in the quiet air like screaming furies. Archie yelped once, turned around, and tugged at his leash. I turned to take him out of there when the machine powered back down. "Sit and stay," I told my dog, then approached the two technicians.

"What the hell is this?" I asked them, although I was pretty sure I knew the answer.

They both turned to face me, and the taller of the two, beaming with almost parental pride, said, "This is a Sanme portable rock crusher."

"No kidding. You mean this thing moves?"

"Well, we brought it in on a couple of eighteen-wheelers, but for short distances, yeah."

The other technician extended a forearm and pointed with an index finger. "This buggy's gonna follow a deep seam of blue basalt that runs in that direction."

I winced inwardly. He'd pointed in the direction of the Aerie, which was barely visible from where we stood. "Oh, you mean right toward that old farmhouse on the ridge over there?"

"Yep. That's the plan."

I kept my cool. "How does the mining work?"

The tall technician stepped forward. "Typically, you blast, skip-load the hopper with rock fragments, crush them in the guts of this thing, and haul the aggregate away in trucks. Demand's high right now, so they'll probably run a twelve-hour operation. Maybe two hundred trucks a day in and out of here."

"That seam of basalt's good for six, eight years of mining," the other tech chimed in.

I swallowed hard and pointed in the direction of the Aerie. "I live in that farmhouse you're aiming for. Does Patterson Engineering realize that this is going to be an illegal operation, that McMinnville Sand and Gravel's not permitted to mine this quarry?"

They looked at each other, then back at me as the mood downshifted. "Hey, we're just here to get this thing running, but I hear they're grandfathered in," the tall tech said.

"Patterson wouldn't touch the job if it wasn't legal," the other tech added.

I handed them each a business card with "Attorney at Law" on it. "Look, I know you guys are just doing your jobs, but this mine's been idle for over twelve years. Grandfather's dead. Tell your bosses at Patterson that if this rig starts up, they're complicit in breaking the law." With that I turned, motioned for Arch to join me, and walked away.

"It's a done deal," the taller tech called after me. "No way you can stop this, dude."

I heard the other tech chuckle under his breath, "Another NIMBY bites the dust."

I kept walking and let the color rising in the back of my neck be my response. *NIMBY?* Not in my backyard. I hadn't heard that acronym in a long time, but I had to admit that it fit. You're damn right, not in my backyard.

"No, I'm not kidding," I said to Marnie Stinson, my contact at the County Planning Commission. "They've moved a humongous rock crusher into McCallister." It was Monday morning. I'd taken Arch out and then dashed across 99W to the Bake My Day for a coffee and *pain au chocolat* break, and was making calls from a back table.

"Are they crushing rock?"

"Not yet, but they sure as hell intend to. I checked with my neighbor, Gertrude Johnson. She's been living next to the quarry most of her life. She told me they stopped mining two months short of thirteen years ago."

"Ten months over the limit. If they start up without a permit they'll be in deep doo-doo."

"Good. I'm driving over to McMinnville right now to tell them that in person."

Marnie paused. "Uh, probably not a good idea, Cal. They won't listen to you. They're notoriously callous about citizen concerns. Let me work it at my end."

I agreed, but only reluctantly, and shook off a feeling of uneasiness by beginning to work the new angle I had on Angela's case. I called Melvin Turner and was put through to his voice-mail, where I informed him that my client had requested me to look into the circumstances surrounding her mother's will. "Angela realizes she may have been a bit naïve about the process," I explained, "and after examining the document, I have a few questions for you and some for your staff. I hope we can handle this informally and avoid the need for depositions." I couldn't help smiling when I hung up, knowing the message would irritate the hell out of Turner.

Brice Avery's assistant put me right through, and when I explained who I was and what I wanted to talk about, he agreed to meet with me at the Wingate Properties headquarters in downtown Portland the following Wednesday. Another midweek trip to Portland. I was starting to feel like a yo-yo.

After dinner that evening, the call I'd been waiting for came in. "Hey," Winona said, "sorry I hung up on you. You didn't deserve that."

"No, it was my fault. It wasn't my place to say anything. I know better than to tell you what to do." We both chuckled at that, and an awkward silence followed. Finally, I said, "Are you okay?"

"No, not really. I'm tired and I'm sick, sick at heart." She expelled a breath. "I'm Native American. We're supposed to be stoic, right? You know, roll with the injustices, live to fight another day. But this is a bitter pill, Cal. We had an injunction; we had them stopped, but that ended with the stroke of the Great White Father's pen in Washington."

Anger tinged with a feeling of guilt washed over me. "Any word on the appeals?"

"No, nothing yet. Our best shot's the one filed by Earth Justice, but even they say it's a candle in a hurricane."

"What are your plans?"

"I'm staying until we get the final word." She sighed long and deep. "I miss you, Cal."

"I miss you, too, Winona. Stay safe."

That was it. I felt let down but grateful for the contact. I wanted to say much, much more, but knew instinctively to keep my mouth shut. I sensed Winona was in a dark place. Better to let her find her way back, a journey she'd do on her own or not at all. Would the anger she felt somehow color her attitude toward me? I hoped not, but guilt by association seemed a valid threat.

That night I dreamed I saw Winona across a wide street, but when I started to cross over to her, the street became a raging river that threatened to sweep me away. I jerked awake just as I lost my footing in the swift current. I must have cried out because Arch came over from his mat in the corner to console me. I swung my legs out of bed and sat there stroking his broad back until I calmed down.

When I got back into bed, my dog lay down next to me on the floor instead of going back to his place in the corner. It was a show of support.

Chapter Eleven

Wednesday morning broke clear, so Arch and I got a run in before heading off to Portland. On the way in, Marnie Stinson called me back. "Our legal counsel contacted McMinnville Sand and Gravel and asked for clarification of their intentions at McCallister," she told me. "He cited neighborhood concerns as the reason. Haven't heard back from them yet, but they won't dare start up now. He said you need to put a letter together substantiating your claim that they've been idle for more than twelve years. Can you do that?"

"You bet." I thanked her, then called Gertie and told her what I needed.

"No problem," she said, "I know several old-timers on the hill who'll back me up on the timing. That was a red-letter day when they stopped mining. Nobody's forgotten it, I guarantee you."

I felt better then, although I still wondered why they'd moved that expensive hunk of machinery back into the quarry. Were they really that reckless, or did they know something I didn't?

After finding a parking space on SW 4th and cracking the windows for Arch, I cut through Keller Fountain Park on my way to the KOIN Tower. Portland had great parks, and this one, with a full acre of cascading waterfalls and pools, was my hands-down favorite. But on this particular morning I was laser-focused on my meeting in ten minutes with Brice Avery, CEO of Wingate Properties.

The firm occupied the entire fifteenth floor of the building, with an understated entry leading into a reception area decorated with photographs of their completed work and a scale model of the North Waterfront Project I'd read about. Nested between meticulous replicas of the Steel and Fremont bridges, the model consisted of low-rise residential units along the waterfront, high-rise office space further back, and what looked like some kind of retail mall near the entry. A yacht harbor ran along the river, a mini-golf course anchored the north end, and in the center of it all, a cylindrical behemoth rose above everything like a gilded phallus. "Tower North."

"I want to live there."

I turned and looked into a pair of vivacious blue eyes. "In the tower?"

The woman laughed. "Of course. At the top." Her name was Brittany. She was Brice Avery's assistant, and she'd come to escort me to his corner office. I followed her shapely figure down the hall.

Avery greeted me cordially, and while Brittany hovered, said, "Join me in some coffee?" I told him I would, and he sent his assistant off to get us some. He showed me to a black leather couch and sat down in a matching chair across from me. Lean and stern-eyed with short, gray-flecked hair and a manicured three-day stubble, he moved with a kind of lithe quickness that people of high energy often exhibit. "So, Cal, you're Angela's attorney," he said with a rueful smile. "She's a pistol, that one. What's on your mind?"

I smiled at that. "I appreciate your meeting with me. As you can understand, the death of Margaret Wingate came as quite a shock to Angela. Now that she's had some time to absorb the tragedy, she has some questions about her mother's estate and how it was handled."

"Margaret's death came as a shock to me and our entire company as well. What are Angela's intentions with this inquiry?"

"I think inquiry may be too strong a word. I'm sure you agree that Mrs. Wingate's will is unusual. Angela simply wants to confirm that the will reflects her mother's true intentions."

At that point, Brittany returned with our coffees, served old-school in bone china cups on a silver tray. Avery set his coffee on the burnished hardwood table between us, dropped in a sugar cube, and stirred. "I'd say Angela did pretty well, considering what she put her parents through. She got the house and the investments, right?"

I nodded. "Angela has straightened out her life, and she and Mrs. Wingate had re-established a strong relationship. Did Mrs. Wingate discuss any of the terms of the will with you?"

"No, she did not. It was a real shocker when I heard what she'd done. I knew she loved the company and wanted to see the work go forward." He looked away, and for a moment I thought he was going to tear up.

"You mentioned the work going forward. Did you and Mrs. Wingate discuss the projects you're engaged in here?"

He sipped some coffee. "Oh, in a general way, yes, but Margaret wasn't all that interested in real estate development. She had her charities. That was her focus."

"I see. She gave you a lot of autonomy in running the company after Charles Wingate passed on?" He nodded, and I leveled my eyes on him. "What about in the last couple of months? Did she push for any changes?"

His eyes held, but a muscle along his jaw line flexed ever so slightly. "Well, she did raise some questions about the North Waterfront Project, but we were down the road on that one. Hell, we already had a green light from the Design Commission and the backing of the Development Commission. By and large, I'd say she was delighted with the direction of the company. This promises to be our best year ever."

"Did you broach selling the company with Mrs. Wingate recently?"

He shot me a so-what look. "Inquiries come in frequently. Portland's hot. Yeah, I think I talked to her about some interest six or eight weeks ago." He laughed. "She made it clear she wasn't interested in selling."

"Did Mrs. Wingate mention that she was revising her will?"

"No, she didn't. But she wouldn't have. It was certainly none of my business."

"Did she discuss any of the provisions in the will with you?" He shook his head. "Did Melvin Turner discuss anything relating to the will with you?"

"No, not before the fact. Like I said, Margaret Wingate's will was none of my business. I was blown away when I heard what she'd done." He met my eyes. "I feel a great obligation to make this company everything she wanted it to be."

I nodded. "Any buyers on the horizon?"

"Let's just say there's interest." He sipped his coffee and added, "Look, Cal, I guess I can't blame Angela for questioning things, and I'm going to assume you're a stand-up guy, but under the circumstances, I think things worked out about as well as they could have. Angela now has a tidy nest egg, the work at Wingate Properties will go forward unabated, and Margaret's beloved charities will get an enormous cash infusion when the company sells."

I nodded again. "Any concern a buyer might balk because of the unique arrangement set out in the will for you and Melvin Turner?"

He waved a hand dismissively. "I don't think that'll be an issue. Most buyers will be looking at the bottom line and how it got there." He smiled again, revealing a sense of confidence that stopped just short of arrogance. "Mel and I know this business, and we know Portland. I think we'll win that one."

I wrapped it up with Avery after a few more questions, and Brittany sashayed me out. The sun was hanging tough, so I hustled to the car, let Archie out, and walked him over to Keller Fountain Park. We found a bench in the warm sunshine. As Arch watched a cross-section of hearty Portlanders wading in the pools, I thought about Avery's comments. I had to admit that what he'd said about the outcome of Margaret Wingate's will— that it was a win for everyone involved—made a lot of sense. The only thing that bothered me was what Avery said about his relationship with Margaret. Were things really as harmonious as he claimed? Not according to what Angela told me. Maybe she exaggerated—although there didn't seem to be any reason why she would—or maybe Avery played the disagreement down.

If he did, he was hiding something.

My second meeting with Melvin Turner went even worse than the first. He met me in the lobby of Turner, Ross, and Steinman this time and showed me to a small conference room. His pudgy, clean-shaved cheeks were slightly flushed. "What is this crap, Claxton?" he began after closing the door. "You have no grounds whatsoever to be challenging Margaret Wingate's will. This is an outrage, and you're skating on very thin legal ice."

I smiled and raised an open hand. "Easy, Melvin. I'm not accusing you of anything, and I'm not challenging anything. I'm simply here to ask a few informal questions. You know very well that Margaret Wingate's will is somewhat unusual. It benefits both you and Brice Avery and cuts my client out of a multimillion-dollar asset. I'm—"

"Margaret wanted it that way," he cut in as a vein surfaced in his neck and his eyes bulged a little. "She wanted Wingate Properties to carry on and leave a substantial sum to her favorite charities. I think what we came up with meets both those criteria. And she wanted Angela to be well taken care of, which she is now. I knew Angela was selfish, but I never expected this." He stopped there and shot me a withering look. "Or is this your doing, Claxton?"

Ignoring the question, I said, "I know it's an imposition, but I'd like to talk to the people who witnessed the will-signing, uh, Arnold Percy and Helen Ferris. We can do it this way, or proceed more formally if you prefer."

Turner dragged a hand down his cheek absently. "Helen's retired now. I suppose you can talk to Arnold for a couple of minutes. Wait here. I'll send him in."

"Thanks, Melvin," I said, flashing a cordial smile. He nodded curtly, and at the door said, "You'd be well advised to drop this now. I'm keeping a complete record of this entire fiasco."

"Thanks, Melvin. I'll consider that as a piece of friendly advice and not a threat."

The chat with Arnold Percy lasted only a few minutes. Yes, he witnessed the signing of Margaret Wingate's will and, yes, she seemed in complete control of her faculties during the time of the signing, and, no, he wasn't privy to any of the discussions leading up to the will. I thanked him and found my way out. I didn't expect to learn anything from Percy, and I wasn't surprised when I didn't. But the timing of Helen Ferris' retirement caught my attention.

Back at the Aerie that night I got a dinner nod from Gertie, something I never turn down since she's a fabulous cook. She served up comfort food—beef stew, biscuits from scratch, and a pear-hazelnut tart for desert that blew the doors off. But the meal came with a price—a game of Scrabble in which I was crushed, as usual. However, I did leave that night with the names, addresses, and phone numbers of six people living in the surrounding Red Hills area who would attest to the fact that gravel mining had ceased at McCallister quarry on June 15, 2004, twelve years and ten months ago.

Later that night in my study I pulled Angela's copy of her mother's will from my briefcase and attached a sticky note to it, on which I jotted "copy" to remind myself to do so and get the original back to her. I don't know why, but I began leafing through it again. I had no conscious reason for doing this except for the fact that it wasn't paginated, which was somewhat unusual. Even given that, the will now seemed much less an issue than it had earlier.

I took another look at the next-to-last page, which consisted of two parts. The first, a "Testimonium," read "In witness whereof, I have signed and do declare this instrument to be my last will and testament, this 8th day of March, 2017, at Portland, Oregon." It was duly signed "Margaret A. Wingate" in clear, left-leaning cursive. The second part, an "Attestation," read "This instrument consisting of thirteen (13) typewritten pages, including this page, was on the above date and in our presence, signed by Margaret Wingate." Below this were the signatures of the two witnesses, Percy and Ferris, and their addresses.

I turned to the addendum, an "Affidavit of Attesting Witnesses," which stated again that Percy and Ferris witnessed the signing of the will and that they believed Margaret A. Wingate "was of the age of 18 years or older, of sound mind and memory, and was acting voluntarily." This was signed by the two witnesses and dated and stamped by a Notary Public.

All by the book, I concluded once again.

I scanned the body of the will a final time. The lower right-hand corner of each page bore the initials MAW and the date in the same slanting cursive as Margaret's signature. I dropped the document on my desk and was halfway out the door when something hit me. I went back and counted the initialed pages in the body again. Thirteen. I read through the Attestation again. It said the will has thirteen pages, *including* the Attestation page. But the document in front of me, if one included the Attestation page, added up to fourteen pages.

There's an extra page somewhere.

I sat back down. Something wasn't right. Since the Testimonium and Attestation were together on a single page, the body of the will was one more page than it should have been. No question. I looked through the will again. The body would be the easiest section to remove and replace with something else, since that act would only require forging Margaret Wingate's initials.

I leaned back, laced my fingers behind my head, and studied the textured paint on the ceiling of my study for a few moments. Margaret Wingate's will was not "by the book," after all. Was this an innocent clerical error or something more sinister?

Chapter Twelve

I stood at the kitchen window the next morning, sipping a coffee and watching the fog burn off in the valley. By the time I finished the cup, only the mist hovering above the Willamette River was left, a gray snake winding through the valley. I was grinding beans for a second cup when the shock wave of the first blast passed under my feet like a subway train. The house creaked, and I saw a puff of plaster dust fall from a corner in the ceiling. The second blast was stronger, rattling the cupboards and sloshing the coffee in my cup.

"*Damn*," I said as a plume of dust rose in the quarry, and the *beep beep beep* of a front-loader kicked in. I went out on the porch for a better look, just in time to hear the deep growl of the rock crusher starting up and to see another plume—this one a black swirl of combusted diesel fuel—rise in the sky.

I stood there in disbelief. Gravel mining in McCallister Quarry had recommenced and Claxton's Aerie had a front row seat.

That's when I thought of Archie. I followed the porch around to the front of the house and called him, but he didn't come. I trotted down to the mailbox, calling his name all the way, but didn't see him. I jogged back to the house, got in the car, and at the mailbox took a right in the direction of the cemetery. Surely he would run away from the source of the blasts, I figured.

I found him standing next to a large stone that marked the

grave of Alexander Johnson, Gertie's great grandfather. His ears were down, and he was still panting. When he saw me, his ears rose a little, but he came to me slowly, like he was ashamed of having run away. I took a knee and embraced him, relieved that he was no longer shaking. "It's okay," I breathed into his ear. "Come on, let's go home."

Then I realized that was the last place he wanted to be.

"You have no right to be mining at McCallister," I said after introducing myself to Mason Goodings, the president of McMinnville Sand and Gravel, and describing the situation. It was twenty-five minutes later, and I'd just been shown into his office by a hesitant secretary.

The borderline obese man with a round face and eyes in a perpetual squint said, "I'm sorry that our operation's inconveniencing you and your dog, Mr. Claxton, but I can assure you we have every legal right to be mining at that site. This county's growing fast and high-quality aggregate's an essential ingredient."

I told him his grandfathered status at McCallister had expired and that I could prove it, but this didn't seem to ruffle him, and he gave me no insight into what he thought their legal basis was. He did tell me they planned to mine twelve hours a day and seven days a week. I said, "I'll see you in court," and stomped out.

On the way back to Dundee, I reached Marnie Stinson. "I'm sorry, Cal. I was going to call you this morning," she said after I dumped my bucket. "It looks like they might have a legitimate position. They're claiming that after they shut down they continued to sell inventory from McCallister for the next twelve months. That means that, technically, they've only been shut down for eleven years and ten months, just under the twelve-year cutoff."

"That's bullshit," I shot back. "Selling gravel after the fact can't be the same as running a mining operation."

A long pause ensued before she told me that, yes, it was the same, that the question had been litigated and was settled law. "I'm sorry, Cal. It doesn't look like you can stop them. Mining interests in Oregon usually get their way."

On the way back to Dundee, I returned a call from Gertie, who took the devastating news with predictable stoicism. "Well," she said, "we took it before, and we can take it again." Then she sighed into the phone. "But what about Archie?"

"Yeah," I said, "good question. I don't think this is what he signed up for."

By the time we got back to the Aerie the mining operation was in full swing, with the ever-present back-up beeping, the whining engines and whooshing jake brakes of trucks coming and going, and, in the background, the steady rumble of blue basalt being crushed—a sound not unlike a distant whitewater river. Even in the absence of blasting, Archie was intimidated and didn't want to get out of the car. I didn't feel much differently.

Our sanctuary was under attack, and I didn't have a clue what to do about it.

I was distracted but managed to get some work done at my office that day. Between clients, I called Marnie back, and she agreed to get me whatever information she could on when and where the alleged gravel sales had occurred. I wasn't sure what I'd do with the information, but I sure as hell wasn't going down without a fight.

I was due at Caffeine Central the next day, which was a relief because being at the Aerie during mining was unthinkable, especially for Arch, whose only coping mechanism was to bolt. After a final conference call, I left him in the office, drove to the Aerie and hurriedly packed enough clothes for the weekend, then looped back to pick him up. On the way into Portland I called Angela and told her I wanted to talk to her.

"I'm at home right now," she said. "Why don't you stop by? I'm on Killingsworth, in Northeast." She gave me the street number.

An hour later, I parked a half block down from her place, an old Craftsman that had seen much better days. Angela was sitting between two tapered columns on the front porch, wearing a pair of shorts, hiking boots, and a sweatshirt with "Resist" written across a clenched fist. A street bike leaned against the porch enclosure next to her. Archie went to her like a long-lost friend, and she laid a sketchpad and pencil down to fuss over him.

"Your bike?"

"Yeah, I have an old Honda I use for work at night, but during the day I try to use the bike as much as possible."

I glanced at the pad, which showed the sketch of a woman jogging. "You draw, too?"

She looked up. "Sort of. I always start a new project with sketches until I get the concept right." She picked up the pad and closed it, making it clear she didn't want to discuss the sketch.

I looked around at the neighborhood. Angela's place looked like the best-maintained house on the block. She watched me, then swept a hand dramatically. "Inner Northeast. Beats the snobby West Hills any day."

I chuckled. "I love these old houses. They have great bones."

She laughed. "Great bones, maybe, but not much else. This place sucks, but it's relatively cheap. I have five roommates. Four of us have bedrooms. The last one in lives in the basement with the mice."

"Are you planning to move?"

She looked past me, down the block. "I haven't faced up to that yet. I like this neighborhood, even though there's a crack house down at the corner, and this is disputed territory between two gangs." Her look turned serious. "I'd feel like a traitor, you know? I mean, this turf's worth fighting for." She paused. "But I'm sure you didn't come to talk about real estate. What's happening?"

I described my meetings with Brice Avery and Melvin Turner. When I finished I said, "So, they both agree with you that your mother's will is pretty reasonable, all things considered." She shrugged, and I continued, "One thing struck me—Avery said that your mother quibbled a bit with the North Waterfront Project but didn't really object."

Her eyes got big, her face incredulous. "That's such bullshit. She hated that project and wanted it redirected."

"Are you sure?"

"That's what she told me. She called it Disneyland Northwest." Another shrug. "But Brice is a smooth talker. I don't know, maybe he convinced her. I'm sure it'll make a shitload of money for the company and put a bunch of hard hats to work."

I considered that. "Are things pretty much the way they were at the West Hills house when your mom died?"

"Yeah. The gardener still comes, and I stop by to pick up the mail, but I haven't been inside since it happened."

"Would you mind if I looked around?"

"Not at all. I'll get the keys." She went inside, taking the bike with her.

On the way there she asked me what I was looking for.

I shrugged. "I'm not really sure—certainly anything pertaining to your mom's will and her activities before the accident. I'm just trying to tie up some loose ends."

She gave me a look, making it clear she knew I was still keeping my cards close to my chest. But she let it slide again. I took that as an expression of trust.

A magnificent, turn-of-the-twentieth-century brick Georgian with a white-trimmed, semicircular portico, the Wingate house exhaled a cool, musty breath when Angela opened the massive front doors. She hesitated for a moment, then plunged in. "Mom's study is back through here." She led me to a small alcove off the dining room. She turned her back with a pained expression on the family pictures covering one wall. "I can't stand to look at those."

"This won't take long," I assured her. I checked the bookshelves lining an entire wall and also the drawers in a fine mahogany library table that doubled as a desk. Nothing of interest. A cabinet in the corner had neatly filed financial records, tax information, a load of family memorabilia and correspondence, and in the bottom drawer, a file marked "Will." I extracted two copies of Margaret Wingate's will from the file. They were copies of the will I had examined. "Do you know where the original copy of the will is?"

"I think Melvin must have it. He had me let him in so that he could retrieve it."

"Did you see him do that?"

"Yeah, I was standing right there." She nodded toward the file. "He took the original and the extra copies, too, I think."

"When?"

"Right after Mom was killed. The next day."

"Did you look through the copies?"

"No. I really didn't want to."

I nodded. "Okay. Did your mom have a computer?"

"Yeah, a MacBook."

"What about an appointment book?"

"Sure. There's a room off the kitchen she used a lot, too. They're probably there."

That room had a computer—but it was an old HP that contained nothing but recipes filed in various folders and a collection of digital photos. There was no appointment book and the drawers of a built-in desk contained nothing of interest, either. We worked our way through the rest of the downstairs rooms but came up empty.

I followed her up an elegant, curved staircase to the second floor. The master bedroom was done in earth tones and had a carpet so thick it practically hid my shoes, but we found no computer or appointment book or anything else that might shed light on Margaret's last days. After going through an antique jewelry box on the dresser, I said, "You should probably put the jewelry in a safe deposit box. Some of it looks pretty valuable."

Angela shrugged predictably. "It's all insured, according to Melvin."

A large walk-in closet separated the bedroom from the bath. I looked through four designer handbags resting on a shelf. Empty. "She must have been using a purse," I said. "Where is it?"

"Good question," Angela said. "I don't see her favorite one, a leather bag with a shoulder strap." I stepped into the bathroom to look around, and Angela called out. "Found it. It was under her robe hanging on the door." She handed me the purse, which was packed with personal items, and looked away. I took a cursory look, opening her mother's wallet last. Front and center was a snapshot of Angela carrying a sign at the Women's March. The sign read "Bitches Get Shit Done."

I showed Angela the photo, and her eyes welled up and overflowed. "Oh, shit."

"Your mom was clearly very proud of you."

She studied her boots, which had taken a couple of direct teardrop hits. "Yeah, well, I can't understand why."

I was putting the checkbook back after scanning through it, when a slip of paper with a grocery list in Margaret Wingate's left-slanted handwriting fell out. On the back she'd written the names Fred Poindexter and Tracey Thomas along with a phone number for each. I knew Thomas was a city councilwoman and thought I'd heard of Poindexter but couldn't remember who he was. I put the slip of paper in my shirt pocket. We went through the rest of the second floor without finding anything else of interest. "Could your mom's computer be in the shop?" I asked.

"It's a Mac. What are the chances?"

Back on the first floor, I checked the windows. They were all locked except for a small one in a half bath. The tile floor of the room was clean and shiny so that the two small, brown shell fragments I noticed stood out. I let myself out the kitchen door and checked below the window. The area had been mulched with crushed pecan shells.

I came back in and locked the window. Angela, who'd been watching me, said, "What was that all about?"

I showed her the pecan shells I'd picked up off the floor. "I think someone came in through this unlocked window and left these behind."

Her big eyes got bigger. "A burglar?"

"Yeah, but not in the conventional sense. He wasn't interested in your mom's jewelry or any of the other valuables in the house. I think he took your mom's computer, her datebook, and probably anything else he didn't want us to find." *And, maybe the burglar replaced the wills in the study with new versions*, I thought but didn't say.

"Holy shit," she said. "This is getting weird."

I had to agree. Weird, indeed.

Chapter Thirteen

Angela peppered me with questions on the way back from our search of her mother's house. I still wasn't prepared to tell her everything—particularly my questions about the will. No way I wanted any of that getting back to Melvin Turner, but I figured she needed to know about the Lexus and Leonard Bateman, so I filled her in. "So, this Lexus that some dude named Lenny the Fox stole in L.A. gets delivered to a crusher an hour and a half after Mom was hit," she said at one point. "Then he winds up dead in a motel that night." I nodded. "Couldn't that just be a coincidence?"

"Yeah, that's possible. As I said, Lenny's death was suspicious, but I've got nothing to connect it to your mother's death, except the timing. I've got some inquiries out on the man seen with him that night, but nothing's come back yet."

"And now you think someone went through mom's house and took her computer."

"Yeah, it looks that way. Look, Angela, until we get a handle on this, I want you to pay extra attention to your surroundings. If you see anything or anyone that doesn't look right, you need to tell me right away." I hesitated, because I didn't want to frighten her, but added, "Why don't you use your car to get around during the day for a while?"

Her eyes got big, and she laughed. "No fricking way! Why would I do that?"

"It would get you off the streets with your bike."

She drew her face into a defiant look that took me back to scenes with my daughter. "Have you noticed the traffic in this town? And lack of parking spaces? I'm not doing that," she said with finality. Then she smiled. "Besides, I'd be a moving target."

So was your mom, I thought but didn't say. I should have known. Caution simply wasn't in Angela Wingate's DNA. When I left that afternoon, I did manage to extract a promise that she would check in with me every day. It was a start.

Later that afternoon Archie and I were busy in Winona's apartment in the Pearl. I was watering her plants, and he was on a general sniff-around. Suddenly he stopped, his ears came up, and he barked a single note as a key rattled in the front door. I swung around, and there was Winona. After a long embrace I managed to say, "Welcome back. I didn't kill a single plant."

Winona returned a wan smile instead of the laugh I expected. "I can't thank you enough for taking care of things, Cal. It was such a relief knowing the apartment was in good hands."

I would've preferred a passionate kiss over a heartfelt thank you, but I let it ride. She dropped to one knee and hugged Archie, who stood next to her wagging his butt and making little whimpering sounds. Was it just me, or did my dog get a warmer reception than I had? She slumped down in a big leather armchair and put a grimy boot on the matching hassock. Her raven hair lacked its customary sheen and was pulled straight back, as if in haste. Her almond eyes were puffy and had little half-moons of discoloration under them. "God, I'm tired."

I took her bags up to her bedroom platform, then circled through the kitchen and poured us each a glass of wine. I handed her a glass and touched its rim with mine. "*Santé.*"

"*Santé,*" she replied mechanically and without making eye contact. "The plane was delayed five hours in Salt Lake City." She shook her head. "I didn't need that."

I drank some wine. "Why didn't you call me? I could've picked you up."

"I got a ride from Hal Lightfeather. I figured you'd be busy, you know, a weekday."

"You hungry? I could go get some food and fix us a good meal."

She looked at me, and suddenly her eyes went bright with moisture. "I think I'll just take a bath and go to bed," she said, her voice thick. "Do you mind? I'm just shitty company right now."

I sat there for a moment, trying not to look stunned. "Yeah, sure. You've been through an ordeal." I resisted the urge to scream, "Talk to me!" I got up, and she continued to sit, her cheek cradled in her palm. "I'll call you tomorrow." And I let Arch and myself out.

I was glad I'd parked three blocks away, because I needed to walk to clear my head. The debacle at Standing Rock was a crushing defeat, and I knew Winona didn't just feel it for herself, she felt it for all the assembled Native Americans there, each and every one of them. *Now she's trying to deal with it as best she can,* I told myself. *She's proud and strong and doesn't want me to see her like this. That's got to be it, so don't take it personally.*

It was good advice, reflecting a mature attitude, but by the time I got to the car, I looked down at Arch and said, "Yeah, but who in the hell is Hal Lightfeather, anyway?"

That Friday at Caffeine Central was as busy as I'd ever seen it, which was fine with me. It kept me from brooding about Winona and the mining going on in my backyard, although it did occur to me at a lull that if it was true that bad luck came in threes, I was really screwed. In addition to the usual real estate issues and immigration inquiries, I found myself counseling a young couple that morning, who were squabbling over ownership of one of the city's newest phenomena, a tiny house. "You wouldn't have sought a mediator unless you were reasonable people," I said after listening to them bicker for forty minutes. "Try again, and if you can't work it out, come back in two weeks and I'll decide it for you. I doubt you'll both be happy with the outcome."

During lunch I got a text from Semyon Lebedev:

Buy me a beer? Same place Saturday around 4.

I texted back that I would be there.

Business dropped off that afternoon, which was a good thing, because I'd identified and scheduled meetings with the two people whose names I'd found in Margaret Wingate's purse. Okay, it was a slim reed, but it was all I had to go on related to her activities prior to her death.

"Yes, Mrs. Wingate came to see me a couple of times about the North Waterfront Project," Fred Poindexter said in answer to my first question. We were through the introductions, which included my telling him I was following up on some issues pertaining to the Wingate estate. Poindexter, it turned out, was director of the Portland Planning Commission. Vegan thin with a neatly trimmed beard, he had a quick smile and eyes that seemed to dart rather than move. "We, um, had some quite detailed discussions about it."

"Why would she come to you about her own company's project?"

"She had some concerns. I think she was looking for an independent assessment. A project of this magnitude's a joint effort between the city and the developer."

"What were her concerns?" He hesitated for a moment. "I'm just curious," I added. "Her daughter told me she had serious misgivings about the project."

He smiled. It looked a bit forced. "She wondered why we weren't insisting on more of a mixed-use project with less emphasis on private luxury amenities."

"And…?"

The smile again. "I explained that our master plan calls for commercial and high-end residential development for that area, similar to the South Waterfront. The jobs created and the potential tax revenues the project will generate are essential to the city." With that, Poindexter launched into a sales pitch.

When he finished, I said, "She agreed, then?"

"Yes, after our second meeting, she was satisfied with the plan."

We talked a bit more about the planning process and Portland's master plan, but that was pretty much it. I told him thanks and left him with a puzzled look on his face. He really wasn't sure why I'd come in the first place.

My meeting with Tracey Thomas was a different story. "Margaret Wingate had profound misgivings about the North Waterfront Project," Thomas replied when I told her what Poindexter had said. She was an attractive, outspoken woman with a quick mind and sharp wit who had been elected to City Council against considerable odds. "I was flabbergasted, you know, when she came in here and told me that. I mean, here's the owner of the biggest real estate development company in Portland doubting the direction of her own project. Wow."

"Why did she come to see you?"

"She wanted my views on the project." Thomas smiled with a hint of pride. "I think she knew my reputation for questioning all the mindless development going on in this beautiful city of ours. We talked at length about what's happening. She was hungry for information, like the newly converted always are." Thomas smiled with genuine warmth. "She told me about the Women's March, how she went to Washington with her daughter, how it was transformative for her." She paused, and her face clouded over. "A shame what happened. Jogging. God. I run every day, just like she did."

I nodded. "So, she was thinking about redirecting the project?"

"Yeah, I think so. She was trying to get up to speed, but that was her intent. Why not mixed-use, instead of ultra-high-end? Just like me, she detested that hideous tower, the golf course, the yacht harbor. Yuck."

"But Brice Avery was resistant? Did she say that?"

"She said it was like trying to turn a battleship. I mean, it's the biggest single project this city's ever seen, and Avery's set to take a lot of the credit." Thomas met and held my eyes. "Fred Poindexter wants it, too, and doesn't want anything negative said about it."

"Will City Council approve it?"

She sighed. "It won't get my vote, but it'll probably pass since the Planning Commission blessed it. The Council's never seen a major project it didn't love."

"What about the mayor?"

She shrugged. "He's new, like me." Her eyes twinkled for an instant. "We'll see if he has a pair or not."

I chuckled. "What about the financing?"

"Funny you should ask. I just heard yesterday from sources that the funds are there. Out-of-state money. That's another strike against the project, as far as I'm concerned."

"Do you know who the investor is?"

"Nope, but I'm working on it."

"If you find out, would you let me know?"

She eyed me with obvious curiosity and smiled. "Your reputation precedes you, Cal Claxton. You've got great street cred, and you've solved some major crimes in this city. I know you're representing Margaret's daughter, but what's really behind all these questions?"

I sensed I could trust her, and God knows I needed help. "Let's just say the terms of the will are a little surprising. For example, it directs the executor to sell the company. I'm taking a look at it as a favor to Ms. Wingate, the only remaining heir."

She came forward in her seat. "Wingate Properties is on the block? That's a shocker. You think the will is illegit?"

I shook my head. "Nowhere close to that. But I am curious about the investor."

She held her eyes on me for a few beats. Wide-spaced under arching brows, they were the color of nutmeg. "Okay, I'll keep my ear to the ground."

We sat there for a while. "What's the endpoint of all this development?" I mused, breaking the silence. "Will Portland just keep growing until it's squeezed out everything that made it attractive and vibrant in the first place?"

She rolled her eyes. "It's a race to the bottom paved with gold. But it's not too late. What we need are leaders who'll put the city ahead of money and politics. And at least the press isn't all-in on the development frenzy. A reporter for *The Oregonian* just interviewed me for a major piece she's working on."

"Cynthia Duncan?"

"Yeah. You know her?" I nodded, and she chuckled. "She let me go on about the insanity of the North Waterfront Project. Had her tape recorder running through my whole rant."

I thanked her and left, thinking that if Tracey Thomas ever decided to run for mayor, I'd volunteer to be her campaign manager. And I came away knowing investigative reporter Cynthia Duncan was still out there. A blessing or a curse? I wasn't sure which.

Back at Caffeine Central, I took Arch out for our usual run along the river. A brisk wind was blowing rain clouds around, but none had managed to accumulate over city center. Cooped up most of the afternoon, he took off like a prancing pony, tugging on his leash, urging me on. It felt good to blow the pipes out, and by the time we got back to the stairs at Burnside, I was huffing and sweating. I felt better than I should have, considering that my personal life had pretty much gone to hell. The saving grace was the Wingate case, I realized. I felt like I was making progress, and that brought a feeling of anticipation and no small amount of satisfaction.

All the same, the accelerating pace of the investigation brought an element of *déjà vu* and a sense that I was, if not on, then damn close to a slippery slope. It was a feeling I'd learned not to ignore.

Chapter Fourteen

Spring got a boost that weekend when a high-pressure ridge parked just north of the state of Washington, holding the jet stream at bay up in Canada. The temperature drifted into the seventies, and the sky turned that achingly clear, cobalt-blue unique to the Northwest. I slept in until about nine on Saturday, got up, and texted Winona:

You up? I'm bringing coffee and almond croissants.

This came back:

Thanks, but I'm off for the Rez. Need a sweat lodge cleansing.

I texted her back, wishing her well, but that stung; not even an indication of when she was coming back, and I was too proud to ask. I looked at Archie. "Let me guess. Hal Lightfeather's going to join her for the sweat?" He looked back with a scolding look as if to say, "Don't doubt her," although it was more likely he just wanted to be fed.

Later that morning I was perusing my e-mail when a note from Marnie Stinson pinged in:

Hi Cal, according to records submitted by McMinnville Sand and Gravel, their aggregate inventory was sold exclusively by H and S Landscape and Construction Supply out of Newberg. The owner's name is Dudley Cahill. The attached PDF shows the sales records in question. It doesn't look good. Sorry. Marnie.

I printed out the attached file—three pages of sales records covering the time after the mine was shut down, each page signed by Dudley Cahill. The sales continued for eleven months and a couple of days, according to the records. Subtracting that from the time the mine was idle—twelve years and ten months— brought the time down to eleven years and eleven months, or a month shy of the twelve-year cutoff. This appeared to confirm McMinnville's assertion that they were mining legally. *Shit.*

I looked through the printout again, tossed it on my desk, and leaned back. A record like that could be altered, of course. Any record can. I wanted more proof, like receipts for the delivery of the gravel. Somebody—an independent contractor, proba- bly—hauled some of that rock from McCallister to H and S in dump trucks, and there should be a record of that as well. The county folded after seeing scant proof of timing, which was no doubt evidence of the clout the mining company had. But this wasn't over, as far as I was concerned. I picked up the phone and called H and S, and was told that Dudley Cahill was out until the following Tuesday.

I made an appointment to see him.

After lunch I put Arch into the car and headed north on the I-5. About a mile from the bridge into Vancouver—Portland's neighbor just across the Columbia River in Washington—the traffic sputtered to a crawl, which even on a Saturday had become a common occurrence. A badly needed bridge expansion project had died in a hail of interstate politics four years earlier. But it wasn't just the bridge on the river. Traffic across the Portland area was becoming more like L.A. every day. Ah, the march of progress.

Helen Ferris, the other person who witnessed the signing of Margaret Wingate's will, lived in Vancouver, just off East McLaughlin, near Clark College. I parked in front of her two- story brick townhouse, cracked the car windows, and told Archie to chill.

The townhouse sat at the end of a row of well-maintained condos that were old enough to have ivy growing on some of the brick walls. She didn't answer the bell, but I thought I heard something inside, maybe a TV or radio. I tried the bell again, then walked around the side of the house to a gate leading to the fenced-in backyard. On my tiptoes, I caught a glimpse of a woman hunched over a flat of flowers. "Mrs. Ferris," I called out, "can I come in?"

"Are you the electrician? You certainly got here fast," she called back.

A little luck now and then never hurts. I didn't answer but let myself in and approached with what I hoped was a disarming smile. "Those impatiens will do a lot better in the shade." I pointed to an area along the walkway. "Maybe over there?"

She looked up at me with a hand shading her eyes. "You're not the electrician. Who are you?" She stood up with the aid of a cane and faced me, holding a trowel with a firm grip. She was tall with soft gray eyes, a square, no-nonsense jaw, and straight, russet-red hair that hung like a fringe below a broad-brimmed gardening hat. I introduced myself and handed her a card. "Oh." Her face instantly clouded over. "Melvin said you might be in touch."

"Well, if you've spoken to Mr. Turner, then you know why I'm here. I apologize for just barging in, but I was in the neighborhood, which, by the way, is lovely," I said, holding the smile. "I'm hoping you could spare me a few minutes of your time."

"I was Mr. Turner's confidential secretary, so there's very little I'm at liberty to discuss. I'm sure you understand that, Mr. Claxton."

"Of course." I'd done some homework and knew she worked directly for Turner for several years and was married, although according to Angela, her husband was afflicted with early onset Alzheimer's and had been in a care facility for some time. "I'm just, you know, tying up a few loose ends for Ms. Wingate regarding the disposition of her mother's will. Everything looks in order, so I'll probably be wrapping this up soon," I lied. "You know these millennials. Such an impetuous bunch."

She smiled faintly. "Yes, Angela's certainly that." *And a lot more*, I read from the lingering ambiguity of her expression.

I took her through a series of questions relating to the timing and process used to update Margaret Wingate's will, some of which she answered and others she didn't. I ended by saying, "And I assume you were the person who typed up the drafts and the final product?"

The question seemed to unnerve her for a moment. "I typed up all of Melvin's work. It was my job."

I smiled warmly. "Of course, and I'm told you were an excellent assistant." Then I locked my eyes on her face and popped the only question I'd really come there to ask. "Tell me, Mrs. Ferris, how is it that the will that was produced has an extra page?"

The throat muscles in the hollow of her neck contracted as she swallowed, and her cheeks lost a shade of color. "An extra page?"

"That's right," I went on, feeling more and more like Lieutenant Columbo. "The will states there should be thirteen pages, including the Attestation page. The copy of the will Turner gave my client has fourteen pages by that count." I smiled. "I'm kind of OCD about details. Just wondering how that could have happened?"

She swallowed again. "Well, apparently I made a mistake. It happens, you know. Whether or not to include the Attestation page in the count can be a source of confusion."

I nodded. "Sure, I can understand that. A will is a complex instrument with a lot of moving parts. Easy to make a mistake."

She folded her arms across her chest and stood a little straighter in a show of confidence, but her eyes looked troubled. "Do you have any other questions, Mr. Claxton?"

I smiled again. "No. That covers it. Thanks for your cooperation." When I got to the gate, I turned back on a hunch and met her eyes, which looked even more troubled. "You know, Mrs. Ferris, if there's something you want to tell me about this situation, or if you need any guidance at all, you have my number. Feel free to contact me. There are more options than you may think."

We stood facing each other for a few moments, and I saw something stir in her eyes. Then it died as she abruptly averted her gaze. "Please leave, Mr. Claxton."

On the way back to Portland, I sifted through what I had so far. No doubt about it, Helen Ferris was hiding something, and it involved Margaret Wingate's will. If the will was tampered with, Ferris certainly had to have been involved. But why do that in the first place? The proceeds from the sale go to charity, not in anyone's pocket. Just to save the jobs of Melvin Turner and Brice Avery? Maybe. Were they both involved in the forgery? Maybe. But somehow saving jobs seemed a weak motive for such a brazen act.

Halfway across the I-5 bridge, my thoughts turned to the hit-and-run. Was it connected? I asked myself. My gut said yes, but the will could have been changed opportunistically after the fact. Was it murder, followed by forgery, or just forgery after an untimely accident? I had no way of knowing. The only thing I did know for sure was that I didn't have a shred of proof for any of this. And I was willing to bet that, in terms of the will, Turner and his assistant had thoroughly covered their tracks. An extra page might have rattled Helen Ferris, but it was evidence of nothing. The will, in fact, looked rock solid.

I felt a flush of frustration. This case just didn't seem to make any sense. I was missing something, something big.

Chapter Fifteen

"If you love her, Dad, set her free. It sounds corny, but I think you have no choice. What happened at Standing Rock was so soul-sucking. She's trying to heal the best way she knows how." It was my daughter, Claire, checking in from Harvard later that day. I'd just finished telling her about the rocky state of my relationship with Winona.

"I know that," I shot back, sounding more irritated than I meant to. "It's just, you know, it hurts to be shut out like this. I want to help her heal."

"Give it some time, Dad." She paused. "Why don't you call Philip? After all, he's her cousin. Maybe he can give you more of a Native American perspective."

"Good idea." Philip Lone Deer was my good friend and fishing buddy, and was, like Winona, a member of the Warm Springs Confederated tribes. "I'll give him a call."

Knowing Claire's propensity to worry, I held back the news about the gravel mining at the Aerie, even though it was weighing heavily on me. Instead I told her about feisty, metal-sculpting Angela Wingate and the case I was working on her behalf, playing down my suspicion that it was murder and leaving out the part about the Russian Mafia. When I finished Claire said, "She's lucky to have you, Dad. I'm really proud of the work you do."

After we signed off, I sat for a while basking in the glow of those words. Every dad wants the approval of his daughter, but it was especially important to me. I always worried that Claire held me responsible for her mom's suicide. She hadn't, and I was eternally grateful for that.

I scrolled down to Philip's number, started to punch it in, then thought better of it. Better to let it ride for a while, I decided. Winona will come to her senses. I wasn't shying away from an intimate conversation with my male friend, a conversation that would reveal my emotional vulnerability, was I? Of course not.

My stomach had just reminded me that it was close to dinner-time when I heard someone knocking at the downstairs door, which set Arch off in a couple of obligatory barks. A window facing the street in the studio apartment was open. I leaned out of it. "Can I help you?"

City Councilor Tracey Thomas looked up. "Oh, hi, Cal. I was out jogging and saw your sign. Can we talk?"

I took the stairs with Archie following, let her in, and introduced her to my dog. She wore a pair of light sweats, an iridescent tank top, and a length of purple yarn that tied off a thick, auburn pony tail. I showed her into my office and took a seat next to her. After looking around, she said, "So this is the famous Caffeine Central. I like the Arthur Ashe quote."

I laughed. "Yep, this is where the magic happens," then waited for her to tell me why she was here.

She smiled a bit conspiratorially. "I didn't just happen by. I checked with my source. The investor for the North Waterfront Project is an outfit called Arrowhead Investments LLC. And you were right. It looks like they're lining up to buy Wingate Properties as well as invest in the project."

"Where are they located?"

"I don't know."

"What's the price tag?"

"Something north of five-hundred million dollars, including the purchase price. That's all I know at this point."

I whistled. "There are going to be some very happy charities out there." She looked at me below scrunched eyebrows. I saw no reason not to tell her. "The will directs the executor to give the proceeds from the sale to Margaret Wingate's favorite charities." I fixed her eyes. "That's not public yet, so I'd—"

"My lips are sealed." She cut off my concern. "Is that why her daughter hired you?"

"No. Other than the choice of charities, Angela Wingate's fine with that provision. She's a sculptor and doesn't aspire to wealth, at least inherited wealth."

Tracey shot me another puzzled look. "So, what's the problem?'

"There are other provisions we're concerned about," I fibbed. She didn't need to know I was actually interested in the will as motive for Margaret Wingate's death. "This source of yours must be well placed." I changed the subject. "What's the motivation for the leak, if you don't mind my asking?"

"Well, you know, sometimes it's the only way people on the inside can get the truth out in the open. As a rule, Oregonians don't trust outside money. But my source values his job, so I can't press too hard."

"What do you plan to do with this information?"

"Not sure yet, but it might give me an edge when the North Waterfront Project gets to Council." Her eyes narrowed down a fraction. "Maybe we can work together on this, Cal. For example, I wasn't able to find anything on Arrowhead. I was hoping you could help me with that."

I nodded, but cautiously. "That could work, but I'd have to know that I can trust you won't go public with information unless I agree." I brought my eyes up to hers. "I know how strong the political winds can blow."

She met my gaze and held it. "You can trust me, Cal. You have my word."

"What about the press? I need to know you won't go to

Cynthia Duncan, for example, without my knowing it. She's a great reporter, but she marches to a different drummer."

"Agreed. The press is out unless we're both on board."

So, I agreed to work with Councilwoman Tracey Thomas. After answering some questions about what I actually did at Caffeine Central, Arch and I showed her out. I offered my hand. "I'll be back to you on Arrowhead. I owe you."

She took my hand. Her nutmeg eyes showed tiny flecks of gold in the sunlight. "I'll think of something for repayment," she said with a playful smile. With that she headed toward the river on Couch with the strong, even strides of an experienced runner.

After she left, I turned to Arch, who stood looking at me with his head cocked. "What?" But I knew what it was. I'd felt a nudge of attraction to Tracey Thomas, and that triggered a vague feeling of guilt.

Damn, I didn't see that coming.

I spent some time on the computer that afternoon trying to find information on Arrowhead Investments LLC, but like Tracey, I found absolutely nothing.

At three-forty-five that afternoon I headed out on foot for Ringlers Annex to meet Semyon Lebedev. Archie didn't like being left behind on a sunny afternoon, but I made the usual bargain—a run when I returned. Semyon was already there, hunched over a beer at a corner table like a bear guarding a pot of honey. He nodded, and I went to the bar and brought back a mug of the dark amber on tap that day, not as well balanced as a Mirror Pond but serviceable.

"How does the investigation go?" he asked when I sat down. His smile was thin and his eyes wary, maybe even troubled.

I shrugged. "Some smoke, perhaps, but I've yet to find any fire." I took his cue and skipped the small talk. "Do you have information for me?"

He took a pull on his beer, glanced around the room, and nodded. "I am told the Lexus you inquired about was treated in an unusual way."

"How so?"

"It was towed directly to the crusher facility without being stripped."

"How often does this happen?"

The corner of Semyon's mouth curled in a smirk. "A first, my friend. The Boyarchenko operation does not like to waste money. A car like that has many valuable parts. And I can tell you this was not done without orders from the top."

My spine tingled a little. "Does your friend know why this was done?"

"*Nyet.*"

"And your friend did not see what damage was done to the Lexus?"

"If he did, he would not tell me. And I asked him again."

I nodded. "Okay. He told you Lenny the Fox dropped the car off at the shop. Was someone with Lenny?"

Semyon drank some more beer. "Yes. Another man. He got out of the car on the street and Lenny went inside to handle the drop." Semyon lifted his eyes to mine, anticipating my next question. "I'm sorry, Cal, but my friend didn't know this man, and he didn't get a look at him."

"Nothing at all?"

"Nothing."

I leaned back in my chair and blew a breath in frustration. "I know very little about Boyarchenko and his operation. What can you tell me?"

The curled lip of a smirk reappeared. "Ilya Boyarchenko came here a few years after me—1995, I think. The Soviet Union was gone, Russia in ruins, but Ilya got out with some family money, which he used to open a small restaurant, The Russia House, on Southeast Foster. His mother still runs it."

I nodded. "I've seen the place but never eaten there."

"It's nothing fancy, but they have good borscht and Odessa sausages, and you can watch Moscow TV live. Anyway, Boyarchenko got into the car theft business early, working for a man named Misko Osmalov. Osmalov was murdered in a car-bombing. Boyarchenko took his operation over after that."

"When was that?"

Semyon stroked his chin. "Sometime in 2006."

"Who killed Osmalov?"

He laughed, a short bark. "It was never solved, but it is common knowledge Boyarchenko did it. He was clever and went on to open a string of legitimate businesses while he branched out into drugs, prostitution, staged auto accidents, bootleg cigarettes, even food stamp fraud, anything that turns a high profit off the backs of working people, many of them honest Russians."

I nodded. "So, he launders his profits through his legit businesses."

"Exactly. He's a rich man now with a pretty American wife and two kids. I think he wants to play the good citizen. There's an article about him in *Dlya Vsekh*, the Russian newspaper, this month. They sing his praises, because he is donating half a million dollars toward a new cultural center in southeast Portland. There's a photo of him with his family, standing in front of the Slavic Emmanuel Church." The smirk again. "The upstanding Russian-American citizen."

"Is his operation strictly local?"

Semyon shrugged. "I think yes. But it is always said that Boyarchenko has ties back to the mob in Russia." He laughed derisively. "That is bullshit, I think."

I looped back through the information, asking more questions, but didn't learn anything further. As our conversation drifted off the subject of Boyarchenko, Semyon announced he was teaching a mixed-martial arts course at the Russian Boy's Club. I was no fan of MMA and he knew it. "It beats having our young boys sit around playing video games, no?" he summed up. I couldn't argue with that.

Semyon left first, but before he did, he fixed his dark eyes on me. "The Portland cops and the Feds have been trying to get something on Boyarchenko for twenty years. He is like a spider at the center of a web. Touch it, and he will know it. I will say it again, be careful. And Cal, my contact said this is the last time he will talk to me."

That evening was clear and crisp. As Arch and I jogged along the Parkway, the arching white suspension cables of the Tilikum Bridge looked rose-colored in the setting sun. My spirits were buoyed by the beauty of the city and by what I'd learned from my Russian friend. The Lexus looked like a potential murder weapon, Lenny the Fox could have been behind the wheel, and the man with him an accessory. With Lenny dead, the only direct link to the murder was the mystery man.

I needed to find this guy.

I also needed to understand the Boyarchenko connection. Why did he green light the destruction of the Lexus, and how could I find that out? I was getting a David-versus-Goliath feeling. The odds were long and the resources short, but I felt like, with a little more digging, I just might find a couple of rocks for my sling.

Chapter Sixteen

I ran out of clean clothes on Sunday. I was tempted to ask Winona to watch Archie while I made a run to the Aerie, but hell, I didn't even know if she was back from the Warm Springs Reservation and her sweat lodge cleansing. No, I would take Claire's advice and not press things. Instead, I called another of my dog's fans, Angela Wingate. "I'm sorry I didn't check in with you yesterday, Cal," she said after I greeted her. "I started a new piece and worked straight through till midnight last night." I teasingly said I'd forgive her if she could do me a favor and watch Arch. "That's totally cool. I'm back at my studio. Drop him by and we'll hang out."

I didn't hear the rock crushing noise until I got to the gate at the Aerie. From that distance, the sound took me back to L.A., where the steady drone of cars on the freeway was never far away. Instead of horns honking, I heard an accompaniment of front-end loader beeps. I watered the outside flowers and my small collection of houseplants, made a coffee, and carried it outside to wait while a load of dirty clothes sloshed in the washer. The black, wrought-iron table and matching chairs on the porch looked like they'd been spray-painted beige. I ran a finger along the meshed table top, disturbing a layer of fine quarry dust. I sat down after dusting off a chair and was halfway through my coffee when the deck rocked, and even though I knew it was a quarry blast, I felt a split second of panic. It took me back to the Northridge Earthquake, which scared the hell out of a lot of Angelinos, including me.

I looked at the dust again, took out my phone, and after writing "Quarry Dust" with my finger, took a photograph. That got me wondering what was in that dust. I fetched a brush and an envelope from the house and collected a sample for analysis. You never know.

I was glad I hadn't brought Archie along, but my heart sank at the realization that if I couldn't stop this operation I would have no choice but to move. Suddenly my coffee tasted bitter. I tossed it over the porch rail and sat there trying to picture leaving the Aerie. I couldn't.

"Let me get this straight. You want me to find who's behind Arrowhead Investments, and you also want me to look for any ties between Wingate Properties and the Russian mafioso, Ilya Boyarchenko?" Nando Mendoza repeated back to me. "Those are tall orders, Calvin." I had called him earlier, caught him at his PI office in Lents on a Sunday, and stopped by after leaving the Aerie with a supply of clean clothes. He looked flashy in an electric-blue workout suit and a pair of Nike cross-trainers, but I knew it was more about looking good than working out with Nando. "Your Russian friend cannot help you with Boyarchenko? My contacts in that community are very limited."

"I've pushed him about as hard as I can. I was hoping you could take a fresh look, come at it from the Boyarchenko side. I'll work it from the Wingate side," I said, thinking of Tracey Thomas' contact.

"I will give it the shot, my friend. Now, finding information on the investment company might be even more difficult. If it is a shell company, as you suggest, it was probably set up to obscure ownership. Such is the way of high finance these days."

"I know that. But you have access to data I can only dream about. I'm hoping you'll get lucky."

After we finished up our business, Nando asked about Claire, whom he was very fond of. I filled him in on her Harvard postdoctoral appointment and the research she was doing. When the conversation turned to Winona, I kept it neutral, saying she was back from Standing Rock and spending some time with family at the Rez. Gifted with intuitive powers, my friend raised an eyebrow as he listened. He sensed something was amiss, but to his credit and my relief he didn't press me.

As I was leaving, I pointed to a spot on the wall behind his desk where a picture of the sitting President usually hung—first Bush, then Obama—placed with care next to a similar portrait of first Fidel, then Raúl Castro. Nando was an avowed capitalist, but he still loved his communist homeland as much as he did his adopted country. He saw no contradiction in this, and I envied the way he dealt with ambiguity. I pointed to the empty spot. "You're missing a President."

"We are all missing a President," he shot back.

Ten minutes later I was searching for a parking space on North Williams when I spotted Angela and Archie out for a walk up ahead of me. I found a slot, and caught up with them. "You two get along okay?"

They both whirled around to greet me. His butt in full wag, Archie came up and licked my hand, and Angela beamed a smile. She wore her signature boots, randomly ventilated jeans, and tee-shirt with *Goldman Sucks* written across the front in gold letters. "Of course. We're best buds now. Great timing, Cal. We're just finishing up a long walk."

We made our way back to the Bridgetown Artists' Co-op and up to her studio. Archie lay down in the only free corner on a mat I'd supplied. After I turned down her offer of tea, Angela gestured toward the beginnings of a sketch on a large piece of paper taped on one wall. It looked like a stickman out for a jog. "I'm, um, working up a full-scale drawing for a piece I'm planning."

As I stepped closer, I noticed a sketchbook lying open on her workbench, the book I'd seen her working on at her house earlier. It was open to a drawing of a woman jogging. Using a patchwork of fine, interconnecting lines, Angela had captured the woman's lean body, flexing muscles, and long, graceful stride, even a suggestion of facial features. The form seemed to be moving right out of the plane of the paper, and the anatomical accuracy reminded me of some of Michelangelo's sketches. I pointed at the book. "I love that figure. You're going to transfer that drawing to the large sheet?"

"That's right. I'm just starting that process. I'll use it for a kind of blueprint for the sculpture I'm planning."

"You're going to reproduce that detail in a sculpture?"

"Yep, the whole thing will be made of interconnected steel wire, welded in place. Just like what's suggested in the drawing."

I whistled softly. "Sounds challenging."

She nodded, and her eyes suddenly glistened in the overhead lights. "It will be challenging, but it's a labor of love." I thought she might cry, but she caught herself by changing the subject. "You won't believe who called this morning. Melvin. He said that he and Brice wanted to meet with me. He told me not to tell you, that you were a hick lawyer, and I was wasting my money on you."

I chuckled. "I've been called worse. What did you say?"

"I wanted to talk to you first, but I didn't tell him that. I told him I was busy and would get back to him."

"Good. Did he say what they wanted to talk to you about?"

"Something about important estate issues that have come up. What should I do now?"

I hesitated. It would be interesting to hear what they had to say, even if I wasn't present. On the other hand, the threat of them manipulating or coercing her in some way wasn't worth the risk. "Tell him you'd be glad to meet, but only if your lawyer's present. See what they say. We'll go from there."

"He called a couple of hours ago. I can call him back now, if you want."

I told her to do it, and when she got Melvin Turner's voice-mail, she left an unambiguous message that was bound to disappoint him.

Hearing that your mother may have been murdered in a most vicious manner is a lot to deal with, particularly for a young, sensitive woman trying to maintain her sobriety, but I decided it was time to level with Angela. She sat down on the mat next to Archie and listened while I laid out what Semyon told me about the Lexus and the implications of that information. When I finished, she leaned forward, hugged her knees, and slowly exhaled. Her face had gone a shade lighter, but her eyes burned with intensity. "What are you going to do now, call the cops?"

I shook my head. "Not yet. All I've got is a bunch of dots. I've got to connect them before I can do anything definitive. I've got a good private investigator helping me with that."

She leaned her head back against the wall and closed her eyes as tears started streaming from them. "Everyone kept calling it an accident, and I guess I sort of went along with it." She sniffed and swiped her cheeks with balled fists. "I feel ashamed now. Deep down I should have known it was no accident." She looked up at me through wet eyes. "I feel like I let her down. She was an experienced jogger. She wouldn't have just run in front of some stupid Lexus. I should have told the cops that."

"You have nothing to be ashamed of, Angela. Don't forget, you came to me because you were dissatisfied with the situation. That shows you had your doubts. Nothing at all would have happened without the action you took. We'll get to the bottom of this, I promise."

She sighed and cast her eyes downward. The room grew silent

except for the traffic noise streaming in through an open window facing North Williams. I was about to speak when she pulled out her cell, glanced at it, and broke the silence. "Hey, I've got to go. I'm due at a meeting over in Southwest in thirty minutes." I must have looked puzzled, because she added, "An AA meeting. I'm leading it today. It'll give me a chance to share some of the feelings this dredged up." She met my eyes and laughed that buoyant laugh of hers, the first I'd heard that day. "Without spilling the beans, of course."

"Excellent." I felt a bit relieved at what appeared to be fortuitous timing.

As I navigated crosstown traffic, I wondered what Turner and Avery were up to. Margaret Wingate's will was settled, so what did they want with Angela now? How would they react when she tells them I'm in, or else? And how should I play it after she hears back from them? I had extracted a promise from Angela to call me as soon as that happens, and I had an inkling of what they might have in mind. I was anxious to see if I was right.

I thought about Angela, too. I admired the courage of this young woman and the commitment she showed to her art and to her sobriety. I thought about my own commitment. I'd just made *her* a big promise. A promise I intended to keep, but could I?

Chapter Seventeen

"*Dobro pozhalovat*," a voice boomed out from speakers on either side of a makeshift stage. "Welcome." It was an hour later, and I was standing in the back at the groundbreaking ceremony in Southeast Portland for the new Russian Community Center. I'd seen a notice in the paper and stopped by out of sheer curiosity in hopes of getting a look at Ilya Boyarchenko, who, I read, would keynote the affair. No surprise there. He was bankrolling the new center.

Rick Holtzman, one of Tracey's cohorts on the City Council, was standing behind the MC and next to another man I guessed was Boyarchenko. The Russian was a heavyset man with broad shoulders and an angular head that seemed at odds with his nearly square body. Holtzman wore a slightly forced, uncomfortable smile. Clearly, was he wasn't happy standing next to a reputed—but never proven—Mafia boss. Maybe he'd drawn the short straw at City Council. Politics does make for strange bedfellows, after all.

After saying a few words in Russian, then in English, the MC handed the mike over to Holtzman, who talked about the importance of the community center and the dynamism of the Russian community in Portland, a city that valued and celebrated diversity. The crowd—a mix of families, teens, young adults, working people—liked the message and gave Holtzman an enthusiastic round of applause when he finished.

Ilya Boyarchenko took the mike next and began his talk speaking in Russian, which elicited a smattering of applause. He then shifted to English and talked about the growing strength of the Slavic community in Portland—some forty-thousand strong, I learned—and the importance of preserving their language, their culture, and their spiritual life. "This cultural center," he told the crowd, "will go a long way toward achieving those goals." When he finished, the applause was polite but well short of the response to Holtzman. The message was clear—we'll accept your money, but we don't approve of you.

Semyon Lebedev was right. Ilya Boyarchenko gave the Russians in Portland a bad name.

The speeches were followed by the usual ribbon-cutting and groundbreaking with chrome-plated shovels. Afterwards I stood on the periphery as the crowd cleared. Several people lined up to talk to Boyarchenko, and then finally he started to leave in the company of his wife and two nice looking teens, a boy wearing a Blazer ball cap and a girl wearing a Portland Thorns jersey. I watched them go, and as they reached a silver Mercedes, attended by a driver who looked like he could bench-press the car, a man approached them. He looked vaguely familiar, but I couldn't place him from where I was standing. I moved in a little closer and realized it was Fred Poindexter, the Chairman of the Portland Planning Commission.

The wife and kids got in the Mercedes while Boyarchenko stood nearby and lit up. I moved back into what was left of the crowd so that Poindexter, who glanced around every so often, wouldn't notice me. The two men talked until Boyarchenko finally tossed his cigarette on the ground, joined his family in the Mercedes, and sped away.

Huh, I thought. I guess it makes sense that the Planning Chief would want to talk to someone who's donating half a million dollars to what amounts to city infrastructure. But there was something furtive about that conversation. Why did Poindexter wait until Boyarchenko was alone at his car to approach him? And why was he looking around like he was nervous?

I didn't know, but it made me wonder.

Commuting from Portland to Dundee that Monday morning instead of the other way around seemed weird, but at least the traffic on I-5 going south wasn't quite as thick. When we arrived at my office, even Archie seemed a little disoriented as he hopped out of the backseat. We went across to the bakery, and I ordered a double cap and a *pain au chocolat* to go. Might as well start the week off right, I figured. It was a slack day, so I busied myself tallying up billable hours for the last month, a boring task that was mercifully interrupted with a call from Claire fifty minutes later. Ostensibly, the call was to tell me she was leaving for the Gulf Coast to do fieldwork on her project—the impact of the Deepwater Horizon oil spill on coastal wetlands—but she quickly steered the call around to Winona.

"She's fine," I said. "I'm giving her lots of space like you recommended." Before my daughter could reply, I changed the subject by asking about her research, a topic she was passionate about. It worked. I got an update on the impact of crude oil on marsh vegetative cover and avoided having to discuss my faltering love life. "Call me when you get down there, and let me know where you're staying," I told her, and when we signed off, I looked over at Arch. "Damn, I'm proud of that girl."

I had reached the halfway mark on billable hours for April when another call came in. "It is going to be even tougher than I thought."

"What is?" I was irritated, as usual, at Nando's habit of launching into a subject without any preamble.

"Trying to find an informant in the Boyarchenko organization. It is what you might call a closed system. One possibility, however, is Boyarchenko's lawyer, a man named Byron Hofstetter. Do you know this man?"

"Wasn't he the lawyer who kept that strip club out on 82nd from getting shut down?"

Nando chuckled. "Yes, the Lusty Devil Club, which the neighbors were up in arms about."

"Right. That case went all the way to the Oregon Supreme Court. Didn't know Hofstetter worked for Boyarchenko."

"Since the last eight years. I am thinking we might take a hard look at him."

I knew that "hard look" was code for hacking Hofstetter's e-mail. Nando used a young freelancer from time to time who was highly adept at this and other digital black arts. I didn't want to know anything about that, and Nando knew it. The vagueness didn't salve my conscience, but I needed the information and knew it wouldn't go beyond me and, of course, would have no evidentiary value. "Uh, yeah, do what it takes. I'm just looking for a connection."

Call it situational ethics.

"I will see what can be done." The line went quiet for a few seconds before Nando added, "This fellow, Boyarchenko, has a nasty reputation, Calvin. You are sure you want to rattle the hornets' nest? I do not have the good feeling about this."

"Semyon gave me the same warning. Yes, I'm sure. Boyarchenko had to have given the order to send that Lexus straight to the crusher. I want to know why." After I punched off, I sat there wondering if I was like that frog before the water boils. Turner and Avery had legal and financial resources that could crush me. And Boyarchenko had muscle that could break my knees or worse, much worse.

That afternoon, I finally got a break to pay another visit to the Swanson Motel, hoping to catch the handyman again, the one person I'd uncovered who'd seen the mystery man with Lenny the Fox. He'd used an incoming call as an excuse to end our last conversation, and I was convinced he had more to tell me. Knowing the information wouldn't come cheap, I stopped at a drive-through ATM on the way out of Dundee and withdrew two hundred dollars in twenties, reminding myself to add this to Angela's tab. The expenses were piling up. An hour later, I pulled into the back lot of the Swanson and couldn't believe my luck—his white van was just pulling out. I followed him to a little bar on SE Foster called Henry's and watched him walk in. When I sat down next to him at the bar a few minutes later, he looked at me through the mirror behind the liquor bottles, then turned. "What the hell now, bub?"

"I'd like to buy your dinner, if you'll join me"—I nodded toward an empty booth in the back.

He turned back and spoke to me using his reflected image. "Dinner? That's not good enough. And if we do any more business, I gotta know you'll keep me out of it."

I forced a soothing smile. "I know, job security. Same deal as before. I don't use your name ever. Could be more in it than dinner, but that depends on you." He sat there for a while then picked up his beer, and I followed his slow amble to the booth. I waited while he drained his glass, wiped his lips with the back of his hand, and held the glass up to alert the waitress.

"I'm still interested in the man you saw that night with the suicide victim." I placed two twenties on the table. Openers.

He reached out and eased the twenties to his side of the table. "What more can I tell you?"

"You're sure you can't remember anything more about this guy?"

He blew out a breath and made a face, as if using his memory was painful. "I told you, all I got was an impression somebody else was driving. I didn't give a shit what he looked like, you know?" He chuckled. "Now, if it'd been a woman…"

The waitress arrived, and he ordered another beer, a steak sandwich, buffalo wings, and a double batch of cheese fries. I ordered a cup of black coffee, and after the waitress left, said, "Was anyone else around that night? A maid? A working girl? Anyone?"

He looked blank for a few moments, then his rheumy eyes suddenly registered something, a momentary flicker behind the pupils. "There's a guy might know somethin'. He was around that Thursday night about the right time." His eyes narrowed down some. "I can tell you how to find 'im, but it'll cost you three more twenties."

"Tell me a little more."

"Name's Spider-Man." The chuckle again. "Least, that's what I call 'im. Don't know his real name, of course. Don't know any of the Johns. Comes in twice a week for a quickie. He was around that Thursday night at about the right time. Could've seen something."

An even hundred to talk to Spider-Man. Worth a shot, I decided, and peeled off three more twenties. "So, how do I find Spider-Man?"

He raked the twenties in. "Comes in Mondays and Thursdays at seven, like clockwork. Drives one of those little Italian sport cars, a Spider. Bright red. Can't miss 'im.

I thanked the handyman, and we ended our session with a handshake just as his food arrived, an event that laid down an aroma of rancid grease. I paid the bill and left him munching his sandwich and fries with a fresh beer at his elbow.

That evening, after we arrived back at Caffeine Central, I weakened, whisked up Archie, and walked over to Winona's loft. I walked past it once. The porch light was on, although it was still light outside, suggesting she hadn't returned from Warm Springs. I turned around, tried the bell, and when no one answered, pecked out a text:

Hey, how was the sweat? Missing you a lot. Call. We need to talk.

I wasn't kidding. We did need to talk. This was getting ridiculous.

Angela checked in with me later that evening. "No, he hasn't called me back," she said when I asked her about Melvin Turner. "Maybe he won't, now that I said I wouldn't meet without you." I agreed that was a possibility but suggested we wait another day before deciding what to do next. I hung up, hoping Turner would make contact.

Winona didn't call that night, which probably explains the weird dream I had. This time I was sitting in a pitch-black room. Out in the hall, I could hear Winona talking, although I couldn't quite understand what she was saying. I got up and began groping around to find the door, but I couldn't, no matter how hard I tried. I awoke abruptly, drenched in sweat and full of frustration bordering on anger.

The next morning I was getting into the car, after letting Arch into the backseat, when my cell phone played a digital blues riff. "Good morning, sir, this is Mel Turner," the voice began. "I'm wondering if you could spare me and Brice Avery some time today? We could come to your office on Couch, if that would be convenient."

Sir? And how did he know I was in Portland, not Dundee? I glanced at my watch. "Uh, sure. How about nine-thirty?" I gave him the street number. "To what do I owe this honor?"

An amiable chuckle. "We'd like to discuss an offer we're willing to make to you and your client, Angela Wingate."

An offer we can't refuse? I was tempted to say. "Okay, see you then."

Turner arrived first, dressed in a summer-weight pinstriped suit and paisley tie and carrying a thin leather attaché case. His eyes betrayed a bit of anxiety, and his clean-shaven cherub cheeks reminded me of a ripe peach. I sat on the edge of my desk and offered him a seat in front of me. After looking around, he said, "Our firm does some *pro bono* work in Portland, mainly for Margaret's charities. We should compare our experiences one of these days." I pushed my lower lip out and nodded. Of course, we both knew that would never happen.

An awkward silence was broken by Brice Avery's arrival. He wore chinos, an open-neck, button down shirt, and boat shoes. After apologizing for being late, he said, "Thanks for meeting with us on such short notice, Claxton." I sat back down on the edge of the desk facing the two of them with my arms crossed. As if sensing I was staking out the high ground as a negotiating tactic, he remained standing, his stern eyes belying the smile on his gray-stubble face.

I got up and sat behind my desk, and Avery sat down as well, ending the dance. "So, gentlemen, what's on your minds?"

Avery leaned back and steepled his fingers. Turner leaned in. "We understand the shock that Angela has gone through, losing yet another parent. No child should have to go through such an ordeal." A quick glance at Avery before continuing. "We, ah, think that Margaret Wingate's will was fair and it certainly represented her last wishes, but we'd like to do more to secure Angela's future." He paused there, inviting me to reply, and when I didn't, he continued. "Of course, we're not suggesting the use of any company funds."

I nodded. "The probate judge would have to sign off on that."

When I didn't continue to speak, Avery broke the silence. "That's right. In exchange, we'd like assurances from Angela and you, as her lawyer, that you'll drop this silliness about challenging the will."

"Where would these funds come from?"

Avery glanced at Turner, then back at me, and offered up a friendly smile. "I think you can understand that's something we don't wish to divulge."

"Not really," I responded but didn't press it. "Why are you so anxious to have us drop the probe?"

Turner started to reply, but Avery cut him off. "That's the right question, Claxton, and the answer's simple. We're in delicate negotiations right now to sell the company, which was Margaret's stated desire. Lawyers are crawling all over this deal. The *slightest* hint that there's someone contesting the will would kill the sale in a New York minute."

"Of course, we also want to do right by Angela," Turner chimed in.

"Of course." I leaned back and regarded them both. "What kind of monetary payment did you have in mind?"

Avery turned to Turner, relinquishing the floor. "We're prepared to offer Angela a one-time payment of two-hundred-fifty thousand dollars, and for your services, a payment of fifty-thousand dollars." I held the neutral expression on my face and didn't respond. Turner glanced at Avery again before going on. "There is, ah, some flexibility in these numbers."

"I'm listening."

"We could go to two-hundred-seventy-five thousand for Angela."

"Tell you what. Make it three-hundred for Angela, and I'll take the offer to her. Otherwise, forget it."

Turner's face flushed as he started to speak, but Avery cut him off. "Fine. But that's our final offer." He nodded at the attaché case sitting on the floor next to Turner. "Give him the non-disclosure agreement, Mel." Then he swung his eyes back to me. "If you and Angela find the agreement acceptable, simply sign it, and we'll make the payments forthwith."

I got up, struggling not to show my contempt. I felt like I needed a shower. "Thank you, gentlemen. That's very generous of you. I'll discuss your offer with my client. We'll be back to you, uh, forthwith."

As I was showing them out, I said, "So, who's the lucky buyer?"

Turner laughed. "Oh, you know how hush-hush these deals are."

Avery cut me a look and smiled with one side of his mouth. "If we told you that, we'd have to kill you, Claxton."

Chapter Eighteen

The full-size drawing of the jogger on the wall in Angela's studio was nearly complete. It was an hour after my meeting with Turner and Avery, and I stood in front of it, admiring the way she had brought the image to life and captured a sense of movement. I had seen a couple of pictures of Margaret Wingate and could see more than a hint of resemblance in the strong nose and the high, prominent cheekbones of the woman in the sketch, all rendered in a crosshatch of intricate lines that would eventually become threads of steel. It was uncanny.

Angela was brewing a cup of tea, and Archie was monitoring the proceedings from what had become a favorite corner, according to his host. When she finished, I took her through what just transpired at Caffeine Central. "Oh, my God," she said, her eyes huge, a hand to her mouth, when I got to the amount of the offer. "Are they serious?" I nodded, and her eyes narrowed down and her face grew rigid. "You know I don't want their money, Cal. They're trying to buy me off."

"I know that, but as your attorney I'm obligated to bring the offer to your attention. It's a lot of money, Angela."

Her eyes shot daggers. "What? You think I should take it?"

"I didn't say that. But I want you to think it through. If you take the money, you'll have to sign an agreement stating you will not challenge the will."

"But that's not what we're doing, right?"

I smiled. "That's right. We're investigating your mom's death, but they *think* we're focused on the will to get more of the estate."

She laughed, then furrowed her brow. "So, we could take the money, sign the agreement, and still keep investigating?"

I frowned. "You could do that, I suppose, but it would expose both of us to a potential lawsuit. In any case, I won't take any money from them under any circumstances."

Her eyes brightened. "Whew! For a moment there, I wasn't sure where you were going with this. I don't want a cent of their filthy money, either. Fuck 'em. That's what I say."

I nodded. "Okay, I'll tell them we're not interested in their deal." At this point I admit to a couple of fleeting thoughts about how nice it would have been to put a new roof on my Dundee office and pay off a chunk of my mortgage. I leveled my gaze at her. "It's possible that what motivated the offer is what they said—that they don't want their buyer to get cold feet. But there's another possibility, Angela. If the will was forged and they're somehow involved in your mom's death, then turning their offer down signals that we're going to keep digging. This could put you in danger."

She held my gaze. "You, too." I nodded. "I understand that, Cal, but no way I'm backing off. If they hurt Mom, they're going to pay big-time."

I left Angela that day not the least bit surprised at the outcome of our discussion. She was young and brash, after all, and intent on finding out what happened to her mother. And money meant nothing to her. Young and brash, but innocent, too, about just how malevolent some people are. The outcome was as it should have been, but at the same time, I felt a new monkey crawl onto my back. It looked like she and I were openly squaring off against some heavy hitters, and it would fall to me to keep her safe.

I made it to my office in Dundee that afternoon just in time for a meeting with a new client. The man, in his late fifties, explained that he'd been fired from his delivery job for refusing to text while he was driving his truck. "That's right," he explained. "My boss expected an instant reply, even if I was behind the wheel. He kept chewing me out, and when I finally complained up the line, he fired me." The man's jaw quivered. "I've got twenty years with the company, Mr. Claxton. I need this job."

I had him take me through the details, took some notes, and summed up the meeting: "You can't be fired in Oregon for refusing to break the law. That's called wrongful termination. I'll contact the company and inform them of our intent to sue unless they reinstate you. If they stonewall us, we'll talk about next steps and costs." The man left looking visibly relieved, and I had a letter drafted fifteen minutes later.

I'd call that a good start to my workday.

I called Melvin Turner's office next, was put through to his voicemail by his secretary, and left a message: "Hello, Melvin. I have discussed your offer with my client, Angela Wingate, and she stated unequivocally that she is not interested in accepting money in any amount in exchange for dropping the probe on Margaret Wingate's will. Neither am I. Good luck with the sale." I hung up and composed a letter summarizing the meeting with Turner and Avery and restating Angela's and my decision. I printed out three copies, signed them, and put them in envelopes addressed to Melvin Turner, Brice Avery, and Angela Wingate. This was evidence of a cover-up, and I wanted it in writing.

The die was cast.

Around three-thirty, I closed up shop, loaded Arch in my old Beemer, and drove to H and S Landscape and Construction Supply, just off the 99W in Newberg. A woman in the office told me I could find the boss, Dudley Cahill, out in the yard. "He told me to send you on out when you got here." She sounded a bit apologetic. "He's probably at the chipper, so follow the noise. He's a big guy wearing a plaid shirt. Can't miss him."

On my way out, I noticed a handsomely framed aerial view of the property showing the layout of the property and where the various building materials were located and stored. At the time, I had no way of knowing how important that picture would turn out to be.

Cahill was huddled with two other men next to a piece of equipment that reminded me a lot of the portable rock crusher behind the Aerie, except that instead of being fed rocks, this behemoth was eating thick tree branches and spitting out compostable material at the other end. A big man with a weightlifter's build and a ball cap facing backwards, Cahill broke off his conversation as I approached. "Mr. Claxton?" he asked, the greeting a bit frosty.

I introduced myself and explained the reason for my visit, although I was pretty sure he already knew why I was there. When I finished, he said, "Well, all I can tell you is that I sent copies of our sales records to the county, like McMinnville requested. I can't help it if it spells bad news for you." He flashed a patronizing smile. "You know, Mr. Claxton, we need aggregate to build roads, just like we need trees to build homes and make your toilet paper." I started to respond, but he cut me off. "I'll bet the folks you bought your farmhouse from didn't complain about living next to an active mine. Comes with the territory in Oregon, you know."

Heat rose up from my neck, but I didn't take the bait. It was a familiar argument between those who wanted unrestrained access to the state's resources and those who didn't. The answer lay somewhere in the middle, but I didn't want to pick that scab with this guy. "I'm just making sure the law's being followed here. You're certain the sales records you submitted to the county are completely accurate?" He nodded. "What about supporting evidence, like receipts for the delivery of the gravel. Do you have those?"

He laughed. "That was twelve years ago. We were lucky to find the sales records." He fixed me with narrowed eyes. "Face it, Mr. Claxton, McCallister's back in business. Welcome to Oregon."

I swallowed a sarcastic comeback and left without saying another word. Probably just as well. I wasn't keen to get fed to the chipper.

On the way out, I passed a row of cavernous, four-sided bins where H and S stored its inventory of gravel. The bins were empty, and a sign posted next to them read: "Temporarily out of stock. Enquire at office for allocation details."

The aggregate was on back-order? No wonder McCallister was being pressed back into service. Demand was high, and there was money to be made. And no question, Dudley Cahill had been prepped by someone for my visit. The air reeked more of collusion than compost that day, and I wasn't sure what the hell I could do about it.

Chapter Nineteen

That afternoon I stopped in the Pearl District for a quick grocery shopping tour. I was missing Winona and flummoxed about the situation at the Aerie and figured a good meal might boost my spirits. Mid-season Dungeness crabs were on sale. They looked so good I bought two big ones, figuring I could freeze one. I added a baguette of sourdough bread, a head of cabbage, a bag of carrots, and a bottle of Moulin de Vries Sancerre to the basket. The meal was shaping up.

Back at Caffeine Central, I fed Arch, poured myself a glass of wine, and had just off-loaded the groceries when a text pinged in:

Hi Cal, I'm in the neighborhood. Free to talk? Tracey.

I texted her back and turned off the burner as my stomach rumbled. When I heard her knock downstairs, I leaned out the window. "We've got to stop meeting like this."

Wearing her jogging attire, she looked up and laughed. "I know. It's my fault, but I run right by here."

Sure you do, I said to myself as I took the stairs down to the first floor. I let her in and showed her into my office, but before she could sit down, I had another hunger pang. I said, "Look, Tracey, I was just fixing dinner. I've got an extra crab. Why don't you join me?"

"Oh, I couldn't," she said, then added with a slightly inflected eyebrow, "*An extra crab?*"

"Yeah, I just picked up two nice Dungeness."

She gave me a faux pained look. "That's unfair. How did you know I have a weakness for Dungeness crabs?"

I chuckled. "Just a hunch. Come on up. We can talk while I cook."

Archie greeted her at the top of the stairs, and after I poured her a glass of Sancerre, she settled in a chair at the small kitchen table.

"I've got a good PI working on finding out who's behind Arrowhead Investments," I said while I put on a large steamer pot of water for the crabs. "He hasn't gotten back to me yet."

She nodded with a look that landed somewhere between disgust and resignation. "Well, I won't hold my breath. Judging from the national scene, if it's a front for offshore money, it'll be next to impossible to trace." She raised her eyes to mine. "I need some ammunition, Cal. The North Waterfront Project looks unstoppable right now. Poindexter's pushing for an early hearing, and I think I may be the only City Council member against it."

"Is there a timeline?"

"Not yet."

"What about the mayor?"

"Still noncommittal."

While she went on about the City Council, I finished grating the cabbage and started on the carrots, and when she tilted another eyebrow, I said, "Coleslaw. Trust me, you'll love it."

"The man cooks, as well," she said with a sly grin. "What other hidden talents do you have?"

I shrugged. "Fly fishing?"

She laughed. "Just living the Oregon dream, huh?"

"When time permits. What about your source? Anything?"

"No. As a matter of fact, he said that the security around the project has tightened up. Brice Avery sent out a memo stating all information regarding North Waterfront should not be shared with anyone outside the company, and leaks are a firing offense."

"Is that unusual for a big project like this?"

"Well, he said the firing threat was a little over the top."

The water was boiling, so I took the crabs out of the refrigerator, one in each hand, my fingers stretching to grasp the heart-shaped shells, the big claws dangling like pairs of industrial tin snips. Tracey sucked a breath. "Oh, those are beautiful!"

I eased the crabs into the steamer basket, put the lid on the pot, and set to work melting butter and toasting some sesame seeds for the slaw dressing. I pointed to the pan with the sesame seeds. "Your job is to make sure I don't burn those. I do it practically every time."

She laughed and nodded, watching as I mixed the dressing— sesame oil, rice vinegar, sugar, salt, and peanuts—and, after tasting it, set it aside. "You don't measure anything, do you?"

"Not if I can help it." After putting plates, silverware, and a crab cracker on the table, I said, "Is your source still willing to help you?"

"Yes, I think so, but he's a little unnerved by the firing threat."

I hesitated for a moment, then decided to risk it. "I'm wondering if he could tell us if there's any connection between Wingate Properties and a man named Ilya Boyarchenko?"

Tracey's eyes enlarged. "The guy who's rumored to be the Russian Mafia czar?"

"Yeah, that Boyarchenko. I'm looking for anything, no matter how slight, that might connect him to the company, to Brice Avery, or to Melvin Turner."

"My God, the Russian Mafia? What's going on?"

I shrugged a shoulder. "Probably nothing, but if there's a connection, it would join a couple of dots I've been wondering about."

She leaned back, crossed her arms, and eyed me. "There you go again, keeping me in the dark. I thought this was *quid pro quo?*"

I smiled. "Bring me something on Boyarchenko and we'll talk."

Her eyes flashed daggers. "Cal, you know—"

Ping. The timer on the stove announced the crabs were ready. Saved by the bell, at least temporarily. I removed the crabs, assembled the slaw, poured the melted butter in a dish, and sliced the bread. After putting everything on the table, I sat down across from her. "*Bon appétit.*"

Tracey must have been as hungry as me, because we both attacked our crabs in silence for a few minutes, dipping each bite in the butter, and passing the cracker back and forth. Like me, she started with one claw then the other, the legs next, and finally, after popping the shell off, the cache of flaky white meat in the creature's body. I was charmed by the look of sheer enjoyment on her face as she ate.

I topped up our glasses, and after we passed the cracker back and forth several more times, our fingers inadvertently touched for an instant. I averted my eyes, but something passed between us, not unlike an electric current. *Whoa*, I said to myself. *No more wine for you.* I was sure she felt it too, but when I glanced back at her, she was tasting the slaw. "Umm," she said again. This goes perfectly with the crab. Where did you learn to cook like this?"

The question caught me off guard, triggering a surge of memories of my wife, then, unexpectedly, thoughts of Winona, whom I cooked for a great deal. I forced a smile and topped up her wine again as a distraction from looking at her nutmeg eyes or the hint of cleavage below her slender neck. "The school of culinary hard knocks."

She laughed. "No. Seriously. I'm curious."

"Well, I, uh, after my wife died, it was learn to cook or live my life eating crappy packaged foods."

I figured the mention of my wife's death would blunt her foray into my personal life, and I was right. After expressing her condolences, she drew her face into a serious look. "So, you won't give me the complete picture of what's going on at Wingate Properties. Why?"

"I can't, Tracey. It's premature, and there are client confidentiality issues. But I can tell you this. I'm working on a theory that could stop the North Waterfront Project dead in its tracks."

She drank some wine and ran a finger along the edge of the scarred tabletop before looking up. "Okay. I want to stop a development Portland doesn't need. What you're working on is obviously much bigger. I can live with that. Just remember that time's running out at City Council."

I thought about my visit from Turner and Avery and chuckled without mirth. "Don't worry. I have a sense of urgency."

She offered to help me clean up the kitchen, but I demurred. Frankly, I wanted her out of my apartment—there was too much going on between us. I walked her down the stairs, relieved that she was on foot, since she seemed a little tipsy. There was still plenty of light, and when we stepped out on the sidewalk, she turned, offered her hand, and when I took it, pulled me to her and kissed me full on the lips. "Thanks for the wonderful meal, Cal Claxton."

I pulled back and looked over her shoulder. I couldn't believe my eyes. Not twenty feet away, Winona stood looking at us with her hands on her hips.

Chapter Twenty

Archie squealed and dashed off to greet Winona, but she spun around and started walking away at a rapid pace. My dog followed her, and I dropped Tracey's hand and took a couple of steps in Winona's direction. "Wait, Winona. This isn't what it looks like." The words sounded pathetically lame. I heard Tracey exhale a laugh and turned back to see her walking in the opposite direction. "Uh, good night, Tracey," I said with equal lameness. She glanced back at me with a puzzled look but didn't break stride.

I caught up with Winona half a block later. "Wait a minute, you've got this all wrong."

She stopped abruptly and stooped to hug Archie, who was still squealing for attention. She looked up at me. "You told me you wanted to talk, but I see I came at the wrong time."

"That was Tracey Thomas, the city councilwoman. I'm working a case with her. She came by just as I was about to eat, so I invited her in for dinner, so we could talk. That kiss meant nothing. It was her idea, not mine."

She curled up one side of her mouth. "Sure it was. Since when do you cook dinner for your clients?"

"She's not my client, and I told you what happened. Look, can we just go to either your place or mine and talk about this?"

She stood up, her jaw set. I could see the warrior side of her kicking in. "That's what I wanted to do, but you were too busy."

"*Too busy?* I've been waiting for you to call, trying to give you plenty of space. What the hell's going on, anyway?"

She studied her boots that were still caked with North Dakota mud, then looked up at me, her almond eyes shiny with tears. "I'm sort of mixed up right now, Cal."

"Who wouldn't be, after what you've been through? Let me help you through this, Winona."

She held me with her gaze, but there was little warmth in it. "I'm not sure you can, Cal."

"What does that mean?"

She shrugged and averted her eyes. "I'm not sure what I want anymore."

"Where does that leave me?"

"I need some time, Cal."

I was hurt and angry at the same time. "Okay, then." I spun around and flicked my head at Archie. "Come on, boy." Then over my shoulder, I said, "Let me know when you get things figured out."

I walked away, hoping like hell she would chase after me, but she didn't. My heart sank like a stone.

Later that night, Tracey called. "Jesus, Cal, I'm so embarrassed about what happened. I was a little drunk, you know, and shouldn't have assumed anything."

"That's okay, I—"

"No, it's not okay. It was my fault, and I apologize." She chuckled softly. "Plying me with French wine's never a good idea."

I made a sound, well short of a laugh. "It wasn't your fault, Tracey. My relationship with Winona has been a little rocky lately. She was on her way over to talk about it when she saw us."

"*Oh, God.* I feel even worse. Would it help if I called her?"

"No, that wouldn't help. If she doesn't believe what I tell her, we're not going to make it, anyway."

"Of course," she said. The line fell silent for several beats. "Do you want to talk about it?" When I still didn't respond, she added, "I'm an expert on crashed relationships, Cal. It always helps to talk about it, believe me."

I hardly knew Tracey Thomas, but she had a forthrightness that engendered a level of trust. I exhaled a breath I didn't know I was holding and told her about Winona's traumatic experience at Standing Rock, and how after she returned things went south.

When I finished Tracey said, "These are threatening times for women and minorities. Being both, like Winona, is doubly hard, to say nothing of the shock of what happened in North Dakota. She's working through some heavy shit, Cal. Maybe you're expecting more than she can give right now."

"Yeah, that's what my daughter said. I've given Winona a lot of space and gotten nothing back, not even the benefit of the doubt tonight."

"This is probably more about her than you."

We talked a while longer, but that was the gist of what she told me. Nothing I didn't already know, but I needed to hear it just the same. We signed off with the tacit agreement to continue working together. This made sense, of course, because we needed each other as sources of information. But the thought of continuing to see her seemed fraught with risk from the standpoint of salvaging my relationship with Winona.

The next day at my law office in Dundee was a busy one, so I was able to keep myself somewhat distracted from the mess I'd made. At the first break, I called Marnie Stinson at the Yamhill County offices and told her I wanted to request a hearing on the County's decision to allow gravel mining at McCallister. "On what grounds?" she asked.

"On the grounds that McMinnville Sand and Gravel and H and S are colluding on this deal. The time line evidence they presented is bullshit."

"The Land Use Board will take the word of two long-standing businesses over your objections, Cal. Do you have any proof?"

"Uh, yeah, but I'm not ready to disclose anything yet," I lied. The truth was I didn't have squat for proof or even a clue about what to do next. But it would take time to schedule a hearing, I figured, and if I didn't have something by then, it wouldn't be from lack of trying. Marnie told me to write a letter requesting the hearing and coached me a little on what to say. I thanked her and signed off.

There's nothing as unnerving as a leap of faith.

After my final conference call that afternoon, I was anxious to drive up to the Aerie, check things out, water some plants, and do some more laundry. However, before I left the office, I made a final phone call. Looking back, I'm not sure exactly what prompted me to call Helen Ferris at that particular time, but it certainly had to do with the visit I'd received from Turner and Avery the morning before, and the fact that I'd left my meeting with her feeling like there was something she wanted to tell me. Archie was at the back door, and when I sat back down to make the call, he gave me a doggie eye roll.

Ferris picked up on the third ring. "What do you want, Mr. Claxton?" she responded to my cheerful opening salvo.

"Well, I'm just wondering if you changed your mind, you know, about talking to me concerning Margaret Wingate's will."

The line went quiet, and I could hear classical music playing in the background. "Why would I want to talk to you again?"

I decided to go for it. "Because it's the right thing to do, Mrs. Ferris. I think you know more than you're telling me. And if you help me, I might be able to protect you."

She laughed, but most of it stuck in her throat. "I couldn't possibly do that." I caught a quaver in her voice.

"Talking to me will beat talking to the police, believe me, Mrs. Ferris."

She went silent again, and I could hear a familiar classical riff, Chopin, I think. I waited. "I can't...talk to you." Click. She hung up.

"*Shit.*"

I started to call her back but thought better of it. The phone was too easy to hang up. On the other hand, a face-to-face confrontation might freak her out even more. Or not. An hour later I stopped arguing with myself. I looked at Archie, whose ears came up when our eyes met. "You up for a trip to Vancouver, Big Boy?"

Of course he was.

Chapter Twenty-one

Traffic across the Interstate Bridge into Vancouver, Washington, that evening was snarled as usual. With Archie's head thrust out the window, we crawled across the corroded steel behemoth, a testament to our crumbling infrastructure. As I caught glimpses of the water below, I pictured the colonies of houseboats on nearby Hayden Island and strung along both sides of the Columbia River. *If I have to move from the Aerie*, I thought, *maybe I'll check out a houseboat. What would it be like to live on the river?* But that flight of fancy backfired as the reality of losing the Aerie crushed in on me. There really wasn't any other place on the planet I wanted to live.

I parked down the street from Helen Ferris' condo and told Archie to stay put. A porch light was on, along with interior lights in the vestibule and in an upstairs room—encouraging signs that she was still home. I rang the bell and waited, and when I got no response, lay on the bell a little longer the second time. Still nothing. Frustrated, I moved to one side of the door, glanced in through the glass panel, and drew in a sudden, sharp breath. Someone was lying on the staircase leading up to the second floor.

I tried the door—unlocked, so I let myself in. Helen Ferris lay facedown with her head jammed against the bottom newel post on the right side of the staircase, and her legs stretched up the stairs. One arm was crumpled under her, the other extended, the fingers splayed. A plastic laundry basket lay on its side between her head and the front door, its contents strewn across the entry floor. Her vacant, unblinking eyes and the horrible angle her head made with her body told me instantly that she was dead. Blood drained from my head for a moment. I fought through it and knelt down to check for a pulse to confirm what I already knew. Her lifeless body was warm. I touched my own arm, then hers, and couldn't feel any difference.

My stomach turned a little as I realized this poor woman died moments ago.

I stood up, called 911, and was told not to touch anything and to wait on the front porch for the police. I glanced at my watch. I had three, maybe five minutes, tops, to take a look around. Okay, it wasn't kosher to creep a death scene, and God knows it wasn't my first time, but hell, I was already in the house. And, although it looked like Helen Ferris had taken an accidental fall while carrying the laundry, the timing of her death was suspicious, to say the least.

Why was the front door unlocked? Unusual for a woman living alone. I hurried through the house to the back door. It was not only unlocked but ajar. I flicked on the back porch light with a pen and looked into the empty yard. I started to turn back when I noticed something along the pathway leading to the garage—she had apparently taken my advice and planted the impatiens there, and they looked trampled on. I took a closer look and confirmed the delicate plants had been crushed underfoot.

Had someone gone out the back way and over the fence in a hurry? Why? Maybe somebody surprised them. Me?

Back in the house, I looked at my watch. Two minutes left. No time to go upstairs, which was just as well. How did I know the killer, if there was one, hadn't retreated up the stairs? The kitchen was immaculate, except for a pizza box crammed into a wastebasket in the corner. A laptop and cell phone lay on the kitchen table, but there was no time to snoop. I heard sirens in the distance and started for the entry. A couple of pieces of opened mail sat on a spindly legged table between the front door and a marble stand containing two pearl-handled canes. One of the pieces of mail was from a nursing home called Windsor Terrace Memory Care, where Mr. Ferris was being cared for, I assumed. A quick glance told me it was a welcoming letter. Huh, I thought, looks like her husband just moved to a new facility. The sirens got louder, so I stepped out the door to wait for the police.

My interview with the Vancouver Police lasted for over an hour. Midway through they allowed me a break so I could let Archie out of the car to stretch his legs. The interview got interesting toward the end, when they started to probe my relationship with Ferris and why I called on her that particular evening. I wasn't willing at this juncture to share my suspicion that Margaret Wingate's death was a homicide, but at the same time wanted them to view Ferris' death with more than the usual skepticism.

"I represent a client whose mother was killed in a hit-and-run in Portland back in March," I explained, giving them Angela and Margaret Wingate's names and walking them through the incident in some detail. "Mrs. Ferris was the secretary of the man who handled the will, a man named Melvin Turner. I came by this evening to ask her a few follow-up questions about the document."

"Follow-up?" the lead detective, a man named Corbin McWhirter, asked. He had brushed-back salt-and-pepper hair, a fleshy nose, and a mouth turned down in a perpetual cop scowl.

"Yes. I talked to her once before, a couple of weeks ago. It was informal, not a deposition."

"What's the issue with the will?"

"It's a little unusual," I answered and went on to explain the sell-off provision for Wingate Properties and the protective clauses for Turner and Avery. "My client simply wants to ensure that those were, in fact, her mother's last wishes," I concluded.

McWhirter leaned in a little. "Is there some reason to believe they weren't?"

I shrugged. "I don't know at this point, but I had a feeling Mrs. Ferris knew something she wasn't telling me. That's why I came here tonight."

McWhirter fixed me with his cop stare. "So you're suggesting this might have been staged, Mr. Claxton, that someone killed Mrs. Ferris to keep her from talking?"

"I don't know, but I think it's a strong possibility." I wanted to tell him about the back door being ajar and the crushed impatiens, but instead I said, "It's easy to fall down stairs, but I'm guessing it's pretty hard to break your neck doing it. The front door wasn't locked, and the body was warm, so maybe I surprised the killer and he went out the back." I left it at that, feeling confident that he and his partner were the good, thorough cops they appeared to be.

I left that night after being told I would have to return to the Vancouver Police Station the next day to read over and sign the statement McWhirter recorded at the scene. The first thing I did back at the car was phone Angela. She hadn't called in that day. When she answered, I sighed inwardly with relief. "Are you okay?"

"Sure. Why do you ask?"

"It's nothing. Why didn't you call me today?"

"My bad. I got busy. At the moment I'm delivering pot to the fine people of Portland. I just arrived at an apartment building on Division filled with people who recently moved here. They seem to have all the money these days."

I didn't think it was a good idea to frighten her by telling her about Ferris' death right then, but I wanted to underline her need to be careful. And I knew better than to suggest she find a safer job or quit altogether, owing to her newly acquired financial resources. I settled for, "You don't deliver in sketchy buildings or neighborhoods, do you?"

"It's a judgment call. If I don't like the looks of the place, I call and tell them to come out to the car. And I carry a penlight, too. It has a switchblade that's wicked sharp."

I almost laughed at that but let it slide. "Good. Keep it that way." After we signed off, I sat there for a while thinking about Angela. My gut tightened a little, picturing her riding her bike during the day and delivering pot all over Portland at night. That was no recipe for personal safety, even in the best of times. And these were definitely not the best of times.

When Arch and I were finally headed back across the Columbia River, I wasn't daydreaming about houseboats any more, or paying the price for daydreaming, either. No. I was focused on the situation at hand. The best lead I had, a person whom I believed was a potential key to the whole case, was now off the board permanently. I hardly knew Helen Ferris, but I felt the same outrage that I did for Margaret Wingate. I felt something else, too. Not guilt, because I didn't know yet how this came about. But I couldn't help wondering if my intervention caused Helen to rethink her actions, and God forbid, maybe she'd said something to Turner or whomever had gotten her involved in the forgery. That would explain why someone decided she had to die.

In any case, her death was a setback, but if I was right—that it was no accident—then at least the battle lines were now more clearly drawn, and the contours of the threat I faced more starkly etched. And I realized something else, too. The killer was as cunning as he was cold-blooded.

It wasn't a comforting thought.

Chapter Twenty-two

"I've checked you out, Mr. Claxton. You may have solved some crimes over in Oregon, but I can assure you we don't need your assistance here in Vancouver." It was the next day, and I was deep into my second interview with Detective McWhirter. It wasn't going well.

"Look, Detective, all I'm saying is don't be too quick to assume it was an accident. The front door was unlocked and the body still warm. Did you find anything suspicious toward the back of the house or in the backyard?"

McWhirter's expression went from scowl to annoyed scowl. "I'm asking the questions here, and I'll decide whether to classify this as a suspicious death or not."

I rolled my eyes. "Just making the point that the killer could have heard me and gone out the back way."

McWhirter's eyes narrowed down, and his annoyed scowl grew more intense. "You already mentioned that. Why are you trying to lead me? Did you by any chance look back there before we arrived? Tell me you didn't crush those flowers on the walkway, Mr. Claxton."

Shit. Overplayed my hand. "I didn't do anything to disturb your crime scene," I said, summoning a look of righteous indignation. It was a true statement, as far as it went.

McWhirter paused for a moment while staring a hole in me.

"Okay," he said, "let's go back over this will business one more time." That took another fifteen minutes, and as I was finally leaving the interview room, McWhirter said, "You were wrong, you know. People, particularly old people, break their necks on stairs all the time. Look it up, Mr. Claxton."

I got up to leave, paused at the door, and turned back to him. "I hear you, Detective, but it's also not very likely Helen Ferris trampled her own goddamn flowers, is it?" With that I turned and left.

Half the day was shot, so I decided to spend the rest of it in Portland rather than Dundee. I had just parked on NE Glisan when Nando's immaculate black Mercedes-Benz S-Class sedan pulled up and parked two slots ahead of me, which reminded me to get my car washed. He called earlier, and we agreed to meet for lunch at Pambiche, our favorite Cuban restaurant. My friend got out of his car with a Gucci man-purse slung over his shoulder. He wore cream-colored slacks, white suspenders, and a black linen shirt that matched the band in his Panama hat. I looked him over admiringly. "You look like you just arrived from Havana."

He flashed a brilliant smile. "I am Cuban. We are sharp dressers."

It was a splendid May morning, so we took one of the small outside tables. "Where is Archie?" he asked as we sat down. "Surely, he is not shut up somewhere on such a beautiful morning."

"He's with his new best friend, Angela Wingate," I answered. "I dropped him by this morning on my way over to Vancouver. They enjoy each other's company."

He nodded. "Have you submitted a bill to this young client of yours?" I told him I hadn't yet, and he fetched a sheet of paper out of his purse and handed it to me. "My expenses for last month." I looked at it and whistled. He smiled. "Quality investigative work is expensive, my friend."

I laid the bill down and proceeded to describe Helen Ferris' death and my fear that the Vancouver Police would view it as an accident. When I finished, he raised an eyebrow. "A hit-and-run that looks accidental, a drunken suicide, and now a fall down the stairs that breaks a neck. This killer is the clever one."

I nodded. "Someone's working hard to disguise these murders. They must have a lot to hide."

"What about your young client? Is she the next one in line?"

I winced inwardly. It was a question I'd been asking myself. "It's possible, although the events so far can be viewed as unrelated. And if they aren't, harming her would make the conspiracy obvious." I went on to describe the three-hundred-thousand-dollar offer tendered by Turner and Avery to Angela and her unambiguous response. "They offered me fifty-thousand, to boot," I added.

Nando rolled his eyes in disbelief. "The price of integrity is very high, indeed." He leveled his eyes back at me. "You may be in even greater danger, Calvin."

I nodded but had more pressing things on my mind. I pointed to the bill he'd given me. "So what am I getting for all this cost?" Before he could answer, our waitress arrived. We both ordered Cuban beer, and I asked for my usual—the fillet of red snapper sautéed in coconut pepper sauce. When Nando ordered the Plato Comunista—a dish made with yucca in a garlic mojo sauce—I did a double take. "You're getting a *vegetarian* dish?"

He smiled almost apologetically and patted his ample stomach. "I am watching the figure."

"So that fancy workout suit you had on the other day's for real?"

"I have lost five pounds, Calvin," he replied, looking hurt. "This is serious. My grace on the salsa dance floor is at risk."

I laughed. "Of course. I see your point." My Cuban friend went on about his latest salsa dancing exploits until our waiter brought our beers, at which point we got down to it. "So, what have you got?" I repeated.

"The reason you could find nothing on Arrowhead Investments LLC is that the company is listed only in the Cyprus corporate registry."

"Cyprus?"

"Yes, Cyprus, where there are nearly as many corporations registered as people. It is a very desirable venue for people who wish to hide money or launder it."

"Now that you know the origin, can you find out who's behind the shell?"

Nando drank some beer and shrugged. "It is very difficult. Cyprus does not require companies to disclose the identity of officers or directors. They can be from anywhere in the world. I did learn that the incorporation was handled by a man named Costas Zertalis, an attorney living in Nicosia. He's a Cypriot who specializes in setting up offshore accounts for wealthy Russians, I have learned."

I set my beer down and leaned forward. "*Russians?*"

He nodded. "Yes, Putin-connected oligarchs have long preferred using Cyprus as a place to park the money they have stolen from the Russian people. We are talking about big money here, Calvin, and very nasty people."

"So, Russians are behind Arrowhead?"

Another shrug. "It is impossible to tell. Zertalis does not deal exclusively with Russians." Our waitress arrived, and after she set the plates down and left, Nando continued, but not before he gazed longingly at my sautéed snapper. "The only hope of finding anything more is through the FBI."

I laughed. "You're kidding, right?"

Nando smiled slyly. "Not completely. I have a friend in the Bureau up in Seattle. He is Cuban. He helps me from time to time, small favors. It is not a lot to ask for the names and nationalities of the people who own a corporation. This should be public information, should it not?"

I laughed again. "What did your friend say?"

Nando took an unenthusiastic bite of yucca. "He did not say no."

I shook my head. The contacts my friend cultivated never ceased to amaze me. "So, what we may be looking at," I said with a forkful of snapper in my hand, "is that someone's using the purchase of Wingate Properties to launder a big chunk of dirty money?"

"Yes, that is a strong possibility. Or the purchaser is simply someone wishing to remain anonymous. People with large amounts of money often act in very strange ways."

I chewed some fish and considered that for a moment. "Would Boyarchenko have that kind of money? We're talking something in the neighborhood of five-hundred-million dollars, right?"

Nando washed some yucca down with a swig of beer. "It is a lot of money and more than he would be able to launder through his legitimate businesses in Portland."

I nodded. "Good point. So he needs something big, like Wingate Properties. Still, that seems like a lot of money to wring out of Portland. Have you found anything tying him or his lawyer, Byron Hofstetter, to Wingate?"

"No, not yet." The sly smile again. "But we have made certain inroads into the lawyer's office. It is a work in progress." That was code for "we have hacked his e-mail, stay tuned" so I let it go without comment. When we finished lunch, Nando picked up the tab in appreciation for the work I'd given him. We walked across Glisan together and stopped at my car. He swiped a finger across the door, held it up, and made a face. "This situation is troubling, Calvin. You may be crossing swords with very powerful adversaries. At the very least you should consider protection for the young woman."

I nodded. "I'm going to see her right now. I'll let you know."

Chapter Twenty-three

The storefront at the Bridgetown Artists' Co-op was closed, so I rang Angela's studio from the back entry, spoke into the speaker, and a moment later she buzzed me in. I took the back stairs, my eyes adjusting to the dim interior lights just in time to see a silhouetted figure at the top of the stairs. It was Darius, the photographer, and he nodded as he passed me on the way down.

Archie greeted me in the hallway, and I found the door open. My eyes were drawn to the image taped to the wall, which was now complete, the figure seeming to move off the paper with power and a kind of elan I associated with gazelles loping through the veld. Angela was busy on a framework that was the beginning of the right leg in the drawing. Resting on a wooden platform in the center of the room, it rose off the wire outline of a foot, followed the shape of a calf and knee, and ended about mid-thigh, the sharp wire struts pointing at the ceiling. She worked quickly, expertly feeding a length of welding rod into the white-hot junction formed by her torch. I had no sooner sat down when her torch sputtered and went out.

She pushed her goggles up and looked at me. "Damn, ran out of gas. Can you give me a hand? Someone borrowed my handcart and hasn't returned it." I helped her move the empty tank out and put a fresh tank in place. "I'm old school," she said. "A lot of sculptors use arc welding, but I like the effects I can get with oxy-acetylene. It's more work but worth it."

"How faithfully will you follow the drawing?"

She laughed. "Sculpting's very intuitive for me. I have to lay in one piece of steel before I know where the next piece goes." She nodded toward the drawing on the wall. "That figure looks detailed, but it's really just a guide." She flipped her goggles back down, ignited her torch with a hand-held sparker, and after adjusting the flame at the tip of her torch, welded in another piece of long, sharp wire. "I'm making the frame now. The detail work will come after I get the shape and proportions the way I want them."

"How long to finish?"

She shrugged, but the look she shot me was a long way from indifferent. "As long as it takes."

When she took a break to brew some tea, I said, "There have been some developments." She took her tea, sat down on the floor next to Arch, and slung an arm over him. I moved my stool over next to the two of them and began bringing her up to date.

"Helen Ferris is dead?" she gasped when I got to that point. "What happened?"

I described what I'd found and told her the Vancouver Police were investigating. We were well past any sugarcoating, so I added, "I think she was murdered to keep her quiet, but the Vancouver Police seem to be leaning toward an accident."

Her mouth dropped open, and her chocolate eyes stood out against skin gone pale. "You mean you think Melvin and Brice killed her?"

"I don't know, Angela. But I think the Vancouver Police will at least check to see if they have alibis for last night, based on what I told them about the will. But if I'm right—if she was murdered—then it was probably hired out by whoever's behind this."

She focused on something past me for a moment. "First Mom, now Helen." She swung her eyes to me. They had welled up and were draining tears. Archie drew closer and licked her cheek.

"I don't have a speck of evidence for any of this, Angela, but I do believe it's bigger than just Turner and Avery." Her face grew expectant, but I stopped there, not wishing to divulge the Arrowhead connection. "Meanwhile, I'm concerned about your safety. How important is your marijuana delivery job?"

Her face tightened. "You think I'm next?"

"I don't want to alarm you, but it's something we've got to consider. Any way you could take a vacation or leave of absence until this gets cleared up?"

"I could just quit now that I have some money in the bank, but it's the perfect job for an artist, you know? Three, four hours a night, great tips. And I like my life right now. I'm not anxious to make any big changes." She exhaled a breath in frustration and shook her head. "But I've been feeling a little freaked out the last week or so, to tell you the truth."

"Did you see something?" I asked, growing anxious.

"No, nothing like that. It's just that some deliveries are in pretty sketch neighborhoods." She exhaled again. I'll have to give my boss a couple of days' notice."

"Good. Let me know. Meanwhile, can you skip the deliveries to questionable neighborhoods?"

"Yeah. I can do that."

"What about your bike? Can you put it up for a while, use the Honda during the day?"

She rolled her eyes. "Jeez. Okay."

Angela went back to sculpting, and I watched her work for a while. Then, after extracting another promise from her to stay in daily contact, I gathered up my dog to leave. At the door, she said with a face full of concern, "What about Herb? What will happen to him?"

"Who's Herb?"

"Helen's husband. I met him a couple of times before he got Alzheimer's. Nice guy. She had to put him in a home last year. Mom said it was a dump, that Helen hated it."

"The police have notified her next of kin by now. He'll be taken care of, but I'll check on him if you want."

"Would you?"

My phone rang just after we arrived back at Caffeine Central. It was Marnie Stinson. "Hey, Cal, just wanted to let you know you're on the Land Use Board of Appeals agenda for June 22."

"Whoa, that's a short fuse."

"Sorry, but don't shoot the messenger. The board's busy as hell, and I had to pull some strings to slot you in." I apologized, and she went on, "I did a little digging on your behalf, Cal. If you want to find who hauled the gravel for McMinnville, you might try a guy named Gus Pembroke. He's retired now, but he ran a big trucking company in the valley for years and knows everyone in the biz."

I jotted down his name and a phone number she had. "Thanks again, Marnie. Your next divorce and restraining order are on the house." She laughed at that, but when I hung up I felt no levity. A hearing in a month and a half? I had nothing to go on at the moment except a gut feel that McMinnville Sand and Gravel and H and S were ripping me, my dog, and my neighbors off. On the other hand, a short fuse meant Arch and I could go home soon if I could figure out a way to stop them. *If.*

I called Gus Pembroke, got his voicemail, and left him a message to call me. Hope springs eternal.

My energy was flagging, so I went upstairs, brewed a double cappuccino and brought it back down to my office. Savoring the almost bitter taste of the coffee tempered by the foamed milk, my thoughts turned back to Angela. She had lost her mother and been warned that her life might also be in danger, but she seemed as concerned about Herb Ferris' welfare as her own. I was beginning to see that Angela Wingate had a heart that matched her courage.

I promised her I'd follow up on Herb, and I was curious about something related to him as well. She said Helen committed him the year before, yet the letter I saw at the scene suggested he'd recently moved to another facility. Why? I tried to remember the name of the place—Windsor something or other. After a couple of minutes on Google, I found it—Windsor Terrace Memory Care. Located on the northeast edge of Vancouver, the website promised a "warm, elegant care environment" that was "gated to ensure the safety of your loved one," and provided pictures of the building and the surrounding acres of manicured parkland that looked more like a country club than a care facility. I called, told the receptionist I had important information regarding the family of one of their patients, and was immediately put through to the facility manager, a woman named Harriet Balfour, possessor of a very soothing voice.

"Thank you for that information, Mr. Claxton," she said when I explained the reason for my call. "The police have already contacted us regarding Mrs. Wingate's unfortunate accident, and we're taking the appropriate steps with Herbert."

Accident? "That's a relief," I said, then added, "uh, I just happen to be shopping for a home for my Uncle Charles. Would you mind if I asked a few questions about Windsor Terrace?" She said of course she wouldn't mind. After listening to a description of their care philosophy, their compassionate, highly trained staff, and their incomparable amenities, I said, "What would it cost me to place my uncle with you?"

"Well," she said, our single rooms start at six-thousand dollars, our luxury suites at seventy-five hundred, not including the cost of medications and non-routine medical care."

"A month?" I blurted.

"Of course," she said, her voice having suddenly acquired a harder edge. I half expected her to say, 'If you have to ask, you can't afford it.'

I thanked her, hung up, and sat there thinking. Angela said

Helen disliked the first facility she'd placed Herbert in, then she moves him to a luxury facility right after Margaret Wingate is killed. Unless she had incredible insurance, no way she could afford seventy-two-thousand dollars a year to keep him there. I looked at Arch. "Looks like a payoff to me. What do you think, Big Boy?" His ears came up in obvious agreement.

I made two phone calls after signing off with Harriet Balfour. First, I called Detective McWhirter, who listened politely as I recounted what I just learned. Judging from some of the details he repeated back to me, at least he took notes, although his tone was decidedly skeptical. "Thanks for the input, Mr. Claxton. We'll be in touch if we have any further questions." I asked how the investigation was going, to which he replied, "The usual, waiting for the ME's report." That's all he would tell me.

I called Nando next. "I know that the Vancouver Police can go for a warrant to look at the medical payment records," I told him after he balked at my request, "but we both know that will be tough and take forever. And, besides, they might not even bother. They're still leaning toward accident."

He sighed heavily into the phone. "Why is it that the jobs you give me are so difficult, Calvin?"

"Because you're the best PI in the Northwest?"

He boomed his baritone laugh. "Ah, the inevitable flattery. You know it is my weakness."

Chapter Twenty-four

That evening I left Archie behind at Caffeine Central, fought the traffic out SE Foster to the Swanson Motel, and parked across the street from the only entrance at six-forty. True to the handyman's word, a low-slung, cherry red Fiat Spider swung off the highway and into the motel parking lot at 6:58, "like clockwork." I followed at a respectable distance and watched the driver park. Tall and thin with dark, receding hair, a hawk nose, and thoroughly inked-up sleeves, Spider-Man got out, knocked at room 328, and was let in. I caught a glimpse of short shorts and spike heels at the door. I parked in front of room 335, feeling, if not optimistic, at least hopeful. Lenny the Fox had died in room 335, and the timing and location of Spider-Man's visit was about right for him to have seen something.

I called Nando, who was expecting my call, and read him the Fiat's license plate number. "That's right, his name, marital status, and anything else you can get me in ten minutes," I reiterated. He called back nine minutes later and gave me what a source in the Portland Police Bureau was able to pull up for him. It pays to have connections.

I got out, walked over to the Fiat, slouched on a gleaming fender, and waited, thinking about my chances. Another long shot. After all, Lenny Bateman's death was six weeks ago, but I was hoping this guy had heard about the suicide, which might make the evening memorable. Chances were he hadn't seen the small item in the paper, but maybe the woman he hooked up with mentioned it. In any case, I was sure the cops hadn't gotten any of the prostitutes or Johns to talk about what they saw that night, and I knew I wouldn't fare any better. Unless, of course, I had an inducement.

Myron Hatcher came out of the motel room twenty-eight minutes later. Quickie, indeed. He looked at me through a pair of small, deep-set eyes and scowled. "Hey, dude, off the car. I just had it detailed." I got up, and he flashed a conspiratorial smile. "You next?"

"No." I handed him a card and introduced myself. "Actually, I'm here to talk to you, Myron."

His smile melted, and his eyes grew instantly alert. "About what?"

"What do you think?"

He dropped his head and studied the cigarette-butt strewn walkway. "*Fuck.* How did Sharon find out, anyway?"

Bingo. He thought I worked for his wife. I would go with that. "You've been a regular here on Tuesdays and Thursdays for a long time. What do you expect?" I gestured toward my Beemer. "Why don't you get in so we can talk? Maybe we can work something out." He followed me to my car and got in, looking distraught. I nodded toward room 335 in front of us. "Did you hear about the suicide that took place in that room on March 16?"

His look turned puzzled. "I thought this was about Sharon?"

I shrugged. "It could be. Depends on you. Did you hear about it?"

"Yeah, I heard. So what?"

"Did you happen to see the victim come in that night?"

He put his hands up. "Hey, I'm not getting invol—"

"Did you see him?" I cut in, putting more emphasis on the question.

He lowered his hands and nodded. "Yeah, I saw him."

"Did you see the other man with him, the one driving?" When he nodded again, I said, "What did the other man look like?"

He looked up at the headliner for a few moments, then released a breath. "The guy that offed himself was a little dude, pretty drunk. The other guy was bigger, well built, uh…short dark hair…

"Caucasian? What else can you remember? Take your time."

"Yeah, Caucasian. Maybe five-nine or ten…"

"Tats, facial hair, glasses?"

"No. Just a regular dude, but in shape."

"How old?"

He shrugged. "I don't know, maybe early-forties, give or take."

That's all he was able to remember, despite several more prompts I threw at him. I skipped the sermon about his needing to contact the police with this information, knowing that, like the handyman, he'd refuse to cooperate. Johns are like that. I said, "Okay, Myron, thanks for your help. You have my card. If you think of anything else, call me immediately."

He looked at me, relief flooding across his face. "*That's it?* You're not going to say anything to my wife?"

"Yeah, that's it, although if I were you, I'd give some thought to what you're up to. It seems obvious from your reaction tonight that you care about your wife. She'll find out eventually, and then you're both going to get hurt."

Myron slunk off to his little red sports car. I watched him drive away, and judging from the look on his face when he left, I figured the Swanson Motel just lost a good customer. I sat back for a moment and let the encounter sink in. Against pretty long odds I'd managed to get a description—admittedly, a sketchy one—of the mystery man I suspected of being behind the killings.

Another piece in the puzzle.

When I got back to Caffeine Central, Archie lobbied hard for a run, but it was late and I was bushed. After I fed him, he settled for a walk and sniff down Couch Street. It had begun to rain, and the light sprinkle irritated my dog, who was no pluviophile. But the gentle downpour seemed to quiet the city and soothe my nerves, and soon I found myself combing back through the case. I now had the vague outlines of a money-laundering scheme that could have driven a forgery, and two, maybe three, murders. I had a cast of suspects, too—a lawyer, a CEO, a Russian mobster, and, if I didn't miss my guess, a hired assassin at the tip of the spear who looked like "a regular dude." I didn't know who was behind Arrowhead Investments yet, but felt they were at the other end of the spear.

It was progress, but on the other hand, the whole construct was circumstantial. A wave of frustration drenched me. It was one thing to see the web of a conspiracy and quite another to prove it. I needed a lot more.

The rain intensified, and I realized I was heading toward Winona's neighborhood. I considered calling her or walking over to her loft but quickly thought better of it. *The ball's in her court*, I told myself. *Stay strong*. Was it wisdom speaking, or was it anger and stubborn pride keeping me from contacting her? I wasn't sure.

I made a nondescript omelet for dinner and fell asleep reading *The Snow Man* while sitting in an overstuffed chair next to the window. I awoke from a dreamless sleep around two a.m. Archie lay curled against my bare feet, the warmth of his body a comfort. I reached down and stroked the fur along his ribs, and he looked up at me. I'm here, he seemed to say. *Stop worrying*.

It was good advice, but I had good reason to worry.

Chapter Twenty-five

It was clear and crisp again the next morning, so I knew there would be no denying my dog. After feeding him, I sat down and began lacing up my jogging shoes while he did his happy dance. He spun and yelped halfway to Tom McCall Park, which was already packed with people—like plants seeking the sun. Taking the lead, with his ears up and stump of a tail down, he guided me expertly through the moving throng. By the time we got back, the black cloud that had descended on me lifted, and after finishing my first cappuccino, I had my mojo back.

"Thanks, Big Boy," I said, and as a token of my appreciation, gave him his weekly bone a day early.

After showering, I went downstairs and opened up Caffeine Central, surprised to see that a queue had yet to form. I chalked it up to the fine weather. The first thing I did that morning was call Nando, describe what I'd learned from Spider-Man, and ask him to arrange an anonymous call to the Portland Police. "He won't cooperate, but I want Portland to know Lenny the Fox wasn't alone. I want them to have this other man's description, however vague it is."

"I can do this," Nando replied, "but it will probably not be enough to cause them to re-open the case."

"Yeah, I realize that, but I can't just sit on the information."

I called Semyon next and caught him at home, where he

felt free to talk. "Do you know who does the enforcing for Boyarchenko?" I asked. When he gave me three names—the Vasilev brothers and a guy named Andrei Mikhailev—I said, "Can you describe them?"

"The Vasilev brothers are behemoths, well over six foot, three hundred pounds. They rough people up, break arms and knee-caps, that kind of thing. Mikhailev is the man Ilya uses when he wants someone dead. He's short, heavyset. Keeps a low profile."

"How short?"

"Five-six, five-eight."

Okay, I told myself after I rang off, *Mystery Man doesn't work directly for Boyarchenko*. Check that box off.

After the call I checked the waiting room, and finding it still empty said to Arch, "Come on, let's take a ride." He sprang to his feet and waited impatiently while I wrote out a sign that said, "Back this afternoon around 1:00 p.m." and taped it to the front door.

Thirty-five minutes later I parked down from Helen Ferris' condo, got out, and leashed up my dog. Now armed with a description of sorts, I wanted to see if I could put Mystery Man at the scene of another suspicious death.

I covered the houses on her block and the coffee shop at the corner, explaining I was an attorney representing someone involved in the case. No one could remember seeing a fortyish, Caucasian man with dark hair and a good build that night. Matter of fact, the persons willing to talk to me couldn't remember seeing *anyone* on the street. *Oh, well*, I told myself, *check off another box. It was something that had to be done.*

I was getting back in my car when I noticed a pizza joint a half block up on a side street—Anthony's Pizzeria, the sign said in a swirling red cursive. A faint ping of recognition made me stop. Of course. I'd seen that logo on a pizza box in Ferris' kitchen that night. I shrugged and started to get in the car when I realized something was slightly off about that—the box was crammed haphazardly into a wastebasket in a kitchen that was, in all other respects, neat and orderly, almost immaculate. I rolled the backseat windows down and told Arch to chill for a couple more minutes.

People are conditioned to answer questions, so sometimes the best approach is to just ask outright, which is what I did to the young girl behind the counter at Anthony's, after flashing a card and explaining I was an insurance investigator. "No," she said, after scanning her computer screen with clear, intelligent eyes, "We didn't deliver any pizza to that address on Wednesday, the second."

"Were you here that Tuesday and Wednesday night?" She nodded, and I went on, "Do you remember if an older woman with distinctly red hair picked up a pizza that evening or the evening before? She lives in the neighborhood."

She scrunched her brow down and smiled. "You mean dyed red hair?"

I chuckled. "Yeah, I guess so. A russet color, no gray at all."

"Not a chance. I would have remembered someone like that. We don't get many walk-ins, you know."

"Thanks," I said, then pointed to the tee-shirts and caps on the wall. "Sell many of those?"

She shrugged. "Not really. But Anthony thinks it's cool to have them up there."

I nodded. "Any chance you remember selling a cap or a shirt or both to a white guy, a little shorter than me, dark hair, around forty years old?"

She didn't hesitate. "Yeah, maybe two weeks ago. A guy sorta like that came in and bought a shirt and cap, no pizza, paid cash. I remember, because that was the first cap and shirt I ever sold, and he didn't look the part, you know?"

"How so?"

"He wasn't from the 'hood, unless he just moved in, and he had on a black wool cap and shades. No way that dude's wearing one of our tees. I figured he was buying it for someone else."

I thanked her and left, and by the time I got back to the car had put it together—the killer appears at Helen Ferris' door carrying an empty pizza box and wearing an Anthony's shirt and cap. She opens the door to him, thinking he has the wrong address. Bingo. He's in. Snaps her neck without leaving a mark. Easy enough for a pro. Carries her body up the stairs and tosses it back down. When I blunder on the scene, he goes out the back door, stuffing the box in the trash in the kitchen in his haste, leaving the back door open, and trampling the flowers.

It wasn't a bad theory. The presence of the pizza box was hard to explain otherwise. Ferris didn't order pizza by phone, and she didn't just happen into the pizzeria and pick one up, according to the young sales girl. Okay, no one saw the killer on the street that evening, but that wasn't hard to explain—we all have our noses in our little screens most of the time these days, right?

In any case, it wasn't a theory I could share with Detective McWhirter. How could I explain having seen the pizza box when I already told him I hadn't gone through the house? But it was another piece in the puzzle, giving me a better idea of how Mystery Man operated.

I was hungry, so on the way back to Caffeine Central I stopped at the Fuego food cart on NW Hoyt and grabbed a bowl of grilled chicken with black beans, salsa, and sour cream to go, along with a side of guacamole and couple of made-that-morning flour tortillas. I ate the lunch at my desk, chasing it with a cold bottle of Mirror Pond. Before taking the sign off the front door, I called Gertie to tell her I was running late on last month's billable hours. "What else is new?" she responded.

"It's slow here today, so I'll be able to get it done," I promised. "What's happening in the quarry?"

"Same old, same old. Five or six blasts a day, truck traffic's building. Just like old times." She grumbled a laugh. "I feel like going down there with a shotgun. I know my husband would have."

"As your attorney, I advise against that." She laughed again, and I went on. "I'm on the agenda of the Land Use Appeal Board in June. I'm working this from several angles," I fibbed, "so keep the faith."

A long pause ensued before she said, "Please. No happy talk, Cal. It's well known that mining interests hold sway in this state." She sighed into the phone. "Considering your location and Archie's reaction to the blasting, maybe you better consider talking to a real estate agent."

Her suggestion felt like a knife twisting in my gut, although I knew it was just Gertie being brutally honest. "What? You trying to get rid of me?" I said, trying to make light of it.

"Oh, God no, Cal. Surely you don't think that. It's just that, you know, being on the lip of the quarry and all, it's going to be hell for you and Arch."

"Yeah, I suppose you're right. Maybe I should talk to someone." But after I hung up, I lost whatever resolve I had in that direction. *Not yet*, I told myself. The operation down there's illegal. Wait to see what Gus Pembroke has to say.

Later that afternoon, Gus Pembroke returned my call. "McCallister," he said, responding to my introduction. "That would be the only gravel mine in the Red Hills. Small, but damn productive for McMinnville Sand and Gravel in its day, as I recall." I proceeded to ask about the trucking firms that had serviced the mine. "Don't recall off the top. Why are you asking?"

I hesitated, figuring I would get stonewalled again if I told the truth, but there was something in Pembroke's voice that led me to chance it. "McMinnville started mining again without any warning, and I think they've passed the twelve-year limit, but I can't prove it. I live on the lip of the quarry."

"My condolences. Never liked those bastards at McMinnville. Always paid late. Hooks in their pockets. I'll ask around, see what I can find out, Mr. Claxton."

By mid-afternoon I finished up my accounting chores and e-mailed a file to Gertie. I'd just returned to my office after making a coffee upstairs when I heard someone enter the waiting room. My office door was partially closed, so I hollered, "I'm back here. Come on in." Tracey Thomas swung the door open and smiled. I said, "I know. You were just in the neighborhood."

"Is this a bad time?"

I got up and smiled back. "No, not at all. Come on in." She wore jeans, ankle boots, and a black silk blouse cinched with a silver belt that matched a pair of dangly earrings. "Casual Friday?"

"*No*," she said with a laugh. "Where is it written a city councilwoman has to wear a pantsuit? I'm taking the afternoon off after my weekly meet-and-greet." She sighed, swept a lock of auburn hair aside, and sat down. "I love talking to my constituents, but it gets old, you know? Nobody comes in without an ax to grind, and of course they all want their problems fixed right then and there, like I'm some kind of omnipotent god." She chuckled and shook her head, her look turning sardonic. "Life was easier when I was an activist, on the other side of the fence."

I laughed. "I don't envy you. Portlanders are a troubled lot these days."

She rolled her eyes. "So true. There's the usual stuff—potholes, aging bridges, taxes—but there's also this collective anxiety that seems to overlay everything—that what's so special about this city's slipping away."

I nodded. "Yeah, I'm seeing it at street level."

She sat up a little straighter and flipped her hair off her shoulder. "I didn't come here to cry on your shoulder, Cal. I have some intelligence about Wingate Properties to pass on."

I leaned forward. "Me, too. You go first."

"You asked me about connections between Ilya Boyarchenko and Wingate. My source doesn't know of any." I nodded, and she continued, "But he just told me there's some kind of important meeting coming up with Wingate's top brass and some unnamed people. A lot of preparations are being made, so the rumor got out. My source thinks it could be the investor coming in for a tête-à-tête."

"When?"

She shrugged. "He doesn't know yet but guesses within the next two weeks. They're looking for an off-site venue that affords a lot of privacy."

"That's interesting. I'd like to know when and where."

"Sure. When he learns more, I'll be in touch." She smiled conspiratorially. "Will you bug the room or what?"

I laughed. "That's illegal and next to impossible, but I might be able to get some photographs or a video of them coming or going. I'd like to know who's there and ID the investor, if he or she's attending. Which brings me to my news—my PI has found that Arrowhead Investments is a shell registered in Cyprus. There's no legal way to find out who's actually behind it, but the attorney who handled the deal's known to specialize in Russians interested in hiding or laundering money."

"Good God," Tracey said, her eyes registering something between surprise and delight. "Boyarchenko?"

"It's possible."

She leaned back, tapped her lips with a finger, and smiled. "If I could say that Ilya Boyarchenko's money is behind the North Waterfront Project, that would help my case immensely."

I put up both hands. "Whoa, Tracey. I don't know that. And if word of any of this gets out, all bets are off for ever getting to the bottom of it."

She placed both palms on the edge of my desk and narrowed her eyes. "I'm not going to say anything, but I just gave you some valuable information. I know there must be a hell of a lot more to this than just a forged will. You owe me the whole story. *Quid pro quo*, remember?"

Sure, she kept showing up at Caffeine Central, flirting, wanting to partner, and anxious to gain information. I was a little suspicious, but I had to admit I was taken by her forthrightness, to say nothing of her charms. And my gut still said I could trust her. Now, with her revelation of the upcoming meeting, she was right. I owed her an explanation, so I laid out what I had, excluding what I'd just learned about Mystery Man.

When I finished, she had a sober look on her face. "My God, Cal, Margaret Wingate and two others murdered by people who want to launder money and gain control of Wingate Properties and the North Waterfront Project? That's horrifying."

"That's what it looks like, but all I have is circumstantial evidence, and events are working against my ever being able to prove it. Margaret Wingate's hit-and-run case is going cold, Lenny the Fox's death was ruled a suicide, and the Vancouver Police are leaning toward declaring Helen Ferris' death accidental."

"What about the forged will? Can you challenge it?"

I shrugged. "Maybe, but proving a document's forged is an uphill slog. All you need for a good forgery is a light table. And it doesn't get me where I want to go, anyway."

"What about Avery and Turner? They're obviously dirty. At the very least, Turner must have been in on the forgery."

"It would appear so, but they've covered their tracks carefully. I need a way into this thing. Maybe the upcoming meeting will give me something to work with."

The room went silent, except for a wailing siren in the distance. Tracey said, finally, "Meanwhile, the skids are greased for the North Waterfront Project. Looks like it will come up for a vote in June if not sooner." Her expression turned bitter. "Poindexter's pushing this like some ass-kissing K Street lobbyist. It's disgusting."

"Maybe he's on the take. Is that possible?" I went on to tell her about seeing Poindexter talking to Boyarchenko at the ground-breaking ceremony for the Russian Cultural Center.

Her look turned thoughtful. "Fred talks to a lot of people in this town, so I'd hate to impugn his motives based on that, but yeah, I wouldn't rule it out based on the way he's behaving now."

We kicked that around for a while, and Tracey agreed to do some digging on Portland Planning Commission Chairman Fred Poindexter. When the conversation finally hit a lull, Tracey eyed me. "How are things with Winona?"

I shook my head. "Not good. We've basically broken up, I guess. I think she's sort of re-evaluating her life right now. I don't know where she's going to come out."

"I'm so sorry to hear that Cal. How do you feel about it?"

"Not good."

An awkward pause ensued before Tracey got up and walked to the door. She turned to me, placed a hand on my wrist, and said, "If you want to talk about it, call me, Cal. Anytime." Her hand was warm, her nutmeg eyes with their little pots of gold soft and inviting, and I could smell lavender in her hair.

When I didn't respond, she turned and left.

Chapter Twenty-six

Helen Ferris' obituary appeared in the Sunday *Oregonian*. Survived by her husband, a daughter, and a brother, she worked for Turner, Ross, and Steinman for twenty-four years, I noted. A loyal employee, no doubt. It wasn't hard for me to imagine her being turned. After all, the forged will basically left the proceeds of the sale of Wingate Properties to charity. Who could argue with that? And as a small token of appreciation, she was able to move her husband out of a flea trap and into a fine assisted-care facility.

The obit also stated that she died from "an accidental fall in her home" and would be buried the following Tuesday. On Monday morning, I called Detective McWhirter to confirm that the Vancouver Police had declared her death an accident. "No," he told me, "we haven't closed her case just yet, but we saw no reason to discourage the family from using that explanation."

"You mean you're still investigating it as a suspicious death?"

He chuckled. "Technically, it's open, but I don't think it will be for too much longer. Turner and Avery both have airtight alibis for that night, and Turner's offered to open up his books regarding Margaret Wingate's will. Meanwhile, the ME confirmed there were no suspicious marks on Ferris' body. Not much to go on, I'm afraid."

"What about her husband's medical expenses? Who's paying that?"

"That's a loose end we're checking, but I doubt we'll get a judge to sign off on a warrant. Look, Mr. Claxton, I've already told you more than I should. There just isn't any blood in this stone."

It was no use arguing. I thanked him and punched off. I'd figured I couldn't count on the Vancouver P.D., and I was right. For a few agonizing moments, doubts crept in. Unlocked doors, a crumpled pizza box, and crushed flowers were flimsy pieces of evidence at best, and maybe Helen put her husband in upscale Windsor Terrace as a gesture of love, knowing he wouldn't live much longer.

But I caught myself. *Nah, she was murdered by Mystery Man.*

On Tuesday morning, I worked from my Caffeine Central office, dressed in gray slacks, a blazer, and a dark tie that I fished out of my closet at the Aerie the night before. Helen Ferris' funeral was that afternoon in Portland, and I planned to pay my respects. I had another motive as well—I wanted to take a shot at Melvin Turner, the weakest link in the conspiracy chain I'd forged. Admittedly a gut feel, I sensed Turner was conflicted by something, and whatever it was, his business partner, Brice Avery, didn't appear to share it. I had no script for the encounter and wasn't even sure the opportunity would present itself, but like Hippocrates said, desperate times require desperate measures.

Clouds rolled in off the Pacific, scaled the Coast Range, and by Tuesday afternoon were shedding a light, steady patter of rain on the city. Out on the street, Portlanders picked up their pace, but I didn't see many umbrellas. In this town, umbrellas were for wimps, tourists, and new arrivals from California. I parked on SW Alder, fed the meter, and headed toward the historic First Presbyterian Church, a stately Victorian gothic with a gabled, copper clad roof, arched stained-glass windows, and a towering, needlepoint spire. Helen Ferris was a Portland native who'd gone to Lincoln High School and Portland State, just a mile from the church. She must have had a lot of friends and relatives, because I saw a long line of somberly clad people waiting to file into the sanctuary.

I hung back across the street and a half block down until they'd all gone in, then started to cross over when I saw someone vaguely familiar approaching on the other side. He was scurrying, pushing his heavy frame along in a near duck waddle. Melvin Turner. I stopped and watched him enter the church, pleased he arrived without his wife and kids, a potential stroke of good luck. I waited a couple of minutes, then entered the sanctuary and took a seat in an empty row at the back.

A funeral can leave people emotionally vulnerable, which gave me a great opportunity to confront Turner. What I forgot to factor in was that it would do the same for me, and when the massive pipe organ kicked in with a godawful dirge, I was swept back to that black day we buried my wife, Nancy, in L.A. Those memories triggered all-too-familiar pangs of guilt and self-doubt, which I fought through as the minister droned on about hope and everlasting life. Finally, brighter thoughts of Nancy emerged. Sure, she'd given up on life, but that was because of her depression, not because she was a quitter. She was passionate about helping the vulnerable—whether it was a stray dog or a homeless person, it didn't matter. I smiled as a fragment of a memory crept in from back before the darkness struck her. We were on our way to the beach with the top down in the old Camaro we owned before Claire was born. Nancy was singing along with Joan Baez to *There But For Fortune* at the top of her lungs. That song pretty much summed up her philosophy. She tolerated my long hours and missed vacations but was often skeptical of my role as a prosecutor. "Why are so many of your defendants the marginalized and persons of color?" she would ask. "When are you going to go after someone wearing a tie?" I was too busy climbing the ladder to respond to her questions in any substantive way. After all, prosecutors were the good guys, weren't they?

But that all changed after her death, when I was forced to examine my life with brutal honesty....

I snapped back to the present as the minister brought Helen Ferris' mourners out of deep prayer. I took a breath, let it out slowly, and felt my moorings reattach. Was I sticking my neck out too far this time? *Hell, no*, I told myself. *Nancy would have expected nothing less.*

I slipped out of the sanctuary ahead of the crowd, went in the direction I'd seen Turner come from, and stepped into an alcove at a side entrance to the church to wait for him. A good fifteen minutes passed, during which the rain abated somewhat. I'd almost given up when he walked by the alcove without noticing me. I fell in behind him, and when he tripped the locks on his Mercedes with his key fob, I said, "How was the service, Melvin?"

He spun around and looked at me, his dark, liquid eyes wide with surprise behind the wire rims. "What the hell are you doing here, Claxton?"

"Same thing as you—paying my respects. I found her body, you know."

He stiffened, and his pinkish forehead grew four evenly spaced furrows. "And you suggested to the Vancouver Police that Brice and I might have had something to do with her death, didn't you? What have you been smoking, Claxton?"

I chuckled. "Hey, all I told them was that I had questions about the will you and Helen produced. They were just doing their cop thing. But since you brought it up..." I kept the smile but fixed him with my eyes. "*Did* you have anything to do with her death?" I hadn't meant to go that far, but saw a chance to get a good read.

His cherub cheeks flushed red, and I half expected the droplets of rain on his bald spot to boil off. He held my gaze, though. "Of course not, you slanderous bastard. Helen was a loyal employee and a good friend."

"Loyal enough that she helped you alter Margaret Wingate's will?"

He took a step toward me, his eyes nearly filling the rims of his glasses. "That's laughable. You have no proof of that. You should have taken the money, you idiot."

"You're right, I probably should have. And now Helen's dead. How convenient."

He raised his arm and pointed a chubby finger at me. "If you think for a moment that I—"

"Is there a problem here, Mel?" We both turned to the street to see Brice Avery, who had pulled to a stop in his forest green Jaguar. He put the car in park, said something to the attractive woman next to him, who I assumed was his wife, and got out. "What the hell are you up to now, Claxton?" he said as he approached. "You chase funerals as well as ambulances, I see."

I shrugged. "Just having a little chat with Melvin here. You're, uh, double parked."

Turner grumbled something close to a laugh and looked at Avery. "He's suggesting Helen's death wasn't an accident."

Avery, who had positioned himself between us, looked at me first and then turned his head toward Turner. "Of course he is. He'll say anything to keep his fake game alive." He turned back to me, his gray eyes narrowing down, hard as gunmetal. "Listen, asshole, you were made a generous offer to drop this witch hunt, but you were too stupid to take it. And, of course, you were professionally negligent in advising your client not to take an even better deal. You've been warned." He glanced back at Turner before continuing. "If you go public with any of this nonsense, we're going to take you down piece by piece, and your liability insurance won't even pay the bar bill."

Turner laughed. It sounded like relief. "Yeah, you'll be defending against lawsuits till you go broke and then some."

I felt heat rise from the soles of my feet. I nodded and swung my eyes from Turner to Avery. "Gentlemen, if you'll excuse me, I've got work to do. If you did nothing wrong, you have nothing to worry about." With that, I spun around and walked away.

I made the message clear—I was not backing off—and I knew there would be consequences. These guys weren't bluffing. Then, again, neither was I.

That night, as I was cooking dinner in the galley kitchen, Angela called. "Hey," she said, "just checking in to let you know everything's cool."

"How's the jogger coming along?"

"Slow, but I've got to get the framework just right or the piece won't work."

"Have you talked to the pot shop?"

"Yeah, they said I'm a star employee, and they'll take me back any time." She laughed. "They're pretty chill. Smoke a lot of their own shit."

I laughed. "When's your last night?"

"Tomorrow." She laughed again. "They even put a note on their website saying goodbye to me."

"Good. No sketchy deliveries tonight, right?"

"Don't worry, I got this."

"I know you do."

I'm not the psychic type at all, but something told me not to leave that last delivery night to chance.

Chapter Twenty-seven

I got a call the next morning from a lawyer representing the delivery company who'd fired my client for refusing to text while driving. "We can't take him back, Mr. Claxton," she told me, "but in view of his length of service we're willing to offer him a severance package."

"What sort of package?"

"Pay for unused vacation of two weeks plus an extra five hundred dollars.

I laughed. "I'm not even going to take that insulting offer to him. Do we really have to do this dance?"

"What dance?" She said, trying to insert some indignation into her voice without success.

I could tell she was inexperienced and felt bad about being rude, but I was in no mood to be patient. I sighed into the phone. "The dance that starts with you making a ridiculously lowball offer as a negotiating strategy. My client's not interested in negotiating. He wants his job back, pure and simple. If he doesn't get it, we'll see you in court. Tell your client that, please, and spare me the charade."

She said she'd relay the message and hung up, glad, I'm sure, to be rid of such a grouch. I looked over at Arch and said, "Lawyers. Spare me." He looked up, as if fully aware of the irony of my statement.

Later that morning, Gus Pembroke called me back. "I found the two outfits that trucked gravel for McMinnville back then," he explained. "Barker Brothers and Tomkins. Called 'em both just to confirm." He paused for a moment. "The news isn't good, Mr. Claxton—they both told me they didn't have records for that period. It was like they were expecting my call."

"You think McMinnville got to them?"

"Yep. I'm sure that's what happened. They're not going to bite the hand that fed them."

I thanked Gus for the help and slumped back in my chair. I had to admit it. I was flat out of ideas. At that point, I did the unthinkable—I tapped "Real estate agents, Newberg, Dundee, McMinnville" into my search engine, jotted down a couple of phone numbers that popped up, and arranged to meet two agents at the Aerie the next week for a walk-through and estimate of market value. It wasn't going to be pretty. A house sitting on the edge of an active mining operation is not in what you'd call a plum location. And you know what they say about real estate— location, location, location.

I left my Dundee office for Portland around three that day, hoping to beat the traffic, but by the time I reached the I-5 from the 99W, things were moving like a conga line of banana slugs. Just like my old stomping grounds, L.A., the concept of a rush hour was losing its meaning. All hours were becoming rush hours. An hour later I parked down from Nando's Sharp Eye Detective Agency. He had called earlier to say he had some new information for me.

"Hi, gorgeous," I greeted his secretary, Esperanza, who, like her boss, was always at the leading edge of the sartorial curve.

She flashed a brilliant smile framed by heart-red lipstick. "Go on in, Cal. He's expecting you." I walked ahead, but Archie parked at Esperanza's desk for the treat he knew was coming. "He can stay out here with me," she said, offering him a Milk-Bone. "We need to catch up."

"I know, my friend," Nando was saying on the telephone, "it is a sad story you are telling me, but I still need the rent by the end of the month." With that, he clicked off, looked up at me, and shook his head. "Being a landlord is not easy. Always the long stories and the short payments."

My capitalist friend owned a sizable assortment of low-rent bungalows and apartments off Division near the 205, which were coming into the crosshairs of developers as gentrification oozed eastward in Portland. He was softhearted, but he loved money, too, and I wondered if he would sell out for what would be a very handsome profit. "You're not thinking of selling your southeast holdings, are you?"

He shrugged. "Why not? There is money to be made."

"Where would those people go? Many are from your homeland."

He shrugged again and opened his hands. "Am I my brother's keeper? In America, profit is king, Calvin."

But I didn't come to discuss the morality of capitalism, so I said, "I know you'll do the right thing, Nando," then sat down across from him. "Now, what've you got?"

"We have, ah, acquired some e-mail records of Ilya Boyarchenko's lawyer, Brian Hofstetter." He slid a single piece of paper across his desk to me. I picked it up, and he continued. "You will note, first of all, that Arrowhead Investments has been in contact with Hofstetter."

I read through a copy of an e-mail at the top of the page. It was dated January 8th.

> Dear Mr. Hofstetter,
>
> Confirming our telephone conversation, you have agreed to represent my client, Arrowhead Investments, in certain business dealings in the city of Portland. I have wired your retainer of $25,000 to the account you specified. We look forward to working with you.
>
> Sincerely,
> Costas Zertalis

I looked up. "So Hofstetter represents Arrowhead here in the States?"

"It appears so, yes. This is not too surprising. As you know, in addition to representing Boyarchenko and others in Portland, his firm has some international clients."

The next e-mail, dated January 29, was from Hofstetter to Melvin Turner and Brice Avery at Wingate Properties:

Brice and Mel,

Enjoyed our lunch. We're impressed with Wingate Properties and the North Waterfront Project, and glad you are amenable to our offer. We'll be in touch with specifics. Arrowhead is anxious to move forward on the proposal.

Best,

Brian

I felt a tingle at the base of my skull. "Looks like the genesis of the offer to bankroll the project and buy Wingate Properties. This had to please Avery and Turner."

Nando nodded. "Precisely. I am wondering why Zertalis didn't contact them directly? Why go through Hofstetter?"

"That's pretty standard for an international deal. He needs an American lawyer in his camp, and it insulates Arrowhead, too, since communications would be privileged. And by using Hofstetter, Arrowhead's also connected to Boyarchenko, at least potentially. That might also play into this."

"I see. Whatever the reasons, they have been very cautious. No details are revealed in any of these e-mails."

I laughed at that. "That would make our job too easy." The third e-mail copied on the sheet was from Hofstetter to Zertalis on February 16.

Dear Mr. Zertalis,

We have run into a major obstacle regarding Wingate. Please advise availability for a conference call involving

your client soonest. We will accommodate to your schedule.
  Brian Hofstetter

I looked up at Nando. "I bet I know what this is about. Margaret Wingate had just told Brice Avery that she'd changed her mind." I chuckled. "Between the Women's March and Angela's urgings, she was balking on the North Waterfront Project, and, of course, no way she's going to sell the company. And it was around mid-February that she let her feelings be known.

"And this undoubtedly upset the people behind Arrowhead," Nando added.

"Right." I read the fourth and final e-mail, which confirmed the timing of the proposed conference call, then looked up again. "Is this all?"

"Yes. After that fourth note, communication between the principals by e-mail stopped completely."

"Hmm. Maybe the conversation took a conspiratorial turn, and they got nervous about leaving any kind of paper trail, no matter how innocuous." Too excited to remain seated, I got up and started pacing. "Maybe this is when Hofstetter and Boyarchenko chimed in with a suggestion for taking care of the problem."

"The problem being Margaret Wingate," Nando said.

I nodded, kept pacing, then turned and looked at my friend. "It fits, Nando. It fits pretty damn well."

Nando's expression turned even grimmer. "There's more. After I took care of the anonymous call to the Portland Police you requested, I gave some thinking to the situation. If you are right about this hit man you described, then he made two murders look like accidents and one like a suicide. This is not the work of your average contract killer."

I sat back down. "Agreed. And according to Semyon Lebedev, Boyarchenko has no muscle on his payroll that fits the physical description I gave you, let alone the MO."

"Not surprising. No one in Portland has this set of skills.

Since I had my computer consultant on the payroll—or your payroll, I should say—I had him go to the Dark Web to search for such a specialist."

My eyebrows bunched up. "Dark Web?" I'd heard the term but had no real understanding of what it stood for, aside from being a digital black market of some kind.

"This is the part of the Internet that is completely anonymous, where criminal activities of all types can be arranged for and even paid for using Bitcoin. Need drugs, weapons, passports, contract killers? No problem on the Dark Web."

"How does it work?"

He shrugged and rolled his eyes. "One must have specific software to log on and communicate anonymously, then other configurations or authorization protocols to navigate the spaces. This is all I understand about it. I consult the Dark Web from time to time, and when I do, my consultant does the strong lifting."

"What did you find?"

He slid another piece of paper across the desk. "What do you think of this?"

I read through what appeared to be a screenshot of a website:

Nightshade Enterprises
Fast, very efficient contract killings with a money-back guarantee if not in full satisfaction. We specialize in incidents that look like accidents or suicides to police and insurance. For low-ranking individuals, price starts at $50,000. For high-rank and political figures, price starts at $100,000. Inquiries will be answered within 24 hours with instructions on next steps. All proceeds in Bitcoin.

A cold chill slithered down my back. *What's this world coming to?* I thought. "Well, this is definitely the required skill set. Surely there's more than one outfit like this out there."

"Not really. We found several killers for hire, but only one with a profile that promises to disguise the crime. This is highly specialized work that requires considerably more planning and expertise than an ordinary hit."

I nodded. "I see your point. I think you may have something here. I don't suppose this outfit can be placed geographically?"

"No. It is not possible."

I read through the screenshot again. "Judging from the weird English, I'd say whoever wrote this is definitely foreign. And 'low ranking individuals' sounds like he might come from a less-than-democratic country."

Nando nodded. "Do you think he is still in the area?"

I massaged my forehead for a few moments. "Okay, let's assume our guy is Nightshade. He started with a single hit on Margaret Wingate. He used Lenny the Fox as an accomplice and either decided he couldn't trust him or didn't want to leave a witness. Then I came along, and Helen Ferris became a problem." I sighed and looked at my friend. "Now I'm a problem along with Angela. So, yeah, if we're right about all this, he's probably still out there."

"What do we do next?"

I hesitated, because, despite the trove of new intelligence, the path forward wasn't jumping out at me. "Well, first off, I want you to keep an eye on Hofstetter's e-mail. A meeting's coming up between Wingate Properties and Arrowhead. Maybe they'll mention the time and place." Nando nodded, and I added, "And if you haven't checked in with your FBI source, do that. I still need to know who's behind Arrowhead."

"I have not heard anything from him, but I will make the call."

"And I need a favor. I need to borrow your car."

"My Mercedes?"

"No. Your jeep." I knew he didn't drive his Mercedes to work because he didn't like leaving his crown jewel parked on the street. "I've got something I need to do tonight, and I don't want to use my Beemer."

Nando agreed, and we exchanged keys. I left his office feeling equal parts exhilaration and dread. On the one hand, I now had a possible handle on the contract killer and knew that Arrowhead Investments and the Russian mobster, Ilya Boyarchenko, were connected—albeit, indirectly—through Portland attorney Brian Hofstetter. Those were huge steps forward. On the other hand, I now knew that the killer was not just good but probably world-class.

Was I out of my league and trying to punch above my weight? Probably. Did I have a choice? Nope.

Chapter Twenty-eight

I drove Nando's Grand Cherokee to Caffeine Central, parked it, and took Archie for a walk down to the river and back. Then I fed him and made myself a quick dinner of two sesame seed bagels slathered with cream cheese, pocked with capers, and filled with smoked salmon, avocado, and thinly sliced red onion. I washed them down with a Mirror Pond and was back on the road an hour later, leaving a disappointed dog behind.

I parked a block down from Angela's Honda, which sat directly in front of her rental house, and waited for her to come out. My plan was simply to shadow her on her last night of pot delivery, using Nando's car since mine could have already been seen by the killer. I called earlier and told her what I was up to and instructed her not to acknowledge my presence in any way. I had my Glock with me, too. I'd finally given in to Nando and gotten my concealed-carry license several months ago, which allowed me to pack a loaded gun within Portland city limits.

She came out at dusk and got into her Honda, and I followed her over to Clinton Street, where she parked down from the Bright Flower Buds marijuana shop, her place of employment. She came out twenty minutes later carrying a box full of what looked like sealed plastic envelopes and, instead of walking to her car, headed in the direction I was parked.

She opened the back hatch of a black, unmarked Prius—of

course, the company car—opened a lockbox with a key, stashed the envelopes, then locked it again and drove off. She made three quick deliveries to a new apartment complex on Division, an architecturally uninspired box thrown up in the rush to cash in on Portland's yuppie explosion. Nothing like a little midweek partying, I figured.

I followed her out Division to Cesar Chavez, where she made two deliveries to well-lit private homes. I began to relax and even felt a little foolish as she led me over to Holgate, headed east, then parked just before a narrow alley that ran between SE 65th and 66th. Twilight was almost gone, and there were no streetlights in this neighborhood, so I strained to follow her movements as she walked toward a dimly lit house on the corner of 66th. She vanished into the shadows of the front porch, and I breathed easier when she reappeared a couple of minutes later. She still carried the envelope. Nobody home.

She was halfway back to her car when something moved in the darkened alley. I leaned forward, blinking rapidly, and saw a hooded man clad completely in black emerge from the shadows and fall in behind her. I got out of my car, and when the door clicked shut I caught the movement of his head as it swiveled in my direction. He stopped, and when I moved forward, he back-pedaled a couple of steps. I kept coming, and he spun around and was immediately swallowed up in the black maw of the alley.

I knew better than to chase him, but all I can say is that a jolt of adrenaline and a flash of anger bordering on rage can really cloud one's judgment. As I sped past Angela I yelled, "Get in your car, lock it, and call 911." I turned into the alley at a full sprint and quickly realized I was flying blind, except for a dim patch of light ahead that was cast by a curtained, second-story window. I hesitated, then saw movement along the edge of that patch and started running again. I blew through the lighted area, but it wasn't long before I realized that the hooded figure had disappeared into the shadows. I pulled up to listen. Nothing. Up ahead, the alley seemed to narrow and get even darker, so I turned around, discretion finally getting the better part of valor.

I was almost back to the lighted area when he jumped me from above. To this day, I still don't know how he managed to mount the low roof of a garden shed so quickly and silently. I caught a glimpse of movement to my right and moved just enough that his flying kick caught the side of my head.

The kick hadn't landed squarely, but it still packed a brutal punch. A shower of meteors ignited behind my eyes as I made an awkward pirouette, dropped the Glock without even knowing it, and sank to my knees. I heard a skittering sound, which must have been the gun as he kicked it away, and the next thing I knew my neck was locked in a stranglehold. He lifted me up, and I could feel his powerful forearm begin to crush my windpipe. I tried to pry his hands apart, but they were locked firmly in place. I reached back with my right hand to rake his face or poke an eye, but he simply ducked away. I flailed wildly, wasting precious energy, but he managed to stay behind me, methodically tightening his hold. The light dimmed, and a swarm of flying ants took wing in the field of my vision.

I sucked a partial breath before my airway was completely blocked, and, using my larger frame as leverage, tried twisting out of his grasp. But he moved with me, maintaining his death grip. In desperation, I flailed at his leg with my left hand, and when my fingers caught his pocket, I clamped onto it and twisted my body again. This time he couldn't move with me, and I was able to swing my left leg behind him. Then, using every ounce of strength I had left, I pushed off with my right leg.

When he realized we were going down with me on top, he let go of my throat and scrambled out from under me. I crashed like a big tree but bounced to my feet, coughing, wheezing, and trying to clear my head. For a moment we faced each other, the reflected light showing the white teeth of a smile before he came at me again. I made the mistake of swinging at him, a poorly placed jab. He grabbed my hand, twisted my right arm violently, and using my forward momentum flipped me over his lowered body. I screamed out as my shoulder dislocated in a blinding flash of pain. He came around behind me for the kill, but when he leaned in for another stranglehold, I swung my left elbow back with everything I could muster. It caught him squarely on the nose, and I felt cartilage give way. He cried out and stumbled backwards. I turned around to face him again, my arm dangling at my side like a broken tree limb, but, just like that, he vanished into the darkness.

That's when I heard the sirens.

I found my Glock and started out of the alley. Angela met me halfway. "Cal, are you okay? Is that a gun? What happened?"

"I told you to stay in the car," I hissed through gritted teeth.

"I called the cops. They're on the way. They told me to stay on the phone, but I was worried about you. What's wrong with your arm?"

"It's my shoulder. Dislocated." The city of Los Angeles made me attend a first aid training course back in the day, and I tried to remember what the hell to do. I pointed at my arm. "Take hold with both hands at the wrist." She did, the movement sending out shockwaves of pain. "Now raise it and pull, slow but steady." She hesitated. "Pull, damn it." Angela was small, but strong. I leaned away from her, and she put her back into it. "*Pull. Harder.*"

Pop. My humerus found its resting place in my shoulder joint again. "Ahhh," I said, as the pain dropped by half. "Thank you, thank you."

We turned to get out of the alley and were suddenly bathed in a spotlight. "Stop right there, and keep your hands where we can see them," a voice boomed out.

"I've got a gun in my belt." I pointed to the Glock.

"Okay, raise your hands and don't move, either one of you."

We did as we were told, and two uniformed officers approached with guns drawn. After retrieving the Glock and patting us down, they began escorting us out of the alley. My arm was immobile, and the pain in my shoulder had settled into a deep, throbbing ache, and a raw welt the size of an egg had risen on the side of my head. But I declined an offer for an ambulance, saying instead, "The guy who attacked me can't be that far away." I motioned over my left shoulder with my thumb. "He went the other way." I gave them a description, such as it was—a couple of inches shorter than me, medium build, Caucasian, wearing a black hoodie and black pants.

The older officer called in the description, while the other, a young woman, said, "Don't worry, Mr. Claxton, we have a unit at the other end of the alley. If he comes out, we'll pick him up. Now, at least let us treat your head and elbow. You're bleeding."

I glanced down at my arm. "That's not my blood. I caught him in the nose with my elbow. You better swab it and keep it as evidence."

She gave me a gauze pad to hold against my head wound, and as she cleaned off my elbow, bagging the swabs, I told them what happed at the scene.

When I finished, the other cop said, "How did you know this person was going to attack Ms. Wingate? Did he show a weapon or threaten her in any way?"

"No. Like I said, he was sneaking up behind her. When I approached, he took off, and, like an idiot, I chased him."

He looked at Angela. "Do you think this man intended to hold you up for your marijuana?"

Angela looked at me, then turned back to him. "I don't know what he intended."

The officers exchanged glances, and the older one turned to me. "Why were you following her?"

"I, uh, had reason to believe someone might be stalking her. Not a thief but a contract killer."

Both cops looked at me and said in near unison, "Contract killer?"

I owed them an explanation, but I was in a lot of pain. I exhaled a breath. "It's complicated, so bear with me."

We finished up forty-five minutes later. No police calls came through during that time, either. Nightshade had apparently made a clean getaway. Angela phoned her boss at Bright Flower Buds, and he agreed to cancel her remaining five deliveries. I followed her back to Clinton Street and waited with my right arm tucked against my chest while she returned the undelivered marijuana and said her goodbyes.

Back at her car, she said, "My boss thinks it was an attempted robbery. I didn't argue the point." She locked her eyes on mine. They registered more excitement than fear. "Do you *really* think he was a hit man?"

"Yes. I think he planned to kill you and make it look like a robbery. He matched the rough description I have, and the fact that he was trained in the martial arts seems to fit. Someone with similar skills probably killed Helen Ferris." The excitement drained off, leaving only fear in her eyes. "I had an uneasy feeling about tonight," I continued. "He could have seen that item on their website about it being your last night and figured he didn't want to miss an opportunity."

She swallowed and blinked a couple of times. "I'm so glad you did that." She moved to hug me, and when I stepped back to protect my shoulder, we both laughed. "Oh, my God, Cal. Thank you," she said. "What do we do now?"

"Find you a safe house."

"Like in spy movies?"

I nodded.

"You're kidding."

"Nope. Chances are he'll get out of Dodge, but we can't assume that."

"What about you? You can identify him."

"There's that, but I didn't get a very good look, and he knows it."

She spread her hands, palms up, and laughed again—the laugh that reminded me of Claire. "Well, you broke the sucker's nose, and we have his DNA."

"We sure do."

That was the good news of the evening. That, and the fact that Angela Wingate was standing in front of me, unhurt and laughing.

Chapter Twenty-nine

We stopped by Angela's place, so she could put some toiletries and a change of clothes in her backpack. I'd been cautious on the road to insure we hadn't been followed. I thought of Gertrude Johnson first, but stashing Angela clear out in the Dundee Hills made no sense at all. I called Nando, but he didn't feel any of the women he was currently dating would be appropriate, and Esperanza had two kids and a husband.

"Call Winona," he suggested.

"I can't do that, Nando. We're kaput."

Five minutes later my cell riffed. "Cal, it's Winona. I understand from Nando that you need some help." I bristled for a moment at my friend's meddling but knew he was right. Winona was the best option. She was coolheaded, resourceful, and her second-story loft had good security. And although I was too stubborn to admit it, I knew deep down that, regardless of our romantic status, I could always count on her for help. I explained the situation, and she said, "Sure. Bring her over right away."

She greeted us warmly, and after examining my shoulder and abraded head, made me a makeshift sling. After rooting around in her medicine cabinet for some Neosporin, she turned to Angela. "This man doesn't believe in hospitals."

"I noticed," Angela said, looking at me. "What's up with that?"

I shrugged my good shoulder. "Just doing my part, you know, easing the burden on our fragile healthcare system."

Angela laughed at that, and Winona shook her head, and to her credit left it there. The truth was, although I considered myself a rational person, I had an aversion to hospitals I really couldn't explain and was glad I didn't have to.

Winona made a pot of black tea next, and we huddled around the kitchen table to talk about the case and what had gone down that night. It was well past two in the morning when she finally showed Angela to the pull-out sofa bed in her living room alcove. I told Angela I'd be in touch in the morning and walked with Winona to the front door. I turned to face her, yearning to hold her. Wearing a thin cotton robe over silk pajamas, she looked up at me, her face unadorned, her big almond eyes dry but tinged with unmistakable sadness.

"Thanks again," I said. "Let her sleep in, and I'll swing by to pick her up in the morning. The Portland Police are going to want to interview both of us." I hesitated for a moment and met her eyes. Surely we could talk this out now. "Winona, I—"

"You're welcome, Cal," she cut in, averting her eyes. Angela's a great kid. She can stay as long as you need."

"Wait a minute," I said, glaring at her. Why won't you talk to me? I know you've been through a heart-wrenching situation, but what about us, Winona?"

Her eyes filled with tears. "I'm sorry. I just don't have any answers right now. Standing Rock turned my life upside down, Cal. How can I worry about us when I don't know what to do about myself?" She laughed. It was laced with self-derision. "Here I am living in trendy Portland when the rights of my people are being trampled on."

I nodded. "I get that. Let me help you."

She took my good hand in both of hers. "You can't help me. This is my work. It isn't fair of me to—"

"I'll be the judge of what's fair."

She squeezed my hand. "Look, Cal. I care for you deeply, but I'm depressed, emptied out. I've got nothing to give you.

And I can't promise anything in the future. *Please*. Do what you need to do."

We stood looking at each other for a long time. Finally, I nodded faintly. "Okay." I pulled her to me and kissed her lightly on the lips. "It's not what I want, but I'll do it. I hope you find what you're searching for." With that, I turned and left with my heart weighing down my chest like a lead balloon.

"Jesus Christ, Claxton, what the hell are you involved in now?" It was the next morning, and I was sitting with Captain Harmon Scott of the Portland Police. He and I first crossed paths in a case involving a street artist called Picasso. Scott and I weren't buddy-buddy—he was a cop and I was an attorney, after all—but there was a wealth of mutual respect between us. His fog-gray eyes looked even more battle-worn through the thick lenses of his horn rims, and the lines in his forehead even deeper than the last time I'd seen him. I wondered how much he thought I'd aged. His smile was thin, almost undetectable. It was all you ever got. "I saw that report come in and decided to interview you myself."

"I'm honored," I said. "I see you got a promotion. Congratulations, Captain."

When I finished going back over what happened the night before, Scott said, "So, this person you saw is either your guy, Nightshade, or some local punk intent on holding up the pot delivery girl."

"It's the former," I said, "and let me tell you why I think that." I had no reason to hold back with Scott, although I couldn't reveal everything I knew, namely what Semyon had told me regarding Lenny the Fox and the Lexus murder car, as well as the recent information Nando gleaned from hacking Brian Hofstetter's e-mail.

Scott peppered my lengthy tale with questions, and when I finished, he leaned back and flashed his almost-a-smile. "Oh, what a tangled web you weave," he said. "Let me see if I got this straight—a Portland socialite, a legal secretary, and maybe a car thief from L.A., are murdered, a prominent lawyer and the CEO of the biggest development firm in the city are implicated, along with a shadowy group called Arrowhead Investments, who want to buy the company and build some gilded tower mega-complex on the North Waterfront. And the dirty work's done by a Houdini-like contract killer from an outfit called Nightshade Enterprises, which is located on the Dark Web." He'd made a face when mentioning the North Waterfront Project, tipping me that he disliked "mega-complexes." No surprise there. I knew Harmon Scott was a fifth-generation Oregonian who harbored a fierce love for the city he worked for.

"That's a fair summary," I said, nodding and speaking in a voice that sounded firmer than I felt. Hearing my theory expressed in its entirety made it appear, well, more than a bit far-fetched, but I pushed down the doubts.

Scott removed his glasses, cleaned them with his tie, and put them back on. "This is so fucking out there that I'm interested, but there's no hard evidence for any of it."

"You have the DNA of the guy who attacked me," I countered. "You can search the national register for a match and also cross-check it against anything found at Leonard Bateman's and Helen Ferris' crime scenes. You have the partial description of my attacker—"

"Did you see enough for a composite sketch?"

I shook my head. "Not really. It was dark. All I can tell you is he has nice teeth. But you can check the hospitals to see if someone showed up last night or today to get treatment for a broken nose."

"We're doing that," he snapped back.

"Good. Also, two other people got a partial look at this guy at the Swanson Motel." I gave Scott the names of the handyman and Spider-Man, adding, "They both said they wouldn't cooperate with the police." Scott nodded, and I went on, "There's also the payments for Herb Ferris' Alzheimer's care. You can pressure

Vancouver to subpoena the records to find out who's paying the tab. And you can put the heat on Turner and Avery. They're both dirtier than clean coal."

Harmon leaned in, his face tight. "Put the heat on them? What the hell does that mean? I don't command a Gestapo unit."

"You can bring them in as part of Margaret Wingate's hit-and-run case. Ask Turner about how Margaret's will wound up so favorable to him and Avery. Ask Avery who's behind Arrowhead Investments. You'll see how cooperative they are. They tried to buy me and my client off, too."

The last statement raised Scott's eyebrows. "How?"

I took him through the whole confidentiality agreement saga and finished by saying, "They're running scared, Harmon."

His look remained noncommittal. "What about Angela Wingate? What should I ask her?"

"Ask her how her mother felt about the North Waterfront Project and selling the company. She'll tell you Margaret Wingate wanted to go in a different direction. There's your motive."

He leaned back and eyed me for a few moments. "Why do I get the impression you know more than you're telling me?"

I gave him the best blank look I could muster. "I've got a gut feeling about this, Harmon. We're looking at three murders, one attempted murder, and a lot of dirty money searching for a laundromat. I know it. I just can't prove it."

He breathed a sigh. "We'll investigate last night's incident as an attempted robbery, which will include running the DNA and seeing what we can dig up on Nightshade. I'll reserve judgment on Turner and Avery until I talk to Ms. Wingate. I'll also call Vancouver and talk to them about the Ferris death, see what their thinking is. That's a start." I nodded my agreement, and he gave me his almost-a-smile. But his gray eyes narrowed down behind his classes. "And, you better not be holding out on me, Claxton."

Harmon Scott interviewed Angela next, while I waited down in the lobby of the Portland Police Bureau's East Precinct, a two-story brick building spanning half a block on SE 106th. As she went in, I told her to just stick to the facts as she knew them and not be drawn into what I'd told her about my theories of the suspected crimes. She was a bright kid, and I was confident she wouldn't fan the flames of Scott's suspicion that I wasn't telling him everything.

She came out an hour and a half later, looking none the worse for wear. "How'd it go?" I asked.

"Okay, I think. He started out with questions about what happened last night, then he got heavy into Mom and Melvin and Brice." She gave me that sly look of hers. "I think you got in his head, Cal. I think he's wondering if they had anything to do with Mom's death."

"Good. We can sure as hell use a friend in high places." I chuckled. "I think he likes the idea of a high-end development on the North Waterfront about as much as you and I do."

We picked her car up, and I followed her back to her studio. She was anxious to get to work on her sculpture, and I wanted to take a closer look at security at the Bridgetown Artists' Co-op building. Entry through the front was open when the gift shop was open, although access to the interior of the building and the second floor was controlled by the clerk working the retail space, who carried a key to the access door located behind one of the sales counters. Reasonably satisfied, I went around to the rear of the building. The back door was steel with a dead bolt activated by key or from within, electronically. Two rows of buttons were located below a speaker providing communications. Only two of the buttons for the second floor had names next to them: A. Wingate and D. Bentley. As a test, I buzzed D. Bentley, and the dead bolt immediately retracted. I let myself in to find a familiar young man standing on the second-floor landing, peering down at me. "Oh, hi," he said, "I'm Darius. You must be Angela's friend."

"Sorry. I hit your button by mistake." As I passed him, I said, "You shouldn't let anyone in you don't know. There've been some robberies in this neighborhood." I made up the last part so he'd get the message. He nodded, but I wasn't sure my warning registered.

As usual, the door to Angela's studio was ajar. I entered and watched as she moved a fresh acetylene tank into place. "I see you got your handcart back," I said.

She'd already donned her leather apron, and her goggles were riding on her forehead. "Good thing," she said with a teasing look. "You're no use to me with that broken wing."

I laughed, then gave her a serious look. "I know you're going to want to continue working here, so a couple of security items." I told her she should tell the clerk downstairs not to give anyone access to the stairs unless she okayed it ahead of time, and she shouldn't buzz anyone in she didn't know. "And tell Darius not to, either," I added. "He buzzed me in without a word."

I took a seat and watched as she began working on the piece I nicknamed Jogging Woman, at least to myself. It had grown since I'd last seen it, the framework of the lower body nearly in place, a second leg jutting out behind the runner. I could see that the frame she was fashioning, although a mere outline of what the final form would take, was astonishingly true to the grace and beauty of the drawing on the wall. As I watched, my eyes began to blur and my insides trembled as I admitted to myself for the first time how close a call last night had been. What if I'd ignored my hunch? What if Nightshade had decided to act a day earlier? I caught myself, sat up a little straighter, and swiped my eyes with a knuckle.

My shoulder ached worse than my head, and I was tired from a poor night's sleep, but when I thought of those glinting teeth set in that leering, disgusting grin, anger quickly swamped every other feeling.

It wasn't over between me and Nightshade. Not by a long shot.

Chapter Thirty

Angela would probably have sculpted through the night, but after I'd gone through every e-mail on my phone, returned a half-dozen calls, and read the *New York Times* from digital cover to digital cover, I convinced her to close up shop. I followed her over to her rental house and had her put the Honda into the rickety garage behind the place. She complained, of course, but I told her that until I got a better handle on the situation, she was going to be the beneficiary of an escort service provided by either me or an operative of Nando Mendoza, the private eye in her employ.

"Wow, my own private eye," she said, then her expression changed. "That sounds expensive. Why won't the police protect me?"

"There isn't enough evidence that you're in danger to compel the police. Don't worry. Nando's not cheap, but you won't need protection for long." The last statement, was, of course, based more on hope than fact. Although Captain Scott was "interested," I knew that, given the scope and political sensitivity of what I'd outlined, his inquiry would proceed slowly at best. Meanwhile, I felt all the urgency in the world but no clear idea of what the hell to do next.

On the way over to Winona's, we stopped off at the Pizzicato on SW 6th and picked up a large puttanesca pizza along with an arugula, pear, and walnut salad. After returning to the car hefting the boxes, Angela said, "Is Winona expecting this?"

"Yeah, I texted her earlier." I smiled with a trace of wistfulness. "She's not very domestic. I figured this was a good idea."

"God, I feel like I'm imposing."

"No. She's the most generous person you'll ever meet. And I can tell she likes you."

I sensed Angela eyeing me as I negotiated the downtown traffic. Finally she said, "Are you eating with us?" When I shook my head, she added, "You two used to be a thing, and now you're on the outs. That's obvious." I nodded, and she continued, "God, Cal, she's so cool and so gorgeous. What happened?"

I wanted to shout "Standing Rock happened, goddammit!" but shrugged my good shoulder instead. That would've required an explanation I wasn't prepared to give. I settled for, "It's complicated."

The next morning, after retrieving Angela and taking her back to her studio, I found Nando waiting for me when I returned to Caffeine Central. We went back over the recent events, and he agreed to put one of his best men, a Cuban American named Bembe Borgos, or BB, as everyone called him, at my disposal. "BB is one of my best investigators. He will take good care of the young sculptor." I thanked Nando, and he said, "By the way, I called my FBI contact in Seattle since I hadn't heard from him. He said that he could not help me with the identity of the Arrowhead ownership. He gave no reason, but I got the feeling it was sensitive, something he did not wish to touch."

"Frustrating."

"Yes. I am thinking the same thing."

When I thanked Nando for calling Winona, he looked at me and shook his head. "It is a shame, you two. I hope you can fix things. I love you both."

It was a busy day of *pro bono* work, which was good because it took my mind off my problems and helped me—along with several ibuprofen tablets—to cope with the pain in my shoulder. Things slowed down around three o'clock, and I started listening for the outside door, hoping Tracey Thomas would show. It was her habit to drop by on Fridays, after all. Sure enough, at a little past three-thirty I heard someone enter, which caused Archie to grumble a single woof and get up from his spot in the corner. I followed him into the waiting room, but he didn't get his customary greeting, because Tracey saw my arm was in a sling first.

"My God, what happened, Cal?" she asked, her nutmeg eyes wide with surprise and concern. I told her the story and answered her questions while she petted Archie, who sat in front of her. "This thing's assuming biblical proportions, Cal. It's good you've got the Portland Police hooked in, but Scott will probably have to get the green light from Chief O'Hearn before he even questions Turner and Avery. Both those guys have political juice in this town."

"I know that. I hope he does question them, because he'll see how jumpy they are, particularly Turner. He's about ready to pop."

She nodded, her lovely face taking on a grim aspect. "The fact that they came after an innocent young woman shows how desperate they are."

"Either that or someone else is calling the shots."

She raised her eyebrows. "Boyarchenko?"

"Who else? Turner and Avery are dirty, no question, but I'm wondering if they would be that brazen on their own. If Angela winds up dead in a botched marijuana heist, they might accept that as a coincidental piece of good luck. Never underestimate what people will believe if they want to badly enough."

She nodded. "That brings me to my news: The meeting between Arrowhead Investments and Wingate Properties is set for next Wednesday night."

"Where?"

"At a restaurant out in the Willamette Valley called Langsted's."

"I know it," I said. "It's south, down by Aurora, high-end rustic. Definitely a private setting. What time are they meeting?"

"Nine-thirty."

"Excellent." I beamed a smile as I jotted down the information. "Did your source pick up anything else?"

"No. He was lucky to get this. The information's being very tightly held." Tracey smiled, and her look turned mischievous. "Can I go with you next week? I want to be in on the cloak-and-dagger stuff."

I chuckled. "If I let you come I'd have to teach you the secret handshake, and you know I can't do that."

She made a face and laughed, then turned serious again. "How's Angela holding up?" It was a topic I hadn't covered.

"She has the courage of a lion. Nothing seems to shake her. She's staying with Winona now, and I'm keeping close tabs on her."

"That's generous of Winona. How are things between you two?"

"Broken."

"I'm sorry to hear that, Cal." She stood up to leave and stretched, the spandex of her jogging pants conforming to her slender, well-muscled legs. "Well, I've got three miles to run."

I walked her to the front door and opened it. She turned to face me, the afternoon light igniting the gold flecks in her eyes. She moved a little closer to me and smiled. "I, uh, don't *have* to run, you know."

I smiled back, involuntarily locked onto her lovely eyes. "What did you have in mind?"

Her look turned mischievous again. She pulled the door closed with her left hand, curled her right hand around the back of my neck, and pulled gently until our lips met. The kiss ramped up from exploratory to pure passion in a couple of mutual heartbeats.

She moved her body into mine and I reciprocated, pressing her gently against the door. It seemed a good fit.

But I pulled away. She moaned, looking up at me. "What's the matter?"

I stepped back. "I'm sorry, Tracey. I can't do this. Not now."

She dropped her eyes and nodded. "Okay, I get it. And I'm a patient woman." Then she looked back up and smiled with more good nature than I thought possible. "But, Jesus, Cal, now I'm going to have to run six miles instead of three."

After Tracey left, I turned to Archie, who was napping in the corner. "Not now? *Really?* Excuse me while I take a cold shower."

Chapter Thirty-one

The big Doug firs swayed in the wind, producing a sound like the sifting of water through fine pebbles; a susurrus of fir needles that always calmed me. It was the following Tuesday, and I sat there listening, eyes closed, on an old wrought iron bench that afforded a view of the valley. Except for the odd clank and shout of a worker, the incessant noise of the gravel mining operation below the Aerie was quiet that day. A day of maintenance for the rock-crusher, I figured. Whatever the reason, I was thankful for the respite. I sat there thinking of the things I loved about the property—the seclusion, the view, the stoutly built old farmhouse resting on fertile soil. But it was the Douglas firs, over thirty of them, many well over a hundred feet tall, that I loved the most. Growing here long before I was born, the majestic behemoths stood like sentinels, watching over the Aerie and every living thing within its five-acre bounds.

I heard a car at the gate, opened my eyes, and glanced at my watch. It was the second of two realtors I'd invited out to get an estimate of my property value. The realtor's name was Valerie Thatcher, a tall woman with a head of ringlet curls that bounced like springs, a firm handshake, and a pre-approved smile. I showed her around the property, then inside the house. "Oh," she said, standing in the dining room, "I adore the crown molding and the parquet floors. Original, right?" I nodded, and she went on, "The wavy cut glass in the built-in cabinets must be original, too. How lovely."

"The place is circa 1920, but they built houses to last back then." I pointed at a large radiator along a wall, its collection of fins thick with countless coats of paint. "That includes the heating system. It's a little noisy at times, but it keeps the place toasty." I felt a certain allegiance to the ancient boiler hunkered down in the basement, and to the antiquated collection of pipes and radiators that delivered the heat, because one of those clanking radiators saved my life once. But that wasn't the reason the system was still around. I couldn't afford to upgrade it.

After touring the house, we wound up on the side porch, which I'd swept clean of telltale quarry dust. There was a low cloud cover that day, but enough light that the spring colors in the valley popped. "Such a beautiful view. Why isn't the quarry operating today? I heard it's a seven-day operation."

I shrugged. "You'll have to ask McMinnville Sand and Gravel." I paused and looked at her. It was time to ask the question. "How tough will it be to sell with the quarry back in operation?"

She shook her head. "Very tough, but with the right price you can move this property due to the gorgeous view. We're talking about a buyer who's not worried about living next to a mining operation." I coaxed a possible asking price out of Valerie, which was about a hundred and twenty-five thousand dollars less than I'd paid for the property. *Ouch.* I did some quick math in my head. By the time I paid off the balance of my mortgage and paid her commission, I'd be in the hole five to ten thousand. My stomach dropped, and I tried again to imagine staying put. Even if Archie could cope, I realized there was no way. I hated the mining as much as he did.

I grimaced. "Well, the good news is your asking price is better than what the guy who just left gave me, but the bad news is it still leaves me upside down."

I thanked her, took her card, and said I'd be in touch. It was even worse than I feared. I watered the plants, did a load of laundry, and left, feeling all the while like I'd been gutshot.

"I've checked out the area around Langsted's Restaurant," I said to Nando. It was later that day, and we were having a beer on the back deck of Hopworks Urban Brewery on Powell Boulevard. Archie lay at my feet, blithely ignoring a rambunctious border collie two tables over. "There's a grove of trees that runs along the west side of the restaurant, maybe a hundred feet from the entrance. Looks like pretty good cover in there, and it's higher in elevation. We should get some good looks before they go inside. You'll have enough zoom to get close-ups, right?"

"More than enough. My Canon XA Thirty has excellent night vision capability and a twenty X zoom. We can make stills from our best shots and enlarge them further, if needed." I wasn't surprised. When it came to PI surveillance equipment, whether it was listening devices, micro GPS tracking chips, or night-vision cameras, Nando kept his firm at the leading edge. My friend reveled in the invasive gadgets, but I always felt uneasy about them.

"Good. I want facial images of everyone attending the meeting." I was aware of the irony of my utterance. This wasn't the time to worry about infringing on someone's privacy rights. The stakes were too high.

Nando nodded after taking a drink of his beer, an IPA the waiter said might come close to Casique, a Cuban favorite of his. From the look on his face after he swallowed, it didn't. "We will get the images, and if we don't recognize someone, I will try to access the FBI Facial Recognition Database."

"What are the chances of that?"

"It is always a challenge, and I try not to play the card too often, but I know the woman who manages the database in the Portland Police Bureau." He flashed a brilliant smile. "Roses—she prefers yellow—and Chanel Gardénia usually work, although I may be called upon to sleep with her as well."

I had to chuckle. "You would do this for me? Such dedication."

Satisfied that Nando and I had a good plan, I gathered up Archie and headed over to Angela's studio. I pushed Darius Bentley's buzzer as a test, and when he didn't respond, buzzed Angela, who let me in. Her studio door was open when I came into the hall. I saw the flash of the torch reflected on it and smelled the now-familiar acrid scent that persisted despite the fan droning in the window. I entered the studio and watched her sculpt for a while. When she finally looked up and closed the oxygen and acetylene valves on her torch, I said, "Great progress. I think she's about ready for arms."

Angela stood back from the sculpture and cocked her head. "Not quite. I don't have the lines of the torso right yet. It's really bugging me." Then she allowed a smile. "But I'm further along than I thought I'd be, thanks to my forced vacation."

After she closed up and we were on the way over to Winona's, she said, "Why don't you have dinner with us tonight?"

"Did you check with Winona?"

"Well, no," she admitted. "I just thought of it. I can call her, but I'm sure she won't mind."

I chuckled inwardly. An unexpected guest for dinner—even one she wanted to see—would throw Winona into a tizzy. "Thanks, but I have other plans tonight."

"*Other plans?*" I felt her eyes bore into the side of my face while I navigated the traffic. "That's such bullshit, Cal."

I shrugged with both shoulders, now that I had my right arm out of the sling. "I can't make it tonight, okay?" I said with a harsh inflection I didn't intend. Of course, I didn't have any plans, but my injured pride was calling the shots at that moment.

"Okay, okay. Jeez, you two make a good pair."

When I turned onto North Flint, I pulled over and let a half-dozen cars pass us, watching carefully as they hurried on toward the Broadway Bridge. Confident we weren't being followed, I pulled out again. Angela knew the drill by this time. "You think Nightshade might still try to find me?"

"It's not likely. He's probably gone to deep cover by now. This is just a precaution."

"Deep cover? Does that mean he's gone back to his Dark Web cave, and we'll never catch the dickwad?"

I shrugged again. "I don't know. He's a pro, and pros don't make a lot of mistakes."

I caught her shudder out of the corner of my eye. "That creeps me out."

When I pulled up in front of Winona's loft, Angela got out, then stuck her head back into the passenger side window. "Hey, almost forgot. I have an AA meeting tonight at nine at the Alano Club. Can I get a lift?"

I wanted to take her myself, but since I'd already proffered my phony excuse, said, "No problem. Since I'm tied up, I'll send BB." She kept her gaze on me for a couple of beats, then rolled her eyes, making it clear she hadn't bought my story. I drove off, and if I had a tail, it would have been between my legs. Angela's lie detection skills were formidable, just like my daughter Claire's.

Back at Caffeine Central, I put on my jogging gear and took Archie for a hard run—hard for me, at least—across the Steel Bridge, down the Eastbank Esplanade, across the Hawthorne Bridge, and back to the Burnside. I took the steep stairs up to street level two at a time, and after crossing the Boulevard, kicked it home with Arch leading the way. I was exhausted, but after feeding my dog and taking a shower, I had enough energy to make dinner—a small pork tenderloin slathered with a paste of olive oil and Dijon mustard, steamed broccoli, and roasted new potatoes, crisp on the outside and soft in the middle.

"Who said I didn't have something to do tonight?" I asked aloud as I stacked the dirty dishes and finished my fourth glass of Carabella Pinot Noir.

I was a little too drunk to read that night. The last thing I remember thinking about before I sank into a deep sleep was the meeting Nando and I planned to document the next day. *Maybe this will give us some traction*, I said to myself. And, as for Nightshade, although he represented an existential threat, in my inebriated state I admitted I didn't want him to go back to his Dark Web lair.

No. I wanted him to stay in the game so I could put the bastard away.

The next morning, Angela and BB dropped by to pick up Archie on their way to the co-op. Angela had agreed to watch my dog for the day. They'd become pretty tight, those two. I hadn't met BB, so I introduced myself. "Nando speaks very highly of you," I said as I shook his hand. He was tall with an athletic build, intense dark eyes, and a smile with more candlepower than Nando's, which was saying something.

"As he does of you," he replied. "I'm glad to meet you, Mr. Claxton. You're a legend at Sharp Eye."

I laughed at that. "I'm afraid your boss is prone to hyperbole. Don't believe everything you hear, BB."

He returned the laugh, and as Angela let Archie into the backseat of his car, she turned to me and mouthed, "He's so hot!" with a big smile on her face.

After a mind-numbing day at my office in Dundee, I met Nando in Wilsonville, and we crossed the Willamette River on the Boone Bridge just as the sun was setting. We took Nando's Grand Cherokee, the one I followed Angela in a week earlier. Had it only been a week since Nightshade tried to kill Angela? It seemed much longer, the result of having made zilch for progress on the case over that time span, I figured.

"Take the Charbonneau exit," I said, as we cleared the bridge and entered the northern tip of the Willamette Valley, "then hang a right on Airport Road and go south for three and a half miles."

"It is very flat out here," Nando said as we cleared the freeway. "My Jeep will stand out like a sore finger."

"No worries," I told him. "I've got a spot for the Jeep." When we passed a lighted sign announcing the turnoff to Langsted's Restaurant, I said, "Go another mile or so. You'll see a dirt road on the left leading into a nursery that's closed. We can park off the road on the right and walk back, using the cover of the trees on the west side of the road."

Twenty minutes later we were fairly close to the restaurant entrance. We were both dressed in black. Nando carried his video camera and a short monopod to steady it on. I had a pair of night vision binoculars slung around my neck. "Okay," I said, "let's walk in through these trees. It's a straight line to a low knoll overlooking the parking lot and the restaurant. We can set up there."

We found a spot with good cover, and after lying prone for several minutes, Nando uttered under his breath, "*Mierda*, we should have brought a tarp. The ground is wet here." So far, two couples had arrived separately for what looked like late dinners. We filmed them both but doubted they were part of the group we were interested in.

"Yeah," I said, "the mulch under these trees holds water like a—"

Before I could finish, another car came into the lot and parked. I trained my glasses on it as Nando started filming. A man got out, locked the car, and started for the restaurant. "I know him," I said. "That's Fred Poindexter. He runs the Portland Planning Commission." No sooner had Poindexter disappeared into the restaurant than another car arrived, a metallic silver Mercedes sedan with highly tinted windows. It stopped in front of the restaurant entrance. The driver got out, opened the rear door, and out stepped another person I was pretty sure I recognized. My pulse ramped up several notches.

"I'll be damned. I think that's Ilya Boyarchenko."

Nando grunted as his camera whirred softly. "It *is* Boyarchenko. Of this I have no doubt." Another passenger got out on the other side. "And that, my friend, is his lawyer, Byron Hofstetter."

"Well, well. This is getting interesting." At that point, another car pulled in behind Boyarchenko's. "Can't wait to see who else—". That's when I heard the crunch of a footstep behind us.

"Gentlemen," a deep, gravelly voice said in a hushed but authoritative tone, "I'm with the FBI. Stop filming, stand up, and put your hands where we can see them. And keep your fucking mouths shut."

Well, shit.

Chapter Thirty-two

Nando and I got up and turned to face the voice as we raised our hands. In the shadows, I had an impression of width and height, and when he took another step forward, there was no mistaking the gun leveled at us. Another, smaller, man came from behind him, patted us down, confiscating my binoculars and Nando's camera, along with the Sig Sauer from Nando's shoulder holster, before snapping plastic cuffs on both of us. "Now," the bigger man said, "we're going to walk out of here *quietly*, am I clear? Not a fucking sound."

When we reached the road, where an unmarked car idled at the ready, the voice opened a badge and shined a light from his cell phone on it. "I'm FBI Special Agent in Charge Aldous Jones. You are going to be transported to our office in Portland for questioning." I was tempted to challenge their right to detain us but figured it would be futile. Jones hustled us both into the backseat of the car and nodded to the smaller man, who was now at the wheel looking back at us through a wire mesh security screen. "Now get them the hell out of here, Harvey."

We took off as FBI agent Jones disappeared back into the woods.

Our chauffeur, Special Agent Harvey Something-or-other, wasn't interested in anything except our names, where we lived, and what we did for a living. Nando and I knew enough to keep it at that, so the trip was long and silent. Only a few office lights burned at FBI headquarters, an uninspired, three-story brick box of recent construction located out by the Portland Airport. Harvey drove us around to the back of the building, where another agent awaited. We were marched into adjacent but separate interview rooms. After my uncomfortable cuffs were removed, I was offered a seat before the self-locking door clicked shut. A pitcher of water and a single glass sat on the table, attesting to our host's hospitality.

I drank some water and took stock. Whatever it was, the FBI sure as hell wanted us out of there in a hurry. Had we broken any laws? Nothing we can't argue, I decided. It's against the law to film someone in a private setting without their permission, but the restaurant's a public place. We weren't trespassing, either.

What should I tell them? That was a trickier question since it had better match up with what Nando had to say. I thought about that and scanned back over the events leading up to this. Like me, he'd tell the truth wherever he could, and, like me, he'd be vague or obfuscate on the sensitive areas. Would our statements be consistent? I was reasonably sure they would be, but there was no way to tell for sure.

I wondered about the FBI's presence at Langsted's. It was pretty damn obvious they were watching the same people we were. Would we learn anything from them? That thought made me chuckle. No way they were going to share any information about an ongoing investigation. This was going to be a one-way pipeline.

I mulled this over and went back through everything a couple more times, hoping Nando was doing the same. Two-and-a-half hours later Aldous Jones came into the room and took a seat across from me. Harvey, whose last name was Branson, I learned, followed Jones and took a seat to his right, and after fiddling with a console built into the table, announced the meeting was being recorded. At least six-three with broad shoulders, a narrow waist,

200 Warren C. Easley

and hair cropped on top with the sides shaved, Special Agent Jones looked like he just stepped off the gridiron. His demeanor was open, almost friendly, but there was intensity in his eyes and a set to his jaw that the observant could not fail to notice.

"So, Mr. Claxton," Jones began, "let's get right down to it. Why you were you and Mr. Mendoza at Langsted's tonight with night vision and video equipment?"

I cleared my throat. "The same reason as you?" I watched Jones carefully, but the only thing he telegraphed was annoyance.

"Please. It's been a long day. Answer my question."

"We were there to identify the attendees of a meeting involving the sale of Wingate Properties, a major development company in Portland, and the financing of a mega-development called the North Waterfront Project. We have reason to believe these people are colluding to launder over five hundred million dollars in cash from an offshore company called Arrowhead Investments. Before you interrupted us, we filmed Fredrick Poindexter, chairman of the Portland Development Commission, Ilya Boyarchenko, the reputed boss of the Russian Mafia in Portland, and his lawyer, Byron Hofstetter, as they entered the restaurant. We believe that the CEO of Wingate Properties and its chief legal counsel are also in on the deal, and expected to see them tonight, as well as whoever's behind Arrowhead."

Jones held a poker face, but when I mentioned money laundering, his eyes flared for an instant. "Money laundering? What the hell do you know about money laundering?"

I smiled. "Not much. We know Arrowhead's a shell that was incorporated in Cyprus by an attorney named Costas Zertalis, who's the darling of Russian oligarchs. Boyarchenko's a Russian with a lot of spare cash." I shrugged. "We put two and two together."

"How did you know about this alleged meeting?"

"From a confidential source."

"Name?"

"Deep Throat?"

Jones didn't even smile. "Don't get cute, please."

"Even if I knew the source, and I don't, I couldn't reveal it."

Jones' eyes flashed for an instant, but he let my evasion slide. "Do you have any hard evidence linking this company, Arrowhead Investments, to Boyarchenko?"

"Not yet," I said, which was the first sensitive area. I knew that Boyarchenko's lawyer, Byron Hofstetter, was Arrowhead's representative in the North Waterfront deal, but I couldn't divulge that without exposing Nando's electronic filching.

Jones glanced at Harvey, then back at me and scowled. "That's all you got?"

"We're not that interested in the money-laundering, per se," I countered. "We think it's the motive for two, maybe three, recent brutal murders in the Portland area, including that of my client's mother." I went on to explain that Nando and I worked for Angela Wingate and began taking them through what we had uncovered regarding the murders and the suspected forgery of Margaret Wingate's will.

When I finished describing the hit-and-run and Mystery Man, seen by the handyman and Spider-Man at the motel, Jones said, "This is all very interesting, but how does it relate to Ilya Boyarchenko?" The Russian again. Jones seemed to key on him.

"We think he set up the hit, or at the very least facilitated getting rid of the car through one of his chop shops. He controls all the chop shops in Portland."

Jones raised his brows. "Evidence for the setup?"

I wanted to reveal what Semyon told me about the timing of the Lexus being dropped off, and Lenny the Fox being the driver, but I couldn't without compromising my friend and his source. I shrugged again. "Working on it."

Jones shook his head. "What else you got?"

I finished by describing what we'd found regarding Helen Ferris' death and the attempt on Angela's life, then summed up:

"So we believe that individuals behind the North Waterfront Project—we're not sure which individuals—resorted to forgery and murder to move it forward. We also think the three deaths associated with this case were murders perpetrated by the mystery man we described."

"Any idea who this guy is?"

"We think he's a contract killer who operates out of a dark website called Nightshade Enterprises. According to his site, he specializes in making murders look like accidents or suicides, which is the exact MO we see here."

Jones' facial expression remained unchanged, and the room fell silent. Finally he said, "Anything else to add?" I shook my head, and Jones leaned back in his chair and folded his arms across his chest. "Thank you for filling us in, Mr. Claxton. This is all very interesting, although I didn't hear much hard evidence." He paused here, and I reflexively girded myself. "I'm sorry for the loss your client suffered, but I'm afraid your investigation needs to stop right now, and you and your private investigator need to button your lips about what you think you know."

"Why?"

"Because you are in way over your heads, and your continued involvement might jeopardize an important federal investigation."

I figured I was going to lose this argument but didn't want to go down without a fight. "Are we violating some federal statute I don't know about?"

Branson barked a laugh, his first contribution to the discussion. "The lawyer speaks."

Jones, whose mouth had drawn itself into a thin, straight line, waved him off. "Look, I'm not going to debate this with you. That's the way it is. Stop mucking around in this."

"What do I tell my client?" I said. "Can you at least give us some idea why you're making this request?"

"It isn't a request, and the answer is no, I can't tell you anything."

I felt heat rising in my neck. I think it was the flat refusal that got my back up. We were deserving of some professional courtesy here. "Last time I checked, this was a free country."

Jones turned, swept his hand like a blade in front of his neck, and waited until Branson flipped a switch killing the recording. Turning back to me, he said, "Look, Claxton, you and your investigator are nice enough guys, but you either cool it or we'll make your lives miserable." He swung his eyes back to me. "You don't want to get on our shit list, believe me."

"It's called an Enemy's List," I corrected. "J. Edgar Hoover coined the phrase, and Nixon embellished it."

Jones leveled his eyes at me, and neither one of us blinked. Finally he smirked, the closest thing to a smile he'd allowed himself. "We'll see who gets the last word, Claxton."

I waited another forty minutes while they questioned Nando in the room next door. After that, Branson was kind enough to drive us back to Nando's Jeep. When he let us off at the road into the nursery, he said, "No hard feelings, fellas. When this gets cleared up, we'll be in touch."

Sure you will, I thought. And by then, the case will be cold as a glacier.

When we were finally back in the Jeep and headed toward Wilsonville, Nando said, "Well, Calvin, that certainly went well."

I laughed, in spite of myself. "Yeah. So much for our interests dovetailing with the FBI. What the hell was I thinking?"

We compared notes and were relieved that are stories jibed. At one point Nando said, "I noticed Jones showed little interest in Nightshade but great interest in the Russian and his connections to Arrowhead. How about you?"

"Same thing. I think they're focused on the money laundering, for sure. That's a federal offense, what they get paid to investigate. But, you know, I have a hunch there's something else here, something a hell of a lot bigger."

"Like what?" I shrugged, and we drove in silence until the

Wilsonville turn-off, where Nando asked the question I knew was coming, "So, what do you want to do now, Calvin?"

I puffed a breath in disgust. "I don't have the slightest idea." And that was the truth.

Chapter Thirty-three

Angela and Archie were waiting for me on Winona's loading dock the next morning. When they piled into my car, Archie leaned in from the backseat and gave me a couple of slobbery kisses between excited squeals. Wearing her pirate head scarf, dangly earrings, and a faded black tee, Angela said, "Late night, huh?"

"Yeah, like I said in my text, I got tied up. Sorry."

"Hey, no problem. Winona, Arch, and I just hung out last night. We got to talking about art, so we went over to my studio, and I showed her what I'm doing."

I didn't like the breech in security but didn't say anything. Knowing Winona, who didn't fear a thing on this planet, it was probably her idea. "What did she think of Jogging Woman?"

"She loved it, wants me to do something for her. She's got a ton of room in her loft. We kicked around a couple of ideas but haven't settled on anything. I'm really flattered."

I nodded. "You should be. She's got great taste."

"I know. I love the art she's collected. She's got a couple of Emmi Whitehorse paintings I'd kill for."

"Maybe you can work a trade."

"Wouldn't that be cool." I could sense her gaze intensify as I pulled into traffic. "So, how was your night?"

I had decided to hold off telling her about the FBI until I had time to think it through, but I hadn't thought of an alternate story, which was a mistake in dealing with Angela. "Oh, you know, I was with Nando."

"Winona told me he's quite the player," she said, teasingly. "Just the two of you?"

I glanced over and caught her skeptical look. "Of course," I said, with more emphasis than intended. Putting me on the defensive—it was uncanny how much she reminded me of Claire.

I had no meetings scheduled in Dundee that day, so I worked from my office at Caffeine Central. Sometime after eleven that morning I was upstairs making coffee when a call came in from Captain Scott. "What's up, Harmon?" I said in response to his greeting.

"Just calling to let you know I haven't been sitting on my hands, Cal. We brought those two potential witnesses in from the Swanson Motel. You were right. Neither one of them would cooperate. They admitted talking to you but said they didn't tell you squat."

"So much for an involved citizenry."

"Yeah, so nothing on your mystery man and the Bateman suicide. We also questioned Turner and Avery about the Wingate hit-and-run and the will. We'd already interviewed them briefly around the time of the accident, but this time the questions were more pointed. They acted insulted but answered our questions. It didn't go anywhere, but you were right about Turner. He was as nervous as a pig in a bacon factory. Strange behavior for an attorney."

I chuckled. "It's different when you're on the receiving end of the questions, I guess. He's either the most high-strung attorney in Oregon, or he's hiding something."

"I wanted to haul Boyarchenko's ass in, too," Scott continued, "but he would've just brought his lawyer and clammed up. Didn't have the grounds for it, anyway. Even so, I gotta admit my cop sense says there's something to this crazy conspiracy theory of yours. But we have a problem…."

I felt my stomach drop. "What's that?"

"O'Hearn came in about an hour ago and told me to drop the entire investigation as it relates to Turner, Avery, Wingate Properties, Boyarchenko, the whole shooting match. Apparently our esteemed colleagues at the FBI have demanded it, in no uncertain terms."

"Shit. I was afraid that might happen." I told Scott what happened to Nando and me the night before, and when I finished said, "Did O'Hearn explain why?"

"Nope. He didn't tell me anything except that failure to comply would constitute a career-ending incident."

"What about the DNA of Angela Wingate's attacker? What if you get a hit?"

"O'Hearn said stop *everything*. I value my job. Sorry." He paused for a moment. "Listen, Cal, I know you like to play the cowboy from time to time, but take my advice—stay out of this. I have never seen O'Hearn more serious. Whatever the hell this is, it's fucking big."

I don't remember what I said to Scott after that. I hope I thanked him for what he'd done before the ax fell. After the call, I sat gazing at the wall in front of me for a long time. Archie sensed my funk, came across the room, and rested his head on my thigh. I rubbed behind his ears absently and considered the situation. I could see the outlines of the conspiracy as clearly as footprints in the snow, but I couldn't prove a damn thing. I'd hoped that at least the Portland Police could continue the investigation now that I was sidelined, but that avenue was closed off, too.

What the hell was the FBI's focus? I wasn't sure, but it didn't seem like the murders were at the top of their list. They were probably chasing the money laundering and didn't want local law enforcement or some small-town lawyer like me getting in the way, or God forbid, stealing their glory. Yes, the FBI was like every other law enforcement body on the planet—they had a vested interest in making sure they closed their cases, and sometimes this meant other people and other causes got stiff-armed.

Where did this leave me? I wasn't sure, but one thing I had no doubt about. I didn't look forward to telling Angela Wingate that the effort to catch her mother's killer and the people behind it had just crashed and burned.

At half past noon, I said goodbye to Archie, drove over to the Bijou Café on SW 3rd, and was lucky enough to score a table toward the back, which afforded plenty of privacy. The best breakfast joint in town, it also served up a great lunch. I ordered a glass of sauvignon blanc and ten minutes later, Tracey Thomas joined me. She wore boots, dark slacks, and a thin leather jacket over a white oxford button-down. Dress on the West Coast was casual, and Portland was at the leading edge of that trend. She sat down, swept the hair off her shoulders, and scowled at me. "You didn't call me last night like you promised. What happened?"

"Order a drink first," I answered. "You're going to need it." I flagged down the waitress, and after Tracey ordered what I was having, I started unpacking the story.

She didn't take the news well. "The FBI can't do that, can they?" she said at one point, her eyes blazing, her face filled with righteous indignation.

"They, uh, made it clear that if Nando and I didn't back off, they would retaliate."

"*They told you that?*"

I nodded. "Off the record, of course, but listen, there's more. Before we got busted, we watched Ilya Boyarchenko go into the restaurant, and just before him, Fred Poindexter."

"*Poindexter?* That bastard! You were right about him."

"Well, he didn't break any laws," I answered, playing the devil's advocate this time. "From his perspective, it could have looked like a meeting of the principals to demonstrate commitment to the project."

"With Boyarchenko?" she shot back.

"Boyarchenko's trying to go legit, you know. He's got money to invest. And Poindexter's job is to spur development."

She considered that for a moment, then shook her head. "No. Fred's job is to spur *healthy* development, and he's never said one negative word about North Waterfront. Not one. He didn't need a demonstration of commitment. He's on the take, Cal."

Our food arrived, and we ate while sifting back through everything we both knew. Finally, echoing the question I'd asked myself earlier that day, she said, "So where does this leave us? Are we just supposed to sit back now and hope the FBI solves the murders and stops a load of filthy money coming into Portland to build an obscene monument to greed and corruption?" Her face had flushed a little, and her nutmeg eyes had a fire burning behind them. "I want justice for Margaret Wingate and the other victims, but I have an obligation to this city." She narrowed her eyes and pointed her fork at me. "If I go public about Arrowhead being a shell investor from Cyprus, I can rally support against the development."

I nodded. "You might win a battle but maybe not the war. And if you out Arrowhead right now, the FBI will know the leak came from me. I gave the Portland Police everything I had."

"So, what then?"

"Give me a couple more weeks. I've got a few leads I want to chase down."

Her eyes widened. "You're going to keep going?"

I nodded again. "Yeah, but under the radar."

She smiled with a warmth that felt like a caress. "One month then. And you better hurry, because the press is on this thing, too. Cynthia Duncan called again for another statement. She said they're planning to run a series of articles on North Waterfront."

I rolled my eyes. "I've been expecting that. What did you tell her?"

"No worries. I just gave her my standard pitch again and told her this was coming up for a vote at City Council in June." She frowned and shook her head. "I wish I'd known about Poindexter. I would have been even more cutting in my criticism of his competency and the direction he's taking the Planning Commission."

I laughed. "Maybe that's just as well. We don't want to tip Poindexter that we might know about his collusion with Wingate and Boyarchenko."

Tracey glanced at her watch, jumped up, and hurried off to a meeting, but not before kissing me on the cheek. I stayed at the table nursing a cup of coffee and thinking about what just happened. I'd come in not knowing what the hell I was going to do and then suggested to Tracey that I had a plan.

Now I just needed to figure out what the hell it was.

Chapter Thirty-four

When I opened the doors at Caffeine Central that Friday morning, the line was four-deep. One of the clients was a young girl, no more than eighteen, with buzz cut bleached-blond hair, sleeve tattoos on both arms, and toting a guitar. "I got rousted from under the Morrison Bridge," she explained when her turn came around, "and when I was packing up my stuff, my Ruger LC9 fell out. It was loaded, so the cops cited me and confiscated my gun. I'm from Wyoming. I thought Oregon was an open carry state, too."

"It is, but in the city of Portland, you can't carry a loaded gun in a public place without a concealed carry license."

"I know that now," she snapped back. "I want my gun back, Mr. Claxton. My daddy gave it to me." Her eyes were clear, bright, and blue as robin's eggs, and they held an unmistakable resolve. Most homeless kids had tragic reasons for their situation—abusive parents, drug use, and the like—but some were out there because of wanderlust and a true sense of adventure. Travelers, they called themselves. This young woman fell into that category, I was willing to bet.

I had her take me through the details, made some notes, and when she finished, I said, "Okay, meet me here at nine the morning of your hearing, and I'll argue the case. I personally don't like guns, but don't worry, we'll get yours back."

It slowed down after lunch, and my office was empty when Cynthia Duncan called. After we exchanged pleasantries, she said, "We're doing a series on the proposed North Waterfront Project, and I'd like to get a statement from you before we go to press."

I laughed. "Well, that won't take long."

"You're Angela Wingate's attorney, right? When I answered yes, she said, "Why did she hire you?" I explained I was handling the legal affairs associated with her deceased mother's estate, and she countered, "Did she tell you that her mother, Margaret, was against the project?"

I didn't like the question, but since Angela was already on the record, I felt a need to clarify. "My client's mother wanted the project redirected toward more public space and affordable housing." Like a hound who'd caught a scent, Cynthia followed that with a barrage of questions designed to get at exactly what Margaret Wingate told her daughter and the implications. I didn't answer any of them.

Out of frustration, she said, "Do you have reason to believe that foul play was involved in the deaths of Margaret Wingate and Helen Ferris?" No comment again. We sparred some more, and finally she said, "Damn it, Cal, give me something to work with here. I know you're involved in this thing, and it has a decidedly foul odor."

I wanted to give her a lot more, but I knew better. I could have asked her to shield my identity, but a leak would have my fingerprints all over it, which would put me sideways with Aldous Jones and the FBI. I figured she could be of use down the road, if all else failed, but there was nothing I could say at that moment. "I'm sorry, Cynthia, but I can't comment any further on this case, either on or off the record." I paused, and when she didn't respond, said, "When are you going to run the article?"

"Soon," was all she said before she ended the call in a huff. I drummed my fingers on the desk and mulled the conversation over. From her questions it appeared Duncan was focused on only part of the puzzle—the possibility of foul play—and hadn't sniffed out the offshore financing and the ring of collusion. I thought about Turner and Avery. They had no idea a cruise missile named Cynthia Duncan was homing in on them. On the other hand, I knew damn well they wouldn't let any claims go unchallenged.

The battle was about to be joined sooner than I would have chosen, and I was right in the middle of it.

I closed up Caffeine Central at three-thirty because I wanted to get a jump on the Friday southbound traffic, but no such luck. My GPS showed a solid red line on the I-5 all the way down to the bridge at Wilsonville, so I took Highway 43, which paralleled the river into Lake Oswego. From there I worked my way over to the four-car Canby Ferry and crossed the river in style, a short distance from the clogged I-5 Bridge. I was headed to the Aurora Airport, a small, regional operation, only a couple of miles south of Langsted's Restaurant, where Nando and I had the misfortune of colliding with the FBI two days before. It occurred to me the restaurant might have been chosen because of its proximity to the airport. If high-rollers were in that second limo, maybe they had their own jet, flew in, had dinner and a discussion, and flew out to keep the profile low. It couldn't hurt to ask a few questions at the airport, could it?

I parked in the lot next to the flat-roofed administration building, rolled the windows down, and told Arch to chill. A brisk wind was busy polishing the air, and Mt. Hood stood in eye-popping domination on the unobstructed eastern horizon. "Can I help you?" The attendant was a tall, gangly young man with an enlarged Adam's apple and a lopsided smile.

I knew very little about how private aviation worked, but I had done enough research to know that the tower at Aurora Airport opened at seven a.m. and closed at seven p.m., and that air traffic did continue even in the absence of guidance from the tower. I also knew that the owner of a private plane could be traced on Google from the airplane's tail number, a six-digit, alpha-numeric code. If the code began with the letter N, the owner had to be an American citizen or American company.

Armed with that trace amount of knowledge, I introduced myself and blundered ahead. "I'm involved in a legal case, and I'm wondering about the air traffic coming in here last Wednesday, the seventeenth." Keep it vague and as close to the truth as possible, I told myself.

He didn't react when I said the date, suggesting the FBI hadn't already been there. "Well, we don't keep any records here, but you can go online and access the tower transcripts." He turned to a female colleague scowling at a computer screen. "What's the address of the air traffic website, Hannah?"

"It's liveatc dot net," she answered. "You can view the last thirty days of inbound and outbound traffic there."

I nodded. "Great. Uh, what about after hours? How does that work?"

The attendant deferred to Hannah, who said, "Well, if they need something like gas or transportation, then we'd have a record, otherwise, not."

"Do you have anything for the seventeenth?" I asked, knowing I was edging out on thin ice.

She met my gaze. "We don't give out information like that. Our customers have a right to their privacy."

I nodded. "Fair enough, Hannah. Forget the names. Could you just tell me whether anyone arranged for services that night? That would be of great help to me." I held her gaze, figuring that my lack of a suit and a tie might work to my advantage out here in the valley.

But she didn't waiver. "Sorry. We just don't share that information. Company policy."

I thanked them both, and on my way out was followed by a

man about my age who had just helped himself to the free coffee in the lobby. "I couldn't help but overhear your conversation," he said after we were both outside. He laughed. "Hannah's a tough nut. Everything's by the book with her."

I stopped and said, "I imagine that's an asset in this business."

"Oh, for sure," he said with a broad smile. "She's invaluable around here." Wearing grease-stained coveralls, clogs, and a neatly trimmed beard, he offered his hand. "I'm Shawn Eastman. Couldn't help overhearing your conversation. I, ah, was here last Wednesday night working on my Piper Cub and watched a Gulfstream come in after hours."

"You did?" I tried to tamp down my enthusiasm. "What did you see, exactly?"

He blew on his coffee and took a sip, making me wish I'd gotten a cup. "It was a little after nine o'clock. I'd just stepped outside when the MIRLs came on—that's the runway lighting that can be activated by an incoming aircraft. So, I go in and turn on my radio, you know, to hear how he announces himself." He smiled. "I'm a hangar jock, I admit it. Anyway, I'm listening, but nothing comes up, and then I hear a jet approaching from the west. I go back outside and watch this sweet Gulfstream G150 land, but not before I turned off the lights in my hangar. I figured this could be a drug drop-off, and no way I wanted them to see me."

"A plane can just land here without using its radio?"

"Sure. After hours, they'd be monitored by Portland ATC, but if they disabled their ADS-B and were squawking 1200 on their transponder, they'd leave a radar signature but without any information on the aircraft."

"What happened after they landed?" I was anxious to hear the rest of it.

"One of the pilots gets out and opens the gate for a black Caddy SUV, which drives up to the plane. Three guys deplane, hustle into the limo, and drive away. No drugs. I left not long after that." He laughed. "I was disappointed. Never seen a drug drop."

"Can you describe the men?"

"They were in that Caddy in a hurry. Two big bruisers came out first and kind of looked around. I took them to be bodyguards. Then a tall, thin guy got out. He had a kind of regal bearing about him. The big boss, I figured."

"White?"

"Yeah. He had a severely receding hairline and a dark mustache and goatee. I had the impression he was foreign, but I can't explain why."

"Notice anything else?"

He paused and stroked his beard absently. "Nah, that's about it. I lost interest. Rich people come through this airport all the time."

My heart sank a little, because my next question was the most important. "Did you happen to notice the tail number of the Gulfstream?"

His face lit up. "I did. November13Bravo64," he said without the slightest hesitation.

I took out a pen and jotted down the code—N13B64—on the back of a card. "You're sure of that?"

He laughed. "Yeah. That tail number jumped out at me. My birthday's November thirteenth."

I silently thanked the fates, but at the same time the skeptical side of my brain kicked in. I looked at him. "Do you mind if I ask why you shared this information with me?"

"No, not at all. I guess it's because at the time I thought the landing seemed a little hinky, but I didn't have any reason to mention it to anyone. When I overheard you asking questions, it brought it back, so I decided, what the hell." He smiled. "And you look like a good guy."

Satisfied I wasn't being played, I thanked him again and gave him a card. If you think of anything else," I said, "call me at this number."

He looked at the card, then back at me with increased scrutiny. "I'm not going to have to testify in court or something, am I?"

"No, no, nothing like that." I paused, wondering if I should tell him the FBI might come around asking similar questions. I decided against it. Mentioning that would raise more questions than I wanted to answer. "But what you just told me might help me get justice for a very deserving client of mine." I left it at that.

Back at the car, I took Arch for a short walk, and once we were on the road, called Nando and told him what I'd been up to. "Well," he commented, "it did not take you long to get into mischief. You are not worried our friends at the FBI will discover you've been snooping around?"

"No, not too much. If they were going to check out the Aurora Airport, they would have done it by now. If they haven't, it's because they know way more than we do."

When I told him the car Eastman saw that night was a Cadillac SUV, he said, "¡*Olé!* The car that came behind Boyarchenko was a Cadillac Escalade."

I breathed a sigh of relief. I didn't know my luxury cars like Nando, so this tidbit was welcome. "That confirms it, as far as I'm concerned—that Gulfstream brought in one of the players in this deal." I read off the tail number and pointed out that it began with N. "If it's not a company plane, it probably belongs to the tall, dark-haired guy Shawn Eastman saw."

"It could be leased," he replied.

"If it is, there must be a way to find the name on the lease."

"That should be possible," he said, then added, "How do you do it, my friend?"

"Do what?"

"Get so much information from people without paying for it. It is impressive."

I laughed. "I'm a good guy, Nando. And people open up to good guys."

I clicked off, and as Arch and I sped north on the I-5 the buzz faded. Just because I'd taken a step forward didn't mean things were going to get any easier. I was still surrounded by uncertainty, but one thing I was sure about—my luck needed to hold if I was going to see this through.

Chapter Thirty-five

I had just passed under the Portland Aerial Tram on the I-5 when Nando called back. "Nothing is simple in life."

"What's wrong?"

"The plane was not leased, but its owner is a Panamanian shell called Global Mandate."

"A foreign shell company? They can't own a plane in this country."

"One would think so, but the company entered into a trust agreement with the Bank of Utah. Apparently, the bank, as trustee, is allowed to sign the FAA registration on behalf of the company. This loophole is used to shield foreign ownership, I have learned."

"Let me guess. You can't find who owns Global Mandate."

"Not as of yet."

"So, foreigners can fly around the U.S. in their own private jets anonymously. Are you kidding me? Did the FAA ever hear of 9-11? Why would the Bank of Utah provide such a service, anyway?"

"Money. It is a profitable business for them. An article in the *Wall Street Journal* stated they have thousands of such trusts."

"In the heartland, no less. What next? Can you dig into Global Mandate's ownership?"

"Yes, but it will take some time."

As I exited onto the 405 beltway the skies opened up, but the tightly spaced traffic didn't slow. This was Portland, after all. "So, another anonymous shell company rears its ugly head."

Nando chuckled. "Global Mandate could be owned by Arrowhead Investments. It is not uncommon for people to use multiple shell companies to hide all manner of mischief."

"What about your Cuban FBI contact in Seattle? I realize he passed on Arrowhead, but could he help here?

Nando paused. "It is touchy. I do not wish to compromise my friend or us. But since you have already defied Aldous Jones, I will risk the call."

I was on my second cappuccino the next morning when I heard someone rapping on the front door. "Top of the morning," I said to Tracey Thomas as I hung out the window. "I'll be right down."

"Check this out," she said as she thrust a copy of *The Oregonian* in my hand when I opened the door. Her eyes were bright with excitement. "Cynthia Duncan's first installment on North Waterfront. I could hug that woman."

The article she referred to was in the left-hand column of the front page, just below a panoramic photograph taken from the river of the warehouses and other industrial sites along the North Waterfront. The headline read: "Proposed North Waterfront Development Stirs Controversy."

"Wow," I said, "they gave her the front page."

Tracey greeted Archie, then followed me into my office and took a seat while I sat on the edge of my desk and read the article. I skimmed the first several paragraphs, which described details of the project, casting it as the largest potential real estate development in the history of Portland, a plan hailed as "audacious" and "visionary" by its supporters. In Brice Avery's words, "This project will transform the moribund North Waterfront into upscale residential, office, and retail space, a small golf course, a private marina, and the capstone, a world-class 200-room luxury hotel, to be called Tower North." Further down, Planning Commission Chairman Fred Poindexter effused, "In addition to revitalizing a key section of our waterfront, the project will provide jobs and deliver significant tax revenues for the benefit of the entire city."

I looked up at Tracey. "Poindexter's selling hard. Why am I not surprised?"

She smirked at that. "Tell me about it."

The state of the opposition was detailed in the next paragraphs, which led with: "But the high-flying project has run into stiff headwinds at City Council and with several neighborhood and grass-roots organizations across the city." Cynthia Duncan put a quote from Tracey front and center: "Rampant, unplanned development is transforming the city we all know and love into something that is, frankly, unrecognizable. The proposed North Waterfront development is emblematic of this madness. We don't need to transform our waterfront into a playground for the super-rich; we need to provide affordable housing for the average Portlander, who is being priced out of this city. I stand ready to work with the Planning Commission and Wingate Properties to move this project in that direction."

I glanced up at Tracey. "Nice quote, and they spelled your name right. What about the mayor? I don't see anything from him."

"He hasn't shown his cards yet. It's hard for an ambitious politician to turn down multimillion dollar projects, but I'm hoping he'll come around." She nodded. "Keep reading. It gets better."

The last four paragraphs caught me by surprise.

According to Bruce Avery, CEO of Wingate Properties, North Waterfront was conceived and developed as an ultra-high-end project. In his words: "From the outset we felt that, given the prime location, the project should be aimed squarely at the luxury segment of the market."

However, Calvin Claxton, attorney for Angela Wingate, daughter of the deceased owner of the development company, disputed this. He said, "My client's mother wanted the project redirected toward more public space and affordable housing." In addition, a source within the Portland Police Bureau revealed that Angela Wingate said in an interview that her mother, Margaret, would have insisted that the North Waterfront Project be redirected, had she not been struck down by a hit-and-run driver. Although heir to the Wingate estate, Angela Wingate did not inherit Wingate Properties. Instead, her mother's will directed the company to be sold, with the proceeds donated to charity.

When questioned about this, Brice Avery said "There was never any question on the direction of the North Waterfront Project." He also stated that a buyer for the company had been identified, and the sale would not affect the company management or the North Waterfront Project. "It will be business as usual for Wingate Properties," he stated.

Margaret Wingate was killed by a hit-and-run driver on March 16 of this year, and the case remains unsolved. This paper has learned that Brice Avery and the firm's chief council, Melvin Turner, are persons of interest in the hit-and-run death and have been questioned twice "in considerable detail." Both Avery and Turner refused to comment on this development. The lead detective on the hit-and-run investigation, Captain Harmon Scott, said, "The investigation into Margaret Wingate's death is ongoing." When asked why it was necessary to interrogate the Wingate executives on two separate occasions, Scott said, "I can't comment on an ongoing investigation."

"Damn it," I said. "I was afraid this might happen. A veiled accusation like this is going to make Turner and Avery even more cautious, and it's going to royally piss them off, too."

Tracey groaned. "Could Angela have leaked what she said in that interview?"

"No. I don't think so. I think Duncan must really have a source within the Police Bureau. Probably someone who doesn't like what Wingate Properties is up to in their city. But I can guarantee you that Turner and Avery will think *I* was the source."

"Will that be a problem?"

I shrugged. "We'll see how they react. This puts them in the public spotlight. They'll hate that, and they'll need a scapegoat."

"Do you think Duncan has anything else?"

"Hard to say. She's cagey." I looked at Tracey appraisingly. "I'm sure she's digging into who the buyer is. She would love to hear about Arrowhead Investments, a source of shady-looking, foreign financing."

Tracey showed a sly smile. "It's my trump card to stop North Waterfront, but I'm keeping my promise, Cal."

"Good. Right now, they don't know we know, and that's about the only edge we've got."

"I won't leak anything." She sprang from her chair and added, "It's a beautiful morning. Let's take Archie for a walk on the river."

Hearing his name, Archie got up from his mat in the corner and started wagging his tail and barking, the doggie equivalent of "That's a great idea." Tracey looked at him, then back at me with an incredulous smile. "Does he understand English?"

I laughed. "You bet, especially the word 'walk.'"

It was, indeed, a gorgeous spring day, and I couldn't help but notice that sunshine was Tracey's friend, enhancing the caramel highlights in her auburn hair and revealing the tiny constellations of gold flecks in her eyes. We took the stairs at the Burnside Bridge and waded into the milling throng at the Saturday Market, an arts-and-crafts bazaar that popped up every weekend and stretched in colorful profusion from Ankeny Plaza down to the river. Three women stopped Tracey on the way to pump her hand and offer words of encouragement. One of the women said, "Thanks for taking a stand against that waterfront abomination, Tracey. Tell the mayor to man up." A young bearded man wheeling a bicycle high-fived her and said, "Keep Portland weird, Tracey." The battle cry of the natives.

"Wow," I said, "you're a rock star."

She rolled her eyes. "Yeah, and I don't feel any pressure at all."

We stopped at the river, where breeze-stirred ripples were darting here and there like schools of fish playing tag on the surface of the water. As we stood at the railing, I told her about my visit to the Aurora Airport and the tall, dark-haired man that flew in on a Gulfstream jet owned by a Panamanian shell company to attend the Wingate meeting. "So," I said, "I think we know all the players in this deal now—Turner and Avery, Poindexter, Boyarchenko, his lawyer, Hofstetter, and our man from Panama."

"What about Arrowhead Investments? Is it owned by Mr. Panama?"

"Good question. Nando tells me shell companies can be interconnected, but we just don't know yet."

"You've left someone out."

I nodded. "I know. Nightshade. But he's peripheral, a hired hand."

Tracey visibly shuddered. "That's a quaint way to describe a cold-blooded killer." She sighed, turned, and looked at me. Her eyes had lost their luster. "It feels like the bad guys are winning, Cal. Not just here. Everywhere. Dirty money, mountains of it, shell companies to obscure identities and motives, people willing to do anything, bend any rule, break any law, as long as they're paid for it—this seems to be the way the world works now. The new normal." She closed her eyes for a moment, and when she opened them they glistened in the sunlight. "Sometimes I wonder if there's hope for the good guys."

I followed a line of ripples as it danced across the water and disappeared. "Yeah, I get the same feeling. But in reality there's hardly been a time when the barbarians haven't been at the gates. It's a struggle to bend the arc. Always has been." More ripples sprang up, and I paused to watch them. "For me, it's the struggle that counts, where I find meaning." I chuckled. "Beats sitting around waiting for calamity to strike."

She reached out and put her hand on mine, which was resting on the railing. We both watched the river for a long time without saying anything, comforted by the silent, inexorable flow. There didn't seem to be anything else to say.

Chapter Thirty-six

"We are crazy people."

"What is it now?" It was midmorning the following Monday at my Dundee office when Nando called and announced himself in characteristic fashion.

"I called my FBI contact in Seattle, and when I mentioned Global Mandate, he said, 'Nando, I don't know what sort of investigation you're conducting, but my advice is to drop it immediately. You are out of your league.' Then he hung up on me."

"So? We already knew we were out of our league, right?"

"We could let the FBI handle this, you know."

"Come on, Nando. We don't know what their angle is. You know as well as I do that Jones showed no interest in the murders. We're going to move cautiously, stay below the radar."

He laughed, a single, derisive note. "I knew you would say that. I spent the morning researching Global Mandate. They were created by a company in the Isle of Man, but I lost the trail there." He expelled a breath in frustration. "Domain ownership, IP addresses, physical addresses of directors—tracing these shells and their owners takes more time, patience, and expertise than I possess. I suggest we put my young cyber expert on it."

"The hacker."

"Don't call him that," Nando snapped. "He is a professional. Expensive, too."

"Okay. We're desperate here. We need the name of our man from Panama. We know he's important enough to come in on a private jet with two burly bodyguards. Maybe he's the one with the dirty money to wash, not Boyarchenko. Maybe he ordered the hits."

"We get his name. What then?"

It was a good question, and I didn't have the answer.

After lunch that day, the real estate agent, Valerie Thatcher called. "Hello, Cal," she greeted me. "I've got a possible buyer for your property. Would you mind if I gave him a walk-through?"

"Who is it?" I managed to say in a normal voice, despite a bubble of red-hot anger that welled up inside me.

"He's a screenwriter moving up from Burbank, who's looking for a hideaway in the wine country. I told him about the mining, but it didn't seem to faze him." She chuckled. "Said he was used to earthquakes. When I showed him a picture of your view, he got pretty excited."

"Let's, uh, hold up on that for a while. I'm still thinking things through."

"Okay, Cal," she said, her voice tinged with a warning tone. It's spring, and the market's jumping. Don't wait too long."

I punched off and sat there deep in thought, my gaze resting on Archie, who lay casually napping in the corner. His eyes were closed, his nose rested between snow-white paws, and his broad chest rose and fell in rhythmical breathing. It was as if he were saying to me "I'm not worried. I know you'll do the right thing." Was I postponing the inevitable? Probably, I told myself and started to call Thatcher back. But I didn't complete the call. I couldn't. Not yet, at least.

On my way into Portland that evening, I swung by Angela's studio to pick her up. On a whim I buzzed Darius Bentley to see what would happen, and he let me in without a word spoken. When he appeared on the landing, I let the frustration show in my voice, "Darius, you gotta cut this out. Make sure you know who the hell you're letting in."

He opened his hands. "Sorry, man. What's the deal? I notice Angela's jumpy as a cat. Is she in some kind of danger? I read that newspaper article in *The Oregonian*."

A little honesty was in order. "There have been some threats. We don't know the origin, but they're credible. Look, Darius, all I'm asking is that you use common sense when it comes to security on this floor, okay?" He nodded and stepped aside as I passed, the look on his face suggesting I'd gotten through this time.

The frame of Jogging Woman's torso was now finished, and she bore the beginnings of two arms. The left arm was thrust back, complete to the elbow, and the right arm extended forward. The sharp, parallel wires that would form the hand reminded me of a flight of arrows. Angela was brewing tea, and when she looked up, I said, "I love it. You're making great progress."

"Thanks. I feel pretty good about where I am. Can't wait to finish the frame so I can start the detail work. That's the most challenging."

When she and Archie finished fawning over each other, I said, "You made the front page of *The Oregonian* the other day."

Her big, chocolate eyes expanded. "I don't read that paper. I told you what I said to the reporter. Was it too much?"

"No, you weren't the problem. Somebody in the Portland Police Bureau leaked inside information about the interrogations of Turner and Avery." I summarized the piece for her, then said, "I'm sure they're furious about now. That was not what you'd call favorable publicity for developers pursuing a controversial, multi-million-dollar project. Cynthia Duncan's planning more articles. She's going to contact you again, I guarantee it. Remember, just tell her you have nothing to add."

She nodded and tried unsuccessfully to suppress a giggle. "Sorry, but the thought of those two feeling the heat makes me giddy. I'd like to hang a medal on that leaker."

I smiled but didn't share her glee, because I figured the leak would spell trouble down the line. "Uh, there've been some other developments, too."

When I finished telling her about the FBI bust and how I found our man from Panama, she said, "Why doesn't the FBI give a shit about what happened to Mom and Helen?"

"I can't be sure what their interests are, but it seems they're after bigger fish."

"What could be bigger than murder?"

I shrugged. "I don't know, Angela. But we're going to keep the flame burning."

I was ready to leave, but she pleaded for more time, so I watched as she welded some of the wire in place and worked on Jogging Woman's left forearm. When she was finally satisfied with the shape, she valved off her oxygen and acetylene tanks, doffed her heavy apron, gloves, and goggles, and followed Arch and me out the door. On the way to the Pearl District I said, "How's Winona doing?"

Angela frowned. "I don't honestly know. She seems depressed, but you know, she puts on a brave front. I think she misses you, Cal. You should reach out to her."

My heart swelled for a moment before my ego intervened. "The ball's in her court, Angela."

After I dropped Angela off, I changed into my sweats and took my dancing, yelping dog on a jog along the river. An hour later we were back on Couch Street approaching Caffeine Central when I saw a metallic silver Mercedes with heavily tinted windows coming the other way. It looked familiar as it passed, then swung a U-turn and cruised up next to us. The back window rolled down, allowing cigarette smoke to billow out, and a smoldering butt bounced on the sidewalk to the left of me. Without thinking, I crushed the butt under the toe of my shoe, and when I looked up, realized I was face-to-face with Ilya Boyarchenko.

He smiled without showing any teeth, the effort contorting his angular face and beard-shadowed cheeks. "Hello, Mr. Claxton. Do you know who I am?" I nodded. "I think you and I have something in common." When I didn't respond, he said, "We both love this city of ours."

Archie, who was straining at his leash to get home to dinner, came back, sat down next to me, and cocked his head.

"What do you want?"

The oily smile again. "Portland can be a great city, a leader on the West Coast, but only with investment and development, don't you agree?"

I knew what he was getting at but surprised he was being so direct. *What the hell*, I thought. *Might as well follow suit.* "Is this about North Waterfront?"

He held my gaze. His eyes were slightly bulged and had the blue tinge of glacial ice. "I'm speaking as a concerned citizen. It is a fine project that will put Portland on the map. Why are you and that young client of yours trying to derail it? What possible harm could come from making our waterfront a showplace and a magnet for people of means?"

"You sound like more than a concerned citizen, to me. Are you an investor in the project?"

He waved an arm dismissively. "That is of no concern to you. I ask again, what is the harm? This is America."

"If you don't know, I couldn't explain it."

He nodded slowly. "I see. This is very disappointing, Mr. Claxton." He brought his eyes up to mine. They were unblinking and held menace. "If you know what's good for you, you'll back off. You are becoming a problem for this city."

"For the city or for you and Wingate Properties?"

His face grew hard, like porcelain. "You're a family man, Mr. Claxton. You need to think about that lovely daughter of yours at Harvard."

I had started to turn away, stopped, and whirled around to face him. "*What did you say?*"

The oily smile returned. "You heard me."

No excuses, but I think it was the events of the last week that tipped the balance and caused me to completely and unequivocally lose it. I leaned forward and put an index finger in his face. "If you touch a hair on her head, I'll rip your eyes out, you son of a bitch." Then I stepped back and looked at his car. "And get this piece of shit off my street." With that, I brought my foot up and slammed it into the car door, leaving a surprisingly large crater. They just don't build cars—even Mercedes—like they used to.

My violent act set Archie off in a fit of high-pitched barking as the driver's side door flew open, and a man came out…and out…and out. He's was the biggest man I've ever seen, at least it seemed that way at the time. He came at me fast and threw a punch that would have easily taken my head off if Archie hadn't launched himself between us and deflected the blow. The man cried out in pain and jerked back.

Boryarchenko yelled, "Dimitri, it's okay. Back in the car."

Dimitri looked at the blood dripping from the bite on his wrist and then at Archie, who was standing in front of me with his blood-stained teeth bared and a low, menacing growl gurgling in his throat.

The bloodied chauffer drew a pistol from a shoulder holster and leveled it at my dog. I screamed, "No," and jumped on Archie, covering him with my body. He struggled to free himself, but I held on with everything I had.

"Dimitri! Back in the car!" Boyarchenko said again. Dimitri stood there, pointing the weapon at Archie's human shield—me. "*Now*," his boss commanded. Reluctantly, the mountain of a man holstered his weapon, got in the car, and the dented Mercedes slunk away like a dog that just lost a fight.

I rolled off Archie, sat on the sidewalk, and hugged him until my breathing and pulse came back to normal. "Sorry, Big Boy. That was my fault." I chuckled with nervous energy. "I've always known you'd take a bullet for me, and now you know I'd do the same for you." He licked my cheek a couple of times as if he understood completely. He probably did.

I pulled out my cell phone and called the first number on my favorites list. When she didn't answer, I left a message: "Hi Claire, it's Dad. Call me as soon as you get this. I don't care how late it is. This is urgent."

Chapter Thirty-seven

A good, hard jog usually guaranteed a night of decent sleep but not that night. I was dead tired but couldn't turn off the encounter with Boyarchenko and his brute of a chauffeur, and it didn't help a bit that Claire hadn't returned my call or answered the texts I'd sent her subsequently. I'd started a Walter Mosley novel, *Cinnamon Kiss*, a couple of nights earlier, but the trouble Easy Rawlins found himself in just made me more anxious. I finally got up, poured a couple of fingers of Rémy Martin and put on Norah Jones' *Come Away with Me*, my go-to album when sleep seemed impossible. I sat sipping and letting the music soak in like a warm bath.

The music worked, although when Claire's call woke me at one-thirty the next morning, I discovered I'd spilled the remnants of the Rémy in my lap. "Hi, Dad," she said, her voice filled with concern, "What's going on?"

"Where are you?"

"I'm at my apartment in Cambridge. What is it?"

"When are you going back to the Gulf Coast?"

"Next week. Why? What's wrong, Dad?"

"Listen, Claire. I want you to go today. Just go to the airport, buy a ticket, and go. I'll cover the expenses. Tell your professor you need a vacation. Can you do that?"

The line went quiet. "Does this have anything to do with the creep who came up to me this morning?"

My gut tightened a full turn. "What creep?"

"I was coming home after an all-nighter at the lab, and this guy steps out of the shadows right next to my stairwell and says, 'Are you Claire Claxton?' I nodded, and he said, 'Tell your old man in Portland that Ila, or some name like that, says hi.' He looked like he stepped out of a *Godfather* movie. I almost jumped out of my skin."

"Was the name *Ilya*?" I spelled it out after pronouncing it.

"Yeah, that sounds about right. That's all he said, then he walked away, but he got in my personal space, Dad. I could smell his cigarette breath. Who's Ilya, Dad?"

"Some local hood who's got a beef with me. What'd this guy look like?"

"He was white, my height, stocky. A thick gold chain and a really bad comb-over."

I relaxed a half-notch. At least it wasn't Nightshade. "Okay. The case I'm working on has gotten a little hairy. This is just a bluff to frighten us, but I don't want to take any chances. Can you leave today?"

"Come on, Dad—"

"I know. It's a terrible thing to ask you." I paused as a tsunami of doubts washed over me. "Look, Claire, maybe I'm being selfish here. Maybe I should stop this whole—"

But she cut me off. "Who's threatening us?" I sketched in the situation for her, and when I finished she said with an edge to her voice, "Screw the FBI and that Russian gangster. You can't back down, Dad. That's exactly what they want you to do. That young woman deserves to know who killed her mother, and those asshole developers need to be stopped. There's an afternoon flight to New Orleans. I'll take it. I could use a break, and the weather should be nice down there."

After we said our goodbyes, I lay back and contemplated the situation. I felt a sense of deep pride that Claire backed me with no hesitation. There was no quit in that daughter of mine.

At the same time I knew that, like Angela, Claire tended to be cavalier about her personal safety, especially when she felt her ideals were at issue. Okay, that probably had something to do with me—the example I set—but as a worrisome parent, it wasn't a trait I wanted her to emulate. I also knew that I could never, ever, put her in harm's way. Had I done the right thing? Would she be safe on the Gulf Coast? For now, certainly, but I couldn't keep her down there for long, just like I couldn't keep Angela at Winona's and BB as her bodyguard for much longer.

The pressure was on.

I spent a busy day in my Dundee office, trying to keep my law practice, if not in the black, at least at break-even. Early that afternoon, I got one of those calls that makes it all worthwhile. It was from the young attorney I was sparring with over the wrongful termination case, and her tone from the get-go was decidedly friendly. It turned out that the delivery company had reviewed the situation and decided to do the right thing—instead of firing my client, they would fire my client's supervisor, the one who had ordered my client to text while driving. "So," she said in summary, "we'd like to meet with you and your client to apologize and explore the possibility of a rehire."

Miracles never cease.

A call came in as I was heading into Portland that afternoon. "Cal, it's Angela. I'm at my studio. Something weird's going on."

I tensed up immediately. "What?"

"A car has been parked across from the Co-op most of the afternoon. Some guy's just sitting there. I'm looking at him right now through my window. It seems like he's watching the place."

"Okay." I kept my voice calm. "Keep the door to your studio locked, and tell your idiot neighbor not to let anyone in. I'll be there in fifteen minutes. What's the car look like?"

"A dark blue Honda Accord. It's sitting between the main

entrance and the entry to the back parking lot, on the other side of North Williams."

The traffic cooperated for once, and I got there in ten minutes. The Honda was still parked where Angela said it was, and I could see someone sitting in the driver's seat as I pulled in behind it. Clearly a nonthreatening situation, I got out, walked over to the car, and knocked on the window. The driver, a young man with head and facial hair the color of rusty iron, looked at me, smiled, and rolled the window down. I said, "Can I help you?"

His smile widened. "I think you just did. Are you Calvin Claxton?" When I nodded warily he held up a legal-size envelope and cleared his throat. "These are legal papers I'm handing you, Mr. Claxton. Consider yourself served. Have a nice day."

He drove off, and I stood there looking at the envelope, which had a Multnomah County Circuit Court return address on it. I had a pretty good idea what was inside, and it wasn't going to be pretty. And I didn't like the fact that he expected me to show up at the Co-op. That meant somebody knew my routine. I glanced up and saw Angela looking down from her window, so I fetched Archie and joined her with the envelope in hand, still unopened.

"Who was that guy?" she said when she let me in. "I saw you send him on his way."

"Just a young man doing a job. He gave me this." I tore the envelope open. There were two legal documents in it, a summons and a complaint. The summons was from the Circuit Court of the State of Oregon for the County of Multnomah, informing me that a lawsuit had been filed against me by Wingate Properties for defamation, and that I had thirty days to file a written response. When I saw the amount, I felt like I was in an elevator whose cable had just snapped. I looked up at Angela. "I'm being sued for fifty million bucks by Wingate Properties. I figured they might sue me after the seeing the newspaper article, and here it is."

"*Fifty million?* They can't do that, can they?"

I shrugged. "We're among the most litigious countries in the world. You can sue anybody for just about anything."

"What are they suing you for?"

I skimmed the complaint, then looked up again. "They're claiming I defamed them by telling the reporter who wrote the story in *The Oregonian* that your mom didn't want to proceed with North Waterfront, and this caused them to be treated as suspects in her hit-and-run. They're saying this negative publicity caused irreparable harm to their reputations and to their ability to attract and conduct business."

Angela was beside herself. "That's such bullshit! *I* told Cynthia Duncan that."

"And I confirmed it with her. But someone in the Portland Police Bureau leaked the bit about them being persons of interest in your mom's murder."

"That's such bullshit. They should be suing me and that leaker, not you."

I nodded. "The absolute defense against defamation is the truth, but this isn't about the merits, it's about intimidating me. My confirmation to Duncan gave them just enough to go after me. This is a SLAPP suit—that stands for strategic lawsuit against public participation—and it's used by people with lots of money and legal resources to shut down someone like me. They probably have five lawyers working on this right now. They plan to put me on the legal rack until I go broke or say uncle."

Angela's eyes flooded with tears. "Those rat bastards. This sucks beyond recognition." She swiped tears from her cheeks with the heels of her hands and sniffed. "I'm so sorry, Cal, I—"

"Hey. It's okay. I don't plan to fold."

"What will you do?"

"Oregon has a strong anti-SLAPP statute. I'll file a motion to have the suit dismissed." What I didn't say was that Turner and Avery would, in response, claim it wasn't a SLAPP suit. If they prevailed, I'd be facing a regular civil action for defamation. This would allow them to file a mountain of discovery demands and a truckload of motions, each of which I would have to respond to—the legal rack, in other words.

Angela eyed me appraisingly, and it was clear she saw through my attempt to play down the situation. She was young but mature beyond her years with a firm grasp on reality. She shook her head. "The fucking universe seems to be lining up against you, Cal. Maybe you *should* get out. For your sake."

I met her eyes and held them. "I don't choose to do that, Angela. Your mother deserves better, and so do you."

She teared up again, stepped forward, and hugged me. "I'm not sure I deserve it," she said, her voice thick with emotion, "but Mom sure does."

Did I mention the pressure was on?

Chapter Thirty-eight

The next morning, when Melvin Turner came out on his front porch to get the paper, I was surprised to see him wearing khakis and a knit shirt instead of a suit and tie. Parked down from his house, I felt like the stalker I was. I decided to follow him into work and try to catch him between the parking garage and his office. A bit unorthodox, I admit, but I wanted some facetime and didn't want our discussion to be in his office, on his turf. Better to catch him a little off balance. Why talk to him? A fair question. With no other obvious actions to take, I'd decided to yank the weakest link in the chain again. That would be Turner, if I didn't miss my guess.

He backed his pearl-white Lexus SUV out forty-five minutes later, and a woman, most likely his wife, had joined him. That complicated matters, but I decided to see where they were headed. Turner worked his way over to the I-5, drove south to the 205, and exited at Stafford Road. When he made a left onto Mountain Road, I was pretty sure I knew his destination, and when he turned onto Pete's Mountain Road, I was certain. The entrance to the venerable, highly exclusive Oregon Golf Club was marked by a graceful iron gate that stood open between stone pillars, and off to the right, a turreted guard house looked like something designed by a Hobbit. Thankfully, it was unattended when I passed through. The long, winding drive into the club descended through conifers and deciduous trees, the view conjuring up a pastoral English countryside, except for the snow-clad volcano on the horizon. I parked a safe distance from Turner and his wife, the rambling, multi-gabled clubhouse rising up behind them. As they removed their clubs from the back of the Lexus, I sat there trying to decide what to do. It wasn't the meeting place I'd envisioned, but the parking lot was deserted. I'd come this far, and I was sure to catch him unawares. "What the hell," I muttered to myself as I got out of my car.

"Good morning," I greeted them as I walked up. "Beautiful day for a round of golf." Turner turned to look at me, and the smile he'd formed broke like a pane of glass. Rearranging her clubs, his wife looked up at me and smiled pleasantly.

"What do you want, Claxton?" he asked. "And how did you get in here?"

Ignoring the question, I said, "I got your love letter yesterday, Melvin. I thought we could discuss it."

He turned to his wife. "Why don't you go on in, Dorothy? I'll be right there." His face was grim, and his neck showed some color, but he managed to impart a soothing tone to his voice. Dorothy nodded and gave me a careful look, her eyes telegraphing concern and something else I couldn't read. It made me wonder what she knew or suspected. When she was out of earshot, Turner swung his eyes back to mine and smirked. "All I've got to say is, see you in court."

I nodded. "Your SLAPP's a joke. I'm filing to have it dismissed. Of course, you know that."

Turner smiled, although his blood had risen, giving his cheeks a pinkish hue. I wondered about the man's blood pressure. "Good luck with that," he said. "If you don't know that we have considerable influence in the Multnomah County Court system, you're going to find out soon enough."

I shook my head, and I'm sure my face registered disgust. "I lied about wanting to discuss your baseless lawsuit, Melvin." I paused for dramatic effect. "Did you know that there was an attempt on Angela's life?"

He held the self-righteous look, but his eyes flared, a tell I'd come to expect. "I'm shocked to hear that, but what's it have to do with me?"

I shook my head again. "If you don't know, you should. Let me spell it out for you. Margaret Wingate was struck by a car, Helen Ferris fell down her stairs, and just last week, Angela narrowly escaped what was intended to look like a robbery gone bad. If I hadn't been there, she'd probably be dead now."

The self-righteous look faded, and he seemed to be listening intently.

"Look, Melvin," I continued, "I think you and Helen Ferris altered Margaret Wingate's will to allow the sale of Wingate Properties after she was killed. The original will must have threatened the sale and left you and Avery without job security, so I can understand why you were tempted to do it. And maybe you didn't realize at the outset that the sale and the financing of North Waterfront would launder a lot of filthy, offshore money." I paused and met his eyes. "But I'm having a hard time believing you'd go along with cold-blooded murder." He started to speak, but I raised a hand to silence him. "These murders are being carried out by a contract killer. A man who specializes in making the deaths look like something other than premeditated murder. I think you may be—"

"Excuse me," Dorothy Turner broke in. An attractive woman with a no-nonsense demeanor, she had approached without either one of us noticing. "Melvin, I've changed our tee time to nine forty-five." Instead of leaving, she stepped up next to her husband and looked at me, making it clear she was interested in what was being said.

"Thank you, dear," Turner said. "Mr. Claxton was just leaving."

I looked at Turner. "Think carefully about what I just told

you. It's not too late. There may be a way a way to extricate yourself, Melvin. Call me if you want to discuss it. I know a lot more than you think I do."

Turner laughed bitterly. "Leave now, Claxton, or I'll call security."

I turned and had taken a couple of steps when I thought of the picture of his wife and three kids that I'd seen on Turner's desk. *Of course.* I whirled around. "Ilya Boyarchenko threatened my daughter two days ago. Is that what's going on with you, Melvin? Have they threatened your family? That's it, isn't it?"

A vein bulged in his neck, and his face took on more color. "Get out of here."

I left the man and his wife standing there in the parking lot of the Oregon Golf Club, framed by the iconic clubhouse and beyond that, a majestic Mt. Hood. It would have made a nice Christmas card, except for the fact that Melvin's crimson face was contorted in a mixture of fear and anger, and Dorothy's held a look of utter confusion.

Later that afternoon, I got a call from Captain Harmon Scott. After a brusque greeting, he said, "Is the FBI watching you?"

"I don't think so. Why?"

"We need to talk. Can you meet me at Kells at four?" I told him I'd be there, and he added, "Don't bring a tail."

The turn-of-the-last-century cast-iron building that housed the original Kells Irish Pub looked like it had been picked up and moved from the historic section of Dublin. I got there at quarter past four and found Scott slouched at a small table in the back with a pint in front of him. I stopped a waiter, ordered an Irish Red, and when I joined Scott he almost smiled. "Behaving yourself, are you?"

I took a seat across from him. "Always. You?"

He sighed and drank some beer. "I'm a cop, I have to behave, but sometimes it wears a little thin, to tell you the truth. Some-times I think the bad guys are gaining the upper hand."

"That's the second time I've heard that this week."

"It's going around." He unlatched a briefcase sitting next to his chair, produced a large, unmarked envelope, and placed it on the table between us. "I, ah, have a friend in the forensics lab, so I didn't pull that DNA sample after all. We got lucky. Your attacker's a guy named Karlo Grabar, a Croatian national who came over here on a Green Card after the Bosnian thing. A high-tech outfit in Chicago wanted him for his computer skills, but he got involved in a white supremacist group, got charged with felony assault, and skipped bail. That was four years ago, and he hasn't been seen since. I also had one of our techs take a quick look at the Nightshade site on the Dark Web. It's been up about three years, so the timing fits, more or less."

"And the fact that he's foreign does, too," I said. "The site doesn't seem to have an American origin."

Scott allowed the thinnest of smiles. "I think I'm warming to your conspiracy theory. I can't see this scumbag suddenly decid-ing to do a two-bit marijuana heist in Portland. That doesn't fit. Anyway, the details are in the envelope along with a mug shot. Needless to say, if this gets out we're both screwed."

"Roger that." I reached for the envelope, thanked him, and said, holding back a smile, "You're assuming I'm going to follow up on this."

He stood and drained his beer, set the mug down, and said over his shoulder as he was walking out, "I know you will. Win one for the good guys, Claxton."

Chapter Thirty-nine

I took the Ross Island Bridge across the river and headed straight for Nando's office. On the way I called Angela, who'd been dog-sitting Archie since early that morning. When I asked about my dog, she said, "He's fine, but I'm afraid he likes me better than you now."

I laughed. "That's called alienation of affection, you know." I explained I was running late and asked if she could continue watching Arch. "I'll have BB pick you two up if that's okay."

"Sure. I'm having a good sculpting day, and I'm always glad to see BB."

I had no sooner tapped off when a text pinged in from Claire. She had found a motel outside New Iberia and was enjoying a spate of fine weather. I breathed a little easier.

With the envelope in hand, I walked into the Sharp Eye and told Esperanza I needed to see her boss right away. "Go on in," she said. "He's on the phone." Wearing a royal purple silk shirt, Nando had his broad back to me, talking in rapid-fire Spanish. I took a seat in front of his desk and looked around. A huge, brightly colored relief map of the island of Cuba dominated one wall, and pictures of his home country, his family there, and more contemporary photos, dotted the other wall. My eyes were always drawn to the picture of him snapped by a U.S. Coast Guardsman. Thin, with a thick, four-day growth and a brilliant smile on his thirty-year-old face, Nando stood in a makeshift raft, clinging to a buoy off the Keys. It was his triumphant arrival in America, and it was easy to see the passion for his new country burning in his eyes.

"*Aye yai yai*," he said, turning to me after he finished his call, "always the problems." But when he saw the look on my face, he added, "You have something." I opened the envelope, pushed the contents over to him, and described what Scott had told me while he gazed at Grabar's mug shot. He tapped the photo with an index finger when I finished. "He has the dead eyes. These are the men to watch out for. We need to find this *cabrón*."

"Any ideas on how to do that? All we have is a photograph. He's sure as hell not using his real name, assuming he's still in the area."

"The motel where you think he hung the car thief, remind me where it is."

"The Swanson. It's on SE 111th, off Foster."

"He wouldn't stay at this motel, but maybe he is staying somewhere in the vicinity," Nando responded. "We could start by showing his picture around the bars, restaurants, and shops in the area. It is mainly industrial, so this would be a manageable task. If we get a hit, we could stake the place out in case he returns."

I nodded but thought of another possibility. "This guy's holed up somewhere alone, right? Suppose he gets horny and starts using one of the women working at the Swanson? After all, he probably knows what goes on there." Nando raised his eyebrows and nodded back. "I could go back there and ask around," I added.

He shook his head. "An excellent place to start, but it should not be you who does this."

"Who, then?"

He smiled knowingly. "BB. All the women love him, and he has experience with the working girls. If one of them knows this man, BB will find out for us."

"I thought all the women loved *you*."

He flashed a smile that lit the room. "It is a Cuban thing, Calvin."

I chuckled. "Okay, BB's our man. Of course, Grabar's a pro, so it's unlikely he'd confide in a prostitute, but it's worth a shot. If BB strikes out, we can try the broader canvassing you suggested."

We settled on it.

Since I'd rattled Melvin Turner's cage and been pretty open about it, I figured I might as well do the same for his business partner, Brice Avery. My hunch was Avery was more deeply enmeshed in the North Waterfront scheme, but of course I had scant evidence of this. I was particularly interested in learning if Turner had talked to Avery about my recent visit. If I was right about Avery, and about Turner being squeezed into compliance by Boyarchenko, then I would expect the lawyer to keep his silence while he mulled over what I'd told him. On the other hand, Avery might be under threat from Boyarchenko, as well.

In any case, I was way past sitting back and waiting for something to happen. Despite the risks, stirring the pot seemed a much better option, and a frontal assault seemed the best approach.

"Hello, Brittany." I greeted Avery's secretary bright and early the next morning. She looked up at me and smiled, her eyes as blue as I remembered them. "I'm wondering if I could pop in to see your boss for a couple of minutes."

She glanced at her screen, then back at me, the smile still intact. "He isn't expecting you, but let's see if I can sneak you in, Mr. Claxton." Impressed with her memory for names, I followed her to his door and waited as she tapped lightly and announced my presence. I chuckled internally but hoped she wouldn't get fired for this. Clearly, she hadn't gotten the memo that I was radioactive, that my alleged defamatory statements threatened the very existence of Wingate Properties.

Avery stood up at his desk, leaned forward propped on both arms, and regarded me. His sleeves were rolled, his striped tie loosened, and his perpetual three-day growth neatly sheared— the picture of a take-charge CEO. He didn't say a word when Brittany announced me, but after she clicked the door shut, he growled, "What the fuck do you want, Claxton?"

I sat down and crossed my legs. "Thanks for seeing me on such short notice, Brice," I said, cheerily. "I thought we should discuss your pending lawsuit."

He cracked a skeptical smile. "Why? You want to make a full retraction?"

"Nah, not really. I—"

"Then I've got nothing to say to you beyond what's written in the complaint." He sat back down, his eyes narrowed to a couple of slits. "You need to leave this building. Now."

I smiled at him, but I'm sure my eyes conveyed a different message. "Funny. That's the same response I got from Melvin when I had a little chat with him yesterday." I watched his face, and it registered pure surprise before he reined the expression in. Turner hadn't said a word to him. "If you think that bullshit lawsuit will intimidate me, you're wrong," I went on. "And having Ilya Boyarchenko threaten my daughter won't work, either. I —"

He cut me off again and pointed at the door. "Out. Now. I don't want to hear your asinine conspiracy theories. You're out of control, Claxton. We're going to bury you and your two-bit law practice."

I got up, walked to the door, then turned to face him. "What I'm wondering about with you, Brice, is how deeply you're involved in this. Was it just to save your job and direct the biggest project Portland's ever seen, or are you complicit in murder? Either way you're going down. Have a nice day."

I thanked Brittany on the way out and was waiting for the down elevator when a hefty guy appeared from a side door down the hall. He had a shaved head, a pronounced unibrow, and wore a white shirt with some sort of insignia sewn on one of its shoulders. When he joined me, he said with rehearsed civility, "Mr. Claxton, I'm security, and I'm here to escort you out of the building."

I looked at him and said, "Tell Mr. Avery thanks, but I'm on my way and don't need an escort." Sent by the big boss to do a job and focused on the mission, he clamped my right arm at the bicep in a meaty hand. I said, "Get your hands off me," and pulled out of his grip. He grabbed my arm again, and when I resisted, yanked it hard. My still-healing right shoulder screamed out in pain, and so did I. Mistaking my scream for a battle cry, he tried to pin my arm behind me, which probably would have re-dislocated it if I didn't react.

My response was pure reflex. I swung my left elbow and caught him in the ribs. He grunted, and I felt something give. But instead of letting go, he wrenched my arm even harder. I screamed again, and in desperation balled my left fist and swung a backhand blow that caught him flush on the cheek. *Whack!*

He let go of my arm and dropped to his knees. The elevator pinged and the doors opened, but instead of getting in, I said to him, "I'm sorry, but that was my injured arm you yanked. Are you okay?"

He gingerly felt his cheek, grimaced, and said through clenched teeth, "Fuck you, man. You're gonna pay for this."

Convinced he wasn't too badly hurt, I apologized again, got on the elevator, and left him there with a dazed look on his face.

My arm was still aching two hours later when two uniformed Portland Police Officers showed up at Caffeine Central and arrested me for assault. I knew one of the cops, and he let me call Angela to have her swing by with BB to pick up Archie. I was too embarrassed to tell her what happened.

To paraphrase Johnny Cash, I've had tougher weeks, but I really can't remember when....

Chapter Forty

The bed was hard as a rock, and my shoulder ached from getting wrenched by Unibrow, so that night in jail was long and torturous. I went back over what happened several times and finally decided I wouldn't have done anything differently. I was pretty sure there was a security camera on that floor that would bolster my side of the story and made a mental note to request a copy the next day as part of my discovery. It was self-defense, but adding another case on top of the defamation lawsuit was unsettling, to say the least.

There was one consolation. As a result of my visit to Brice Avery, I was now fairly confident he was knowingly involved, not only in the money-laundering, but the murders, as well. Why else would Melvin Turner not have told his partner about the revelations I laid out at the Oregon Golf Club? Because he was afraid, that's why. Okay, this wasn't proof, but it made a lot of sense. And, by suggesting an out to Turner, maybe I'd succeeded in driving a wedge between them. I hoped that wasn't wishful thinking.

At my arraignment in Municipal Court that morning, I was expecting to be charged with assault four, a misdemeanor, since I hadn't used a weapon. However, I learned that I'd cracked one of the security guard's ribs and broken his cheekbone, so the county prosecutor saw fit to bump it to assault three, a felony, which for a lawyer was a one-way ticket to disbarment. The news was like a well-placed kick to the groin.

I pleaded not guilty, and since the judge knew me, I was released on my own recognizance. Afterwards, I called Angela to check on my dog. "He's fine," she told me. Always the perceptive one, she added, "Are you okay? "You sound a little down."

I ignored her question. "I'll pick Arch up as soon as I get my car. It's pouring outside, so it may take a while to get there. I'm at the courthouse and my car's at Caffeine Central."

"Hang on a sec." I heard muffled voices, then "Winona's here checking out Jogging Woman. We'll come pick you up." I tried to object, but she insisted.

I stood in the courthouse entryway, and when Winona's Prius C pulled up, I dashed to the street and hopped in, much to the delight of Archie. I wasn't anxious to explain the situation, but I saw no way to avoid it. When I finished, Angela said, "So Brice sends a security guard out to rough you up. What a douche move." She tried to suppress a laugh but couldn't. "Boy, did that dude get a surprise."

Winona glanced at me in the rearview mirror with a less sanguine expression. "If you're convicted, you'll lose your license, right?" I nodded. "What about the guard? Could he sue you for the assault?"

"Theoretically. He could claim damages of some kind in civil court, where the burden of proof's less. I can beat the felony charge, but civil suits are a crapshoot."

She glanced back again. "And Angela told me you're being sued by Wingate Properties, too. Jesus, Cal, is this as bad as it looks?"

"Nah," I said, mainly for Angela's benefit. She looked like she was going to cry, and I couldn't handle that at the moment. "There's a clear path through this whole morass." I chuckled to lighten the mood. "But maybe I should consult my horoscope to see how many planets are lined up in opposition to me."

Angela smiled at that, but the reflected look Winona shot me was pure skepticism.

Angela insisted on being dropped off at the Co-op first, which I suspected was her playing Cupid with Winona and me. She didn't know the little cherub had already blunted his arrows on our romance.

"I want you to know how much I appreciate you putting Angela up," I told Winona as we skimmed over the Willamette River on the Broadway Bridge. "We know the name of her attacker now, so I'm hoping we'll get a break and take him out asap"

"I hope you get the bastard, but don't worry about the timing. I've grown very fond of Angela, and she needs a woman she can confide in right now." She shook her head. "Thank God she made it through. A lot of rebellious kids don't these days. So many ways to go wrong. She's still mad at the world—what rational person isn't? But she's using the anger to drive her creativity now. She's a talented sculptor, Cal."

"I know. I'm fond of her, too. She reminds me a lot of Claire."

We drove in silence for a while, and when Winona finally pulled up in front of Caffeine Central, she turned to me. Her eyes were more hazel than green in the overcast light, and she smiled just enough that the tiny whirlpools of her dimples appeared on either cheek. "You look well," I said. "How have you been?"

She shrugged and sighed. "Better, I guess. I'm sorry to hear about all the trouble you're dealing with. Is there really a light at the end of this tunnel?"

"That remains to be seen, but one thing's for sure—the only way out is going to be through." She smiled knowingly. I weakened. "Look, why don't you come up? I can fix us both a late breakfast. I'll make your favorite, blueberry pancakes."

She averted her eyes and shook her head. "I can't, Cal. I'm driving out to Warm Springs today for a meeting. I'm looking at a job there. The Tribal Council wants someone to put a comprehensive ecological plan together and lead it. They asked me to apply."

"Oh." My heart knew better, but it sank just the same. "They'd be lucky to get you. You'd move out to the Rez?"

"If I take the job, yeah." She sighed again. "After what I witnessed at Standing Rock, I know I need to do more. You're standing up for Angela, and I'd like to do the same for my people." She swung her eyes to me and forced a smile. "I've made a little bit of progress, at least."

"You've made a lot of progress. Uh, good luck with the job interview. That's exciting."

Archie and I got out of her car, and after she pulled away I looked down at my dog. "I'll be damned, Big Boy, it turns out rock-bottom has a basement."

At close to two the next morning my cell phone dragged me out of a deep sleep. It lay on the kitchen table, and I stumbled down the hall, catching it on the eighth or ninth ring. "We have found him."

My mind cleared in an instant. "Grabar?"

"Yes," Nando said. "A woman named Blaise out at the Swanson Motel recognized the photo. She said she's been to his place twice. Grabar sent Uber to pick her up because he had an accident."

"Let me guess—he broke his nose."

Nando laughed. "Precisely. He did not wish to be seen in public, but the sex urge was not to be denied, just as you thought. BB is there now, watching the place. It's a rental house off Stark on SE 215th. The lights are out."

"He's being cautious, right? Grabar's no one to mess with."

"Of course."

I chuckled. "You were right about BB."

"Yes." I could hear a tinge of pride in his voice. "The young man is top notch. I suggest we join him. That way, when Grabar goes out in the morning, BB can follow him, and we can search his place."

I wasn't keen on breaking and entering. On the other hand, I was reluctant to involve Harmon Scott and the Portland Police. Scott could be compromised, and, besides, all they could charge Grabar with is assault, and that was a stretch because he didn't lay a hand on Angela and could claim that I attacked him. Let it play out a little more, I decided. "Okay," I told Nando, "Grabar got a look at your Jeep, so I'll swing by and pick you up."

Twenty minutes later, we crossed the Ross Island Bridge and headed east. According to BB, Grabar was staying in a one-story ranch set back from the street on a long driveway lined with trees and shrubs, probably a short-term furnished rental. The street was unlit. We parked about a block south of the driveway. "BB's a block north." He punched in a text announcing our arrival. When BB didn't answer, he said, "*Mierda*. I told him to keep his phone on."

When BB didn't answer the second text, I said, "Stay here. I'll go wake him up." I said it half in jest, but the hairs on my arms had risen. When Nando asked if I had my Glock, I opened my coat to show it tucked in my belt.

"Good. He's in a black Camry."

Clouds masked a thin sliver of moon, so I moved in near total darkness along the tree-lined road. The Camry was where it was supposed to be—a block past Grabar's driveway on the other side of the street —but BB wasn't in it, and it was unlocked. I looked around, wishing I had the eyes of an owl. Nothing moved in the shadows on either side of the street. That's when I heard a faint ping, the unmistakable sound signature of an incoming text. I smiled, figuring it was my impatient friend sending another text to BB, who must've gotten out of his car for a pee. The sound came from further up the road, a section that lay in even deeper shadow. But the hair on my arms was still standing, so I reached for my Glock, took a deep breath to center myself, and moved toward the ping's location.

As I drew near, I stumbled on something lying across the

pathway and went sprawling. Miraculously, the Glock didn't go off. I got to my knees and reached back to find what had tripped me. It was a couple of jogging shoes attached to a pair of legs. I gasped, took out my cell phone, and activated the flashlight.

Bembe Borgos stared back at me in the garish light, his cell phone visible in a shirt pocket. A perfectly round, half-inch hole lay directly between his blank eyes, and a thin thread of blood had seeped from the wound, tracing a path down his nose and across his cheek like a bloody tear.

I rocked back on my heels. "No, goddamn it, no."

Chapter Forty-one

The rest of that early morning is a swirl of bad memories soaked in guilt. I texted Nando to join me, warning him to be careful, that Grabar might be lurking somewhere on the street. I went back part of the way to intercept my friend, and when he loomed out of the shadows, I grabbed his arm and pulled him behind a tree. There was no gentle way to say this. "It's BB. He's been shot. He's dead," I whispered.

Nando ripped his arm from my grasp. "*No. That can't be. Where is he?*" He tried to whisper, but his voice carried in the stillness. I led him to the body, and after recoiling from the shock he knelt next to his friend and colleague and said something softly in Spanish I didn't catch. When he got back up, I pulled him behind a swath of large rhododendrons that at least provided us some cover from the street. He clamped his hands on my shoulders, holding me at arm's length. "This is my fault, Calvin," he said in a thick, quavering whisper. "If I hadn't sent him to the stakeout alone he would still be alive."

"We're both to blame," I answered, feeling like the weight of Nando's hands would buckle my knees. "I should have realized the danger and given BB more warning about who he was dealing with."

Nando stabbed a finger in the direction of the rental house and said through clenched teeth, "If he's not on the street, that *hijo de puta* could still be in there. You watch the front. I'm going to bust in through the back."

I shook my head. "You can't do that, Nando. This is touchy. We weren't supposed to have that picture of Grabar or his name. We can watch the place until the cops get here, and let them break in. Grabar's almost certainly long gone anyway."

"What are we going to tell the cops?" His voice shook with anger.

I paused before answering. "We tell them BB was working off the general description I gave him, *not* a photograph. That way, Scott doesn't have to lie if he gets questioned by his boss."

"What about Blaise, the woman who recognized the photograph?"

"We say BB didn't tell us who he talked to at the Swanson. Blaise is unlikely to contradict us, because she won't want to talk to the cops. Everything else is *exactly* as it happened. If Scott wants to admit he knows Grabar's name and came up with a photo, that's his call." I shook my head. "I don't like it, but I can't see any other way to handle this without compromising Scott."

"And the FBI?"

I shrugged. "Good question. If they're pulled into this, I'm not sure they'll care that much about us pursuing Grabar. Remember, they seemed to disbelieve our theory of the murders."

"I do not give a shit, anyway." Nando's voice was low and menacing. "Grabar is going to pay for this." He started striding toward the rental house. "Now, let's call in the cops," he said, over his shoulder as he drew his gun.

Before the cops arrived, I called Harmon Scott on his cell to give him a head's-up, explaining what had happened and what Nando and I planned to say about it.

"I'm damn sorry to hear about your friend, Cal," he responded, "and thanks. I owe you big-time for this. I need my pension to retire."

"We're even," I told him. He went on to say he would arrange to meet us at the eastside precinct later that night to complete the formal interviews. He gave me no clue as to how he planned to handle the fact that he knew Grabar's name and had a mug shot of him. As it turned out, that conundrum was overtaken by events.

The crime scene investigation passed in agonizing slow-motion. As I expected, Grabar had cleared out of the rental house, leaving it "antiseptically clean," as one of the techs put it. I wondered how the killer knew he was being watched by BB. After our preliminary interrogation and while the techs were scouring the house, I strolled down to the end of the drive and examined a dogwood standing at the edge of the property. A wide-angle surveillance camera strategically placed in the tree would have provided a clear view of the street. Either that, or somebody at the Swanson tipped Grabar. There was no question about how he'd surprised BB. The victim's pants were unzipped, and he had fallen next to a patch of his own urine.

When we finished up at the eastside precinct, I went with Nando to tell BB's mother what had happened. It was one of the worst experiences of my life, conjuring up dark memories of the death of my wife in L.A. all those years earlier. Afterwards, we went our separate ways, both of us needing to be alone to come to grips with what happened.

Back at Caffeine Central, I fed Archie, then called Claire. I just needed to hear her voice. "I'm fine," she told me. "I'm actually getting some work done, but I'm going to need to get back to Boston at the end of next week."

Not to alarm her, I said we were making progress on the case but left the details vague. When I tapped off, I sat back and looked at Arch. "*Progress?* Are you kidding me? Grabar's in the wind and tipped that we're on to him, and I can't prove that forgery and murder were committed in a money-laundering conspiracy, even though I know most of the principals involved. What a joke, huh?" My dog looked back at me, and I swear there was compassion in his eyes.

I needed that.

I called Angela next, picked her up at Winona's, and took her to the Co-op. She took the news about BB especially hard. It was no secret she was very fond of him, and I had the impression he was beginning to reciprocate. I held her for a long time while she cried and then she abruptly broke away and began sculpting. Diving into her work was her way to cope. Archie took up his spot in the corner, and I sat down on the floor next to him and watched her work, trying to divert myself from the sadness, guilt, and anxiety racking me.

Jogging Woman's frame was nearly complete, and Angela had begun the detail work that would bring the figure to life. I marveled at how she cut and bent finer pieces of wire and welded them in place, the cross-hatching like a painter using fine brush strokes to add detail and dimension. She was concentrating on the face, and I could see that the shape of the nose and the bone structure of the cheeks and around the eyes were beginning to bare an uncanny resemblance to her mother. I was moved by that, in spite of my dark mood. Curiously, both of Jogging Woman's hands were still straight strands of ridged steel wire. When I asked about this, she said, "The hands are critically important and the toughest to flesh out. I'm saving them for last."

There's something to the idea that it's darkest before the dawn, because when my cell phone riffed that afternoon, I was as low as I've ever been, and that's pretty damn low. "Hello, Mr. Claxton, this is Mel Turner's wife, Dorothy," the call began. "I, um, I was wondering if we could meet this afternoon? I have some questions I'd like to ask you." I told her sure, and we agreed to meet at Caffeine Central in an hour.

Well, whaddaya know?

Dorothy Turner had a pleasing round face with soft eyes marked with crow's feet and double parentheses on either side of her mouth, suggesting she smiled early and often. But she wasn't smiling as she entered my office, and her eyes looked deeply troubled. After greeting Archie like a person who knew and loved dogs, she took a seat across from me. "If Mel knew I was here, he'd pitch a fit," she began, "but I have to talk to someone." Her eyes filled, so I got up and handed her a tissue. She dabbed them and looked at me. "I don't know who to turn to. You seem like someone I can trust. Can I trust you, Mr. Claxton?"

I met her eyes. "Yes, you can," I said. "If you confide in me I'll do everything in my power to help you and your husband. I think he's in a situation he doesn't know how to get out of."

She held my eyes for a long time, taking my measure. Finally, she said, "You asked Mel if someone was threatening our family. Why did you say that?"

"Because someone your husband is involved with—a man named Ilya Boyarchenko—threatened my daughter if I didn't stop an investigation into his real estate dealings. I think he may be threatening your husband the same way to keep him in line."

"Is this about the North Waterfront Project? Is there something illegal going on?"

"Yes. And I think your husband wants out but is afraid for you and your kids."

She straightened a little and fixed me with her gaze. "Whatever Mel did, it had nothing to do with the deaths of Margaret Wingate and Helen Ferris."

"I believe that," I said. "Otherwise, I wouldn't be talking to you." I sensed that's as far into the conspiracy as she wished to go, which was fine with me.

Her chin trembled, and she lowered her eyes. "That must be it, then," she said, almost to herself. "He's so troubled. He's not sleeping or eating much. He's continually on edge. I've never seen him like this." She brought her eyes back up. They were wide with fear and anxiety. "What should I do, Mr. Claxton?"

I leaned in and opened my hands. "You have to get him to come forward, Mrs. Turner. He doesn't want to go to the police because he's made some mistakes, and I think he's ashamed. But he's a good man, I sense that. That's why I showed up at the golf club. Tell him to come to me so that we can work together to resolve this. He holds the key to stopping them."

"Will this endanger the children?"

"Not if he uses discretion, and I know he will. Tell him there's a way out without putting you and the kids at risk. And, as for you, don't say a word of this to *anyone*, especially Brice Avery."

Her eyes narrowed down. "Brice's part of the threat, isn't he?" I nodded, and she stared at the marred surface of my desk for a long time before looking up again. "Mel's a proud and stubborn man, Mr. Claxton. I'll tell him exactly what you said, but I don't know how he'll react." Then she shifted in her seat. "He's been getting more and more nervous and agitated. It feels like something's about to happen? Is it?"

"A lot has already happened that I can't share, but I agree there's more to come." I wasn't just saying that. It felt like something major had finally broken loose.

I showed Dorothy Turner to the door, and before she strode off down Couch Street, she turned and did something that totally surprised me. Her hug was firm and unselfconscious. "Thank you, Mr. Claxton. I feel a little better. I'll be in touch one way or the other."

I watched her walk away, more secure in the knowledge that my hunch about Melvin Turner was right. He may have been caught up in an ugly mess and was suing me for defamation, but I was convinced that at core he was a decent guy. Otherwise, he could have never attracted someone with the character of Dorothy Turner.

The question now was could she get him to come forward?

Chapter Forty-two

That Sunday in late May was cloudless, although I awoke in the shadow of BB's ghost with issues and obligations stacked squarely on my shoulders like so many sandbags. I just finished a double cappuccino when my cell went off. "Hey," a cheerful voice said, "it's Tracey. Do you and Arch want to go for a run?"

Thirty minutes later, the three of us were pounding down one of the ramps on the Eastbank Esplanade after having crossed the Steel Bridge. With Archie leading the way, we passed the Hawthorne and crossed at the Tilikum Crossing—the cable-stayed bridge that accommodated pedestrians and the MAX Light Rail—and stopped at Elephant's Deli, where we ordered coffee and croissants and found an outside table. I was feeling a lot better, but by the time I brought Tracey up to date regarding the lawsuit, the Boyarchenko threat, my arrest for assault, and BB's death, I felt overwhelmed again.

I wasn't looking for sympathy, and when I finished, Tracey didn't give me any. Instead, she reached across the table and squeezed my hand, her eyes lit with determination. "We're going to get through this, Cal. You told me the other day you found meaning in the struggle, right?" She paused, smiling with a hint of wryness. "Well…?"

I laughed at that. "Yeah, I've had about all the meaning I can stand right now." She returned the laugh, and I said, "I hope the news is better at your end."

She sipped her coffee and eyed me over the rim of the cup. "The council's split on North Waterfront, two leaning for and two against. The mayor can break the tie, but he's been non-committal so far. Poindexter's going to give a final report and a set of recommendations in two weeks. He's all in, of course, and his glowing report might tip the balance. The Oregon Industries Association and the Metro Business Alliance are both leaning toward support. The final vote will come in June." She paused. "I know I promised you a month, Cal, but the timing's tightened. I can't wait much longer to tip Cynthia Duncan about Arrowhead. She'll need time to dig in, then get an article published."

"You think that will be enough? All we know is that Arrowhead was incorporated in Cyprus. We still don't know for sure whose money's behind it."

She shrugged and made a face. "It's all I got, except for some vague accusations about Brice Avery, Melvin Turner, and Ilya Boyarchenko that sound like a conspiracy theory."

"I've got another iron in the fire." I told her about my visit from Dorothy Turner.

When I finished, Tracey's eyes brightened with hope. "You think Turner will come forward?"

"If Dorothy Turner has anything to say about it, he will."

Her look turned conspiratorial. "I've got an iron in the fire, too. Fred Poindexter's secretary, a woman named Mia Cantrell, came to me yesterday and said he's been making unwanted advances and saying inappropriate things to her. He's married, too, the slimeball. I told her to file a formal complaint, but she doesn't think it'll stick. It's just 'he said-she said,' at this point. Anyway, I recruited her."

"Recruited her?"

"Yeah," Tracey said, looking proud of herself, "I told her I suspected him of other improprieties and would be very interested in hearing about anything unusual going on in his office—communications with strangers, unexpected or hastily called meetings, anything that looks unusual or outside the normal routine to her. I gave her a list of names and key words to look out for, too: Arrowhead Investments, Ilya Boyarchenko, Byron Hofstetter, Costas Zertalis, Cyprus."

"How did she react?"

"She jumped on it."

"Can you trust her?"

"Absolutely. She hates the bastard, and she's a straight-shooter."

"Nice work. You're good at this stuff."

Her eyes turned to pure flirtation, and she smiled at me across the table. "I have a good teacher."

The weather held as we walked back along the river through Tom McCall Park. The park was a riot of happy Portlanders engaged in all manner of spring activities, reminding me that the dark, smash-and-grab forces I was up against—the "new normal," as some were calling it—hadn't touched everyone. Not yet, at least. It was as if the scene was a mirage, something out of the nostalgic past that could never be reclaimed. I hoped like hell that wasn't the case. A couple of times, Tracey took my hand and squeezed it, and I sensed the same thoughts were going through her mind, although neither one of us spoke.

We crossed Burnside at 3rd and when we reached Couch Street, Arch and I took a left, while she continued toward her condo on Hoyt. But before parting, Tracey sealed it with a kiss on my cheek and a hug for my dog. It was unspoken, but firm, that whatever was going on between us was on hold until this mess got sorted out one way or the other.

That Monday morning, back at my Dundee office, I still felt the weight of the world on my shoulders, but at the same time, a vague feeling lingered that things were finally moving. I spent my first working hour talking to the owner of one of the larger wineries in the Dundee Hills about his upcoming divorce hearing.

It was the usual, joy-numbing story—two people, once in love, were now locked in a struggle over the material things they once freely shared. If I didn't need the money, I wouldn't have taken the case, but there you go.

I tackled the response to the charges in the Wingate defamation lawsuit next. It wasn't due for twenty-four days, but I had an itch to get it off my to-do list. Halfway through the first draft, a call came in from the real estate agent, Valerie Thatcher. After we exchanged greetings she said, "What's the latest on the mining at the Aerie?" When I answered that nothing had changed, she said, "That screenwriter I told you about is still interested. Would you mind if I showed him the property?"

I paused while my gut did a flip and looked over at Arch. "Uh, I guess it wouldn't hurt to see how he reacts." I glanced at my calendar. "The hearing at the Land Use Board isn't for another three weeks, but I haven't uncovered anything to stop them from mining. There's a house key hanging on a nail on the side of the front steps, second step from the bottom on the right." She thanked me and went on her way. I knew she was just doing her job, but her cheerful demeanor annoyed the hell out of me, and the thought of some stranger walking around in my place, let alone buying it, was almost more than I could stomach.

I finished the first draft of my response to the defamation suit and had just sat down at the bakery for a quick lunch when my cell riffed. "We have something big, my friend. You must come to my office immediately."

It was Nando, and he made it clear he didn't want to talk on the phone. There was also no mistaking the excitement in his voice.

Chapter Forty-three

"You look stunning today, Esperanza," I said, as I stood watching her making a fuss over Archie an hour later.

She looked up, swept a lock of hair from her dark eyes, and smiled mischievously. "Flattery will get you everywhere, Cal Claxton." I laughed at that, and she nodded in the direction of Nando's office. "Go on in. He's expecting you."

Nando and a young man stood up when I entered the room. Nando said, "Calvin, this is Mohinder Gupta. He's the cyber expert I've been telling you about." We shook hands, although I think a fist bump would have been more to his liking.

Looking all of twenty, Gupta wore a plaid shirt, a dark leather bow tie, and skinny jeans rolled at the ankles above powder-blue canvas shoes. He was thin, with a mustache like a smear of coal dust and a pile of dark hair with all the order of a windblown haystack. "Call me Mo," he said.

"As you know, Calvin," Nando continued, "Mo's been looking at Global Mandate and Arrowhead Investments to see if there is any connection, and who's behind the shell companies." He placed a hand on the young man's shoulder. "Take Calvin through what you've found."

"Okay." Mo glanced at me with eyes radiating intelligence. "I started with Global Mandate, the Panamanian company. They bought a Gulfstream G150 for 14.1 million in 2015 using a Bank of Utah trust arrangement. As far as I can tell, that's the only legitimate transaction that Global Mandate ever did. I tracked down all their listed directors and shareholders. All of them are shams." I raised my eyebrows, and he explained, "People behind the shell paid what are called sham directors to use their names on the company's documents. It's a big business. The shams have real names, titles, addresses, so it lends an air of authenticity." Mo laughed. "One of the directors has been dead for three years."

I glanced at Nando. "Surprise, surprise."

He nodded. "Indeed. The shell was created to buy the expensive airplane that could be registered in the USA."

"That's right," Mo said. "So, who set GM up? There were several possibilities, and all of them appeared to be blind alleys. I finally traced a wire transfer for the 14.1 million dollars to a law firm in Bermuda who represents a company in the Isle of Man called Morning Star." I must have looked incredulous, because Mo smiled and said, "I'm not making this shit up. Anyway," he continued, "judging from its bogus website and another set of sham directors, Morning Star's also a decoy. From there, I found the company that set up Morning Star in the British Virgin Islands, another bogus shell called Hyperion Finance, which had set up yet another shell in the Cayman Islands"

I laughed, half in amazement and half in disgust. "I'm starting to see a pattern here."

"Right," Mo said. "These kinds of networks are built by lawyers to obscure the identity of their clients. The origin of the Cayman Islands company was the toughest to trace, but I finally wound up with the daddy of them all—Arrowhead Investments, LLC, out of Cyprus. The money for the Gulfstream originated there and zigzagged all over the globe before landing at Global Mandate."

"Bravo," I said. Excellent work."

Nando beamed a broad smile and looked at Mo like a proud father. "There is more."

Mo said, "So, what stood out was the law firm in Bermuda that was right in the middle of this deal. It's a big-time outfit called Appleton. It turns out the scumbags work with the Bank of Utah and banks all over the world to provide these kinds of strategies and other shady shit to help the uber rich hide their identities and their money." He smiled slyly. "But the dudes got their asses hacked recently. I checked around and found a source." He glanced at Nando.

"We bought the information, Calvin," Nando said. "It cost five thousand dollars. But I will pay half," he added hastily."

I nodded. "So, you found who owns Arrowhead?"

"Yes. It is one man, a Russian national named Stanislav Anapolsky," Nando answered. The name didn't mean anything to me. "He is one of the richest oligarchs in Russia, a protégé of Vladimir Putin. He controls massive oil and gas holdings but has been long suspected of being a key figure behind the global cocaine trade. From the little that's available online, I learned Mr. Anapolsky is a big fan of the U.S. lifestyle, and enjoys traveling in our fair country."

I shook my head. "And he needs his own private jet to do this."

"Of course. Is there any other way to travel? He must keep up appearances as he searches for suitable places to launder his ill-gotten gains."

"And the tail number of his jet can't be traced back to him, so he can travel anonymously once he's in the country," I added, then glanced from Nando to Mo and back again to Nando. He caught my drift and asked Mo to give us some privacy after we both thanked the young man profusely.

When Mo stepped out, Nando handed me two photographs of Anapolsky, a headshot and a picture of him standing with a group of golfers. "How did your friend at the Aurora Airport describe the person who got out of the Gulfstream that night with his bodyguards?"

I looked the photographs over. Tall and thin, Anapolsky stood out in the group of shorter, mostly overweight golfers. The head-shot showed a man with intense dark eyes, a receding hairline and a neatly manicured mustache and goatee. I looked up. "The description he gave me fits perfectly."

"Hail, hail, the gang is here," Nando said.

I got up and started pacing. "Yeah, I think we know all the players and have a complete picture now. It looks like Anapolsky is fronting the money to buy Wingate Properties and finance the North Waterfront Project. Investing in a red-hot market like Portland would beat hiding his money in a low interest-bearing account in the Caymans or some other haven. He either knows or knows of Boyarchenko, so he uses Byron Hofstetter to help set the deal up. Maybe he cuts Boyarchenko into the deal to guarantee cooperation. It's smooth sailing until Margaret Wingate goes to the Women's March in Washington and comes back a changed woman."

Nando's face darkened. "So they bring in Karlo Grabar, and that sets off the whole nasty chain of events."

An image of BB's blank eyes flashed in my head, and I had to shake it off before I could continue. "That's right. They were planning on just one hit, but it spun out of control." I stopped and faced my friend. "There's one thing I haven't told you. Melvin Turner forged Margaret Wingate's will, but I'm certain he didn't know she'd been murdered. Brice Avery was in on it, and I think he talked Turner into the forgery." Nando gave me a questioning look as I continued. "His wife came to my office last Saturday and asked me for help."

Nando's thick eyebrows rose, and his eyes enlarged. "You are making a joke. What did you tell her?"

"I told her to convince him to come forward, that I would help him. He's an attorney, he knows he has leverage with the police if he wasn't in on the murders. But he'd face disbarment and humiliation, and they're threatening his family, so he's frozen."

"What if he doesn't come to you?"

"I'm going to wait another day, then go see him again. He's the only chink in their armor, Nando. I've got to convince him to tell what he knows. If that doesn't work, I'm going back to the FBI with my hat in hand and fill in the rest of the picture for them."

Nando leveled his dark eyes on me. "I will go with you, Calvin."

I left Nando's office that day, feeling a mixture of satisfaction and frustration. It was satisfying that we now had a handle on all the players and their motivations in the North Waterfront scheme, but intensely frustrating that there was still no direct action I could take to bring down the whole house of cards. There was also a deeper feeling underlying it all—I raged at the thought of someone like Stanislav Anapolsky using his filthy money to wreak havoc on my city.

Without Anaposky, none of this would have happened.

If I were a religious man, I would've prayed for a special circle in hell for the oligarch and the opportunity to send him there personally.

Chapter Forty-four

Late that same afternoon I drove back to Portland and picked up Angela at the Bridgetown Artists' Co-op. When she told me Winona was still out at the Rez, I said, "I'm starving. You like Thai food?" She told me she did, and fifteen minutes later we had a table at the Lemongrass on NE Couch. We ordered spring rolls, larb, gaeng pah curry, and a couple of Thai ice teas. I'd ordinarily have a Singha beer with Thai food, but I skipped it in support of Angela's sobriety.

After we ordered, Angela said, "Can you take me to my AA meeting Wednesday night? I'm getting my three-year sobriety coin."

"Absolutely. That's a great accomplishment. Congratulations." She thanked me, and I said, out of pure curiosity, "What's the key to AA?"

"For me, it's support, I guess. The best advice comes from people who've been there, people in recovery. And structure, you know, the twelve steps. Even after I got sober, I flailed around, not knowing how to forgive myself for my shitty behavior. It wasn't until I started making amends to people I'd hurt or insulted—that's the ninth step—that things really turned around for me." She hesitated then brought her deep brown eyes up and met mine. "Would you sit in on the meeting tomorrow night, Cal?"

"I would be honored." And that was the truth.

While we ate I told her about Dorothy Turner's visit, and also about Stanislav Anapolsky. When I finished she said, "So, you think Melvin's just a forger and not a murderer?"

"What do *you* think?"

She wrapped some larb in a lettuce leaf, took a bite, and seemed to contemplate the question while she chewed. "Melvin disliked me, for sure, but I always thought he admired Mom. Maybe that's why I felt more betrayed by him than by Brice Avery. Now that I think about it, Melvin isn't a hater. And Dorothy, she was always kind to me, even when I was acting like a little bitch."

I nodded as I put some more gaeng pah on my rice. "That's the way I read it. What about Avery?"

She shrugged. "Aloof. Cold. It was always about the business with him. I wasn't surprised when you told me you suspected him." She lowered her fork and looked at me. "Do you think Melvin will cooperate?"

My turn to shrug. "I hope so." I told her about my plans to confront him again if I didn't hear from him soon, but left out the bit about going to the FBI and back to the police if that failed. I was afraid she'd see that as capitulation, and frankly, that's what it was beginning to feel like to me. I had a strong, internally consistent theory but was still short on incriminating evidence. What if the FBI was only interested in the money-laundering, and the powers that be in Portland let the matter drop?

That was unthinkable, come to think of it.

That evening, Tracey called. "Hey Cal," she began, "Mia Cantrell told me something interesting today. Fred Poindexter had her cancel a dinner he had planned with his wife for their twenty-fifth wedding anniversary. He'd booked a table at Andina weeks in advance. She asked him why, and all he said was he had a conflict. Mia thinks this must be a big deal, because she overheard Fred trying to smooth things over with his wife. She told me he said something like, 'I have to be there. I have no choice.' Anyway, I thought this might be important."

"Does she know where he's going?"

"No. But I asked her to stay alert tomorrow and let me know immediately if she learns anything more."

"Good work. Keep me in the loop. Maybe there's another meeting coming up." Tracey wanted to talk more, but I wasn't good company that night, so I took the first opportunity to sign off.

I awoke the next morning stiff and tired after a restless night filled with frustrating dreams I couldn't even remember. My reverse commute to Dundee was slowed down by an accident on I-5, and I had just cleared Newburg when my Bluetooth lit up. "Good morning, Cal," Valerie Thatcher greeted me with irritating cheerfulness. "The screenwriter loves your place and would like to make an offer. What do you think?"

"Come on. I thought he just wanted to look the place over."

"He did, and it was love at first sight."

"Was the quarry operating?"

She laughed. "Oh, yeah. In fact, they set off a blast while we were there. Didn't even faze him. Cal, I think he'll make you a very generous offer. What shall I tell him?"

I paused for a long time. "Tell him he can make an offer, provided it's effective the day after the county hearing—that's June twenty-third. I'll give him my answer then."

"That might cost you the deal. Didn't you say you weren't likely to prevail at the hearing?"

"That's my position. He can take it or leave it."

At midday I called Tracey to see if Mia Cantrell had come up with anything. "Not yet," she told me, "Poindexter's been in his office all morning, so she hasn't been able to snoop around. Don't worry. I'll call one way or the other this afternoon."

It was after three when she called back. "The news isn't good—he left his office abruptly, and Mia has gone through everything without finding a clue to where he's headed tonight. Sorry, Cal."

I thought about calling Nando to see if he could try tailing either Turner or Avery. If a meeting was planned, they were sure to attend. But that would require him picking one or the other of them up at rush hour. That didn't seem feasible, and the whole thing could be a false alarm, in any case.

I decided against calling him.

I left my Dundee office that evening feeling restless. Something was up. I could feel it. But what? I was back at Caffeine Central, had finished dinner, cleaned up the kitchen, and was pacing around like a caged lion when I got my answer. "Mr. Claxton?" the voice on my cell phone said, "This is Dorothy Turner. I'm frightened and worried sick about Mel."

"What is it? What's happened?"

"He just left, but he wouldn't tell me where he's going. He was really agitated. The worst I've ever seen him. I asked if he was coming to see you. He said no, that he was going to take care of the situation himself. I demanded to know what was going on, but all he would say was that he was doing this for me and the children. I begged him not to go, but he wouldn't listen."

"Did he say why he had to leave?"

"I heard him talking to Brice on the phone. I think he's meeting him, but I don't know where."

"Does he have an office in your home?" She said yes. "Go in and look around. See if he left any clues to where he might be headed. Can you do that, Mrs. Turner?"

"Yes, I'll do that right now and call you back."

I sat by the phone until it rang again seven minutes later. "Mr. Claxton? I don't see anything in his briefcase, his appointment book, or his e-mail. He did scribble something on a notepad next to the phone. It looks like a code or something."

"What does it say?"

"It says, 'November13Bravo64 at ten p.m.' Does that mean anything to you?"

My pulse jumped ten points, and a surge of electrical current sluiced down my spine. "Yes, Mrs. Turner, it certainly does."

Chapter Forty-five

"So, they are having a board meeting," Nando quipped. It was forty minutes later in his office, and I had just explained what Dorothy Turner told me.

"I'm sure of it," I said. "They're landing late, so maybe they're planning to meet on the plane. That would make sense. The airport should be deserted."

"They have much to talk about, I think," Nando said.

"For sure. I've had confrontations with Boyarchenko, Turner, and Avery, there's been an unfavorable newspaper article, and we put that Nightshade bastard, Grabar, to flight. About now I'm sure Anapolsky's wondering if the view's worth the climb."

Nando chuckled. "Perhaps he would like to wash his money in a more welcoming city. What do you want to do, Calvin?"

"I already called Aldous Jones, but he hasn't returned my call. I think the FBI will be all over this, but we can't be sure."

"Did you leave a message?"

"I just said it was urgent for him to call me."

"What if he doesn't call?"

"We go to Aurora and get some video of the board meeting, a nice group shot showing the whole happy family."

Nando nodded, and his eyes narrowed down in a cold, murderous look. "I would like to go there and kill them all."

"I know," I said. "One step at a time."

Fifty-five minutes later Nando's big bolt cutters sliced through the padlock on the service gate at the Aurora Airport like it was made of balsa wood. I called Jones again, but he still didn't answer. After all, I was just a small-town lawyer, in way over my head, right? Once inside the gate, we moved quickly and silently along the east side of the airport, using as cover a wide swath of low trees that ran behind a row of hangers. I put a hand out to stop Nando and pointed between two of the hangars to an open area maybe seventy-five yards ahead of us. The area was pooled in dim light cast by a series of security lights. "The hangar jock told me the Gulfstream taxied into that staging area last time," I whispered. "It's a good bet they'll do the same this time."

We crept out of the trees and into the shadow of the closest hangar and worked our way forward from one structure to the next. We were well below the central administration building, but across a service road there was a smaller structure that provided an unobstructed view of the staging area. I pointed in that direction. "We'll have to chance crossing the road, but it looks like we can set up in the shadows behind those foundation plantings along the side of the building. That will give us decent cover."

Nando nodded, we dashed across the road, and once we were in place, breathed a sigh of relief. I carried the night-vision binoculars again, and Nando manned the camera. We were both armed. Nando said, "If the FBI is here, they are well hidden."

I smiled and shook my head. "Finding us again would just make Jones' day, wouldn't it?"

At 9:56, the runway lights to the west of us popped on, and several minutes later we heard the distant, high-pitched whine of a jet lining up for a landing. The plane approached from the north, touched down, and used most of the runway to come to taxiing speed. After it made a U-turn onto the service strip and was heading back toward us, I was finally able to focus my binoculars on the tail. "November13Bravo64," I said under my breath. "That's Anapolsky's Gulfstream."

"I am rolling the camera," Nando replied.

I followed the jet with my glasses as it turned off the service strip, entered the staging area, and powered down. The hatch popped open, the stairs deployed, and a man got off and hustled on foot in the direction of the main gate, blocked from our view by the building we were crouched next to. "He's going to open the gate," I whispered. Meanwhile, two more bodyguards got out and stood on either side as a tall, thin man came down the stairs.

"Anapolsky," I whispered.

"The oligarch himself," Nando uttered as the camera whirred softly.

Anapolsky stood erect with his arms crossed as two cars pulled into the staging area and parked near the plane. I recognized both cars—Turner's pearl-colored Lexus and Boyarchenko's metallic silver Mercedes. The Mercedes had a large primer patch on the passenger door, I noted with satisfaction.

"Boyarchenko," I said, as his driver, the Incredible Hulk's twin brother, opened the passenger door and let the Russian gangster out.

"And Hofstetter," Nando added, as the lawyer emerged on the other side. "I have them all in my sights. Too bad this is a camera. I would rather have a sniper rifle."

I swung my glasses to the other car. "That's Turner standing on the driver's side and Avery on the passenger side of the Lexus." The rear door opened, and a third passenger got out. "Poindexter."

Nando grunted. "All present and accounted for."

The Portland welcoming committee approached Anapolsky as his bodyguards looked on. After smiles and cordial handshakes all around, Anapolsky nodded to the bodyguard to his right. The man produced a narrow black cylinder that resembled a flashlight without a lens. "What's that black thing—?"

"A radio frequency detector," Nando whispered. "He's going to sweep them for wires or recording devices. He is a cautious man."

The bodyguard swept Poindexter first, then Avery, and when he came to Turner, the pudgy lawyer stepped back. With my binoculars, I could clearly see fear forming on his face. The bodyguard glanced at his counterparts, then stepped toward Turner again, who backtracked another step. That was enough for Anapolsky's security team. "Oh, shit," I said, as they surrounded him, stripped his coat and shirt off, and tore off something taped to the ribs below his right armpit. One of the bodyguards held up something so small I couldn't make it out. "What the hell is that?" I hissed.

Nando zoomed in. "It looks like a voice-activated recorder."

Anapolsky shouted something in Russian as the Portland contingent stepped away from Turner like he had the plague. One of the bodyguards removed a gun from a shoulder holster and clipped Turner with the butt of it. He staggered and when he went down, the other two bodyguards began kicking him viciously. I lowered my binoculars after one of the blows rocked his head violently. "*Shit.* They're going to kill him. We've got to do something." But what? It was mostly open space between us and the Gulfstream. Anapolsky's team was certain to be trained marksmen, and although Nando was a good shot, I wasn't. Intervention looked like suicide to me.

Nando put his camera down, pulled out his Sig Sauer, and looked at me. "We have no choice, my friend." I swallowed, drew my Glock from my waistband, trying to remember whether the clip was completely loaded or not, and we both stood up. Nando pointed to a panel truck parked to our left, halfway to the Gulfstream. "We take cover there. I will shoot the two men kicking him. You shoot the other one." Sure.

We made it to the truck without being seen. I held Nando back and stepped out without exposing myself completely. "Stop beating that man," I called out. Everyone in the group whirled around to face us, and all three bodyguards drew their weapons. "Put your guns down," I shouted. As pure a bluff as there ever was.

The bodyguard nearest to us crouched down and squeezed off two rounds. Pop, pop. The bullets thudded into the body of the panel truck where I had stood. So much for peaceful negotiations. Maybe it was all that salsa dancing, because, despite his size and bulk, Nando moved like a cat as he jumped out, lowered to a crouch, and aimed at the man trying to kill us. A single report rang out in the night air. The bodyguard pitched back, and his gun flew out of his hand.

"*You got him*," I cried out.

Nando looked at his Sig Sauer, then at me in utter confusion. "The hell I did. I didn't pull the trigger."

CRASH.

The sound reverberated in the still night like a thunder-clap. We looked to our right as an armored Humvee slammed through the sheet metal door of a hangar and started toward the Gulfstream, bathing us, the jet, and the party in front of it in a blinding swath of light. "This is the FBI," an amplified voice warned. "Drop your weapons and raise your hands, all of you."

The command was repeated.

Behind the Humvee a dozen agents wearing FBI vests and armed with automatic weapons fanned out on either side. Nando and I put our guns down, but one of the two remaining bodyguards raised his weapon while the other began hustling Anapolsky up the stairs of the Gulfstream. That was a big mistake.

This time I saw the muzzle flash from a sharpshooter on the roof of the central building. The bodyguard next to the oligarch pitched off the stairs and landed flat on his face. Loyal to the end, the other bodyguard laid down, covering fire as he backed toward the plane. He got off a couple of volleys before he, too, was cut down. The rest of the group scattered in panic, and Anapolsky disappeared into the Gulfstream as the turbines began to whine. But an instant later the tires on the plane were shot out.

It was all over in less than a minute. Once the FBI secured the scene, Nando and I ventured toward the plane with our hands held high. Aldous Jones was standing at the periphery barking orders, and when he saw us said, "Oh, no, not you two again." He looked at me. "I should bust your balls for this, Claxton."

"I called you twice, Aldous."

"I know. I know. I saw your calls, but we were in position, and I was busy." He pointed at Nando's camera. "Did you get any decent footage?" Nando nodded, and Jones added, "Leave the cartridge. We can't have too much evidence in this case. Now, stay out of the way, but don't go anywhere."

Melvin Turner was sitting up and being attended to by two agents. His face was bloodied, and he looked dazed, but he was alive. That wasn't the case for everyone. In addition to the three bodyguards, whose bodies were already covered, there was a fourth corpse, conspicuous by the boat shoes on the feet protruding from a makeshift cover. We both looked around, then Nando said, "I don't see Brice Avery."

"Me, neither." I nodded in the direction of the fourth body. "I think that's him."

It *was* the body of the CEO of Wingate Properties, Brice Avery. He'd taken a stray round through the temple, and it wasn't until two weeks later that we learned the bullet came from one of the bodyguard's guns.

A group of agents huddled around another victim. Nando and I moved along the periphery until we could see it was Ilya Boyarchenko. He was lying in a pool of blood, but he was still alive.

The Gulfstream was surrounded by a phalanx of armed, Kevlar-vested agents, and we watched as the two pilots got off first, followed by Stanislav Anapolsky, the renowned Russian oligarch who was on a first-name basis with Vladimir Putin. By the look on his face, this wasn't the friendly Northwest welcome he'd expected. A black sedan appeared out of nowhere, and Anapolsky was immediately placed in the car and whisked away.

The rest of the suspects—Fred Poindexter, Byron Hofstetter,

280 Warren C. Easley

and Boyarchenko's hulk of a driver, were all standing handcuffed under the watchful eyes of three more agents. The Hulk looked defiant, but Poindexter and Hofstetter looked absolutely terrified. I was reminded of Rosencrantz and Guildenstern, except the two of them were still alive.

Nando and I stayed at the scene for the next couple of hours, then drove ourselves to the FBI regional headquarters, where we each spent another two and half hours undergoing intense debriefings. When we finally pulled up in front of Caffeine Central, it was nearly four in the morning, but we were both wide awake. "Come on up," I said. "I have a bottle of Rémy Martin VSOP."

Archie greeted us like he'd been shut in for the last month. I filled his water bowl, gave him a doggie biscuit, and poured Nando and me three fingers of the gold liquid. We sipped in silence for a while, letting the liquor slide down our throats and warm our insides. Finally, Nando chuckled. "So, Melvin Turner was not wearing the recorder at the behest of Aldous Jones. I would have thought it so."

"That's right. Turns out he was on his own evidence-gathering quest. He told his wife he was going to take care of the situation. I guess this is what he had in mind. Jones said he recorded some useful stuff on the way to the airport, though."

"He didn't think Anapolsky would check him for a bug?"

"Apparently, the Russians didn't wand them last time, so he thought he was okay. That's what Jones told me."

Nando sipped some Rémy and looked at me. "Jones seems to have changed his opinion of you."

I shrugged and smiled. "He did say he was impressed that you and I had this whole thing figured out, that it was a fine piece of investigative work."

"Did he mention Grabar?"

"Lip service only. They have Anapolsky. That's all they're really interested in." I shook my head. "Melvin Turner precipitated this whole thing. Jones was prepared for anything, but he was planning on only documenting who was there, like us. They wanted to get a GPS tracker on one of the wheels of the plane, too, if they could get close enough. I think he's worried he doesn't have enough on the oligarch."

"Even now?"

I shrugged. "I don't know. Anapolsky's a big fish. There's a lot of international politics involved."

We sipped some more cognac in silence. Nando focused on something across the room and said, finally, "I find it interesting that you and I were ready to put our lives on the line to try and save that sniveling lawyer."

I laughed, but it was more nervous relief. "We would have been toast. And don't forget, you were the one who said we had no choice."

He smiled wistfully and nodded. "I did, didn't I? Why did I say that? That man means nothing to me."

"You said it because it's built in. You hate bullies and injustice as much as I do. And you said it because you are a man of great courage. Who else would willingly go into a gun battle with me?"

His laugh shook the room like a *basso profundo*, then he swung his dark eyes in my direction and clinked his glass against mine. "To friendship, Calvin."

"Yes," I said, "to friendship."

Chapter Forty-six

It was a little after seven in the morning when I returned Tracey Thomas' calls from the night before, four of them. "Are you sitting down?" I said.

"Actually, I'm lying flat on my back," she shot back in a groggy voice. "What's happened?" When I finished telling her the story, she said, "Well, I'm standing up now, Cal. That's incredible news. My God, what a scene that must have been, the FBI coming in like the cavalry in a John Wayne movie. North Waterfront's history now, for sure. Is Turner going to be okay?"

"I think so, but they took him away on a stretcher. He surprised me, to be honest with you. I thought he might come to me or go to the police, but I never expected him to go it alone."

"Well, they obviously made a mistake when they threatened his family. What about Poindexter? Did you see him?"

"Yeah, I did. He was cuffed and looking like PTSD was in his future."

"How deeply involved do you think he was?"

"Hard to say. My guess is he was on the periphery, there to insure the project got approved by the city with lots of generous tax incentives. We'll see what charges they bring against him, and whether he decides to cooperate in exchange for leniency."

When Tracey and I finished up, I called Claire in New Iberia and told her I thought it was safe for her to go back to Cambridge.

When she asked why, I said, "Because the man who threatened you is under arrest and in the hospital in critical condition," and went on to fill her in.

When I finished, she paused for a long time before saying, "You need to find a safer line of work, Dad."

She had a point.

Three days later, I picked up Angela and we drove to the Good Samaritan Hospital in Northwest Portland, where we met Dorothy Turner. "Thanks for coming, both of you. I'm very grateful," she said as she shook my hand, then gave Angela a hug. "His room is at the end of this hall." We followed her, and after a policeman at the door scanned for our names on a clipboard, checked our IDs, and stood aside, we entered Melvin Turner's hospital room.

"Come in, come in," he said, forcing a smile that was more of a grimace. "My jaw's wired shut, so I can't speak very well, and I'm still a little loopy from the concussion." He looked like hell, with a sutured gash above his left eye and an even longer, vertical wound running from his eye to his jawline. Angela sucked a breath as he motioned her to take the chair next to his bed. She sat down hesitantly, and he turned his head toward her as his eyes filled with tears. "I didn't think you'd come. I, uh, don't expect you to ever forgive me, Angela, but I wanted to humbly apologize for my behavior. I'm so sorry for what has happened and for the role I played."

Angela nodded faintly, her hands folded in her lap.

He pointed to an envelope on a portable table next to the bed, glanced at me, then back at her. "Your mom's actual will is in that envelope. I want you to take it with you, and read through it with Mr. Claxton. Your mother, uh, passed before it was fully executed, but that's not going to be a problem. Mr. Claxton can see to that. She left everything to you except for some money for her brother and sister. She saw the growth in you, Angela, and figured by the time she was gone, you'd be ready to keep Wingate Properties on a course of social responsibility. That was her dream."

"What about you and Brice Avery?" Angela asked.

"Well, if I was still able, she wanted me to stay on to help you. But Brice isn't in the will. She had decided to get rid of him and take the reins of Wingate Properties herself." He forced another painful smile. "That was your doing, young lady."

Angela showed a hint of a smile in return. "The Women's March in Washington had more to do with it than me."

"She knew you loved art over business," he went on, "but she figured you would be smart enough to hire the right leadership down the road."

Angela's hand went to her face to stem the tears. "She said that?"

"Yes, she did." Melvin let a breath out slowly and glanced at his wife before continuing. "I, uh...I made the mistake of telling Brice about your mother's plans, and he convinced me to forge the will after the hit-and-run. It was an inexcusable act of cowardice and greed. And I was such a fool to think that Margaret's and Helen's deaths were both accidents." He swung his eyes to me. "I finally woke up, thanks to Mr. Claxton, but when I started asking questions, they threatened to kill Dorothy and the kids." He lowered his eyes. "You know the rest."

The room went completely silent and motionless. Finally, Angela reached out, and when Melvin realized she was offering her hand, he grasped it with his. She said, "Thanks for telling me this, Melvin. It means the world to me." She sniffed hard. "I'd be the worst hypocrite ever if I didn't forgive you. God knows how much I've screwed up, and I've learned how hard it is to ask for forgiveness." A faint smile spread across her tear-stained face. "As a matter of fact, you and Dorothy are on my list of people to make amends to."

Silence reigned again, and when a nurse came in shortly after that to chase us out, there wasn't a dry eye in the room. As we were leaving, Melvin added, "Mr. Claxton, my firm's dropping the lawsuit against you, of course. I hope you'll forgive me for that, as well." I nodded to assure him I did.

After we said our goodbyes to Dorothy Turner and were walking back to where my car was parked, Angela said, "What will happen to Melvin now?"

"Well, he'll get disbarred for life, that's for sure, and he'll be charged with forgery and conspiracy to launder money. But he's the government's star witness against Stanislav Anapolsky, who's a top target of the FBI, so he's got considerable leverage to cut a deal. He'll be okay, I think, but life as he knew it is over."

"What will they charge the oligarch with?"

"International money-laundering, narcotics-trafficking, and racketeering, among others. The charges are enough to put him away in a U.S. federal prison for quite a while."

"No murder charges?"

"I doubt it. It looks like Karlo Grabar was contracted by Boyarchenko, and he's not cooperating."

"Yeah, but Anapolsky put him up to it."

I nodded. "Most likely. I'm just not sure the case can be made."

"What about Grabar?" Her look turned to disgust. He's long gone, isn't he?"

I shook my head in frustration. "I don't know, Angela. The trail's cold, for sure, and he doesn't have any reason to hang around. But he'll make the FBI's most wanted list, I'm sure."

I slept in that Sunday and awoke feeling fully rested for the first time in a long time. I fed Arch, took him for a short walk, then after a couple of cappuccinos, made blueberry pancakes that I served with Canadian maple syrup and a rasher of crisp bacon. While I cooked and ate I listened to some early Lucinda Williams and when she came to *Big Red Sun Blues*, I found myself singing along.

But the bubble burst around midmorning, when my realtor, Valerie Thatcher, called. "I've got the offer for the Aerie, Cal," she said with that ring of enthusiasm I found so irritating, "and it's dated June twenty-third, the day after your hearing, like you requested." She went over the numbers with me, and I had to admit it was generous. I'd still take a beating, but it wasn't nearly as bad as I thought it was going to be. "My advice is that you lock this in right now," she said. "It's not binding on him until the effective date, and he might change his mind. You won't get another offer like this."

"Nope. I'm going to wait for the hearing."

I spent that afternoon going back over all the sales records and other information I had on the quarry situation, and then reviewing all the pertinent land-use laws and regulations. I found nothing I could build a legal argument around, which of course was no surprise. I was promised the results of the quarry dust analysis I'd requested but didn't have much hope I'd find a stopper there. No, it looked like the only chance I had was to appeal to the emotions of the members of the Land Use Board. I could bring in Gertrude Johnson and other long-term neighbors and have them testify about how the mining degraded their quality of life—the blasting, truck traffic, diesel fumes, crusher noise. But it would be just that—an emotional argument. Meanwhile, McMinnville Sand and Gravel had the law on their side, as their counsel would quickly point out.

I'd pushed away from my desk in disgust when the aerial view of H and S Landscaping and Builder Supply that I'd seen that day in their office popped into my head. I still can't explain why that happened. It made me think of satellite imaging. I logged in and started a search....

Arch and I got in a good run that afternoon, although the sky opened up on the way back, and we both got soaked. I just changed clothes when Angela texted me that she'd nearly finished Jogging Woman and wanted me to come by to take a look. I jumped on it, anxious to see the latest version. Since Arch was snoozing on his mat and smelling like a wet dog, I left him there with orders to guard the castle. Angela buzzed me in fifteen minutes later, and when I walked through the open door of her studio, my head became the clapper in a bell.

The last thought I had as I spiraled into unconsciousness was *how could I be so stupid?*

Chapter Forty-seven

I heard somebody groaning, and then realized it was me. As I came to, I tasted blood, which had found its way down my face from the blow that knocked me out. I opened my eyes and saw Angela staring at me in terror. She sat in a chair at one end of the studio, her hands bound with plastic handcuffs, her feet tied together with nylon cord, and her mouth taped shut. Her floor mate, Darius, lay next to her, bound like she was. The side of his head was bloody, and his eyes were closed. I looked carefully and was relieved to see he was breathing. At the other end of the studio, a man was busy with his back to us at the workbench. I was slumped in a chair against the wall that ran along the street, my hands and feet done up like theirs. In the center of it all, Jogging Woman stood mute, her legs striding, her arms pumping.

Angela gave a muffled sob and swung her eyes in the direction of the man. Hearing the sob, he turned around and looked at her before settling his eyes on me. They were flat and hard, like I'd seen in the mug shot, and his body had the well-muscled tone of the man I'd faced in the alley.

"Oh, you've come to," he said. "I didn't tape your mouth because I wanted to chat. If you raise your voice, I'll immediately execute the boy and the girl. Are we clear?"

I nodded. "This isn't necessary, Grabar. It's all over. You won't even get paid for this. Ilya Boyarchenko and Stanislav Anapolsky are both in jail."

He put his hands on his hips and faced me. "I know what happened. And it's not the money, it's my *reputation*. I was supposed to take care of this young woman, and you got in the way. I can't let that stand. Bad for business." He flashed a smile. "But don't worry, the three of you won't feel a thing, and the cops will think it was a tragic accident." He smiled again. It was laced with pride. "It's what I do."

Grabar turned back to whatever he was working on at the bench. I glanced over at Angela and saw she was straining to loosen one of her boots. I understood immediately—if she worked her boots off, she might be able to slip the nylon cord off her small feet. But then what? I had no idea, but I nodded encouragement and tried loosening my own shoes, but without success.

I looked at Jogging Woman, who was poised between Angela and Grabar as if striding to catch the assassin. Her face and the rest of her body were now fully detailed, the only exception being her right hand, whose stout wires still thrust forward, unshaped. Jogging Woman's face was haunted by Margaret Wingate's visage, now more than ever. Did Karlo Grabar see the resemblance of the statue to the woman he murdered? If he did, he wasn't showing it.

Grabar finished at the bench, walked over to the oxygen and acetylene tanks chained to the wall, and with a small file set about gently abrading the flexible hoses that carried the gases to Angela's torch—first one, then the other. Then he repeated the process at two other points on the hoses. When he finished, he looked up at me and smiled. "Worn hoses can be such a hazard in this type of work. Both these gases are colorless and odorless and highly explosive, you know." He pointed to the abraded areas. "These are for the forensic team to discover in the ruins, if there's anything left of them."

"Think about it, Grabar," I said. You're just incurring more risk here. The FBI's in the middle of this. Look what happened to Analpolsky and Boyarchenko and the others. Cut your losses, man. Get out of Portland while you can."

He looked up again with annoyance. "I explained to you why I can't do that." From the gas tanks he went over to the exhaust fan, where I watched as he loosened one of the electrical connections at the back. "Well," he said with a satisfied look on his face, "it looks like the exhaust fan is not working properly. Such inattention to safety." He looked in Angela's direction and added, "By the way, young lady, I wanted to thank you for your website. The pictures of your studio here were invaluable as I planned this." He glanced over at Darius. "And it was kind of that young man to let me in. Saved me a lot of trouble."

From there, he went back to the bench and busied himself unpacking items from a briefcase. Meanwhile, Angela had one boot loose and was now focused on the other, a look of deadly determination on her sweaty face. I didn't know the plan, but my attempts to talk Grabar down sure as hell weren't working.

Grabar turned to face us, holding a small ampule between his thumb and index finger. "This is succinylcholine, considered by many to be the perfect poison. Why? Because the metabolites are natural body constituents. Can't be traced at low dosages. But relax, I'm not going to poison you, I'm just going to inject enough to incapacitate you for fifteen minutes or so. Then I'm going to unshackle you, turn the gas tanks on, and leave. I'll be blocks from here when I detonate a digital fuse on the workbench by cell phone. Boom." He smiled and the satisfied looked returned to his face. "I might have to put this at the top of my hit parade."

"You'll never fool the FBI," I said. "Don't do this, Grabar." But he ignored me, turned back to the workbench, and began withdrawing the chemical from the ampule with a syringe.

I glanced over at Angela, who had slipped off one boot and was working on the other. She grimaced and tugged, and the second boot popped off. She slipped her feet out of the rope, rose to her feet quietly, glanced at me for a moment—I'll never forget the look on her face, a mosaic of rage and fear—then sprinted toward Jogging Woman. She hit the wire statue going full tilt, which ripped it from its temporary moorings. Grabar whirled around at the sound just as the statue arrived with Angela riding its back. He screamed as the sharp, stainless steel wires of the unfinished right hand drove through his neck, knocking him back and pinning him to the wooden floor like an insect in a collection. He howled in agony but was unable to move as his blood began pooling on the floor.

"You little bitch," he snarled in a gurgling, barely audible voice. "Get this off me."

Angela stayed on top of the statue, staring straight into his face without saying a word. When I realized she wasn't going to move, I said, "He's not going anywhere, Angela. Come over here and get the rope off my feet.

She did, and after we clipped off each other's handcuffs and I removed the tape from her mouth, I had her call 911 while I set about trying to staunch Grabar's bleeding. Judging from the blood loss, one of the wires must have nicked his jugular, and the fact that he could breathe meant his windpipe had been spared by the second wire impaling his neck. The other three wires had missed his neck but were as firmly imbedded in the floor like the two that had done the damage. I was afraid of trying to unpin him for fear of making it worse, and I didn't know if there was a pressure point for neck veins. I ripped off my shirt then my undershirt, folded the latter, and pressed it against the left side of his neck. The bleeding slowed but didn't stop, and by the time the paramedics arrived, Grabar's face was the color of wet plaster, and he was babbling weakly in a foreign language I assumed was Croatian.

Unfazed by the bizarre scene of a man pinned to the floor through the neck by the hand of a steel sculpture, the paramedics set to work on Grabar. First, they clipped the wires above his neck and righted Jogging Woman, then they eased his head up just enough to get a pair of wire snips under him. Once the wires were cut, they wrapped his neck, put him on a stretcher, and hustled him out of the studio. By this time, Grabar had lost consciousness, and as he passed by Angela, she said, "Will he make it?"

The lead paramedic said, "He's got a shot. It's a miracle he's alive."

While Grabar was being extricated from *Jogging Woman*'s grasp, I called Harmon Scott to tell him what had gone down. A long silence ensued when I finished. "Jesus, Claxton," he said, finally, "with you it's never a dull moment."

"Yeah, it's a long story and he's in a bad way, but you better tell your first responders here to send an armed guard with him to the hospital. "He's not to be underestimated, even with a couple of steel spikes in his neck."

"Put one of them on."

I handed one of the uniformed officers my cell and said, "Captain Scott wants a word with you." The young officer looked at me incredulously but took the phone, then nodded a couple of times, said a couple of yes-sirs, and left with the stretcher.

They carried out Darius Bentley next. As he passed by Angela and me, he looked dazed but decidedly sheepish at the same time. "I'm sorry," he implored. "I never should have let that maniac in." Angela patted him on the shoulder, and I just shook my head.

Angela held up like a trooper through the rounds of questioning, which began at the scene and then continued at police headquarters until late that night and included spending time with Special FBI Agent in Charge, Aldous Jones. When we were finally released, I called Nando, who came across the river and picked us up, and it wasn't until Angela was sitting in the front seat of his Lexus that she broke down crying. We let her cry for a while, knowing this was a common reaction after the fact for people who have been called upon to do extraordinary things. When she regained control, she turned to me and said, "Thanks for saving Grabar's life, Cal. At the time, I wanted him to bleed to death, but I'm glad I don't have that on my conscience now."

"Thanks for saving *my* life. What you did tonight was an act of true heroism." I smiled and shook my head. "I wasn't sure what you were up to with taking your boots off. What gave you that brilliant idea, anyway?"

"Grabar didn't tie my legs very tight." She smirked. "I guess he figured I was no threat to him. Anyway, I got those boots at Goodwill, and they're a little big for me, so I figured I could get my legs free. The idea for the rest of it just came into my head." She smiled wistfully and her big chocolate eyes filled with tears. "It was like Mom was there, you know? In the flesh."

I nodded. "I think she was, Angela. I think she was."

Chapter Forty-eight
June 22nd. The Yamhill County
Land Use Board of Appeals

"To conclude," Mason Goodings, President of McMinnville Sand and Gravel, said to the five board members, "we have every right to start mining again at McCallister Quarry. As you've heard from the testimony and seen from the evidence, although the quarry was idle for twelve years and ten months, sale of our gravel continued for another eleven months at H and S Landscape. Therefore, the operation as a whole has been idle for less than twelve years." He paused and looked confidently at the panel. "It's as simple as that, ladies and gentlemen. I ask you to allow us to continue to mine at this quarry to provide this valuable resource to the people of Oregon. Thank you very much."

Prior to Goodings' concluding remarks, the attorneys for the gravel company entered into evidence the sales and shipping records from the mining operation and the gravel sales at H and S. I made no objection to the quarry records but noted to the panel that the records from H and S were not backed up by their tax returns or any trucking invoices. "And you heard the testimony of the owner, Dudley Cahill," I pointed out, "that the records were not available that far back in time. This means their accuracy can't be independently verified, ladies and gentlemen."

A glancing blow, at best.

When Goodings stepped down, I began my appeal by having several of my neighbors, including Gertrude Johnson, testify about how the resumption of mining was, once again, degrading their quality of life. I finished with a personal description of what the blasting did to Archie, hoping there were some dog lovers on the board. It was a spirited, emotional rebuttal but nothing board members hadn't heard before. Living near an active mine had consequences, after all.

Next, I held up a large copy of the "Quarry Dust" photograph I'd taken on my deck that day and introduced into evidence the analysis of the dust I'd collected. I caught a break there—the analysis showed the dust contained a high content of crystalline silica, a known human carcinogen, owing to its presence in the blue basalt being mined. I went through the dangers of silica, playing it for all it was worth, but the reality was there were was no way to prove an actual threat to human health. The limits weren't established for this type of operation and data simply weren't available.

Another glancing blow.

When I finished, the chairwoman looked at me a bit impatiently and said, "Is that all, Mr. Claxton?"

"No, I'm not quite finished. I'd like to ask Dudley Cahill a few more questions." Cahill looked surprised, then angry, when he was asked to take the chair again. After he sauntered up and took his seat, I approached him with a folder in my hand. I opened the folder and handed him a large photograph. "Do you recognize this?"

He took the photo reluctantly and examined it. "Uh, yeah, this is a satellite photograph of our operation."

"What's the date on it? It's in the right-hand corner."

He looked at the photo again. "Uh, it's dated April 2, 2005, I guess."

"There's no guess work, Mr. Cahill. That's the capture date for the satellite image, the date the photo was snapped from space. Can you see the bays that hold the gravel?"

"Sure, they're those four rectangles on the southeast side of the property."

"Are they stocked with gravel?"

He looked again. "You bet."

"You can see that they're stocked?"

"Yeah. They're obviously full. And you can see a truck being loaded at Bay Three."

"Have you ever sold gravel from any other location on the property?"

"No. We've always sold out of those bays."

"Thank you." I took the photo from his hands, turned to the panel, and explained again what he said, to make sure they understood. Then I handed the photo to the chairwoman of the panel, so she could pass it around. "This was the heyday of the McCallister operation, when things were booming," I added.

"Now, Mr. Cahill," I went on, "I'd like you to examine and comment on this photo, please." I handed him another print, and right on cue a sheen of sweat appeared on his forehead. "What's the status of the gravel bins?"

"Uh, they appear to be empty."

"They *are* empty. What's the date?"

"It looks like March 15, 2006."

"That's correct." Turning back to the board, I said, "That is the capture date for that shot, meaning, again, this was the day that Google decided to update their data about thirteen months later. And, behold, the bins are empty now. I handed Cahill a copy of the H and S sales record for that day. "How much gravel did you sell that day, according to these records you submitted?"

The sheen on his forehead had become drops of sweat. He glanced over at Goodings, then back at me, avoiding eye contact. "Uh, it says here we sold twelve truckloads."

"*Twelve truckloads?* That's impossible. The bins were empty."

At this point, the hearing room had gone completely silent, and the panel members were leaning forward in their seats. I stepped closer to his chair. "Come on, Mr. Cahill, you stopped selling gravel from McCallister Quarry on March sixteenth of that year, if not sooner, and you know it. You simply ran out. But you faked these sales records to help out your buddies at McMinnville Sand and Gravel and allow you to start selling again."

He shook his head. "No, that isn't—"

I cut him off. "I don't need your admission." I turned to the panel again. "I obtained this information from Google Satellite. The photographic evidence is conclusive, ladies and gentlemen. At the *latest*, H and S ran out of gravel on March sixteenth, which is only five months and some change after the quarry shutdown. You can do the math. This proves the quarry was idle for more than twelve years. I ask you to examine these photographs yourselves and then rule against the resumption of mining at McCallister. Thank you."

McMinnville Sand and Gravel's attorneys tried to object and tossed out several alternative theories, but there was simply no way to argue against the photographic evidence and Cahill's admissions. We were asked to leave the room, and forty-five minutes later were called back and told that the vote had been four to one to deny the right to any further mining in the quarry. "If you wish to mine at the site, you'll have to apply for a new permit," the chairwoman informed the mining company. And everyone in the room knew that permit application would be dead on arrival.

A cheer went up from the gallery, and that set Archie off barking. Angela had smuggled him into the hearing, claiming he was a service dog. We filed out of the hearing room, and I was surrounded by well-wishers and grateful neighbors for a while. Gertie patted me on the back and said, "Cal, I was feeling pretty uncertain there until you put that liar, Cahill, back on the stand." She laughed. "I guess I'll have to change my opinion of all that technology we have these days. Google really saved our butts. Who would've believed it?"

The Board of Appeals gave McMinnville two weeks to affect an orderly shutdown, but the blasting was ordered stopped the next day. We swung by the Aerie on our way back to Portland, so Angela could see the place. On the way, she said, "Those satellite photos were so cool. What made you think of that?"

I laughed. "Believe it or not, it was an aerial map of H and S I saw hanging on their wall the only time I was there. I was holding my breath by the time I figured out how to find the capture dates. Turns out, Google doesn't update with any set pattern, but that update in 2006 came at just the right time."

I stopped at the gate to the Aerie, and Angela and Archie jumped out and did a laughing, barking dance across the field. I sat there and watched, my vision suddenly blurred.

It was damn good to be home.

Epilogue

That Fall

I sat on my favorite bench listening to the soft sifting of the wind through the Douglas firs. Archie lay snoozing next to me with his chin on his paws. We were taking a well-deserved break after cleaning the gutters and raking the leaves under the maple trees on the east side of the house. My dog supervised while I did the heavy lifting. The air had a sharp nip to it, and across the glittering thread of the Willamette River, muted patches of vermillion, ochre, and yellows unfurled between the Coast Range and the Cascades, like a comfortable old family quilt.

My thoughts drifted back to the events that followed the FBI bust at the Aurora Airport and Grabar's attempt to murder Angela, Darius, and me. After two major surgeries, the Nightshade assassin had pulled through, although I heard from Harmon Scott that he now talked in a harsh, barely audible whisper, a remnant of Jogging Woman's revenge. Now that the entire scheme was unmasked, the FBI wanted to establish a link between him and Anapolsky, so they could charge the oligarch with murder, in addition to money-laundering and drug-trafficking. But there was a problem—Grabar could only be charged with counts of *attempted* murder—the attempt on Angela followed by the attempt on the three of us in Angela's studio. Apparently, his lawyers liked his chances because they were advising him not to cooperate with the Feds.

That's when I thought of something I'd asked my friend, Semyon Lebedev, at the beginning of this case. I called him immediately. "Remember when I asked if your friend could put aside the cube of the Lexus that was the hit-and-run murder car?" I asked him. "Did he?"

Semyon told me he would check and called me back an hour later to say that yes, it was there, tucked away in a small shed. And access to the yard would be easy, he explained, because Boyarchenko's organization collapsed after his arrest. I called Aldous Jones with the news that I had located the weapon used to murder Margaret Wingate, and he graciously invited me to watch as an FBI team spent a day sawing and prying their way into the cube. On the passenger door handle they lifted perfect thumb and index prints, and on a small section of the front bumper they found tissue and dried blood.

Two weeks later, Karlo Grabar was charged with Margaret Wingate's murder, and a week after that, he agreed to cooperate with the Feds to avoid the death penalty. My hunch that Ilya Boyarchenko had set up the Nightshade contracts was correct. The contract for Margaret Wingate was done anonymously on the Dark Web, but it turned out that Grabar and Boyarchenko had met face-to-face in Portland to discuss the Ferris murder and the attempt on Angela's life. This break in Dark Web protocol allowed Grabar to implicate Boyarchenko and led to the Feds charging the Russian mobster with murder in addition to the money-laundering charges already in place.

Not surprisingly, it didn't take long for him to turn on his Russian countryman, Stanislav Anapolsky, who had supplied Boyarchenko with the software and protocols for the original Dark Web contact.

As Aldous Jones put it to me: "It was like mad dogs turning on each other."

From what I read in the paper and what Jones shared, the arrest of Stanislav Anapolsky caused quite a stir at the Kremlin, particularly after he was charged with murder here in the U.S. Just last week, Aldous told me that the oligarch had been accused of tax evasion in Russia, and Putin was asking for his extradition back to the motherland. It was a move designed to rescue his friend and political ally.

"Surely we won't extradite the bastard?" I asked Jones in utter disbelief.

"Without the murder charge, it could have happened. You know, Putin might offer up someone we want, like Edward Snowden, in exchange. The politics get tricky at that altitude. But no way he's getting extradited when he's charged with first-degree murder. I'm damn glad you had that Lexus cube set aside, Claxton."

"Me, too," I told him.

My thoughts turned to happier topics. Just last week I attended an unveiling of Jogging Woman at the Portland Art Museum, which had purchased the statue and placed it in the commons between their two main buildings in downtown Portland. The event drew a sizable crowd, and Angela gave a moving talk about her mom and what an inspiration she was to her.

"Mom wanted Wingate Properties redirected toward more socially responsible development," she said at one point, "and, as the new owner, that's exactly what I intend to do." Her first action, she explained, was to begin a search for a new CEO who would transform the development company into a nonprofit. At my suggestion, Tracey Thomas was chairing the search committee. "I've also put the North Waterfront Project on hold, pending a complete redesign," she added. "That ugly tower, the yacht harbor, and the golf course are out, and a block of affordable housing and a large-scale complex for artists, featuring studios and a retail space, are in. My dream is that this new artists' cooperative will be a mecca for creative people across the country."

That last line received a burst of applause from the audience, which caused the speaker to blush and tears to form in her big chocolate eyes.

Nando attended the ceremony. He had become a fan of Angela and her work and commissioned her to do a sculpture to be placed outside the Sharp Eye Detective Agency. They're collaborating on a design that will honor Bembe Borgos. She offered to donate the piece, but Nando would have none of it. "You caught BB's killer and saved my best friend's life," he told her. "I can never repay you for that."

Winona also attended the ceremony. We were on opposite sides of the crowd and when our eyes met, I thought I saw the flicker of something in hers—longing perhaps? But when it was over, she slipped out before I had a chance to talk to her. She had taken the job at the Warm Springs Reservation, and from what I hear from her cousin, Philip Lone Deer, she's a lot happier. She certainly deserves it. With the perspective of time, it seems to me our breakup had more to do with the state of this country than anything either of us did or intended to do. Affection for her still smolders in my heart, and that's not apt to change any time soon.

As for me, I'm just taking it a day at a time, which will include a lot of steelhead fishing this fall. The felony assault charge against me for roughing up that security guard was dropped some time ago. He decided not to press charges. It might have had something to do with the fact that he now worked for Angela Wingate, not Brice Avery, but I can't say for sure. Tracey and I continue to see each other, although neither one of us is sure where the relationship is heading. She's focused on city politics, and I'm trying to pump some new life into my law practice in Dundee and do what I can at Caffeine Central.

Best of all, I'm back at the Aerie with my dog.

To see more Poisoned Pen Press titles:

Visit our website:
poisonedpenpress.com
Request a digital catalog:
info@poisonedpenpress.com